The Cancer Club

a crazy, sexy, inspirational
novel of
SURVIVAL

By Lucinda Sue Crosby
Award-winning Bestselling Author

LuckyCinda Publishing
USA
www.luckycinda.com

Endorsements

"Through the main character in The Cancer Club, Lucinda Sue Crosby takes the reader on an emotional journey from struggle to self-discovery and forgiveness. Her writing skills artfully employ the use of pathos, honesty and humor."

Roberta Kay
Psychotherapist, Memoirist

In The Cancer Club, the reader is invited to accompany Marly Mitchell on her cancer-recovery journey. Her world does not stop or even slow down enough to let her catch her breath and calculate the next move. In fact, the rollercoaster ride speeds up, twists, shifts into reverse and stops suddenly before cranking up again.

Marly's sense of humor; her desire to survive; a positive attitude; the acceptance of the strengths and weaknesses of those around her; and hope for the future provide an insightful window into one woman's survival experience.

I have outlived two cancers because I received love, support, comfort, acceptance and help from my husband, my family, my friends, medical personnel, other cancer patients and even some strangers.

Thank you, Lucinda Sue, for a novel that touches our hearts and teaches us that bald is beautiful!

With love,
Grace Elliot
Survivor

Although *The Cancer Club* is a work of fiction, it is based on actual events. Significate inspiration was provided by the writings and life of stage and TV actress and Jim Henson puppeteer Eren Ozker (1948-1993).

The author has taken creative liberty with names, characters, places, plot and incidents. Some book characters are composites of real people but names of actual persons have been changed for privacy reasons.
Half- Moon Bay Hotel on Antigua; the airplane graveyard in Arizona; and Las Hadas Resort are all real locations.

Copyright © 2014 by LuckyCinda

All rights reserved. Published and Printed in the United States.

www.luckycinda.com

LuckyCinda USA

Book Design by Laura Dobbins
Cover Design by Laura Dobbins

Cataloging-in-Publication Data is on file with the Library of Congress.

ISBN-13: 978-1481983259
ISBN-10: 1481983253

MANUFACTURED IN THE UNITED STATES OF AMERICA

First Edition

No portion of this work can be reprinted, copied, distributed, resold, used digitally or otherwise, without the permission of the publisher: laura@luckycinda.com

To order more copies or to contact the author:
LuckyCinda: www.luckycinda.com
laura@luckycinda.com

Acknowledgement

This book is dedicated to my friend, Eren Ozker, 1948-1993. In a thousand and one ways, this compelling, dramatic, gorgeous daughter of Eve, the first woman puppeteer ever hired by Jim Henson, reflected back to me the best parts of myself – and spurred me to first investigate more thoroughly and then embrace my talent for writing.

Our friendship wasn't long lived but it was shining and powerful. My boyfriend at the time was the best pal of her urbane husband, distinguished character actor and wicked good joke teller William (Bill) Bogert. A group of us gathered often to play a game I still adore: First Lines of Novels, at which Eren excelled. We also comingled on the tennis court, dressed up for Old Hollywood-style Halloween parties with complex treasure hunts, knocked back good wine with scintillating discussions on far-flung yet significant topics and shared self-mocking and humbling tales of our lives in the TV and movie Biz.

The last three years of Eren's life were anchored by a merciless struggle to beat a rare and aggressive lung cancer. The cancer won but it didn't touch the soul of my Eren ... as you'll see for yourself if you take the time to read the bulletins included in this book through which she kept her friends apprised of her condition.

She's the one who came up with the term "Cancer Club." She's the one with the wit, nerve and communication skills to chronicle the ghastly truth in a way the reader can't help but gather up and breathe in. Before she died, I asked and received her permission and Bill's to use this remarkable last testament as a springboard for the novel I hoped to write one day. You will find all but the first bulletin reprinted in their entirety at the end of the story.

This book is also dedicated to all the cancer survivors of this world. Having had a cancer episode myself in 1992, I know and understand the withering effect this terrible disease has not only on the afflicted but on anyone involved in loving and caring for him or her. Of course, cancer episodes are as varied and nuanced as human beings, so I don't pretend to speak for all. Still, if you are intimate with cancer for any reason whatsoever, I pray this story resonates and lifts!

Lucinda Sue Crosby

Chapter 1

1992

Believe it or not, it is impossible to commit suicide in an airport. I have good reason to know this, as I exhausted every conceivable possibility during an eight-hour-and-sixteen-minute daytime nightmare on March tenth of last year.

John F. Kennedy International was the scene. I had taken the red-eye from Los Angeles after having recently suffered, and only partially recovered from, A BREAKDOWN. As I'd had to change my travel plans at the last second, it was the only flight available. I was done—physically, emotionally and spiritually done. My bones felt rubbery, my skin sagged, and the hollows underneath my eyes had taken on a spectral life of their own. On top of everything else, I had endured the continuous staccato wailing of a baby one row back, who added a delightful last-straw quality to my trials.

Once I had dragged my strung-out self from the winged torture chamber and slumped onto a row of rock-hard, fake-Naugahyde airport chairs, people shied away from sitting beside me. And who could blame them? It wasn't a comfortable seat to sit on, and I wasn't a comfortable person to sit next to. I noticed them weighing my state of mind with some hidden human yardstick. Not that anyone was purposefully unkind; their collective flinching at the shadow I had become was simply beyond their control. I couldn't blame them for the subtle fear that flicked, for a brief moment, across their eyes. It was the same flick I'd become accustomed to each morning when I looked at my own face in the mirror.

It had been a nice face once, even-featured and fine-boned. I especially like my eyes, as they constantly change color from gray to blue to green. It made people want to look more deeply into me without my having to try. I like my smile, too. But the best part of the pretty picture that was me was my skin coloring. I had one hell of a pelt, a gift from my father's Native American quarter of the family. Bronze without being ruddy, the blush in my cheeks was perpetually rosy and sun-kissed.

Not now. There is a listless grayness about me now ... a melancholy that tints my once-bright personality with shadowy earth tones. I've always looked lousy in earth tones. They bring out the yellow, and yellow makes me look sick. But of course, *I am sick.*

An accented voice spoke liltingly over the loudspeaker. English was obviously and charmingly her second language. "We are truly sorry, ladies and gentlemen. We just received word that the mechanical misbehavior of British West Indies Airlines Flight 469 will go on and on for a while. We are apologizing again for the delay, but everything our people have been thinking of to do is being done. We will be providing updates by this loudspeaker but urge you to check with flight information from time to time. They will politely give you information even if there is none."

To a chorus of groans, I slung my purse and carry-on bag over my shoulder and picked up my computer. I slogged over to a harried man with a billowing Afro, wearing the BWIA Caribbean blue uniform. I didn't wait my turn; I'd lost all interest in being polite 312 disappointments before.

"Is there a real restaurant somewhere close by …," I began testily, interrupting two fistfuls of other irate passengers who waved their collective arms and shouted at me, as if I were going to listen. I shouted right back, meeting each decibel of theirs with two more of my own, "… *with real chairs and real drinks?*"

My rudeness even astonished me. Weighing my obvious physical condition for a nanosec, Afro man yelled over the hubbub, "Yes, ma'am. Back through security. Taking the moving sidewalk to the end and turning right. You can't be missing it."

When I found the restaurant, I chose a table for two across from the window and relinquished my increasingly heavy luggage to the chair opposite mine. The place was filling up, and I didn't want anyone to even think about sharing a table. I ordered a Bloody Mary from Tina, an impossibly fresh-faced waitress with a voice like Joan Rivers, and set about engaging my new go-to hobby: brooding.

The too-big watch that used to fit told me it had been five hours and fifty-three minutes since I'd touched down at Kennedy. Suddenly, the idea of committing suicide sprang into my mind, full-grown, like Aphrodite sprang from the head of Zeus. Hmmm. The table was set with cheap stainless steel. Idly, I ran my fingers across the cutting edge of the knife. It was barely sharp enough to slice through butter, much less the skin stretched taut over the blue veins in my wrist. After I stirred my drink with it and set it down on the pink tablecloth, it spread a little pool of vodka-laced, blood-red Mr & Mrs T mix.

I tried to remember how much I enjoyed New York, a fine city, bursting with an energy that engulfed you miles before your plane kissed the tarmac. I had visited there many times. Never been mugged. Never lost any baggage. Never been cheated by a cabbie. Never regretted leaving, either. That particular morning, the huge airport was shrouded in a late winter storm. Fingers of heavy mist drew mysterious designs on the wall of windows opposite me. Waiting in that place, feeling tired and sick to numbness, I couldn't dredge up any amicable feelings for the The Big Apple.

"You want anything else, like?" asked the Joan Rivers impersonator of the dewy skin.

I looked up into those clear brown eyes, gushing youth and health. "Bring another in fifteen minutes," I said, tapping my glass.

As she sashayed away, I started to think about my life. Again. It's a subject I suddenly find endlessly fascinating, endlessly confusing. What have I missed? Is this it? Oh, Peggy Lee, "Is this all there is?"

My curiosity has always been my rudder. Even as a toddler, I had to know why, a trait that has been my greatest blessing and my greatest curse. I constantly steered into uncharted territory, propelled by a bone-deep preoccupation with The Unknown. This is a great game plan for settling a continent or discovering a cure for Bubonic Plague, but it is rarely a recipe for a satisfying life. Just about the time I'd get the hang of something or someone, off I'd tear in a brand-new direction. I made some serious mistakes, because I passed up things that were right under my nose in favor of what was around the next bend in the road.

Luis; he was a primo example of that.

We met at UCLA in 1973. He was sleek-looking, with hair the color of milk chocolate and skin to match. He sported a thin moustache and a delicate scar over his left eyebrow that I always referred to as his dueling wound. (Actually, it arrived after a flip off the old bicycle at age six.) He was a second-generation Spanish-American with a passion for life and me.

He always smelled great. I can remember standing in front of his half of the closet and drinking in his aroma, his own masculine aura coupled with a mixture of honey-dipped Sherman cigarettes and lemon soap.

He was majoring in physics and Russian and predicted that the Americans and Soviets would one day develop a peaceful coexistence—share technologies, lead the world into a different dynamic of power. "When that day comes," he used to confidently say, "I'll be sitting in the middle of the action, translating the latest mind-bending concepts of infinite possibility."

He knew. I envied that. He had a plan for his life. Luis was on his way to someplace in particular and understood exactly how to get there.

I, on the other hand, was a mess in those days, the quintessential California blond looking for a party. I was free—maybe a little too free, and admit I cared more about having a good time than getting an education. Not through a lack of intelligence, no. Actually, I'd been something of a scholar in high school: Honors at Entrance; National Merit Society; National Who's Who in The High School Students' Handbook; blah, blah, blah, blah blah … At age sixteen, when I finally escaped the rigid Catholic environment my parents had chosen to "help give me some direction in life" and entered UCLA, I felt I'd been liberated. EEEEEYOWEEEE!

For the next two years, I tried just about every course of study and dated every boy that interested me. History. Philosophy. Music. Sociology. Psychology. Tom. Dick. Harry. Larry, Moe, and Curly. By age eighteen, I'd discarded them all.

Luis was my first real love. He was only twenty when we met, but he was a most unusual young man who finessed the boundary between sensitivity and wimpishness. Why I suddenly had the good sense to recognize his particular value, I couldn't have said.

We met at an afternoon basketball game at Pauley Pavilion. He insisted I order my hot dog first, though he was ahead of me in line. As I drowned the foot-long in ketchup and mustard, he asked me to dinner for later that night. His manners were exquisite, his conversation literate and literary. He treated me like an intelligent and desirable woman: heady stuff. We fell in love and moved in together. Everything went along swimmingly for months.

Then came spring break.

My family tradition dictated we troop down to the La Jolla Beach and Tennis Club. I'd invited Luis to join us, but he'd been invited to a seminar thrown by Caltech for gifted science undergrads from across the nation, a huge honor. Was I magnanimous and supportive when he chose Caltech and physics over La Jolla and me?

That was a rhetorical question.

In case you haven't heard, La Jolla is a charming and well-heeled resort town on the coast of Southern California, just north of San Diego and just west of Paradise. In those days, the Beach and Tennis Club was an elegant old lady with Hollywood, horse racing and cereal empire royalty in her past.

Emblazoned with sea green tile seahorses everywhere you looked, she boasted tennis courts, a pitch-and-putt golf course, a pristine beach and some of the most glorious lifeguards this side of heaven. The big joke was: forget about CPR; a guy just had to have blond hair, blue eyes and perfect teeth to lifeguard at the Beach and Tennis Club; it was written right into the contract.

That's where I met Sandy. He had—Surprise!—blond hair, blue eyes and a perfect smile. He was a jock god clothed in bronze-coated muscle, as different from Luis as a three-masted schooner is from a cigarette boat. He asked me out on my first Saturday afternoon and I accepted. You understand, I wasn't intending to hurt Luis, though we had made a promise not to date other people. But Sandy was gorgeous and uncomplicated and no rocket scientist, three attributes which made him alluring ... please don't ask me why; I'm not ready to answer that question yet.

Besides, Luis would never know.

The sexual revolution was in full swing in 1973. It wasn't difficult to get around my parents, who were concerned about the seriousness of my feelings for Luis, anyhow. Besides, I was on the pill, and Going All The Way was still an adventure, pure and simple.

Sandy bowled me over. He kept doing silly man things to attract my attention: double flips off the low board and a round of arm wrestling matches, all of which he won. A highly polished example of genial machismo, he showed me off at parties every night. Did I enjoy watching all the other high school and college girls hissing with envy?

Rhetorical!

On Thursday night, Sandy took me back to his summer digs at the back of the hotel. He poured me a tall glass of Lancers Sparkling Rose and put a Doors record on his Blaupunkt. I have always been turned on by "Light My Fire," the long version, and that night was no exception.

The foreplay wasn't creative, as Sandy displayed little imagination and less staying power.

My climax was predictably anticlimactic ... there wasn't one.

The next evening, a Friday, Dad invited Sandy to have dinner with us at The Marine Room, a restaurant attached to the hotel. Even then, it oozed this old-fashioned, comfortable, high-rent vibe, with tiled floors, leather banquettes, and picture windows on the surf side. Every summer evening at nine P.M. or thereabouts, the incoming tide pounded against the glass, sending a cascading shiver through the long, low dining room.

It was also at nine P.M. that Luis appeared in the doorway. As he checked the crowd for our party, I remember trying to become invisible. I hid my head behind my braided hands and slowly craned my neck around to stare at the phosphorescent sea surging against the window. Peripherally, I felt Luis hesitate, taking in the scene. Then I heard him stride purposefully across the parquet floor. Click, click, click.

"Why, Luis ...," I heard the surprise in my dad's voice.

"Good evening, Mr. Mitchell. Mrs. Mitchell. Marly."

He sat down a tad too close to Sandy, looking incredibly relaxed. "Hi, I'm Luis Mendinades."

"I'm Sandy. Good to meet you."

Where is a time machine when you really need one? God! How I wished I could catapult myself into the future! There I sat, my lover's arm possessively around my shoulders, looking into the dismayed face of the man I loved. The five of us remained mute for eternity plus one, pouring unbridled attention upon our water glasses.

"So," Sandy finally blurted, "you a friend of Marly's, or what?"

"Actually," Luis replied coolly, "we live together."

You could have heard that silence in San Francisco. If my parents were stunned by this information, Sandy was shocked. His arm fell away from my shoulders. "I see," he said softly, over an uneasy glance my way.

Mom took a deep breath. She was and is a wonderfully put-together woman in every sense of that phrase, with Loren-esque hips and bosom. Her chest cavity swelled to the breaking point. "You two live together?" she asked.

I bobbed my head.

My parents weren't prudes. They would have happily conceded, in theory, that a young woman's interest in sex was a natural part of growing up, as was a relationship which included intimacy. But then, I wasn't just any young woman; I was their daughter. I hadn't kept my feelings for Luis a secret from them. I just hadn't told them every little niggling detail of the relationship ... like the fact that we were living together.

My dad drummed his fingers on the tablecloth. He looked at Luis. He looked back at me. He looked at Sandy. He looked back at his fingers. Then he looked at Mom and raised his right eyebrow. He sat back and lit a cigarette, awaiting the next incoming.

Mom leaned forward and spoke softly to Sandy. "Perhaps you'd feel more comfortable sitting somewhere else? At a bar in downtown San Diego, for example?"

Sandy straightened up. "Actually, no, Mrs. Mitchell." He turned his face to mine and gazed dopily into my eyes. "I think I'm in love with Marly."

Oh, my God ...

I finally got Sandy out of there with a promise to call him the next day, a promise I didn't keep. Luis sat making small talk with my folks while I shoveled Dover sole into my mouth.

At 10:30, Dad paid the bill. He stood up and helped Mom out of her chair. "Marly," he said, "I ..." He shook his head, took Mom's arm, and they joined some bridge-playing friends at the bar. Luis and I were left utterly alone.

He started to speak half a dozen times, lifted his open hands once or twice, shrugged his shoulders. Finally he whispered, "Why?"

I hung my head and spoke the absolute truth. "I don't know."

Luis never raised his voice or even narrowed his eyes. His calm was unnerving. "I don't believe you."

"I don't know! I don't know!" Through gathering tears now, his and mine.

Luis and I stumbled out to the beach which, thank heaven, was deserted. The air was balmy; the sky glistened with starlight; it was a gorgeous moment to embrace Planet Earth. In the midst of that earthly perfection, I shivered with a cold that seemed embedded in my very soul.

Luis looked up at the sky. "I wish I could understand," he said. I could hear pain in his voice.

"I wish I could understand," I answered.

"Do you care for this man?"

"I could never love him the way I love you."

"You slept with him, didn't you?"

I thought hard about lying. I probably could have gotten away with it. But when I looked into his chocolate eyes, I had to acknowledge the terrible chain reaction my behavior had set into motion.

"Yes," I answered.

Luis walked down to the water's edge and lit a cigarette. He squatted on his haunches and studied the waves rolling, rolling.

"Could I have one of those?" I asked.

"But Marly, you don't smoke."

"Seems like the right time to start."

We stood there together, smoking, watching the waves ebb and flow. I could hear music from a boisterous party coming from one of the hotel rooms behind us. People were laughing. Someone put on "The Tracks of My Tears," by Smokey Robinson.

"Maybe we should ... try a separation," Luis said at last. "You can figure out what it is you're looking for, what you want."

He never blamed me. Not once. I would have felt better if he'd ranted and raved, but he wasn't the ranting type.

I started to cry. "But I love you. I love you!"

He frowned. "I believe you ... I do. But your kind of love doesn't respect my kind of love, does it? You know, sometimes two perfectly fine people bring out the absolute worst in each other." He kissed me on the cheek. "I'll stay with Tony until you decide what you want to do." And he was gone.

"You want another?"

It was the lovely Joan-ified Tina, startling me out of my daydream.

"No, thanks. I'll take the check."

When she brought the bill, she noticed my computer case. "Are you a writer, or something?" she asked shyly.

I was about to come back at her with venom-laced sarcasm until I saw the spark of real interest in her eyes.

"Yes," I said simply.

"Wow; one of the sweet jobs. I could never be a writer."

"Tina, my dear, anyone can be a writer, believe me."

Chapter 2

Outside the restaurant, I noticed a duty free shop to my right and decided to do a little browsing. Electronic gates were making their first appearances, clanging to beat the devil when some absent- or pilfering-minded citizen carried out a city-themed silk scarf, celebrity-endorsed perfume or chocolates in gold foil boxes that hadn't been desensitized by a computerized register. Thankfully, the man monitoring the gates insisted on keeping my carry-on luggage, so I stretched out my back muscles and strolled unencumbered down the aisles full of high-rent foreign goods. As I browsed, the suicide conundrum wafted its way back to the front of my consciousness.

A gun is a popular self-offing tool, but getting hold of one in JFK was out of the question unless I mugged an airport policeman. Frankly, summoning the physical strength for that seemed a flight of fantasy (the only flight I was likely to take that day?). Besides, committing suicide with a gun produces predictable and unavoidable gushes and tidbits of blood and brain matter, not to mention unwanted attention. And what if I misfired and had to live the rest of my life as the answer to a sick trivia question? I don't think so.

Hmmm ... perfume bottles. They were made of leaded crystal. I picked up a bottle of Fracas from an almost-naughty counter display featuring a delicious bare-chested male and held it in my hand. The broken pieces probably wouldn't be hefty enough to exert the kind of pressure I needed to slit an artery. There were larger examples on the next shelf down, but it dawned on me that if I cut myself in this place, help was sure to reach me before I could quietly bleed to death. Which meant that, instead of "borrowing" it, I'd have to buy the damned thing and take it to a ladies' room stall.

On the up side, it'd be a lot tougher to get me to pay for it after I was dead. Would an international company sue an American suicide's estate for $672.26—the price of the largest bottle? And, practically speaking, wasn't that a terribly high price to lay out for a second-class suicide method?

"May I assist?"

I looked up.

"With the perfume, madam. May I assist?"

I wondered if the slim, thirty-something woman had read my mind and seen the dark thoughts swirling there. She might have been my age. I find it depressing when people my own age call me ma'am. "Madam" is even worse.

She was severely French, très chic in her navy blue. (Did I miss the memo? When did all official airport apparel become blue?) Her auburn hair was pulled back tautly into an obedient chignon at the base of her long neck. She reached out a graceful hand and picked up the Fracas I had recently discarded as too small a weapon with which to commit a proper suicide.

"A very good value, no? No government tax, you understand."

"Yes. Actually, I was just looking."

"Ahhh, window shopping. I see. My name is Cecile. Well, should you need the assistance, you have but to ask."

I saw her search my face and recognize the gray tinge of my skin.

"Is there ... anything else I can do?"

It was an unexpected meeting of minds that sometimes occurs between strangers.

"No. Actually, I've been ill, but I'm better now."

"I am glad to hear it," she said with a smile that showed one slightly crooked tooth in the front of her mouth. "I will be right over there," she said and walked away, the navy skirt outlining her trim figure.

Now, where was I? Chemotherapy burn-out wreaks havoc with the little gray cells. Oh, yes. I continued walking slowly down the aisles, past leather purses with ugly gold initials and what seemed like acres of clocks and watches. I finally stopped in front of a shelf full of music boxes. I love music boxes, have been collecting them since I was a child. I light up at the silvery melodies and the dancing figures and the scratching sound the tiny keys make as I wind them. Sometimes, when my life is at its bleakest, I set all my lovely boxes in motion at the same time and allow the pleasing, tinkling cacophony to envelop and soothe me.

That's what I did in that duty-free shop. When I had them all going, I closed my eyes and didn't open them again until the last box stilled.

It shouldn't have been surprising that I had gathered the attention of every other shopper and even some folks in the main concourse. Yet I felt as though I'd been caught naked, performing some ancient Druidic ritual.

As I hurried straight back to the electronic gates, gathered up my bags and insinuated myself into the disjointed bustling and jostling, I noticed that the day seemed to have brightened.

In order to return to my gate, I had to reenter security ... which meant I had to prove my computer was really a computer ... which was the main drawback of being a writer and flying. First you unpacked the damned thing. Then you hooked it up to some juice source. Then you turned it on and booted it up and waited until at least four lines of script appeared on the lit screen. Then someone from security had to witness the four lines and the lit screen. Then you unplugged and repacked, making sure to disengage any diskettes. You handed the diskettes to a security guard, placed your various carry-ons on the conveyor belt, passed through the electronic doorway, retrieved your diskettes and picked up your bags.

In the middle of this exercise, I sometimes felt like hurling my laptop into the machinery, smashing everything to smithereens. I imagined the sounds of breaking glass and buzzing alarms and the yelling of voices and the footsteps of the armed response team that would materialize within seconds. I imagined that I would look around innocently and ask, "Gee, is something wrong?"

As I rode the moving sidewalk, I looked out the huge gray-tinted windows and watched an aircraft begin to taxi away from its gate. I wondered if I could somehow make my way down onto the tarmac. And once I was there, what the odds were of my being run over by an L-1011. Of course, the tires on any jumbo jet were quite narrow. And how fast did they taxi, anyway? Four miles an hour? What if some camera-crazed tourist captured me on videotape, crushed and flattened? Or worse, what if the pilot somehow missed me entirely?

Maybe a baggage truck would be a better choice.

The end of the ramp rushed up to meet my feet, and I stumbled onto the tile floor, considering the various possibilities. Surely if I were leveled by a baggage truck, that would be the end of me. Or would it? What if I only sustained a couple of broken legs? God, what if I was paralyzed? The idea of spending more months or years in a hospital, taking physical therapy from some too, too cheerful twenty-five-year-old do-gooder wasn't too appealing. The idea of spending the rest of my days in a wheelchair was insupportable.

Back at the gate, the harried young man was still surrounded by irate passengers. Just then, a telephone rang. Holding up a hand to fend off the next assault, he turned away from the mob and plucked the receiver mounted on the wall behind him.

"Yes?" he asked hopefully.

He listened for a moment then nodded his head twice.

"Thanks be to God," he finished and hung up. He turned back toward the menacing mass of humanity and said simply, "Departure at 4:30 P.M. Boarding at 3:45."

Running his hands through his magnificent 'fro, he disappeared behind a door marked "Airport Personnel Only."

We were finally getting somewhere.

Now that the major data gap had been filled, there was a general exodus toward the main terminal. I guess everyone decided to eat at the same moment, which left some empty chairs. I looked around and found two together, one for me, one for my stuff. It felt good to sit. I was weary. As I stretched out my legs and leaned back, my eyelids felt heavy. In the good old days, which means any time at all pre-disease, falling asleep was a feat I could only accomplish in a darkened room at night, on top of a bed with clean sheets stretched tight over a firm mattress. Forget napping. Forget sleeping in a car or on a plane.

Things are different now. I can fall asleep anywhere, any hour, on or in any conveyance for any amount of time: a ten-minute taxi ride; an hours-long, choppy crossing of the English Channel; at my desk in my Eames rocker morning, noon, or night. An airport chair, rock-hard or otherwise, was no match for my newly intimate relationship with the Sandman.

Of course, the nightmares can be a little rough, especially the ones that come in the broad light of day. And it's unpleasant to awaken soaked to the skin when you're dressed for a business meeting. But the ability to drop off is one I've always envied in other people, and I choose to indulge my napping capability in spite of the attendant terrors.

For some reason, the nightmare that visits most frequently is The Lump. It always starts out with me in the shower. I am singing "The Dance," a poignant Garth Brooks country mega-hit. I reach for the soap, which slips off its dish and onto the yellow tile floor of the shower. As I bend down to retrieve it, I notice a large lump in my left breast. I can't ever remember having seen it before. I press my hand to the lump and attempt to flatten it. But it's too hard to suppress and continues growing slowly, inexorably, right before my eyes. I try to scream, but I can't get any air into my lungs and begin to gasp for breath. I realize that the lump is sucking the very life out of me. That's when I wake up.

I had that dream for the first time three weeks before the mammogram that started it all. I'd been examining myself like the good doctors on Oprah Winfrey's show advised and never felt anything the least bit ominous.

The Cancer Club

I recall plainly waking up from The Lump Nightmare that first time in a cold sweat. My sheets and nightgown were soaked through. My heart banged haphazardly against my ribs until I thought my chest cavity would burst. I switched on my bedside lamp and waited for the fear to ooze away. That's what usually happened with the infrequent scary dreams I'd had in the past. But somehow, I couldn't shake the awful cold that shivered up and down my spinal nerve endings.

It was an omen. As sure as I lay there, rigid with what-ifs, it was an omen.

As I dozed fitfully on the Naugahyde seat in the BWIA terminal at Kennedy International, I felt The Lump Nightmare tiptoeing into my subconscious. I was just about to fall headlong into that dreadfully familiar scenario when a voice came over the loudspeaker.

"Ladies and gentlemen, we are elated to announce our boarding of British West Indies Airlines flight 469 to Antigua, Tobago and Trinidad. Please have your passes at the ready. We will be pre-boarding anyone needing assistance, the infirm, and those flying with young children."

A cheer went up from the throng as I came fully awake, thankful for having escaped a trip down the rabbit hole. I gathered up my gear and got on the airplane with the rest of the folks needing assistance, the infirm, and those flying with young children.

Chapter 3

Antigua is a lush island nation in the Caribbean. Variously, it is a place for lovers, newlyweds, college kids on vacation and lone writers needing a break from deadlines and unwelcome plot suggestions. When citizens of the frozen north dream of the Garden of Eden, Antigua is the image they conjure up.

My destination was a hotel there called Half-Moon Bay, a place I had visited three years before over Easter week, by accident, when the adjoining Saint James resort was full. It wasn't posh in the least. What it did have in abundance was that air of studied neglect that is common to all one-time British colonies with hot, humid climates.

Riots of hibiscus and bougainvillea cascaded in balletic grace over white split-rail fences. The rooms themselves were small and simply decorated and contained no clocks or telephones.

Each room did have a miniscule veranda overlooking the gray-green ocean, furnished with a table and two sailcloth chairs. The sea caressed the beach incessantly, in hypnotic rhythm, and when mixed with the sound of nightly trade winds, the result was a soft and haunting lullaby. It was an enchanting place, and Lord knows, I needed some enchantment.

As I settled back into my first-class seat, I began to think about what the hell I was doing. Changing my entire life around, that's what I was doing. Okay, okay, it needed changing, but even if suicide wasn't the answer, something had to give.

The previous eleven months had been the toughest, most humbling and most draining period of my entire life. I could pinpoint the exact moment when life's guillotine dissected my past from Everything Else: the moment I awakened from The Lump nightmare for the very first time.

Fighting cancer is like fighting the Hundred Years War. It is an interminable campaign that demands voluminous amounts of re-education, strength of purpose, a physically and emotionally shattering array of weapons/treatments, horrifying choices, and every ounce of love and support you can squeeze from whomever you can squeeze it out of.

There is also the matter of fear.

It paralyzes. It affects the ability to make decisions. It muddles awareness and saps strength. Fear has become my mortal enemy. In order to get a better fix on Fear, I have imagined it with a human form and character, the better to recognize it, my dear.

Fear is definitely male. Tall and skinny to the point of gauntness. His hair is the color of a rainy-day sky, and his cheeks and eye sockets are carved sharp like ravines. His gangling limbs are covered with gray clothes of excellent quality and cut. His voice is gentle, soft, cool, and he broadcasts his dangerous message in a whisper that is always present inside your head: there's nothing you can do about it, anyway ... why not let go? Give up? Give in?

As the plane took off, I felt gravity push against my chest. Mentally, I pictured the indentation in my left breast where all had once been round plumpness. The scar only hurt occasionally now, but there was still a dull ache in that empty space. It's known as a phantom pain. Dr. Phyllis Dent (an appropriate name?) carefully explained the phenomenon.

"It's perfectly normal," she said kindly.

I remember pursing my lips and considering the situation. "You mean that it's perfectly normal to feel pain in tissue that's been chopped off?" I glared down at the offending site. "How can it still be hurting if I don't have a there there?"

Dr. Dent shook her head. "What can I say? It's a mystery. The pain is real enough. It's the body part that's the phantom. Ergo, the name ..."

"Phantom pain," I finished. "It pisses me off."

Once the fasten-your-seatbelt sign had gone out, a flight attendant named Ginevra began taking drink orders.

"And what can I be getting for you now, ma'am?" she asked in that musical way I have always loved hearing. It sounds happy even when it isn't meant to.

"Something tropical with scads of good, dark rum."

"Oh, I see," she said with a grin. "It's one of those vacations."

"Yes, one of those."

"Well, then, my only recourse is to conjure up an old family recipe. It's been handed down, don't you know, through six generations of my family's women. It's gorgeous and packs quite a wallop."

"Just what the doctor ordered."

"Are you travelling all the way to Tobago?"

"No. I get off in Antigua."

"Will you be renting a car?"

"No. Actually, someone is meeting me." I felt myself blush.

"I see," she said with another grin. "Then you can have as many Aunt Minnie's Surprises as you wish."

It was a good drink. The tall glass came frosty and rimmed with pink sugar. I couldn't begin to describe the subtle blending of juices and liqueurs that seduced the tongue and the nose oh, so gently.

The seat next to me was empty, and after my second Aunt Minnie, I spilled over into the adjoining space. If my mother could only see me now. Actually, I'd asked her to join me, knowing how she appreciated exotic drinks and balmy weather. But she begged off politely. "Three's a crowd. Maybe when you get to ... know him a little better."

"Does that mean 'know' in the biblical sense?" I'd asked sarcastically.

"Yes, actually, I think it does. For your sake, I hope it does."

"Mother!"

"Don't 'Mother' me, Marly." She took me in her arms. "You've been through the wringer these past months. It's not your fault that Don was such a prick."

"Don't you think he had good reason? I'm not exactly the woman I once was."

"Bull," my mother said with a snort. "And even if you were only a tenth of the woman you once were, you'd still be twice the person Good Ol' Don will ever be in his wildest dreams."

That's why I love my mom. She's a pithy, man-eating tiger whose ferocity has never been minced when it came to my defense. God bless her.

"In fact," she continued with a grin, "I've brought you a little bon voyage gift."

She searched through her huge handbag for more than a minute before plucking and brandishing her prize. It looked like a small plastic bottle filled with water.

"What is this," I asked, "miracle H20 from Lourdes, to ensure my complete remission?"

"No," she said with a laugh. "It's called AstroGlide."

"Again, please?"

"It's made by the AstroLube Company of North Hollywood. See?" she asked, showing me the label.

"I'm almost afraid to ask," I said, rolling my eyes.

"It's a sexual lubricant."

"Mother!"

"It doesn't contain any petroleum products, which means it's totally safe for women. And it has a light, lovely taste."

"Oh, my God!" I plucked the bottle from her and waved it in her face. "Let me get this straight ... At the moment of truth, I'm supposed to whip out my little bottle of AstroGlide and casually pour it over myself and wait for the fireworks to begin?"

"Something like that."

I shook my head. "Right."

She put her arm around me then. "Don't you think I know how difficult this all is for you? I'm just trying to help."

"He'll think I'm nuts."

"If he does, then he's not the right man for you."

"Mother, the right man for me doesn't exist in our galaxy."

Chapter 4

As the plane cruised toward the rendezvous point, I began to think about the man I was going to meet. We'd been introduced some months before by mutual acquaintances in the Studio City hills, not far from where I make my home. He was visiting them from Ohio, and they put together a small dinner party in his honor.

It was my first official social outing since the lumpectomy. (Isn't that a charming term?) As I was in between chemo episodes that particular night, I felt scrappy and sarcastic and insecure, although I was fairly confident I'd be spared throwing up. This man and I had intentionally been seated next to one another by the hostess, who thought she was being subtle and clever, a circumstance that made me grate my teeth and lock my jaw ... as unnoticeably as possible. What woman has any zest for the idea of flirting with a new man when she's only got half a boob on one side?

"This seems like the perfect setting for a food fight," he said as he sat down beside me. "Hi, I'm Chris Lockehead."

Rhymes with "blockhead?"

"Hello, I'm Marly," I said, sticking out my hand. "A food fight, you say?"

Hmmmm.

"One of life's little pleasures in the right company. That's how Janet and I met." He picked up a sourdough roll from his Spode bread plate and began wadding up the soft inside. "In Mazatlan, at a place called Señor Frog's. It was an accident, actually. I bit into one of those little hot peppers they serve in relish bowls down there, and I ended up squirting Janet and Richard, who were sitting at the next table."

This was no kid talking, but an eminently successful something-or-other somewhere in his forties. I took a closer look at him then.

Not a classically handsome man by any means, he was medium height and blondish. I remember how inviting I found his nice, open smile and the way his eyes twinkled when he tossed the first small piece of bread at our hostess.

"Uh-oh ... I'm going to have to warn you all," she said, pointing her finger at Chris with a gay laugh. "Our friend down the table there is a food-fightin' fool. Watch out for incoming missiles!"

I watched the developing hostilities with bemusement, careful to remain detached. The antipasto made up the first wave of armament, as a couple of raw carrot pieces and a celery chunk zipped through the air at carefully timed intervals. The trick, it seemed, was to launch an attack without being observed by the enemy. Chris marshaled his forces in an expert manner, readying two projectiles at a time. Janet was much more casual, hurling tiny bits of vegetables whenever the mood struck.

The war escalated and ebbed in turn. We were all invited to join in the melee, but no one else did. Janet's husband, Richard, a dour and desperately critical self-made poop, paid no attention whatsoever to the goings-on. He dominated a discussion about fallen real estate prices and groused about money in general, as though it were the most natural thing in the world for an occasional glob of sun-dried tomato to whiz by his face.

"A recession is tough on everyone. A ton of people bought houses purely for investment, and they got greedy. Now they're paying the price." He grinned at his own witticism.

Whiz.

"But Richard," said an older woman named Dot, with outrageously teased hair, "don't you think it's rather pathetic that a college professor can't afford to buy a decent house in this city?"

"What's decent?" he asked, scowling. He leaned back into his $600 Saarinen chair and opened his arms expansively, symbolically hugging all the pricey furniture and objets d'art in his eyesight. "Not everyone can afford this. Why should they be able to? I worked my ass off for it."

"You don't suppose," I ventured, "that an Ivy League education and a trust fund had anything to do with it?" My relationship with Richard was one of casual animosity. His self-importance wore me out.

"Oh, minimally," he conceded.

Whiz, whiz.

"But let's all remember, Marly," he said, clasping his hands behind his head, "that luck is merely that moment when opportunity meets preparation."

Dot's husband, skinny Nat, got into the act. "But some folks just don't get the same number of opportunities. Doesn't matter how prepared you are if you never find yourself in the right place at the right time. Am I right?"

"People overlook opportunity every day of the week," Richard said smugly.

"C'mon, Richard," I said in exasperation. "You didn't have to scrape three pennies together when you started out. Your money was family money. You had a leg up on the rest of us from the get-go."

Chris picked up two baby peas on his fork and said, "I can appreciate the seriousness of Richard's position. I, too, have given away huge sums of money ... to ex-wives." He whizzed the peas at Janet, who ducked and stuck out her tongue.

Everyone laughed except Richard.

"I'm not bitter about that," Chris continued. "Although I am thinking about throwing an end-of-alimony-payments party in May. It irritates me that women always get a settlement when they're just as able as men to make their own living."

Whiz.

"That sounds good, but it's not the whole truth, though, is it?" asked Dot. "Because while women make up 51% of the work force, they only earn seventy-seven cents for every dollar made by a man with the same educational background and experience level."

My respect for Dot expanded.

"Is that true?" asked Janet.

"That's not my fault, dammit," Richard said in a tone of voice closely akin to a sneering growl.

"No one's blaming you, Richard," I said with fabricated patience. "And I wouldn't dream of taking anything away from your success. I'm only saying that you had a little help along the way. And now, in your turn, you've helped a couple of women along their way."

More laughter.

Janet urged, "Marly, Marly, tell them your theory about men and money."

"Oh, Janet, I don't know ..."

Chris turned to look at me. "I'd be interested in hearing this."

I thought about it for a long moment before deciding I might as well leap from the frying pan into the fire. "Okay. Men have an odd umbilical-type cord which runs from the center of their souls straight to their bank accounts." I smiled prettily and waited for rebuttal. When none was forthcoming, I continued. "When a man gets divorced, he hates like hell to pay any of his money to his stay-at-home wife and/or children, even if she worked to support him in the beginning, because what he is being separated from in this transaction is actually a piece of his soul."

Richard's face and neck reddened.

Chris said, "Ouch" but didn't interrupt further.

Nat asked, "You really believe this?"

"Think about it," I answered. "How many men still insist their working wives do all the housework, handle all the child care and expect to see dinner ready when the workday ends? A ton of men, that's how many. It's always the woman who interrupts her career for childbearing and rearing. Usually it's the woman who moves with the man's business opportunities. It's the woman who doesn't scale up her own corporate ladder, because she can't or doesn't care to put in the same amount of overtime and weekend hours as her male counterparts. Why, you may ask? Because her husband/boyfriend/lover/children/parents or whatever know she will eventually sublimate her own wants and needs to those of everyone else. That has always been the custom of civilization. Rosie the Riveter and her sisters went out into the work force en masse in the forties for the very first time. Ten thousand years of culture can't be undone in fifty. It's gonna take time. The sooner men wake up and smell the coffee, the better for us all."

Chris picked up his demitasse of coffee and sniffed.

I turned to Richard, who looked as though his masculine plumbing may have been tightening up.

"I've heard you complain that Janet isn't financially independent enough," I said. "Don't deny it; we've all heard you. And yet, if she had a real job outside this house, and had certain hours and days that had to be allotted to her business activities, and wasn't available to travel with you to Mexico or Tahoe or Timbuktu at the drop of your hat, you'd be aggravated."

Nobody said a word for at least three minutes. Finally Janet laughed nervously and announced, "Dessert!"

The dessert was wild blueberry pie, which brought about an unconditional cease-fire, announced by Richard in no-bullshit tones. "Blueberries stain. I'd prefer to keep my white walls white, if you don't mind. And it might be nice to have a little peace at the table while we're at it." He punctuated this with another one of His Looks.

Damned if I didn't agree with him.

I helped Janet take the dirty dishes to the kitchen. "Are you sure you should be lugging those?" she asked.

"Unfortunately, I'm recovered enough to reengage in all sorts of menial tasks," I sighed, lifting the dishes into the sink. "Richard's having a good night."

"Is he? I never pay one bit of attention."

That was true.

"God, you were acid tonight, Marly. I just love it when you talk like that. Hey, have you made up your mind about reconstructive surgery? I know a wonderful man. He goes right through the nipple and never leaves a scar. See?" she said, whipping up her top with her dry hand to show me the good doctor's handiwork.

I shook my head in wonder. Janet had grown up relatively poor. She was a striking-looking woman with innocent blue eyes and baby blond hair. One of the things I liked best about her was the way she openly adored her newly acquired wealth-by-marriage. She was obviously delighted with the width of her wallet, even a little heavy-handed about it, but never malicious. There was no meanness in her. So when she bragged and paraded and gifted her friends with expensive and thoughtful trinkets, it was impossible to hold it against her. Besides, she had great taste, and I have always enjoyed receiving presents, particularly when given just for the hell of it.

She also knew a lot about surgeons, plastic and otherwise.

"I've considered rebuilding my boob," I said. "Sounds like a post-war period, doesn't it? But for some reason, I've become perversely proud of my missing pound of flesh. I consider it a kind of Purple Heart." I then patted the poor little indentation.

"So what do you think about Chris? Isn't he sweet?"

I had to admit that he was.

"He's getting over someone, I guess. Richard and I only met him last year. You know, Marly, he's a lot like you."

"He is? Is he missing some vital anatomical part?"

"I'm serious. He's funny and likes people, and he doesn't cat around ... At least, I don't think he cats around. Plus, he's very successful, if you know what I mean."

I knew what she meant.

"He likes you already," Janet went on blithely as she continued stacking the dishes in the sink. It was Sunday and, therefore, Maria's night off. But that good Guatemalan woman would return first thing Monday morning to a dirty kitchen and party leftovers. Janet did as little around the house as possible and made no excuses. It was another thing I liked about her.

"Janet, don't be an ass. After the tirade I blew through? Besides, how could you possibly know how the man feels about me?"

"Because I asked him."

"Oh. Well ... Does he know about the Big Valley?" I asked.

"I didn't think it was my place to mention it."

"Ah ... then he still has that fantastic and marvelous surprise awaiting him."

"He won't care. He's not shallow like that. He's had five years of therapy."

Oh, my God ...

"And how many wives?" I asked.

"Well ...," she equivocated.

"How many?"

"Three, actually."

"And his latest ... She's the one he's getting over?"

"No ... I don't think so. I think there might have been an alcoholic girlfriend since."

Oh, brother.

A sane person would have written the whole thing off right then and there. The logic was unassailable: I was still in the recovery period from my surgery. Chemo was proving to be hell on heels. My brain was stressed out and stretched taut. Chris, it seemed, was still nursing some significant wounds of his own, not to mention the fact that he lived in bloody Ohio, which made him FUGU (fucking unbelievably geographically undesirable). How easily I could have written the whole damned thing off.

But I didn't.

After dinner, I walked out onto the veranda for a cigarette. Chris followed me and pulled out a silver cigarette case. The three-quarter moon was low-slung and sepia. I inhaled and watched the city lights flickering in the distance below. We smoked companionably for a time.

"So, Chris," I found myself asking, "where exactly do you live in Ohio?"

"Cleveland. Don't laugh."

"Why would I laugh?"

Chris laughed. "People do. Cleveland is funny, I guess. I also spend a lot of time in Bentonville, Arkansas."

"Which is probably not more than a stone's throw from Pea Ridge."

"How in the hell did you know that? I'm impressed."

"I've done some research on the Civil War battle sites. Pea Ridge was significant."

"If you say so. Anyway, I'm on the outskirts of retail sales, and Bentonville is to us folk as Mecca is to a Moslem. It's the headquarters city of Sam Walton's businesses." His voice was flat, its rhythm measured.

"Wasn't he the Walmart guy?" I asked.

Chris looked rather pleased with me. "You do get around. Yeah. He was one hell of a man, down-to-earth, smart as a tack. Drove a pick-up with two black Labs in the way back. Sam knew retail."

"You work for his company, then?"

"Not exactly. I'm a consultant."

I've always found people who style themselves as "consultants" to be slippery as eels. What do they do, exactly? What are they selling? I spoke these thoughts out loud to Chris, who chuckled good-naturedly.

"I'm attracted to women who can make me laugh. It's unusual."

"For you to laugh? Or have you concluded that women were brought forth upon this earth solely to bring you pain?"

"You're doing it again."

"Am I? And you evaded the question."

"Did I?" he asked with a grin; he grinned a lot. "You know, I get out to Los Angeles once in a while. Why don't you give me your number? The next time I'm in town, I'll take you to dinner and tell you just exactly what it is I do. It'll take me about that long to figure it out."

This sounded uncomfortably like a "date." Ugh.

"I don't know ..."

"Look," he said, "I've never met anyone like you before. You're smart and pretty, and you've got my favorite kind of legs—long and shapely. I bet you even pump your own gas. Let me take you to dinner."

Any man who thought I had long legs was a man I wanted to get to know better. Of course, eventually, if things progressed far enough along, I'd have to tell him about ... it.

"I have an idea," I said, looking straight into his pale blue eyes. "Are you a letter-writer?"

"I'm no author like you, but I've been known to put pen to paper."

I stood up a little straighter and blew a perfect smoke ring, pleased that he'd heard of me. "You've heard of me, then." It was a statement, not a question.

"Not exactly. Not much of a reader. But Janet told me how good you are."

The blind leading the blind there.

"But I think it'd be a gas to correspond with someone who makes their living as a writer. I'm game."

And so we traded addresses and began to write back and forth on a regular basis.

I wrote first. It was a chatty sort of letter, a kind of lengthy how-de-do. I asked him about his life and where he lived, and I told him something about my life and where I lived. I didn't mention having had cancer. What was the point of his knowing then?

His response stunned me. It was your basic life history, beginning at the beginning. It ran seven double-sided pages and didn't pull any punches. His mother was an emotional abuser, critical to the point of cruelty. His father was a mild-mannered ineffectual who didn't spend enough time defending his children from the Dragon Lady. Chris had three sisters and two brothers, and none of them were apple-pie normal.

He'd been your classic asshole/success and poured all of his energy, from his college years onward, into showing his mother how terribly she'd misjudged him and his potential. In the meantime, three wives and several girlfriends were swept by the wayside, all victims of his consuming need to prove over and over his own worth to his mother and himself and the world.

He touched on his relationship with the alcoholic. Apparently, he'd met her in his group therapy and should have known better. He wanted to help her, but she didn't want to be helped. He made her sound like a tragedy waiting to happen and stated plainly that he thought he was pretty much over her now.

Again, I could have stopped the whole thing dead in its tracks. I actually thought about it. I could have, but I didn't. Oh, shit.

Chapter 5

I could feel Ginevra bending down over me, peering into my face, gauging whether I was asleep or awake. I opened one eye.

"Will you be wanting lunch, then?" she asked.

"What is it?" I asked, stretching languidly.

"There's a choice in first today. You can either have steak or fish."

"What fish?"

"Sea bass, grilled in butter and herbs. It's the best of a so-so lot."

"That's a good enough recommendation for me, Ginevra. What would you say to another Aunt Minnie as a side dish?"

"I'd be saying coming right up."

The fish wasn't bad, for airplane food. Which is like saying rubbing alcohol isn't bad, for sipping whiskey.

I passed on the cuisine and gazed out the window. The sky is always so salute-the-flag blue at that altitude. On this particular journey, the clouds looked like fat powder puffs. My great-grandmother, Francesca, loved to contemplate clouds and could name them properly: cumulus, stratus, cirrus. It was something she'd picked up during her years as a pilot. I remember visiting her and great-grandfather Matt when I was eight. That would have been the summer of 1968, when I'd flown from Los Angeles to Des Moines all by myself and felt very grown-up.

Francesca and Matt had owned a flight school in Iowa together for ten or twelve years before retiring to Francesca's family property just outside of Lost Nation, a small town in the Wapsipinicon River Valley. It was a twelve-acre apple farm with a pond, a bridal cottage, a barn, and a rambling white frame main house called—no imagination there—Main House. It was a gorgeous, gracefully aging place, the perfect setting for Francesca, who was still a gorgeous woman, even in her seventies.

Matt was younger by about twelve years. They'd met when he was forty-seven and divorced, and she was sixty and widowed. I've heard the most provocative stories about how their love affair scandalized the little town. My mother, Sarah, was so taken with the story, it ended up being the subject of her first really successful novel. Did I mention she was a writer, too? Her style personifies a kind of innocence I can't seem to infuse into my own characters.

Matt and Francesca were obviously still crazy about one another. In the firefly-lit dusk of the midwestern evenings, we'd all sit on the front porch, where I'd luxuriate in their fantasies about the cloud formations that rolled by.

"Those are horse-tails," she'd say. "They're attached to the rumps of the Celestial Herd. When the wind comes out of the west, they kick up their heels and race toward moonrise. I can almost hear them neighing. Can't you?"

I could.

"Now that ...," Matt would say on another evening, pointing upward at the deepening purple dotted with cottage cheese, "that is a buttermilk sky. Watch the curdles as they continuously meet and separate. I've always been partial to buttermilk, especially in Frannie's Death Ball biscuits."

"I have always been and will always be partial to you, Matthew Mosley."

Then they'd kiss. Not a peck on the cheek like my Grandmother Rachael's usual buss with Grandpa Clay. And not an air kiss in the manner of my great-great Aunt Maude. No. Francesca and Matt's kisses were usually lingering and soulful.

Great-grandfather Matt died in 1989 and Francesca in 1990. She was over 100 years old by then but still possessed of all her faculties. Even on her deathbed, there was a most compelling quality about her physical beauty, as though she were lit from within. She used to say that Matt had kept that fire inside of her alive despite time's efforts to extinguish it.

I have recently begun to wonder if I'll ever be lucky enough, blessed enough, to have a relationship like that. Hell, these days I'm wondering if I'll have the opportunity to break out the AstroGlide sometime before it evaporates.

Now that I was actually on my way to Antigua, I was nervous as a bug on a cat's paw. I hadn't been with a man in many months, and those last occasions had been humiliating. I couldn't blame the cancer for that, not exclusively. So it was comforting to think that when I ran out of bad luck to curse, there was always Good Ol' Don.

I was engaged to Don when I first experienced The Lump nightmare. He was a Sooner man/child, whipcord lean and slightly bow-legged. He was ruddy-haired and ruddy-faced and a hell-raiser, was Ol' Don. My mother, bless her heart, still can't understand how I ever could have been attracted to him. He was, in her words, "a lump of coal in the rough."

He was charming in a bronco-busting sort of way, if petulance can be charming. A cowboy by birthright and a screw-up by profession, Don was a hard-drinking, motorcycle-riding daredevil. He loved fast cars and speedboats and bull-dogging. He was proud as a peacock of being a man who lived on the edge. I came to think of him simply as a man with a death wish.

I have met others like him ... people who are at their best in crisis situations, people who are hell-bent on setting up those same damn crisis situations on a regular basis so they can make the heroic effort and come galloping to their own rescue. Yokels addicted to this kind of adrenaline rush never consider the hell they put everyone else through. They're too self-absorbed and too busy flinging monkey wrenches into perfectly good works. When everyday life doesn't get screwed up enough, racetracks and defensive driving schools and bungee cord outfits fill the need to defy bad odds.

I certainly wouldn't want to give the impression that I'm a goody two-shoes. I had my share of turmoil during my hormonally ruled adolescence, which led to my reputation for being wild as the west Texas wind. By the time my mid-twenties rolled around, though, I'd had my fill of inviting myself onto life-threatening roller coaster rides. I'd come to the conclusion that thrilling adventure should not be confused with downright stupidity. Although Don was in his forties when we met, he'd never had the good sense to come to the same conclusion.

I could have put up with the strained muscles and broken bones and contusions and maybe even the topsy-turvy temperament that came with the realization that he was getting too old for the whirlwind he made of his life.

It was the women that drove me nuts. Zaftig women, athletic women, Ph.D.s or high school dropouts ... Ol' Don was like a kid in a candy store, with a drive to taste every single jelly bean, licorice whip and peanut cluster. Not that he had affairs with all of them or any of them. It's just that he couldn't let a daughter of Eve pass by without making an effort. It got so I hated to go out in public with the man. He'd get this look in his eye, and off he'd go down the rabbit hole.

Why, you may be asking, would a sensitive and reasonably intelligent woman like myself put up with such a man? One, he was totally different from any other man I'd ever been with. And two, he was a remarkable lover.

My mother has always maintained that any woman who finds two or three truly satisfying lovers out of a possible ten or twenty during a, well, ... distracted lifetime, is living a miracle. For those lucky or ignorant women who manage to stay faithfully married to one man all their lives, with no previous sexual experience, the point is moot. Since they have no practical basis for comparison, they don't know what they're missing. Both my mother and I do have a practical basis for comparison.

My romantic case history, unfortunately, is the usual tacky mixture of unrequited loves, bad choices, and curiosity killing the cat. My mother's story, on the other hand, is wonderfully convoluted. She married the same man twice: my father, Talbot. Once at nineteen, when she was pregnant with me, and again on my twelfth birthday, after they'd been divorced for two years.

Good Ol' Don had a naturally slow rhythm to his lovemaking, which complimented mine like trade winds compliment tropical summer nights. Since he was on the plus side and I was on the small side, our coming together, so to speak, could have made for a very uncomfortable ride. Fortunately for me, he didn't hang his hat on staying power. Because of his flirtatious nature, securing his undivided attention was a tall order, but once I had him lying quietly by my side, my deliberate caresses usually did the trick. He was a slave to his lust.

Hell, he was a man, wasn't he?

Because I owned him in bed, I felt lush and powerful in his arms, free to experiment. I tied his hands together with silken scarves and sometimes pleasured him with ice cubes in my mouth.

I'm not a word-mincer. I know all the slang sexual expressions, and am not averse to tossing them into the conversational stream on occasion. But writing them here, in the midst of my own storytelling, makes me nervous. "Penis" is a slight and somehow ridiculous word for an appendage whose cravings have changed the course of history. It sounds cartoonish, especially if you say it over and over. (I'd recommend trying this exercise in the privacy of your own bathroom.) So what are the alternatives? "Dick" isn't too bad, I guess. "Throbbing member" sounds like a Young Republican with a headache. I've always been partial to "schlong," though I've never been quite certain of the spelling. But isn't it more of a stand-up comic's term that doesn't seem appropriate when describing passionate clinches including penetration and nudity?

Okay, let's try it again ... I'd fill my mouth with ice cubes and his dick(?) prick(?) until I heard him catch his breath and felt him quiver with pain-tinged pleasure.

To give him credit, he searched for all my secret places. He had solid instinct with his tongue and sensed when to press harder and when to lighten up. He had patience and knew when I was ready. Actually, it was all a lot more fun than it sounds here.

The cancer came between us. It must have pushed the button of his own mortality too piercingly. I remember our last night as lovers: he seemed remote, distracted. As we drew apart literally and figuratively, I lit a cigarette and watched him watching me. He looked troubled.

"Speak to me," I said.

In answer, he got up and walked over to the window. With his back to me, I could see the tension in his shoulders and neck. From overhead, the rare sound of California rain drummed on the roof.

"I'm thinkin' of sellin' my business and tryin' to start up someplace else. Maybe Utah or Washington State. Maybe Alaska," he said finally.

"And?"

"And I thought ... well, things might be kinda tough at first. I couldn't ask you to come with me. At least for a while."

"Really? Why?"

He turned to look at me then. He scratched the late-day stubble on his cheek, warming to the lie he was about to tell. "Well, you bein' sick, and all ... yeah. It's askin' too damned much."

"I'm not sick. I have ... I had cancer. They cut it out of my body. Right here." I jabbed at the scar with my finger. I was beginning to get angry. "Eventually, I'll be done with the chemotherapy, and that'll be that. So what's the big deal? I'm a writer. I can support myself just fine, thank you. Anyplace in the world."

He folded his arms and got that stubborn look in his eyes I had come to dread. He said, "I'm only thinkin' of you, Marly."

I laughed harshly. "What a crock! You never did or said anything in your whole goddamned life that wasn't first and foremost for your own benefit." It hit me then. "You're scared!" I hurled the words at him. "What're you afraid of, big guy? That you'll catch it, for Christ's sake? You don't have tits, you know."

"I don't know what you're talking about, Marly. I can sure as shit tell you that you're not the same woman you used to be."

"Brilliant! I have a three-inch hole in my chest and a scar that itches and burns constantly. I've only just started chemo, and already my hair is falling out in handfuls, and half the time I feel like I've got a dead puppy in my stomach. How could I possibly be the same woman, you son of a bitch?"

Hot tears burned at the corners of my eyes. I sniffed them back and set my chin.

"I have needed you these past few months like I never needed anyone before. And I hate it. But as much as I hate it, I can't help it. Don't you think I've seen the repulsion in your eyes when you look at my body? When you touch me?"

"That's a damn lie. That scar has nothin' to do with it."

He walked to the closet and reached for a pair of old jeans, shrugging them on almost violently.

"I feel like I been livin' here by myself," he said. "I'm tired of it. So you're sick. Well, I'm sorry as hell and all about that, believe me. But I am tired to death of your whinin' and mopin' and draggin' around here like some paralyzed dog. I just can't take it!"

I screamed at him then, a cry of rage from the depths of my despair. He grabbed a sweater from a bureau drawer and whipped it on over his head. I sprang from the bed and lunged at him, my hands like steel talons. I tore at him and then I pounded him with my fists.

He gripped my arms with his large hands, those hands that had given me so much pleasure, and shook me. When I suddenly collapsed against him, sobbing like a child, I felt him freeze up. He took a deep breath and let the air out of his lungs in slow motion. Then he reached over to touch my face but thought better of it. Gently, ever so gently, he guided me to the bed and sat me down.

"I'll get you some water and a Kleenex."

By turns, I cried and moaned and shivered and pummeled the mattress like a madwoman.

Don returned with the water and a wet washcloth. He sat down on the bed and waited till my inner furies subsided before handing me the glass and the tissue.

I remember how I shuddered, aching to be held, horrified of being pitied. Yet I was stuck in the eye of a hurricane of self-pity. I hugged myself to keep my soul from spilling out through my pores. Outside, the storm shook the foundations of the house as the wind rose. Inside, my personal cyclone shook the foundation of the person I had come to think of as myself. I took a deep breath and looked up at Don.

In the shadowed room we had shared, he resembled nothing so much as a lost little boy. I could tell he needed to look to me for comfort, and I had none to give. On the bedside table, the clock ticked the minutes away, along with the shards of our relationship.

"Ladies and gentlemen, this is your captain. We will now begin our approach to formerly Coolidge, now V.C. Bird International Airport. We should be landing in ten minutes or so. We would appreciate your passing all cups and glasses to the center aisle, where an attendant will gather them up. You must fasten your trays properly and return your seatbacks to their full and upright positions. Thank you."

Ginevra came by, and I gathered my empty Aunt Minnie glasses.

"Awfully good, Ginevra. Refreshing, with a soft finish." I fixed her with my most serious look. "I don't suppose you'd give up the recipe without a fight ... but I think I'd be willing to pay hard cash."

"Sadly, the recipe doesn't belong to me. It has been a secret in my family since the earliest days of rum shacks. But I tell you, if you'll be sending me an autographed copy of *BloodHounds*, signed to my grandmother Kaydee, I think we just might be working something out."

I flushed with pleasure. "You know me?"

"Gran is a great reader. She's thoroughly enjoyed everything you and your mother have ever written."

"Give me an address, my dear, and it shall be done."

Chapter 6

The three-point touchdown was smooth. I stepped out into the humid evening and breathed in the unmistakable smell of Antigua: pungent, sweet and sour by turns, equal parts refinery smoke, ripening fruit, and jet fuel. The sun was setting as I made my way into the shed laughingly called "terminal" and prepared my visa information.

V.C. Bird is classified as an "international" airport solely by virtue of the planes that land there. It is not grand or automated, and the air conditioning system is a disaster.

"And you are here for business or pleasure?" asked the square-built immigration agent.

"Pleasure."

"Fine. You'll be picking up your luggage there," he said, gesturing with his pointer finger, "and then you'll carry them through customs there." He looked at me squarely and waggled his chin. "Remember, it is against our law for any unhappy people to vacation in this tropical paradise." His wide smile showed off two gold-capped teeth. He stamped my entrance date with panache and motioned me on. "You be enjoying your stay now, you hear? You be enjoying your stay. Next!"

Since all baggage at V. C. Bird is moved by hand, I wrangled my patience as the ground crew got with the program, blotting perspiration with my sleeve. A young man in jeans and a tee shirt sucked up my things like a human Hoover and hurled them onto his pushcart. He deposited me in front of the main building next to the drive-by, where I began looking for Chris.

Who was nowhere to be found.

Shit.

There's nothing like feeling sweaty, exhausted and slightly tipsy after a long, debilitating trip, unless it's feeling abandoned and lost after a long, debilitating trip. I wrestled my big bubba suitcase onto its side and fell upon it in a wrinkled heap.

"Taxi, Missus?"

"I don't know ..."

"Where you going, then?"

"Well, I ..."

"I have the truly best rates on the island and no mistake."

"Actually, I'm waiting for someone."

Most of the cars on Antigua are past their last legs. The climate is tough on the metal inner workings, and the island-time, laid-back lifestyle is tough on the outer workings. Even the rich folks, many of them European and American second home-owners, let the little things slide. Like brake pads, plumbing oddities and electrical outages.

I hadn't started to panic when the sun sank into the sea. The night air soothed my jig-jangled nerve endings. One by one, my fellow passengers went off in taxis or the cars of friends until, finally, I was alone, still reclining across my big bubba in a rapidly moistening jumble.

The little dark man who had first spoken to me approached me again. "Do you need a taxi, Missus? Very, very reasonable to wherever you may be heading?"

He was asking.

"I have reservations at Half-Moon Bay."

"Ahhh ... very nice place, very nice. A proper and lively destination. I can take you there fast and give the most reasonable rates on the island."

He was wiry and not young, judging by his hair, which was shot through with gray. He had long arms and short legs and a chartreuse nameplate on his faded flowered shirt that said, "Hi! My name is Felix."

"Felix ..."

"I'm not Felix. I am Felix's first cousin, Felip. He loans me this fine badge."

"I see. Well, Felip, I was expecting someone to come and get me."

"But Missus, Missus, the plane came very out of time. Perhaps there is confusion with the arrangements? Please allow me to take you to Half-Moon fast."

Without waiting for an answer, he hefted half my stuff and walked to his taxi. What could I do but follow?

The main thoroughfare on Antigua wends a tortuous, pothole-filled route from one end of the island to the other. Felip's shock absorbers had given up the ghost years before, and we bumped and jittered along the road like a drunken sailor on camelback.

"Very nice ride. The best on the island," Felip assured me, after one encounter during which the top of my head met on the fly with the top of the cab.

"I remember these awful holes from my last trip here. Why doesn't somebody fix them?"

"Oh, Missus, somebody does indeed fix them. With the most luxurious-grade gravel obtainable. But after forty or fifty cars pass over the pocket, all the gravel is rudely interrupted and spilling out."

Pitch-black it was out in the open country. I remember making out ghostly outlines of large animals standing by the side of the road.

"What was that?" I asked once, in alarm, as we swerved to miss something.

"That was a cow, Missus. There are horses and sheeps along this road as well, but mostly cows. It's public land, do you see? Free grazing."

"Isn't that dangerous? So close to the traffic, I mean?"

"They're mostly tied with a chain to a stick hammered into the ground. They can't be wandering far unless they unhitch themselves. We love our cows here on Antigua."

Three or four times during the trip, Felip and I suddenly found ourselves on the tail of an old truck with no taillights, pooting out a billowing black exhaust. Barely hesitating, Felip honked twice and passed the slowpoke almost casually, seemingly without regard to what might have come barreling along from the opposite direction.

The quaint turn into Half-Moon Bay encompasses an expanse of flower-bordered drive, dotted here and there with soft yellow lights situated low to the ground, glowing like little moons. The hotel is divided into three wings that sit at soft angles to one another and are married by one long, vine-covered breezeway. Felip pulled around the circular drive and stopped with a spin of his balding tires in front of the reception area. He leaped out and opened my door with a flourish.

"Very fast," he said proudly.

As soon as I stepped out of the car, I heard the sea. The tide was up, and the crash of the waves echoed rhythmically. There was always a lovely breeze on this side of the island, and the night was scented with jasmine and citrus blossoms. I took in a deep breath and filled my lungs with the perfume of the Caribbean.

All I wanted at that moment was a bed. I didn't care about a meal or a drink. I didn't care about scrubbing the travel grime off my body. I didn't even care about the picture I must have presented, standing in the small lobby, gray of face, dumpy of bearing. I most certainly didn't give a flying fuck about Chris. Sleep. That was my all-consuming passion.

"Surprise!"

Janet, Richard, Dot, Nat, and Chris rushed toward me, engulfing me in a round of energetic hugs.

Oh, my God ... I burst into tears. "Where've you been, for Christ's sake? Why didn't you meet me?"

"We have been waiting forever!" squealed Janet. "We've been calling the airport, but you know how BWIA is. Here; taste this!"

"Surprised to see us? Chris' idea," said Nat. "Pretty wonderful, us all showing up like this, isn't it?"

Oh, my God.

"I already checked you in, Marly," said Richard. "Are these your bags?"

"At my age, I prefer the term 'luggage.'"

I thought Janet would laugh her three-carat diamond studs out of her ears.

Dot took me by the hand. "We've made special arrangements for a late dinner. By the pool. It's so beautiful here. Well, c'mon, Marly."

In a blur, I was catapulted along, suppressing a scream. If I'd had any real hair, I would have pulled it out. I wanted dead quiet and a darkened room. I wanted to lay my head on a down pillow and escape into oblivion. What I got was a welcoming party peopled by two dozen strangers limboing to a steel-drum band.

"Wait, wait!" I said, digging in my heels like a stubborn mule. "Wait!"

When the party stopped on a dime, I looked into Chris' face and felt his sudden unease.

"What is it, Marly?" he asked.

"I ... just thought maybe I could ... clean up." I gestured weakly. "Wash my face. Brush my teeth."

Dot seemed to understand and whispered into my ear. "Have we done something really terrible here?"

I shook my head no. "Just give me a couple of minutes in my room." I looked around at the festive group and managed a small smile. "You've all gone to a lot of trouble, and I really do appreciate it. Just a couple of minutes, all right?"

I started to walk purposefully toward the nearest pool area exit before it occurred to me I hadn't a clue where my room was. I turned back in some confusion and found Chris at my side.

"This way, Marly." He took my arm gently and steered me away from the throng. "Maybe this wasn't such a good idea," he said, nodding his head back in the direction of the Mongol Horde. "I thought we'd be more ... comfortable ... if some friends came with us. All very last-minute."

I missed the significance of this admission entirely.

"No ... I mean yes." I pushed out a bone-deep sigh.

"Here," he said, stopping in front of room number 153. "Here's your key. Do you need any help, or anything?"

"No, thank you." He looked abject, hangdog. "I'll be fine, really," I reassured him. "Just give me a few minutes. Hey, I never ruined a good party in my life."

He took me in his arms then and pressed me into him. I stiffened for a moment.

"I've been looking forward to this," he said softly.

He kissed me once on the cheek, turned on his heel, and left me standing in the flood of light streaming out from the open door to my room.

"There's a light at the end of the tunnel, and I hope it ain't no train."

Chapter 7

The first thing I did was shrug off my high heels and rub my swollen feet. A terrible heaviness invaded my body, as though my bones and muscles had been cast in cement. Suddenly, dying didn't seem like such a bad alternative.

Uh-oh ... Mr. Fear talking! I recognized that seductive lure to give up and give in as coming straight from his metal-gray lips, and it galvanized me into action.

I unpacked everything carefully and took the cosmetics, toothpaste and shampoo into the miniscule bathroom. The builders of Half-Moon Bay hadn't lavished money on upscale niceties ... like square footage. After all, they must have reasoned, what did the room matter when a guest spent so little time in it? Like the old joke: my bathroom was so small, I had to step outside to change my opinion of it.

All at once, a flickering visual tickled the gray cells, something interesting that hadn't registered properly. I walked back into the bedroom and saw the bottle chilling in a plastic ice bucket. The attached card read, "To our getting to know each other better. Love, Chris."

I grabbed the Veuve Clicquot firmly by the neck, stripped the foil and unwound the little metal necklace. Using my right thumb as a lever, I eased the stopper from its nestling place. Booouuuuf! The first soothing yet uplifting sip came straight from the bottle, filling my mouth with golden bubbles. Better. Better and better.

As long as I can remember, I have used hot water as a remedy for everything that ailed me. Baths, showers, Jacuzzi tubs ... all offer holy liquid for the cleansing of both my physical frame and the state of my spirit.

When I turned on the hot water tap full blast, steam immediately began to rise up from behind the shower curtain. I let the water run a long time, pouring over my skin, thinking how nice it was to be away from the drought in California. I waited for the calming warmth to spread and the attendant peaceful glow to creep up through my body from my toes. Often when I'm naked, my fingers find their way subconsciously to the scar on my breast.

I was soaking in the tub the night my Ob/Gyn, Dr. Stephan Yavinovich, telephoned me with the results of my mammogram. It was after 8:30, which was, and is, significant. A call from a medical doctor after 8:30 at night is never good news.

"Hello?"

"Marly? Dr. Yavinovich."

The lateness of the call prodded me like a bony finger.

"This can't be good news," I said in a flat voice.

"It isn't. I'm sorry."

"Oh, shit."

"There is a small but definite mass in the upper left quadrant of your left breast."

"I see."

Silence on both ends lingered.

"What the hell do I do now?" I finally asked.

"We have a couple of ways to go." His voice was low and professional and full of concern.

"First things first: we need you to meet with at least two surgical oncologists—cancer specialists, that is—and pick out someone you feel good about ... that you have confidence in. I'd be happy to make some suggestions. Or not."

That word 'cancer' had cut through me like a knife. I think I actually gasped for breath and quickly covered the receiver with my hands so Stephan couldn't hear my cowardice. Then, "I want to hear every single piece of advice you can dredge up."

"Fair enough. Let's see ... you'll need to have an excisional biopsy or a needle aspiration to determine if the lump is malignant. That's standard at this point. It might not be. Malignant, I mean. Ordinarily, I'd give you the rah-rah and true speech about most of these things being benign. But in your case, the diagnostic radiologist discovered a cluster of micro-calcifications ..."

"English, please, for scary shit," I interrupted.

It was his turn to take a breath before continuing. "... Tiny specks of calcium that can signal the presence of cancerous tumors."

There was that word again. It was just like in The Lump Nightmare. Christ, it was The Lump Nightmare.

"Marly? You still there?"

I managed to push out a grunted "yes" from the back of my esophagus.

"I would prefer to have the rest of the diagnostic techniques performed by your oncologist. Shall I make some appointments for you, or would you prefer to make the calls yourself?"

"You."

"The sooner we get on it … You understand."

"OK."

"Good. What's your schedule like this week?"

"This week?"

"No time like the present." His tone was severe, purposeful. "You have any plans to hit the road?"

"No."

"Fine. I'll have Dorothy make a couple of appointments and call you with the times tomorrow."

"Tomorrow," I echoed. It's only a day away.

We both took an extra-long pause. Finally, Stephan said, "Marly?"

"What is it?"

"Waiting. You're going to be doing a lot of waiting. It's the damnedest thing—the toughest thing you'll be up against, at least in the beginning. I've been around this dance floor a few times, sad to say, and I can tell you that all sorts of possibilities will run through your mind, all of them ugly. A case, I guess, for the idea between the devil you know and the one you don't. God, it sounds hollow, but don't borrow trouble. And call me any time, day or night. I mean it. I like to think that we have a relationship besides …"

I hung up the phone without saying good-bye.

By the time I got back to the hotel pool, the wind had died down. The uneasy celebrants of my pity party were waiting to gauge my condition. I stood for a moment and watched them milling like lost lambs in a storm, sipping their Planter's Punches and Piña Coladas, nibbling on crab claws and fricasseed squid. I wondered what they were thinking. How much did they know about me and the party Chris had organized on my behalf? What had they felt about my sudden disappearance? Hopefully, they were too drunk to care.

I ran my hands through my wig and searched my soul for … what? Guidance? Inspiration? Intestinal fortitude? An entrance line?

Suddenly, an image invaded my melancholy: my great-grandmother, Francesca, watching the clouds from the porch of Home Farm. In my memory, clear as glass, I watched her rocking back and forth, pictured the elegant sweep of her neck and the glow of devilishness in her bold eyes. Her sheer joy of livingness swept over me. She reached out her arms, beckoning me to the safety of her bosom. Even now, years after her passing, she had the power to soothe my agitation, and the sweet warmth of her kiss enveloped me like the calmed sea that lapped gently on the beach beyond.

I squared my shoulders, stepped into the light, and waited until they all noticed me. As I walked to the microphone stand, I realized that I was the only person in the crowd who felt comfortable. It was time, past time, to grab the bull by the tail and face the situation. I saluted the steelies and adjusted the microphone.

"Hello. I guess you all know who I am. Wait ... let me amend that. You know that I'm your guest of honor, and the booze is free. Funnily enough, I don't know who you are, most of you. We'll see soon enough how long the welcome wagon survives. Somebody ... anybody ... could I borrow a glass of something potent?"

Janet immediately scooped up a glass and a bottle of Veuve, delivering same with a mocking curtsy.

"Thank you, little handmaiden," I said and waved her back imperiously.

I cleared my throat.

"Ten months ago today, I learned something truly dire about myself."

I took a significant swig straight from the bottle and listened for the shifting feet in my captive audience.

"It is, therefore, an anniversary of sorts. Since that day, my Herculean journey through hell and back engenders in my fellow men an appropriate amount of pity. I have suffered indignities too numerous to mention and too awful to relate in polite company. I have been miserable, as only a human being can be when confronting her own mortality."

I took another belt.

"But, in all that slowly passing time, I have never, and I mean never, experienced a more sorry example of a party than this. Steel-drum music excepted."

I had them squirming.

"And so, to enliven the proceedings a touch, I'd like to share a rule of life, which I have recently adopted."

I waited a moment here and observed my little band of supporters. Richard looked embarrassed. That pleased me. Dot and Nat seemed intimidated. Janet was Janet: getting a kick out of my wacko display.

And Chris? Whatever. I was busy burning bridges.

"Prince Philip, long quasi-faithful mate of Queen Elizabeth, was asked some time ago what was the single most important thing he had learned from his many years as the consort to the world's most wealthy and dutiful woman monarch. He answered on the spot, 'Never pass up an opportunity to relieve yourself.'"

I raised the bottle once again, poured the remaining liquid over my head, and hollered "Cheers!"

Chapter 8

"There's supposed to be some fabulous trail that goes all around the peninsula," said Janet chirpily. "It even has a blowhole! Doesn't it sound like a kick, babe?"

"Rock climbing?" I let the concept sit at the base of my skull and worm its way slowly up, over and around the acid remains of dead alcohol fumes. "It sounds ... slightly insane." The inside of my skull was chock-a-block with jagged shards. My eyelids scraped across my eyeballs. I took a sip of cold water and swirled it round and round in my mouth before I swallowed it, to muffle the shock of it going down my throat.

Let's take inventory. I'd finished 2.4 bottles of champagne by myself. I dimly remember an unscheduled fall into the pool, which turned the bottom half of my wig into spaghetti-squash tendrils. Later still, several disastrous yet potent attempts at recreating Ginevra's Aunt Minnie's Surprises found their way down my gullet.

Chris had remained quiet throughout. He and Janet had poured me onto my bed a little after four. In the too-bright morning light, as I shielded my eyes from the assassinating sun, I felt him glancing at me from behind the safety of his menu. About then, I bet he was wondering what in the name of hell he had gotten himself into.

"You're supposed to wear tennis shoes or boat shoes," Dot read aloud from the hotel guide. "The rocks can get slippery. Absolutely no bare feet."

"Delightful," I said, smiling grimly.

"She's obviously not up to it," Richard said with his usual disdainful expression.

Chris glanced at me under his brows.

"Oh, no," I said, dredging up the first lie of the day, "rock climbing sounds like just the thing for what ails me."

After a meal that seemed to my black-and-blue taste buds like mayonnaise mixed with wood shavings on a slab of granite, we met on the beach, just above the water line. A narrow, well-worn dirt trail led upward into the cliffs.

"This is it!" said Nat. "See?" he said, shading his eyes. "It turns left by that boulder. Isn't that what the guidebook said, Janet?" He flung himself forward.

"Does anyone have the slightest idea where we're going?" I asked.

"Don't be silly, Marly," answered Janet. "This is an adventure. Maybe we'll discover pirate treasure!"

Yo-ho-ho and a gallon of rum.

Actually, the first third of the climb wasn't too bad, just a few twists and turns and a reasonable incline. We were passed, in fact, by a couple in their seventies who didn't look to be in all that great a shape.

After several minutes, Janet began to sing. She couldn't carry a tune in a bucket, but she loves to sing. "I got friends in low places where the whiskey drowns and the beer chases my blues away ..."

The others shouted down her choice of music. Thank God. Garth and a hangover do not blend well, especially when trying not to heave cookies into ocean depths.

Without warning, we came to a sudden halt, bumping up against each other like a routine from a Three Stooges movie. Nat, in the lead, was standing on a ridge next to an outcropping of fat, egg-shaped, foot-long rocks wedged tight up against one another. He tested for solid purchase with his right shoe. "This doesn't seem too sturdy here ..."

Richard, impatient as usual, opened his mouth to give imperious marching orders. "Oh, for Christ's sake, Nat ...," when all the egg-shaped rocks came loose and skittered down into the sea.

We watched in awe. Richard swallowed his complaint.

"That could have been one of us," said Dot.

"You know," I piped up, suddenly feeling lighter and brighter, as I always do when the Cosmic Forces of the Universe nudge Richard in the ego, "I'll bet we took a wrong turn somewhere. Let's go back."

Janet grabbed my arm. "No way. You're in this with the rest of us. C'mon."

Richard set his jaw. "Well, if those two old coots made it past this point, then we certainly can."

"Maybe they know where they're going," Dot offered reasonably.

"And maybe they're not a bunch of wusses," Richard shot back. He took off in the lead.

Richard thought of himself in heroic terms, mistaking his confrontational nature for leadership. I felt beads of irate perspiration ooze out of my forehead. Just for a moment, I indulged in a daydream of pushing him into the sea. Instead, I lagged back a little and found myself just ahead of

Chris, who was bringing up the rear. He watched his feet with concentration, placing them with atomic precision.

"Maybe you should be in the lead," I said.

"This is exactly the kind of situation that used to set me off. I hated not being King of the Mountain, The Man in the Center of Things. You talk about a control freak. But I've learned there are some things I gotta let slide. Slide?" He laughed at his own joke and rubbed the sweat from his face on his shirt sleeve. "You remind me of me, sometimes."

"The old you or the New Improved you?"

Chris pretended he hadn't heard. "God, what a selfish bastard I was. You know," he said, turning to me, "my therapist is still warning me to watch myself every second so that I don't slip back into those old bad habits, those old relationship traps."

"That doesn't sound right. I mean, if you're still monitoring every little thing, then how visceral can the change be?"

Chris was silent for a time, as we picked our way up a relatively steep slope. When we crested, he said, "I have a history of falling in love with ladies in dire distress and then coming to their rescue so forcefully, they stop living their own lives."

I thought about my performance the night before. Strike three.

"Not that I blame you," he continued too hastily. There was something in his face...

"It's okay. I understand," I said, the umpteenth lie of the day rolling trippingly off the tongue. "You don't want to get hurt again." It pisses me off that men can be that vulnerable and never admit it. But I can't deny that I understand the whole defense mechanism dance. I wrote the music for it.

"I just think if everyone took care of themselves, it'd be an easier world to live in. Women need to be self-sufficient emotionally and financially. But then, we all do."

I smiled weakly. "Discovered Ayn Rand in college, did you?

"You can snark if you like, but I honestly believe life is about self-reliance. Autonomy."

"I know!" I said cheerfully. "You need to meet a normal woman. Someone who had a nice, normal upbringing and comes to the Year of Our Lord 1992 with no mountainous cartons of emotional baggage dragging behind. Good luck with that."

"Don't be ridiculous. I am aware that model is extinct!" Chris said with a laugh, and the gray tinge of his concern passed into sunshine. "So how are you feeling?"

I let out a moan and grasped my throat. "Like I'll live," I rasped, "but I'm still not sure I want to."

He looked at me then, stared at me really, as we began the next stretch of climbing. "I can't help but think," he started in, "that there's something about you I don't know. Something vital that you haven't told me."

Oh, shit. Little dark secrets stashed nicely under rocks get uncovered at the most inopportune moments. You see ... I hadn't exactly explained the entirety of the cancer thing yet. Fine, call me a coward. But honestly, what would have been the point? Chris and I had barely seen one another enough to decide which of us was the more adventurous eater, and the ticklish subject of sex had barely reared its complicated head. Of course, I'm not naïve ... No man invites a woman to a lush tropical paradise without having a hormonally-motivated agenda.

But for the first time since my diagnosis, I was attracted to a man. From the outset, he seemed fun and sensitive and trustworthy, and in my experience, it's rare and admirable when a man examines his life and living as Chris had been doing. But the more attracted I became, the less inclined I was to confess, until I suddenly found myself on a plane to Antigua and the sands of time had run out. Now that I'd absorbed his little self-sufficiency speech, I felt more loath than ever to expose myself further—in any way.

"What is it?" he asked, grasping a large, dead branch with his right hand and pulling himself up onto the ledge where I already stood. "What's the big mystery?"

"It's not that big a mystery," I said, "but I suppose you have a right to know. If we live through this," I said, with a shake of my head in the general direction of the others, "I promise to spill out the whole shoddy story."

The trail steepened and narrowed. We climbed and clawed our way up over the highest crest of the peninsula and stood looking out across the whitecaps, which sat up prettily, posed like dollops of whipped cream. It was a perfectly glorious day. I had regained enough equilibrium to appreciate the beauty that surrounded me and drank in the salty air by the lungful, hungrily, greedily. There is a lovely kind of clear-headedness that comes when you give yourself over to a stiff sea breeze. As it buffeted me, I swayed back and forth, now leaning into its power, now leaning against it. Chris offered me a sip of water from a plastic jar he'd carried on his belt.

Below us, the ocean pounded in and out of the famous blowhole. Janet, the photo-opportunity freak, directed her victims to stand and sit and smile while she checked light readings on her Nikon.

"Over there! No, Richard, there!"

"It's a little close to the edge, isn't it, dear?"

A thought flickered: I could still shove Richard into oblivion.

Janet laughed and stamped her foot playfully. "But the light's perfect. Okay. Now, Dot, move a little to your right. No, no, I mean Richard's right. Naaat! Where do you think you're going? Get back there."

She fiddled with her camera some more.

"All right, everyone say cheeeese ..."

Nat pointed up at Chris and me. "But aren't you going to make them join in the fun?" He didn't say it like he was having fun.

Chris turned to me. "Coming?"

Janet walked over and shoved Chris in the direction of the blowhole. "Marly hates having her picture taken," she said. "I stopped arguing with her about it long ago. Okay, are we ready? Cheeeese ..."

The downhill part of our Special Services Excursion into the Unknown proved much tougher than the uphill part. A little like life. We laughed and hollered and handed one another over the roughest spots. A little like life. Don't tell anyone, but I was actually enjoying myself.

"Watch out," Janet teased, "Marly's beginning to have fun. You can tell by the way she's gritting her teeth."

"Hallelujah," said Richard. He'd often opined that I was being overly dramatic with my cancer. He compared me to a hammy actor chewing the scenery during a lingering death scene in a third-rate summer stock melodrama. Or he would have, if his mind ran to literary comparisons. It was a difficult point to argue. I had never been ill before. Not life-and-death ill. I hadn't realized there were rules.

Richard instructed me once. "There's no excuse for bad behavior. Any therapist will tell you that. Reasons, maybe; excuses, no."

He was fiddling with the engine of his Donzi ski boat that had recently arrived at the Malibu Marina after a lengthy and costly delivery from its European manufacturer. So far, Richard had only been able to get the powerful engine to cough and sputter.

"Hand me that screwdriver, will you?" he asked. "You're smoking like a chimney and drinking like a fish. Hand me that roll of paper towels. Very destructive. And I'm hearing a lot of acid in your voice these days."

I drank down a glass of wine to prevent myself from kicking him in the groin.

"Janet may think you're funny, but I can't see how any decent man would even consider putting up with that kind of behavior. Start the engine now."

The knocking noise was deafening.

"Turn it off!" he yelled.

"Why don't you swear?" I asked.

"Swearing will not help the situation," he answered.

"Possibly not," I said. "But wouldn't you feel better if you let a good, loud 'fuck' roll out of your mouth once in a while?"

"I've learned to deal with my anger in more appropriate ways."

I poured myself another glass of Graves and studied its golden color. "Bullshit."

He sniffed. "You should learn to do that, Marly: redirect your anger. Make it work for you."

"Richard ..." I was about to redirect my anger.

"I know. I'm being critical. I have a habit of being critical, especially when it'd be better to mind my own business. But at least I'm aware of it, and I'm working on it."

He turned to face me. "You're a crazy-maker, but I care about you. I wouldn't waste my time telling you these things if I didn't."

"If you think it's such a waste of time, why bother?"

"Get that wrench for me, will you?"

I leaned across the captain's chair and grabbed the heavy tool from its box. A searing pain shot up through my arm, and I gasped.

Richard scowled and walked over to where I was sitting. He squatted and picked up the entire tool chest. "You haven't been doing your rehab exercises, have you?" he asked accusingly. Lugging the chest, he struggled back across the boat and heaved it down on a towel next to the open motor-housing.

I wanted to scream at him. I wanted to rage at his insensitivity and bash in his head with a ball-peen hammer. Instead, I lit a new cigarette from my old one and churned the smoke out in angry puffs.

"I can feel your hostility." He bent his head over the engine.

The most awful part of his little speech was the kernel of truth at its core. At times, I was behaving abominably, crazily, stupidly, even cruelly. But

I felt like a doe frozen in the headlights of an onrushing car: scared to death and distraction. There wasn't time or energy to ponder the civil war in Yugoslavia or the plight of perpetually starving Africans, or the little investors snagged by the savings and loan fiasco, much less the day-to-day suffering of my friends. Fuck 'em. I just didn't care about anything other than the place where my breast used to be. The woman I used to be. I felt the ever-lurking tears well up in my eyes and covered my face with my hands.

"I know a lot about rage, Marly. And I can't always say what I feel without pissing people off. But I care."

He really thought he was being helpful. Didn't he know that no good deed goes unpunished? One biting comment, and I could have sent him back toward the place in his soul he was trying to escape from. I resisted the temptation.

"Richard, I'm scraping along here," I said without malice. "Goddammit, I recognize me in what you're saying. But it all seems so ... unfair sometimes. And I'm exhausted. By my doctors and my group therapy and even my self-pity. If I'm gonna go out, I'll go with an acid remark on my tongue and a good, stiff drink to wash down the taste. So thanks all the same."

He glared at me. "It's your funeral."

"You said it."

"Cancer?" Chris spit out the word.

We were sitting on my little terrace, sipping Planter's Punches and eating melon slices. We'd been back an hour or so, and the rest of the gang was playing tennis.

"Cancer?" he said again, shaking his head. "Wow. I've wondered about your wigs ..."

"Breast cancer. Here," I said, patting the spot with my hand.

I have become a chronicler of the various ways in which people react to the announcement. Fear, loathing, curiosity, fascination, dismissal, blankness. Sometimes it's fun to predict which way the ball will drop on the roulette wheel: leaning a little toward curiosity ... no ... now bumping up against fear ... hmmm, dismissal, maybe?

I watch people inspect and discard comments and questions. Where was it ... is it? Are you terminal? Are you suffering? Will you live until next Tuesday? Have you bought any term life insurance? Would you buy some from me?

Chris is the kind of man who looks open but actually lives close to the vest. It was hard to know which direction I should take him in. I decided on the clinical approach and rattled off the facts, medical journal-style.

"I first detected a lump by routine self-examination in the upper left quadrant of my left breast. Shortly thereafter, a mammogram affirmed the presence of the mass and its size, T1, which was measured at something less than two centimeters. Also observed were micro-calcifications, or fine sand-like calcium deposits, an indication of possible malignancy."

I gazed steadily on Chris' face, watching his eyes flick and flinch as I spoke. I kept my voice matter-of-fact and took a perverse satisfaction at ticking off the grim steps one by one.

"I consulted surgical oncologists and one plastic surgeon the next week, all of whom had been recommended by my own Gyn/Ob. I chose a woman. Phyllis Dent. Three days later, I underwent an excisional biopsy as part of a two-step surgical procedure. The material was examined by both frozen-section and permanent section methods. The verdict was malignant."

Chris had tossed down the last of his punch, so I poured him a refill from the pitcher. A readily available attitude adjustment aid seemed a humane precaution.

"It was on the advice of Dr. Dent that I sought for and received a second opinion. The verdict was the same: malignant. Bone and liver scans showed no signs that the disease had metastasized. After discussing three treatment possibilities, including lumpectomy and radical mastectomy, my doctor and I opted for segmental resection with lymph-node dissection."

I raised my left arm and showed him one of my scars, which still puckered angrily (and itched likewise) under my arm.

"I received radiation therapy, which is quite standard these days. And because a small amount of unattached cancerous cells had been detected in my nodes, I also underwent intravenous chemotherapy over a period of months. To destroy those cancerous cells that might still have been present. More punch?"

Amazing to think I could compress the agony of an entire year into those few sentences.

Chris leaned back in his chair and stared out at the sea. Without looking at me, he said, "I can imagine how awful it must have been."

"No, you can't. Honestly, you can't imagine."

"And you didn't tell me, because ..."

"Because I couldn't bring myself to spoil our friendship." The sex part, you ass.

He looked at me then. "It hurts me to hear you say that."

"Oh, shit. Men are lousy confronters."

"That's a generalization."

"It is. But I do remember so many of the things you wrote to me."

"Like what? That I spent five years in group therapy, for God's sake? You know, most of the people in my group were women. I heard them tell horror stories about their lives ... You can't believe what they suffered through. I didn't flinch from the truth then, and I wouldn't have with you. I'm here. Until we find out what we can feel for one another."

"You didn't want to sleep with any of them, did you?"

"What the hell does that mean?"

"Did you?"

"No. I wasn't attracted to any of them."

"Because they were needy, Chris?"

"That's unfair."

He stood up and walked around to my side of the table. He began to knead the tense place between my shoulder blades. His hands were rough.

"Life's unfair." I relaxed against the pressure of his hands and picked up a package of Chris' cigarettes from the table.

"Actually," he said, "I'd prefer it if you smoked your own. I can't get those here."

"I beg your pardon?"

"I can't buy those here. Would you mind smoking your own? I'll get 'em for you."

"No." I remember I felt jarred out of the moment, pushed to the side of something. "That's okay. I didn't really want one anyway."

Which was true, I realized with a start. Chris continued to massage the nape of my neck while I brooded and drank. Neither of us spoke. Finally, the sun and the punch melted my mood, and I felt a kind of dreamy letting-go. The afternoon had turned to dusk and the light of the day to lilac.

Chris spoke softly, his voice more caressing than before. "A terrible lot of pain, Marly. And some terror maybe thrown in for good measure." His hands worked their way down my arms in firm, measured circles. "But you're here now. You're alive. Tempered steel. Stronger than ever. Whatever it is you lost, you could afford to lose."

I shook my head lazily as my eyes closed.

Chris' voice was now a murmur. Intimate. Delicate. "You're tough; I like that. You're a survivor, and you didn't need a man to help. Oh, you lost little bits of things when you looked at death in the face. But you spit in his eye."

It was the oddest lullaby. I felt his breath on my cheek. Then his lips. He took me by the hand and lifted me gently out of the chair. I felt his arm go around my back as he pressed my head onto his shoulder.

"I want to love you."

I was scared. He seemed to think I was somebody else. Or maybe he saw a part of me that had disappeared. The flint. The steel. I felt stunned and confused. I didn't want to pretend I was something I wasn't. But I hadn't a clue what I was in the process of becoming. Besides, I was suddenly horny as hell. Funny how powerful the sex urge is even when half your left boob is missing.

What would he think when he touched my scar? Who cared? What if I'd forgotten how to react? Could I fake it? Who the hell cared?

I let Chris lead me into the bedroom. As the sun sank into the sea, I pulled the curtains together, and everything was cloaked in a richly deepening gloom. I shrugged off my shorts and pressed my tank top close against my chest with both hands. As Chris moved to switch on the light by my bedside table, I touched his hand.

"Not yet," I said. I began undoing his shirt buttons, and the salt-air scent of his skin rose up and tickled my nose. "This time, it has to be in the dark."

Chapter 9

How to explain it? It wasn't great lovemaking by any means. We were both skittish, as our hands started to explore. Chris' body was a skosh endomorphic, listing a tad more to the Pillsbury Doughboy side: soft in the middle and pear-shaped, not fat but rounded. He had a saucy bikini imprint that left him tan-on-white two-toned. (It's amazing how much you can take in in a nanosecond.)

I hadn't been with a man in so long that I began to shudder almost as soon as we turned the spread down. I had no need whatsoever for the AstroGlide, as I was awash between my legs, between my toes, between my breasts, down the crease of my ass. The humidity and my own impatience greased the track.

And then, it was done. We didn't break any longevity records. I didn't hear bells and banjoes.

Chris' first comment was, "There's hope for us."

My first thought was, "God ... I'm glad that's over with."

Why is it that in fiction, sexual tension always lends a delightful spice to a relationship? In reality, especially in the days before pre-marital intercourse was commonplace, the wedding night loomed like a swinging pendulum. Since men weren't required to please women in any way, they often didn't. (Swing left.) And no one bothered to tell the woman a damned thing. (Swing right.)

I can remember my great-grandmother Francesca telling me how she hid in the closet because she thought her brand-new (first) husband was trying to kill her. And she'd grown up on a farm where animals were expected to "be fruitful and multiply"—i.e., copulate regularly! Eventually, and give all due credit to Grandpap, she decided she quite liked sex, and I can imagine how my grandparents' lovemaking changed after that.

Now the game has grown much more complex. It's still a question of waiting, I guess. Forget marriage; love that includes body parts is tough enough. We females gyrate through all sorts of contortions, just trying to get them to say it before we do it. Of course, men are still swinging along on the other side of the pendulum, there having been little change in the aims of the male libido during the past gazillion thousand years. Any "relationship expert" will tell you it's easier for a man to admit he loves a woman who's already turned him on between the sheets ... It's a closeness he can maneuver.

Women like me, who've pretty much given up on happily-ever-after, also insist on trying the milk before buying the cow. Which is a lot of convoluted explanation for a very simple phenomenon: giving some serious thought to the threat of HIV floating around out there, sex has become, in too many instances, something to be negotiated to safety (my testing lab or yours?) and then gotten over with. Think about it: if he's too big or too fast or too naïve or too uncomfortable in his nakedness or creativity; if he's a whips-and-chains kind of guy and you're a lace-and-roses kinda gal; if he won't use his fingers delicately or can't stand to look inside a naked woman ... it's better to know before you've fallen head-over-heels. Because trying to get him to change his style of lovemaking after the fact will be impossible. It has to do with the ego, darling, the most vulnerable part of a man's anatomy. From the ego comes the wardrobe, the car, the house, the sex. Ergo, ego-driven sex is a like a fingerprint. Unique. Something you can only alter with acid.

Okay, okay, I'll get on with it.

With Chris, I'd remained stiff throughout, no pun intended. Disquieting thoughts raced across my mind. How would he react to my "deformity?" (When he elected to bypass the area altogether, I'm not sure who was more relieved.) Once we got going, how would I respond? I'd started out wet, sure. My body was ready-Freddie after a long, dry spell. But how long would I stay wet? Would he perform oral sex? Did he like it? I craved the feel of his tongue inside me ... to feel that friendly fire at the tip of my nerve endings. But there was no way I was able to tell him that.

My response was animalistic. I don't remember feeling romantic. I don't remember wondering about love. Chris was an object, a way to satisfy my curiosity and my lust and my need to be a whole woman. I still wasn't healed in any sense of that word and was therefore incapable of sustaining a real relationship.

On the one hand, I was ashamed of myself. I felt guilty, like a woman who's taken to whoring purely for sport after a righteous upbringing. On the other hand, the act was a release and an affirmation of my being present in the world. I was finally physically attracted to a man. I fucked him and had an orgasm in the process.

I can't tell you how important that orgasm was to me. It meant that I was still here. That I was still a woman, boob or no boob. That I was still alive.

Chris the throbbing member had a lot more to do with all this than Chris the human being, although I had no intention of telling him anything of the kind. In fact, we both might've gone on our merry ways relatively unscarred, with some dignity intact. Except that Chris turned out to be the kind of man who refuses to let sleeping neuroses lie. Maybe he was feeling out of his depth and element? How else could a man with five years of therapy be so fucking insensitive?

"I've never been to bed with a woman wearing a wig before," he said. "Why don't you take it off? Isn't it hot?"

I couldn't believe my ears and tried to ignore him.

"No, Marly, I mean it. What's the big deal?"

Why couldn't he just disappear? I thought to myself. "No big deal," I answered, feeling jarringly threatened. He was looking at me in that steady way of his. "It's not the right time," I added.

"You don't trust me?"

Warning, warning. "I didn't say ..."

"It must be an issue of trust. What's so terrible about a bald head? I'll have one of my own in a few years" He sounded playful, for Christ's sake. Who the fuck did he think he was?

"Are you shitting me?" I asked, bamboozled. "And why are you so interested, anyhow? Are you a voyeur? Itching for a nasty thrill?"

Chris sat up. "That's an acrobatic overreaction. Why are you suddenly pissed at me?"

"Why am I pissed at you? Why are you as dense as a post?"

"You know, insulting me isn't going to solve anything."

"Maybe not, but it'll make me feel better."

"All I asked was ..."

"I know what you asked, Chris. And I'll answer you. My bald head is none of your damned business."

He threw his hands in the air. "Again, I ask, what's the big deal?" It was the loudest I'd ever heard him. "I'm going to see ... whatever, sooner or later." His smile glowed evil, I swear.

I flattened my hands across my head. "Don't touch me. Don't."

He backed off then. "It can't be all that terrible." He suddenly sounded the essence of sweet reason, just like my Mr. Fear.

Hey, I never pretended to be sane.

I slouched on my robe, curled up on the edge of the bed and smoked a cigarette. We didn't speak. At last, when my heartbeat had slowed to a mere

120 beats a minute, I poured two glasses of flat champagne from the bottle on the bedside table.

"I don't feel comfortable enough with you, Chris. I don't know why, but I don't. I know it sounds screwy." I took a swig. "Going bald was the single most awful side-effect of chemotherapy. It was so ... debilitating. So humiliating! De-womanizing. I even lost my eyebrows and eyelashes! They're just starting to grow back now ... You must have noticed."

He shook his head.

"No? That's odd." I looked skyward. "Thank God, my pubes stayed put. I don't think I'm quite evolved enough to wear a merkin, much less shop for one."

"What's a merkin?"

"It's a hairpiece for a muff."

Chris started to laugh, and though he tried to hide it, there was no way. I puffed and watched him laugh himself to tears.

"It's not that funny. Will you stop?" I offered, a little pissed now.

His belly was quivering like jelly. His shoulders shook. He was gone.

"Look, Chris, I'm tired. I'd like to rest a bit before we meet for dinner. Would you mind? Going?"

He took a deep breath and tried to contain himself. "Marly, listen ... I'm sorry ..." And off he went again. "Hahahahahaha."

Now, I'm usually the kid that will get right in the middle of a good guffaw. God knows, my family's been known to pee their pants in jocularity. But for some reason, this episode was proving nothing but irritating. And the more I scowled at Chris, the more he shrieked and gasped.

"I'm sorry, Marly. I don't know what's ... hahahahahaha!"

"Look ... I'm kinda tired. Maybe we can take this up later?"

"Marly ..."

"Chris ... please."

"I can't help ... hahahahahahahaha."

"I know you can't help it." I took him firmly by his quivering arms. "And I'm not blaming you. Merkins are inherently hilarious." Of course, this drove him to new heights of hilarity.

It must have been another five minutes before he was able to gather himself back together. He tried to put his arms around me, but I pulled away.

"Marly ...," he said, and took three long breaths.

"I'm not angry. Really." I managed to smile. "I'll see you later, okay?"

He kissed me on the forehead and left.

He couldn't have been five steps from my door when I heard him. "Hahahahahahahaha ..."

How could I possibly explain? What could I say to make him understand?

It wasn't so much the way I looked, although that was a part of it. My wigs were the magical shields I held up to ward off the onslaught of cancer against my female-ness. The process of selecting them and caring for them was heroic, mythic.

They were both made of the real stuff, both the same delicate honey blond of my childhood. Hey, if I was going to have to buy my hair, I was going to buy the best damned hair on the market. I remember how I nodded my head sagely when Dolly Parton announced, "Home is where your hair hangs."

When I first started investigating OPH (other people's hair), I inevitably began to notice people who wore hairpieces or wigs. And it hit me: Why is it that so many men wear such terrible toupees? I mean, the idea of a hairpiece is pure vanity, right? Because the bald thing makes him look older? So he chooses to resemble a turtle sporting a coonskin cap instead? Honestly! Some of those rugs look like real rugs. They look like they're made from the same synthetic fiber originally developed for shag carpeting. And the colors! I don't mean to be cruel about this, but I'm not talking about some poor homeless folks. I'm talking about lawyers and TV producers and junk bond kings. Incredible.

I was not going to be caught dead (literally or figuratively) in anything but the best. So, dragging my gal pal Lark behind me, we ventured out to the wilds of deepest West Hollywood to investigate.

Lark is in her early forties. At nineteen, she married an older man who was already well-established in the movie biz. She was naïve and easily controlled, so her vulnerabilities dovetailed nicely into her husband's controlling personality. Besides being a neat-freak beyond all comprehension, he manipulated everyone around him using the twin cattle-prods of verbal abuse and sulking. Lark was a bird in a platinum cage.

I first ran into her at a screening of one of the more infamous megamoney flops five years ago, give or take. I was struck by her softly rounded face, her large brown eyes, and her sweetness. The quintessential stay-at-home super-mom, she'd never learned how to say "no." In those days, she was an absolute doormat, but she had potential.

We bumped over a chilled silver bowl filled with jumbo shrimp and scarfed down like it was The Last Supper.

She laughed out loud, a mellow sound, rounded like her cheeks. "It's an awfully expensive send-off," she said, motioning to the lobster and crab spread at the next table. You'd never know the reviews on this picture are mixed ... terrible and horrendous."

"But these folks have discovered one of the great truths of life ...," I said, dipping a couple of tasties into the tangy red sauce.

"Which is ...?"

"Which is," I continued, mouth full now, "that the greater your disaster, the bolder face you have to put on it."

She laughed again.

Encouraged, I developed my theme, swinging my plastic fork around. "When you're fired in this town, you get a call from your agent that evening. He addresses you as 'pally,' even if you're female, consoles you for twenty seconds, and counsels you to purchase a BMW from his good friend The Used Car Salesman Who Used To Be A Studio Head. In the case of a big-budget crash-and-burn, you're required to buy a place in Aspen, as long as you detest skiing and cold weather."

"I see. I'm Lark."

"Really? What a great name. I'm Marly."

We wandered around the subdued after-screening party together, sipping champagne and feasting on tabouli, hummus, stuffed grape leaves, and shellfish until we were properly sated.

"The perfect meal," I said. And it was. A little of this, a little of that, munched zestfully with no regard for calories or cholesterol count, accompanied by bouzouki players and dancing waiters, and washed down by retsina and a couple pieces of baklava.

"Actually," she said with a frown, "I don't care much for baklava."

"Actually, neither do I. But when someone else is paying, I make it a point to be a good guest."

It was the beginning of a strange and wonderful friendship. The one fly in the ointment proved to be Lark's husband, Tom, who took an instant aversion to me and everything I represented: a little intelligence and a lot of independence.

His disapproval oozed out of his pores like snake venom whenever Lark and I played tennis at their house in Encino. His face was set in a studied scowl, and he hmmphed a lot.

"Tom, you remember Marly."

"Hmmph." Scowl.

"Hi, Tom," I said breezily. "Why don't you hit a few with us?"

"Hmmph," he responded. Scowl.

"Well, okay," I said, patting him on the back condescendingly. "But you're missing one hell of a good time."

"Hmmph, hmmph." Scowl, scowl. Glare.

Tom and Lark have been divorced now for over three years, and Lark is close to completing her Masters in psychology at UCLA, specializing in family counseling. I don't take any credit for this development, but I gotta admit I didn't discourage her. I may even have voiced one or two pithy opinions ... Hey, I'm not a saint. But I made a concerted effort not to lecture her or push. And I certainly never attempted to cut Tom down in her eyes. He didn't need my help.

"But I don't know anything about wigs," Lark protested. She was nervous. She often felt intimidated when faced with new challenges. It was a smoggy summer day, and the heat shimmered across the pool water behind the house Tom once owned but had grudgingly vacated, bag and baggage, in a hmmphy huff.

"Neither do I," I admitted, tying my head scarf for the third time. "But since I'm about to go bald as an ostrich egg, I figured it was time to do some research with the experts. Damn this thing! It keeps slipping off."

"I have some electrician's tape. Maybe we could fasten it to your head somehow."

"Won't it pull out the few lonely strands I have left?" I sighed.

"Welllll," she said, drawing out the syllable à la Jack Benny, "you could shave ..."

"That would solve the problem. Got a razor?"

Something about my melon-shaped skull set Lark off on a laughing jag.

"God!" she sputtered, "it's just the color of cantaloupe rind!"

"But not nearly so wrinkly," I said as I stared at myself in the mirror. A weird-looking and pathetic woman with a large, round head and a hollowed, pinched face stared back. The bank of make-up spotlights over the sink reflected light from my shiny dome as ably as Venetian glass. Any Boy Scout worth his merit badges could have used my pate to ignite a pile of kindling.

"Think it will glow in the dark, like those Tinkerbell wands from Disneyland?" I asked, posing.

"Marly! Stop it!" she said with a belly laugh that came right from her toes.

I ran my fingers across the top of my head. "Gee. It's smooth as a baby's butt. Here," I said, bending over her, "touch it, Lark."

"No!" She shrank away from me. Her laughter died.

"C'mon, touch it. It's just skin, you dolt."

"I don't want to touch it, and you can't make me touch it!"

Frozen in that place and time for the briefest heartbeat, we were close enough that she could plainly make out my pencil-drawn brows and my lashless eyes. I saw her suddenly struck with terror by this alien figure standing in her bathroom, by the awful, hideous caricature of a female that was me. A strangled wail escaped from my lips, and I rushed outside, slamming the French doors with a bang.

I heard an anguished cry from inside. "Marly! Come back!"

I threw myself down on the lush carpet of grass behind the pool, covered my face with my hands and wept. I don't know how long I lay there like that; it might have been a minute or an hour. But I do remember Lark's soft voice in my ear and the feel of her hand on the top of my head.

"I don't know whatever made me behave that way," she said wonderingly. "I'm sorry."

She didn't try to stop me from crying. She just stroked me the way my mother would have, until I finally quieted down. I liked her tremendously just then.

"What did you have in mind, then?" asked the springy young man who sashayed out from the back of the shop. He seemed to insinuate himself, rather than walk, from one place to another. His hands were delicate and darted through the air like small birds.

The place was called "Jess's Tresses." It'd come highly recommended from the folks in my therapy group, which we'd all come to think of as "The Cancer Club."

The shop looked like a jungle conceived by Rube Goldberg with an assist from Charles Addams. Every wall, every tabletop, every glass case was festooned with hairpieces. I half-expected ectoplasmic heads and hands to pop up, shaking and tossing the disembodied shag cuts and afros in some weird ballet.

"Hi. I'm Jess, the proprietor. And you must be Marly and Lark. Dar-

The Cancer Club

ling scarf, Marly. Adolfo, isn't it?"

We were stunned into silence by the place.

Jess gestured vaguely. "It does take some getting used to." He grabbed a beard from his desk and stroked it like a Siamese cat. "But I can assure you, they're harmless! Now, what did you have in mind?"

"Well ..." I began, not knowing where to begin. I glanced around at the storefront window and noticed the people passing by. "Is there someplace a bit more private?"

"Of course! Right this way."

Jess led us through the maze of manes and moustaches to a small room near the back of the building.

"Bill? Watch the shop for me, will you?" he called.

From somewhere nearby, a muffled and peevish-sounding voice yelled back, "Oh, all right."

"He's the artiste, you know. Such a temperament! Now, sit right here and tell all."

Jess flipped a switch, and the bold light of day was softened by two pink bulbs. I undid my scarf and tossed it to Lark, who perched on edge like a bird ready to bolt.

"I hadn't realized there were so many choices," I said.

"Oh, yes! We do it all here. Punk. Ethnic. Peter Pan. Lady Godiva. Eva Gabor. Let's see ..." He turned my swivel chair slowly, studying my head in the glass. "What a lovely shape. Good bone structure. I wish I had those cheeks. To die for!" His face collapsed. "Oh my, I am sorry."

"No problem."

"I detest insensitivity."

"Really, it's okay."

He relaxed into a chair. "You're very understanding. Now ... Have you decided between real and synthetic? There's a big difference in price and a big difference in effect."

"How much difference in price?" asked Lark.

"Several hundred dollars, taking shoulder-length as the starting point."

"I see," I said, rapidly computing.

I wasn't poor, but fighting the cancer had proved to be expensive, even with insurance. I wasn't due for another royalty payment until July ...

"Cost is no object." Lark's voice was firm. "My treat."

"Lark, I can't ..."

"Of course you can. What good is a humongous divorce settlement if I can't treat my friends to a little hair once in a while? Just pretend Tom is paying."

Jess nodded vigorously and remarked, "Ex-husbands can be so convenient. Now what color was ... I mean is your hair?"

"I honestly don't remember. I've streaked it since high school."

"You bleached your hair in high school?" asked Lark. "I thought you went to a Catholic school."

"The nuns were very progressive."

We discussed various options. Most recently, by bottle, I had become honey-toned, streaked with pale yellow. Before my diagnosis, I'd taken to wearing my hair cropped short, tapered above my ears and down the nape of my neck. Jess was knowledgeable and brought out seven or eight different styles and lengths to try on.

"Oh, my," he said of the first, his eyes popping, his jaw clenching. "That won't do. No, no, no. That won't do at all."

"Don't be dispirited, Jess. I'm accustomed to looking absurd."

"'Dispirited.' What a lovely word. So much more refined than 'demoralized,'" he said. He tried another style.

"That's because people resent being moralized and don't mind being spirited," I said, turning my head back and forth. "I look a little too much like Nancy Reagan's niece in this, don't you think?"

"It is on the Young Republican side, isn't it? Ah ...," he said with a smile, "now this ...!"

He was right. The hair was buttery colored and Veronica Lake-ish. Jess lifted the bangs with a tease comb and brushed the rest softly over my shoulders.

"I like that," Lark said. "It's ... sexy."

It was, rather.

"I'll take it. And would you have something similar with a perm?" I asked.

"I don't think I have it in exactly your color. But Bill is a frigging genius. Bill? Bill, we need you." This last part was almost sung.

A huge, blocky man with ham hock arms attached to beefy shoulders filled up the doorway.

"Football?" I asked.

"Discus," he answered. "University of Southern California. That's smashing on you. And those cheekbones ..."

"Aren't they to die for? Oh, I am sorry." Jess sighed again.
"You threw the discus?" Lark asked uncertainly. "For USC?"
"Before he became an artiste," said Jess.

"She wants another, shaped just like this, with a perm. When can we deliver?"

Bill looked at me. "Are you ... in a hurry?"

I knew what he meant. He was asking about life and death. My life and my death.

"No."

"Good. I can have it for you in a week."

"That'll be fine."

Lark flashed her AmEx while Jess packaged my hairpiece carefully.

Bill drew me aside and whispered in my ear. "You're with The Cancer Club, aren't you? I hear great things."

"It's been a lifeline for me."

"Do they take men?"

It was my turn to take a long look at him. I raised my penciled-on eyebrows inquiringly.

"Kaposi's sarcoma," he mouthed. "Jess knows about the HIV but not about the cancer."

I touched his massive arm. "Oh, my dear, I am so very sorry."

He shrugged. "Do they? Take men?"

"Yes, they do. I'll be happy to write down all the information."

No, I wasn't ready for Chris to see my naked head.

Chapter 10

Every night, Half-Moon Bay showcases a different exotic brand of island entertainment. For my money, the two most invigorating are the weekly crab races and a trio of scantily clad native dancers whose specialty is fire.

By the time the crab races scuttled around, Chris and I'd settled into an uneasy, lust-filled course. Who the hell knew where we were headed? Had the cancer scared him off? God knows, I couldn't blame him for that ... It scared me off.

I was certainly thankful I had my own room and that he hadn't seen my bald head.

As time and distance separated me from my last course of chemotherapy, I had begun to look and feel human. A touch of the old, familiar stubbornness even slipped back into my psyche, and I was delighted to reacquaint myself with it.

When it came to the nightly repast, the six of us always ate together at one large table, the better to pass around bottles of wine and conversation.

"They paint the crabs' shells?" Janet asked.

"So you can tell them apart," Dot explained. "The paint is water-soluble." She was a civilian with a scientist's penchant for investigating life with a magnifying glass and took large satisfaction when subsequently explaining the subtleties to us less-obsessive/compulsive mortals.

"The colors are the same for each contest: red, green, yellow, black. You can bet on each of four heats. There's a race-off between the four heat winners, complete with auction, which is where the real action comes in, apparently. The take can be hundreds of dollars."

"I know. Let's form a syndicate!" Janet said. "The six of us." She turned to me. "You'll be our investment advisor."

"What the hell do I know about crabs?"

"Crabbiness?" Richard asked.

Chris quickly interrupted the brittle smile that gave away my thought process. "It was a joke, Marly. You remember those?" He thrust his eyebrows toward heaven and waggled them at me.

Dot patted my hand. "He can be insensitive, so male in that aspect, for all his analysis. Don't pay any attention."

That's the problem, though, see? I do pay attention. Seems I've lost the capacity to swallow my anger ... The taste is just too sour these days.

Richard pushed back from the dinner table with a condescending sigh. "Count me out. Sounds ... childish."

"Really?" I asked.

"I see," said Janet.

Chris had mysteriously and suddenly acquired the same smug look on his face. "I think I'll sit this one out, too."

Hmmm. What was this; what was this? "Fine," I said. "We'll be outside."

Nat, Dot, Janet found a table near the action and ordered banana daiquiris.

"What's their problem?" asked Nat.

It had to do with me. I just knew it. Paranoid? Not when they really are after you. "Fuck 'em." I dismissed them. "Let's get this cabal organized. How much money have we got?" I asked.

"Does it have to be cash?" asked Nat.

"Gamblers on tropical islands don't take VISA. Give. Okay ... two hundred forty-seven, eight, nine, fifty, fifty-one. That's not going to be enough."

"Are you kidding?" asked Janet, wide-eyed. "How much can a crab cost? It's not a racehorse, babe."

"You crowned me investment advisor, and I suggest the three of you cash some traveler's checks. We'll meet back here at exactly twenty-two hundred hours."

"Huh?"

"Ten o'clock, Janet." I turned to the nearest waiter and said, "Give this table away and forfeit your life."

He bowed and grinned in response.

By the time we'd finished with the hotel cashier, the pool area had begun to fill up. I waved to Captain George, King of the Crabbers and the evening's emcee. A towering man with a huge belly and a basso profundo voice, he sported a nautically-inspired costume of crisp white slacks and navy blazer that was too narrow by half to enclose his girth.

"Laaaaadies and gentlemen," he called out, causing the din to die down, "I am Captain George. Good evening and welcome to the Wednesday Night Crab Races at the beautiful Hotel Half-Moon Bay."

When he clapped his hands twice, one skinny youngster grabbed an ice cream carton and set it in the middle of the dance floor.

Captain George was big with manual gestures. He pointed to a folding table directly behind him. "This is the wagering booth. Make your wagers according to any scientific measurement you wish to employ, but betting must be completed before the race begins, at which time the final odds will be calculated." Captain George then swung his massive, graceful hands toward the sea. "Please examine our contestants over there without touching them." He finished by waggling his finger in warning.

"What do we do now, Marly?" asked Janet.

"Like the man said, we examine the contestants."

The crabs had all been captured that afternoon by Captain George's numerous progeny, working alongside nieces and nephews. As I bent down to get a closer look at the scrabblers for Heat Number 1, someone tapped me on the back. I thought it was Chris, so I answered without looking, "Decided not to be a prig?"

When I felt the person bend down next to me, I turned my head and found myself face to upside-down face with Ginevra.

"Since you were assuming I was someone else, it has turned out to be an interesting vacation?"

"Most interesting, Ginevra." I admitted truthfully. "What are you doing here?"

"Captain George is my cousin, my father's brother's oldest child. I always attend the crab races, unless I'm crewing for BWIA."

I introduced Janet, Nat and Dot.

"How do you pick a good crab?" asked Dot. "You must have the inside dope."

I rolled my eyes, but Ginevra only laughed and whispered, "Two things. Nominate someone of your party to keep track of the winners of each heat, as they repaint them straightaway. And when it comes to crabs, bigger isn't necessarily faster."

Everyone had a theory: every bartender, every three-year old child, every cab driver. In fact, at one point, I ran into Felip.

"Ahhhh, Mrs.! Looking very, very much better this perfect night."

"Felip! How's the taxi business?"

"Very, very fine."

"How much do you know about crab racing?"

With supreme dignity, he answered, "I know all. Captain George is my cousin, on the side of my mother's brother-in-law. I apprenticed as a crab gatherer."

"What an interesting family tree you all have."

With five minutes to post time, Nat was antsy. "Jesus, they all look the same to me."

I was listening with half an ear when I noticed Richard and Chris lurking in a shadowy corner behind the bandstand. I punched Janet in the ribs. "Look!"

"Ouch! What? What?"

"Over there. Richard and Chris."

"So?"

"Janet, is something going on? They're behaving like cretins. Have been all day."

She didn't look at me.

"What is it, Janet? Hey, are you my friend, or what? C'mon."

She eyed the bar for an avenue of escape. The crowd was too dense. Finally, she took me aside. "They had a talk about you."

"Really." I took a deep breath. "What'd they talk about?"

"Things."

"Really. What things?"

No answer.

Nat, Dot, Ginevra and Felip huddled together, pretending they couldn't hear us, but their six collective eyes popped out when I grabbed Janet by the shirt. She blurted out, "Richard said that you weren't ... stable. That you had a wild streak and couldn't be trusted. That you were a militant feminist and Chris should watch himself so he didn't get hurt."

I let it all sink in.

Dot stared at me. "Is there a problem, Marly?"

"Those assholes! Those sons of bitches!" I managed to keep this utterance down to a dull roar. But it was full of invective.

Dot took a step back. She looked at Janet uncertainly.

"What did you say in response, Janet?" I asked.

"Well ... I said you were my friend. And that I liked you just the way you were. That you're so different from everyone else. And funny. Of course, I had to admit that you are a ... a little wild."

"And what did Chris say?"

Janet hung her head. "He said he knew all those things about you already and that he'd have to make up his own mind.

What to do, what to do? Wild, was I? Too wild for Richard, that conservative, misogynistic, tight-assed son of a bitch? Suddenly, I thought about what my great-grandmother Francesca used to say: Never wrestle with a pig; you get dirty, and the pig likes it.

Okay, running over to them like a madwoman and chewing their asses into little pieces was probably going to shore up Richard's argument. God, I hate when that happens. So, what to do; what to do?

A bold yet sleazy alternative strategy darted across my brain. I couldn't. I wouldn't dare. What would people think?

Wouldn't it be amazing to get away with it? Yes.

I pushed my way through the crowd and sidled up to Chris, just beside the bandstand. "Where's Richard?" I asked.

"Getting a drink."

I spotted Richard at the bar and waved daintily. Then I reached up and grazed my lips against Chris' cheek. "Are you sure you don't want to buy in?"

"One minute, ladies and gentlemen," said Captain George. "One minute to post time."

Chris put his arm around me. "You look beautiful in the moonlight." He kissed me like he meant it. Looking over Chris' shoulder, I saw Richard stiffen. Yep, I thought to myself, I can definitely pull this off ... pun intended!

The second the bartender handed Richard his drink, he began to press his way back through the crowd. When I could tell I had both men's absolute attention, I pushed my pelvis against Chris' playfully. "It's such a gorgeous night," I purred, "for a fire."

Chris laughed and pushed back.

There was a last-minute flurry of activity before the betting windows closed. Captain George's tallest girl assistant scooped up the plastic carton and carefully set it upside down in the middle of the dance floor.

Chris put his arm more firmly around me. "Are you trying to seduce me? Right here in front of everybody?"

Richard stood just a little behind us now. He'd definitely heard Chris speak.

"Oh, I don't think Richard would approve of that," I said to stop Richard from coming any closer. "It's so ... public here."

"Remember," Captain George boomed sternly, "touching the contestants will disqualify." He blew on the silver whistle round his neck and nodded to the youth, who then bent over the carton. "Ready ... and ... go!"

As I kissed Chris passionately, the container was whisked away and the crabs began to stir. Everyone pressed toward the dance floor, pushing our bodies together even more tightly. In front of us, a demure-looking elderly woman wearing a lacy outfit and a hat resembling a bridal bouquet screamed, "Go, red! Red! You can do it!"

I darted my tongue in and out of Chris' mouth. He sucked at my lips hungrily. Richard's eyes were locked onto us. He tried to wedge and sidle closer, but there wasn't an inch of space.

The elderly woman sank to her knees. She began to blow in the direction of the crab. "Go, red!" she screamed again.

I folded my body into Chris and slipped my hand down the outside of his Bermudas. Apparently, the blue crab sidled toward the bandstand, because the musicians were jumping up and down lustily. "That's my blue!" I heard one of them shout.

When I felt Chris swelling to my touch, I reached underneath the material and scratched his balls through his bikini underwear. He gasped in pleasure. "Don't," he protested and made a halfhearted attempt at pulling away.

"Don't worry," I whispered softly into Chris' ear. "No one's paying the slightest attention."

Which was a lie; Richard was paying attention. I'd turned my body enough in his direction that he could glimpse my wandering hand. Though Richard pretended not to look, he was obviously fascinated.

"Oh, God," Chris said softly.

"Red!"

"Blue!"

"Black!"

"Damn yellow. Why isn't he moving, Martha?"

"I don't know, Sid. But I've always hated yellow. Makes my skin look sallow. I told you to get on the black."

I began pulling on Chris. He closed his eyes and slumped against me. His breathing became ragged.

"Just think where you are and what's happening to you. Let yourself go," I whispered. "No one will ever know."

"And the winner ... but wait!" Captain George screamed above the din as the red began moving forward again.

The red and the black were claw to claw, the black taking his time, the red gaining momentum.

"See the red and black fighting it out, ladies and gentlemen!" Captain George boomed out.

Chris shuddered. I grasped him tightly now and proceeded with the coup de grâce.

Captain George announced, "It's going down to the wire! See them push!"

The crowd yelled wildly.

"Go, yellow!"

"Go, black!"

"Now," I whispered into Chris' ear.

"And the winner is ... red!"

A chorus of hoorays and groans covered Chris' shuddering as his warm spray pulsed into my hand. We were still invisible to the crowd, most of whom screamed delightedly or disgustedly and hustled over to the betting table to either collect winnings or grouse.

Captain George's Uncle Freddy, working furiously on his battery-operated calculator, handed over the winners' take and announced with a vocal flourish, "And the red paid seven-to-two, ladies and gentlemen. Now while we're settling, please to take a look at the next batch of contestants."

"Wasn't that fun?" I asked Chris, who managed a dazed nod. I took him gently by the arm and led him to the men's room. "There's more where that came from." I kissed him again. "I'll see you later, darling."

I found a stray cocktail napkin, carefully wiped all traces of my activity away and playfully dropped it into Richard's shirt pocket. I don't think he quite got the entire significance of that gesture, which only augmented my satisfaction.

"Enjoying the floor show?" I asked.

His face reddened.

"Don't have a heart attack, Richard. I'll bet you had almost as good a time as Chris did."

We were joined by the rest of the gang.

"Yeeeeaaaahhhh!" This from Janet, who was waving a fistful of paper money around her head. "Isn't this great? We won! Whoo hoooooo!"

"Should we take our winnings or let it ride?" Nat wondered aloud.

"It is very, very comforting to wager with house money," Felip offered sagely.

"Guys," I said, "in celebration, Ginevra and I have a surprise for you.

Wait right here."

"I just love surprises!" said Janet.

I waltzed Ginevra to the outdoor bar and pointed to my friend. "Do whatever she says," I instructed. "Five times."

"Oh," he said with a knowing wink, "you'll be wanting Aunt Minnies then!"

I turned to Ginevra. "Family secret, huh?"

"Well, actually, he's my cousin. He is!"

Chris came out of the men's room with a shit-eating grin on his face. He practically waltzed to my side, catching up Richard along the way.

I wondered if Richard would ever admit to Chris that he'd seen. He was bound to tell Janet and God knows who else. I'd be infamous. What his opinion of Chris would be, I couldn't begin to imagine. Or could I?

Life was sweet sometimes.

The other races passed away in a blur until it was time for the championship round. Ginevra touted the red from the first race.

"The most compactly made," she advised. "The most rested, having won the first heat. And she will be in the greatest hurry so as to avoid being dinner for one of her larger brothers."

"Ah, yes," Felip agreed. "Very, very fine crab."

"She'd better be fast," Nat groaned, "She cost us seven hundred frigging dollars, for God's sake!"

That dear, sweet, heroic, divine little yellow crab was everything Ginevra and Felip had promised. She zigged. She zagged. She got the hell out of there. Once she'd crossed the finish line, she headed straight for the water, down a path lined on both sides by cheering customers.

When Richard and Chris rejoined us, I looked at Richard and said, "The female of the species is more deadly than the male."

"You're utterly amazing sometimes. Totally unpredictable." To punctuate this thought, Chris kicked a piece of seaweed with the toe of his Bali loafer. We were alone on the beach.

"You think?" I asked a bit warily.

"That wasn't a criticism," he said.

I waded into the sea, high heels and all, to underline his observation. "You meant that as a compliment?"

"You'll ruin your shoes." He closed his eyes. "I've never done anything like that before."

"Ruin your shoes in the surf?"

"You know what I mean. I'm trying to understand. I want to ..."

"Dissect it, right? Analyze it? So you can assure yourself that your dance-floor Big O was a one-time aberration?"

He ran his hands through his hair. "I'm afraid of what you bring out in me. I don't like it. And ..." He hesitated.

"What else?" I asked.

"You ... need."

"Of course! Doesn't everyone? You need! It's part of the goddamned human condition."

I threw up my hands in surrender. "I don't understand this thing of yours, Chris, about everybody running around in their own little worlds, never needing comfort or help from anyone else. You knew all about me from Janet before we ever met and yet, despite everything, you were attracted to me. You came on to me."

Chris said, "Yes, I was. I did. But I can't help wondering if it's a good thing or a bad thing. I want to get better. To heal. I need to heal, and I honestly believe we're all here to learn to be self-sufficient but that women especially need to learn to ..."

"Not depend on men for a life? To be saved? OK, I'll give you that. But even the sanest relationships sometimes require rolling up your sleeves and pitching in."

"I was there for Becky ..."

"She was an alcoholic, an addict. She busted you flat because you tried to help when she didn't want your help. Can you at least admit you picked her just as much as she picked you?"

"I hate feeling responsible for another person's life."

"Wait a minute; you think human weakness is an invitation for you to step in?"

I watched him start to deny and then I watched him reconsider. "I don't know." He turned his back to me. "People take advantage. Women take advantage. Richard says you take advantage."

I bit back my frustration and said in softer tones, "Shades of Mr. Darcy. Richard is absorbed with possessing and controlling. He's the one who takes advantage."

Chris wheeled around and grabbed me. "Caring: it takes too much energy."

I considered this and then asked, "What the hell do we do now?"

"I have no idea," he answered, "but I want you more than ever."

Chapter 11

Janet and I were lying together on the sand a discreet distance from the hotel, in a sheltered area of the bay where topless sunbathing was permissible. A short typewritten note from the hotel management placed on the dressing table had informed us of this fact in very polite though somewhat strangled English.

Janet toed her towel this way and that. "He really cares for you, Marly."

Four or five other women of various shapes and sizes were enjoying the warm sun on their nakedness, and I glanced around wistfully, even at the elderly women. Their tits may have succumbed to gravity, but they hung down whole and unscarred.

"And he's such a kind man. And so much fun! Marly! Pay attention! I'm solving all your problems for you."

"Huh?"

"Chris. He really cares about you. It's obvious."

For some reason, I couldn't get the picture of rounded, swinging breasts out of my mind. "Marly!"

"What?"

I don't think I was deliberately ignoring her.

Janet lowered her voice. "So how's it going?" She made a circular motion in the sand with her hand. "You know ..."

How was it going? In answer, seventy-odd phrases passed through my mind, most of them inexplicable. I turned to face Janet and randomly picked one from the pile. "Well ... the sex is pretty damned good."

Janet's face lit up. "Really? But that's great! You know, if you two get married and he insists that you go to Ohio, he'll have to support you."

"Janet, that is one strange observation."

"It would only be fair, considering you'd have to move your entire life."

"No one's moving anywhere. Besides, I can write on the dark side of the moon. And have, actually."

"What's bugging you?" she asked.

I threw my hands into the air, reaching for the right words. "He's nice

... but reined-in."

Something flickered across her eyes. "Reined-in?"

"Well, he says all the right things and references struggles I can relate to. He does lots of the right things. I guess I could admit that we communicate on a reasonable scale."

"Oh, I see. That would bug me, too."

I couldn't blame her for being sarcastic. "Do I sound a little nuts to you?" I asked.

"Well ..." I studied her face as she thought it over. "You do a ton of writing about ... mostly about what people feel. And you do it in a way that makes it easy to feel the way your characters feel. In fact, I don't know how you get it down in writing like that. I mean ... I identify with their problems."

"So?" I asked, searching for the bottom of this circuitous declaration.

"So ... You're always writing about people who don't pay close enough attention to their gut hunches. Even when they know better. You always point out stuff about people's instincts and how they relate to their emotional stuff."

"I am?"

Janet rolled her eyes at me in disgust. "Don't be dense, Marl. If you're feeling something strong at your gut level, then ... your heroines would tell you to ... pay attention." The set of her face changed to real interest. "What are you feeling? And don't be jokey."

"Jokey?"

"I demand a serious answer."

I rolled over onto my stomach and propped up my face with my hands. My tone was only partially sarcastic. "I want to lay me down and die in his arms. I want to shelter myself inside the safety of his embrace. I crave his touch, which is like tongues of flame on my skin. I want to marry him and have his children. Then I want to murder him in his sleep with a baseball bat. He's inflexible, Janet. His ability to be vulnerable may be almost as damaged as mine."

Her mouth dropped open. "Are you shitting me? Chris?"

"He looks playful. And charming and full of fun. But he's not comfortable inside. There's this grasping, echo-filled place where his heart and soul should be."

"Have you told him this?"

"Not exactly." I laughed a bit too cynically. "I mean, who is shitting whom?"

I reached for the tube of sunblock #45 and slathered it over my arms and hands. It was cool on my skin.

"The only thing ..." I started hesitantly.

"Yes?"

"So ... when we finish, and we're lying next to one another, he tells me how 'wild' it was. That's the word he uses. 'Wild.' He loves me when I'm not scaring him to death."

Janet screwed her eyebrows together in an effort to follow the trail of breadcrumbs I was tossing out. "Does that mean that you and Chris actually did ...?"

"I didn't think Richard could keep his mouth shut." Her jaw dropped. "What, will there be an article in tomorrow's *Island Crier*?"

Janet shook her head in wonder. "I never met anyone like you."

I said, "What a sheltered life you must have led."

"That wasn't very nice."

"You're right, it wasn't. I wonder about myself sometimes. Maybe I'm just not ready to have a real relationship yet."

Janet thought for a moment. "All this stuff sounds pretty real to me."

Besides the ever-beckoning trappings of Paradise, one of the attractions of Half-Moon Bay is the entertainment. On Thursdays, three exotic native dancers perform a kind of primitive fire ballet. I remembered the sensuality of their presentation from my previous visit and made sure we all had front row seats.

The night was still and warm, with the temperature hovering near seventy-eight degrees. The tide was low, and the sea sounded like rustling taffeta.

Most of the hotel guests had gathered by the pool for an after-dinner cordial. There were a couple of backgammon games in progress as the band members moseyed in one by one and started their set-up and sound check.

Chris sat on a lounge chair, his body flush against the backrest, his legs stretched out in a vee in front of him. I nestled back into that vee while he massaged my neck and shoulders, his fingers sticking delicately to my skin with the humidity. Richard and Nat were discussing our coming shopping expedition into St. John's, the capital city of Antigua. Felip, who I'd contracted to take us, warned me that we'd be disappointed. But I believe in being a real-live tourist when I travel. If it's there, I want to visit it, absorb it, photograph it, drink it, swim in it or eat it. End of discussion.

Dot, as usual, had a number of pamphlets spread out on the table in front of her. She idly picked one up, examined it, then handed it to Richard. She observed, "Admiral Nelson spent a lot of time in these waters."

Richard nodded. "Isn't there a marina somewhere near here? Named after him?"

Dot bobbed her head like a myna bird. "Yeah, there is. Nelson's Dock. Maybe we could stop there on our way back from town."

Chris said, "Marly, are you sure you want to drag us all along with you?" He began playfully finger-walking the flower patterns of my dress.

"I'm sure," I said, leaning toward him with pleasure. "Even through drunken stupors, on the night I arrived I clearly remember you all promising to do whatever I wanted. I intend to hold you to it."

"You were the one in the drunken stupor," said Richard.

"Technicalities!" I protested loudly.

The lights dimmed to black.

One of the musicians began to beat on a hollow-sounding drum. The cadence started softly, almost gently, and oh-so-slowly. The soft, deep rhythm seemed to echo back upon itself as it came and went, just on the edge of conscious perception, not unlike the heartbeat of a dying man.

Two deep red spotlights sprang into life, revealing our three entertainers. The two young men, black to the point of blueness, boyishly thin, graceful, loose-limbed and triple-jointed, stood fiercely erect. They wore black tights underneath thong-style briefs, decorated with feathers and brightly-colored artistically primitive symbols. Their faces were streaked with dye, one red, the other blue.

The woman was creamier complected, lusher of figure, rounded at the breast and the buttock and even the belly. Where the young men were stern-looking and presented ferocious faces, she was mockingly coy. Where they challenged and taunted silently, she seduced and beckoned.

They started out like liquid shadows, so insinuating was their movement, and seemed to have no edges as their bodies flowed back and forth, giving to and taking from the darkness. They wrapped themselves gracefully into and out of impossible positions, solitarily at first and then, as the drumbeat turned up a notch and then another notch, around one another. They were ebony smoke and sylph-like.

You could sense the crowd inching to chair edges with delectable fascination. Beads of perspiration broke out on the foreheads of the women in the audience while the men shifted their crotches inside their trousers. I saw Richard's hand move unconsciously to Janet's thigh.

Dot leaned closer to Nat and lolled her head back, her eyes shut, her smile dreamy. I even noticed that I had begun to sway but couldn't remember when. I felt Chris' hands move to my arms and pressed against his chest.

The tempo of the beat quickened. The sound was darker and cruder. The three dancers separated and began to take solo turns.

The blue-faced boy, for his figure still had the unformed musculature of lingering adolescence, moved to the center of the dance floor. His brother threw him a circle of wood, like a primitive hula-hoop. Lithely contorting his body, he slipped it over his left arm, his head, his right arm, down his chest, over his hips down the right leg, up to his crotch, and down the left leg until it was free. He held it up for our inspection, to show the impossibly small space through which he had maneuvered his entire frame.

We were all too enrapt by his presentation to applaud.

The woman/girl took his place. She began to shimmy, all the parts of her body moving independently. Her two partners appeared at either side and lifted her gracefully into the air. They easily passed her back and forth over their heads, through their legs, winding her around the fronts and backs of their bodies. When they set her on the ground, she extended her legs into the splits. Each boy grabbed a foot, and they carried her around the stage area, all three bending and weaving to the drumbeat. When they set her down again, she gracefully stood on her hands. The blue-faced dancer picked her up. Grabbing his thighs, she moved herself through the wicket of his legs. On the other side, she was met by the red-faced boy. When she had worked her way, hand over hand, up his body until her face was the same height as his, he placed his biceps under her armpits even as she threw her own arms wide. The red dancer turned around and pressed himself against the other two for a moment before sliding his own biceps next to those of the other boy. They carried the girl around like that for some seconds, as the red spots faded to black.

Now the drummer turned up the tempo, and the solo dancer appeared in a single spot at center stage. He bowed low, his face passing his knees. When he righted himself, a small piece of wood appeared, as if by magic, in his right hand. In a breath, he had somehow ignited the wood, which burst into flame. As the music escalated in tempo, the youth began to spin and twirl. He waved the torch wildly, flicking its flaming head like a cat-o'-nine-tails.

He began to jump and somersault and flip, the fiery tongues licking at his skin.

When he suddenly plowed through the audience, we responded just as he had planned, by screaming delightedly. He vaulted tables and jigged on one leg, the ever-present fire punctuating each rapid movement like an exclamation point. Finally, he sped back to the dance floor and spread his legs wide. Slowly, slowly, he bent over backwards until his chin nearly rested on the cement. He moved the torch through his legs and, bent into a complete circle, crab-walked several steps. He rested for a long moment, his chest heaving with his exertion, his body glistening and stretched taut. Then he raised the fiery baton slightly above his head, and when he doused it by inserting it into his mouth, the spotlights went out.

The applause was riotous. The hotel guests stood and whistled and clapped and banged on tabletops and one another with their fists. The lights came up, and the four artists bowed together, almost demurely, eyes downcast, and ran into the night.

"Wow," said Nat, exhaling heavily, "I need a drink." He signaled for a waiter.

Janet's eyes were popping out of her head. "Did you see that?" She blotted her forehead with a cocktail napkin and turned to Richard. "Now that was sexy. Didn't you think that was sexy?"

Richard ran his hands through his hair distractedly.

Dot said, "I've never seen anything like that in my life. Never, never, never." She glanced at Chris. "I'll just bet they don't dance like that in Ohio."

I said, "I'll just bet they don't do anything at all like that in Ohio."

Everyone laughed.

Janet stood up. "I need to pee. Ladies?"

I know ... I know. It's a hackneyed scene straight out of the fifties, with all the female-types gathering up minute evening bags and, arm in arm, traipsing to the restroom. Here, in decades past, they would dab and blot, comb and gossip, compare recipes, bemoan their husbands' expanding midsections, and the scarcity and price of What Everyone Is Wearing. The updated nineties totally-happening topics included plastic surgery, mate-bashing, sex, and the scarcity and price of What Everyone Is Wearing.

We elected to repair to my hotel room, where the line was sure to be shorter. And the conversation promised to be depth-defying.

I haven't spent a great deal of time in men's bathrooms. Notice I don't say I've never spent any time in men's bathrooms ... after all, any port in a urine storm. But it has never ceased to amaze me how personal conversations can be in ladies' rooms.

Two women sitting in their respective stalls, who have never even seen one another before, can start a conversation over the lack of toilet paper and wind up discussing the unusual sexual proclivities of their significant others. It's a weird but consistent kind of casual intimacy.

I can't imagine some man standing over a urinal turning to the stranger on his left and discussing the weird curve in his dick or his prostate enlargement. On the other hand, I have actually overheard women previously unknown to one another discuss vaginal vs. clitoral stimulation, the last man who broke their hearts and stole their money, and/or medical problems of a most personal nature. It's quite democratic, as anyone in the john is free to kibitz with an opinion or a related experience. No question is taboo, no subject too off-the-wall.

So it didn't surprise me when Janet said, "That girl had such high-standing breasts. She couldn't have been more than twenty. Did you see the way those two guys sandwiched her? I've never done that. Have you, Dot?"

"Had high-standing breasts? Oh, you mean ... no. In fact, I was a virgin when I married Nat."

Janet eeeped. "Eeep! You were? How old were you?"

"Twenty-three."

"You mean to say that Nat is the only man you've ever slept with?" I asked.

"I didn't mean to say that at all."

Janet and I looked at each other.

"Does Nat know about this little detour?" I asked.

We listened to a tinkling sound, followed by the flushing toilet.

"No." Dot swept back into the bedroom, and it was Janet's turn. "We were having some problems with our marriage. When I pressed for counseling and Nat refused, I went by myself."

"And fell in love with your therapist," I predicted.

"No. With a fellow member of my group."

The toilet flushed again. Janet reentered the room and said, "Dot! You never told me that."

It was my turn to pee. While still inside the bathroom, I heard Dot say to Janet, "Oh. Thong panties? Too uncomfortable for me. I hate the feeling of something riding up my crack."

"I hate panty lines," Janet explained. "Besides, you get used to it."

I flushed and took my place in front of the bureau mirror beside my friends. "I don't think women are as interested in having sex with two men as men are in having sex with two women."

"Actually," Dot said, "I've lusted after plenty of men. Chastely, of course, like Jimmy Carter lusted."

Janet and I laughed.

Dot continued, "But if I actually had the opportunity to try it ... I probably wouldn't."

"Doesn't it depend on the men?" asked Janet. "I wonder if you could find two normal guys who wouldn't flip out at the thought of sharing a sexual experience with another male?"

I brushed through my wig. "What's normal? Maybe just the fact that a human being is interested in a threesome makes him or her kinky."

We finished primping and walked slowly back to our dates/mates. We were still discussing the subject when we got back to the table.

"I think men are more liable, Janet."

Janet nodded her head reluctantly.

"Liable to what?" asked Chris.

"Liable to dream about sexual sandwiches," I answered as I kissed the top of his head.

"Sexual sandwiches?" That was Nat.

"Like an Oreo cookie with hormones," I explained. "C'mon, guys. Are any of you gonna sit here with a straight face and tell us you've never thought about having sex with two women?"

Nat put his hands up in a classic gesture of surrender. "I'm not gonna tell you that, Marly."

"I'd like to know who you fantasized about," Dot said. "Anyone I know?"

"Oh, hell. I was a kid."

Dot stared at Nat, arching one eyebrow.

"Okay," he admitted, "it wasn't that long ago. But I never did anything about it. You're my one and only."

Actually, this might have been the truth. Nat and Dot had a pretty good marriage, and they were obviously still crazy about one another.

Richard stroked his chin. "Well, of course, I too am happily married." He smiled at Janet and blew her a kiss. "Our therapist feels that subjecting a marital relationship to that kind of stress is very unwise. Too volatile."

"Ka-boom." That was me. I turned to Chris. "We Californians are a little more open about these matters than the rest of the world. But be honest ... the idea of a threesome or even two women together isn't ... horrifying, is it?"

Chris scratched his chin, then drank deeply from his white wine. "Two women together."

I watched Nat's eyes come back into focus. "That dance ... if that's what it was ... really stirred things up. For me, anyhow."

"I know exactly what you're saying," agreed Janet. She looked playfully at Richard and nudged him with an elbow.

"Ah ...," I said, "the children's hour. Why don't we call it a night?"

"That's really what women talk about in the john?" Chris asked as he began to undo his shirt buttons.

I slapped at his hands softly and took over the job. "Yep," I said, "and a lot worse." I flicked my tongue over his right nipple. "Did you mean that? About two women?"

"Yeah. You ever ... had sex with a woman?"

"No. But I watched two friends of mine once, a guy and a gal. They asked me to."

Chris shook his head. "What was it like?"

"They were performing more for me than one another. It wasn't sexy or anything."

"Did you ... join in?"

"No. I was merely an innocent bystander."

Chris thought about this. Then, "For me, the idea of two men together is kinda disgusting. But seeing you with a woman ... I'd be ... intrigued."

I began tonguing circles around his nipple. "Well," I whispered, as I sank to my knees and started to unfasten his belt, "if I ever arrange it, I'll send you an engraved invitation."

I am skipping the gratuitous sex scene here. Suffice it to say that our coupling was exotic and animated as in: 1) he never lost his hard-on and 2) within a very few seconds of completing lap one, we'd started lap two.

"How long has it been," I murmured into his ear, "since you last needed no recovery time?"

"I ... can't ... oh, God. Oh, God ... remember."

When my scarf came off my head sometime during the fray, neither of us noticed.

Chapter 12

That night, The Lump Nightmare broke through my subconscious with a vengeance. Covered in fear-scented sweat, I can only thank God Chris had already returned to his room. My travel alarm showed 3:37 as I thrashed myself awake. With moonlight pouring into my room like glowing Karo syrup, I began to sob uncontrollably, as I felt The Wall move in on me.

The Glass Wall. The Wall of Death. It's a psychological symbol I learned to identify in my group, equal parts terror and numbness, compliments of the ubiquitous Mr. Fear, my imaginary enemy. And yet, when you feel it/him pressing down on your body, pressing in on your spirit, the suffocation effect is as massive and cold as an Alaskan glacier. Horror of horrors, The Wall isn't stationary. At various times during your treatment, it moves closer or farther away, depending on the nature of your prognosis or the amount of pain you happen to be in. It's unpredictable, debilitating, crazy-making. Your therapist will attempt to convince you that you control its proximity, that when the unbearable pressure is closing in, you have the power to push back.

Or succumb to it.

Shivering and shaking, I managed to drag myself out of my soaked sheets and into the bathroom. I turned the shower on full blast, waited while steam filled up the stall and slipped into that healing liquid warmth, still dressed in my shorty nightgown. I let my body go limp as the surge of spray beat down on my shoulders. I closed my eyes and began to breathe deeply. In ... Out ... In ... Out ...

My heart, which had been ricocheting around my rib cage in frenetic, uneven beats, slowed down to a dull roar. I could feel the muscle tension in my neck ease. I massaged my shoulders with slow, circular motions and tried to think of something pleasant.

An image of my grandmother, Rachael, popped into my mind. A brisk, competent woman, she spent the first half of her life on a small farm in Iowa and the second half in various large and airy apartments overlooking Fifth Avenue in New York City. It was a challenging transition to make, and my grandmother made it in the same manner as she'd undertaken every other challenge during her life: crisply and energetically.

She eventually became a woman who learned to appreciate what I have come to think of as the high life, including but not restricted to a whirlwind of shopping, card playing, golf and tennis and always, always some new place on the map. She and my grandfather, Clay, weren't jet-setters, by any stretch of the imagination. She would have snorted at the absurdity of that idea. Yet he made a more-than-comfortable living from travel writing, and she was only too happy to pick up and take off at a moment's notice. I think my wanderlust came straight from their mutual DNA.

Lying akimbo in the shower, willing my heartbeat to return to normal, I recalled the first time my grandmother and I had ever flown together.

We were on a plane to La Paz, a small harbor town on the Baja Peninsula. I was only about four years old at the time, and I don't recall why Rachael and I were making the journey alone together. I do remember the bone-jangling turbulence we ran into shortly after the plane crossed over the border at San Diego. I vividly recall the gasps and retching sounds of several of the other passengers, as our craft was thrown helter-skelter through the sky, bouncing from one air pocket to another.

Grandma Rachael was a strong-minded, cheerful sort, pragmatic and quick-thinking. She'd run a thriving business out of the family home before Clay's unexpected success as a writer, and she would have made a fine frontier general; she had that kind of bustling drive and organizational skill.

I clearly remember the moment when the plane began to rock and how I turned, wide-eyed, to Rachael for reassurance.

She laughed and patted my arm. "This is what the guys up front call 'interesting weather.' Here," she said, reaching for a small paper bag inside her purse, "chocolate chip cookies, just in case. Made them myself." She popped a half a cookie into her mouth. "You know, this feels a lot like a ride on a roller-coaster. Whhheeeeee!" she cried as the plane dipped and swerved. When she began flapping her arms over our heads, I relaxed and allowed the turbulence to carry me up and down, under and over. I started to giggle and yelp with delight, clapping my hands. "Yay! Yay! Yay! Yay!" You might have expected this behavior to have been irksome to everyone else. But honestly, our fellow travelers began to laugh at my antics and clap their hands and yell, "Yay! Yay!"

I turned off the water then, and with my head propped against the shower tile, I clapped my hands and yelled, "Yay! Yay!"

A knock on my door startled me. I hoped it wasn't hotel security, come to throw me out on my ass for practicing to wake the dead. I threw a towel around my wetness and asked, "Who's there?"

"Chris. Are you all right? I heard some noise coming from your room."

I opened the door. "You did? God, I must have been a lot louder than I thought."

"Well, I'm right above you, actually. It was you, then?"

"Yes."

He looked me up and down, sopping wet, practically naked, with no doubt the look of chaos in my eye. "Are you okay?" he asked in a solicitous tone.

"I had a nightmare."

I suddenly realized I wasn't wearing any head covering. Without thinking, I drew the towel from around my body, tossed it over my head and slammed the door in Chris' face. I had stopped shaking by then, but I felt sick to my stomach, knowing someone outside the magic circle had seen. I'd let my mother gaze upon my baldness and one or two others, like Lark and Jess. But this was a man I hardly knew, a man who'd pleasured me and, more importantly, breathed new life into my sense of myself as woman. I'd just about given up hope that any male would ever lust after me again, when Wham! Chris waltzed into my life and turned my hormones back on.

I started to cry.

"Marly? Let me in. Please?"

"Go away," I hiccoughed between sobs.

"Let me hold you. I can't make it better, but maybe I could make it easier."

"Go away," I repeated, louder this time.

I felt him standing there, listening to my crying. I wanted to let go, to surrender my sorrow to his embrace. I wanted to lay down my burden, just for a moment, and rest in his arms. But if I allowed myself to do that and our relationship came a cropper somewhere down the line, I wasn't sure I'd be able to recover.

Oh, hell.

I opened the door and fell into his arms.

It was quite late (or hideously early) by the time Chris finally got me quieted down. Snuggled in his arms, I asked him to tell me something I didn't already know about his life. I wanted just to listen, to just drink him in and find peace in the softly rolling vowels of his accent.

"That's a tall order. You know a lot about me already. Let's see ... They're trying to get me to sell the rest of my land, the bastards."

Oh, well.

"They're building a country club all around me. Fine; no problem. But they've decided the architecture of my house is an eyesore." He laughed grimly. "I designed it myself."

Unconsciously, he drew me closer, and I could tell that he desperately wanted me to listen, to understand something about him that was basic.

"They've offered to buy low. They'll sell high. In short, they're trying to screw me."

"But didn't you tell me that all the other houses have been negotiated out?" I asked. "I mean, you used to live in a neighborhood, with people and dogs and backyard barbecues. Didn't you?"

"Everyone else sold out a long time ago."

"Isn't it lonely?"

"Private. It's private." He began to rock me gently back and forth. "My house is beautiful—ranch style with lots of picture windows and different levels. The living room's creamy white." He kissed my wisps of hair. "I want to see you on my couch, in front of a roaring fire, a proper thunderstorm lighting up the night sky." He lifted his head, as though he were listening to the call of something far away. "I'd take two million, but they're too stupid to anticipate what a stubborn sumbitch thorn-in-the-butt I can be. They could offer me one of their attached condos at cost. Then I'd do some serious thinking."

It was an odd lullaby he was crooning. Oh, it came straight from his soul, all right ... that was the problem.

I have spent most of my adult life in pursuit of things which can't be measured by bank balances, in the belief that my bulletproof youth would last forever. Not to say I despise money. Money is the perfect medium for buying your way out of games you've grown tired of playing. It's good for treating your friends and avoiding your enemies. It's a hedge against the cruelties and vagaries of the world; all this I admit. But as an end in itself, it sucks. A tinny alarm bell went off in my head.

He kissed me softly. "I want to bring you to my house. Meet my boys. See what I've made for myself. A few years ago, I almost lost everything, but I regrouped, borrowed, begged, almost stole, and got lucky. And I'm back. Come and see what I've made for myself."

He kissed me again. The talk of his success seemed to work on him like an aphrodisiac. His hands moved across my belly, up my ribs, over my breasts. He found the indentation on my left side and stroked it gently. Then he bent his head down and ran his tongue across my scar.

"If I sucked on it hard enough, do you think I could pop it back out? Like a car fender?"

This made me laugh, as it was intended to do.

"Chris ... have you ever heard of AstroGlide?"

As I mentioned earlier, there are no clocks or telephones in the rooms at Half-Moon Bay. You fill out a breakfast menu each night and leave it at the front desk, designating a time for delivery. The next morning, a young woman, carrying a laden tray on her head, knocks on your sea-side door. "Loooo ... missus. I be setting up out here, and you be getting up in there."

That's the standard wake-up call at Half-Moon Bay.

I rolled over onto my back and felt for Chris. He wasn't there. I sat up and looked around the room. He wasn't there. I checked out the bathroom, but I already knew: he wasn't there.

I remembered his saying he had the room above mine, so I threw on a bathing suit and ran up the nearest stairs. I found him packing his bags. I could feel my stomach muscles knotting up.

"Going somewhere?" I asked, as casually as possible.

Chris barely glanced up at me. "It's my son, Jeremy. Got a call from his mother this morning. He really needs to see me. She was pretty adamant about it."

"In the middle of your first vacation in three years?"

"I've been traveling a lot. He's going through a difficult stage, hard to handle. With the divorce, and all. Sometimes, only his dad will do. You know what kids are."

I wished, just for a moment, that I was a child again and the center of my parents' universe—or anyone's universe but my own. I wanted to ask why he was really going, but somewhere in the back of my brain, I knew the real why. So I just stood there watching him, frozen in my tiny spot, which grew smaller the longer I stood on it, feeling uncomfortable and a little lost. Something in my manner must have tipped him off. He suddenly changed his direction mid-stride and walked purposefully over and took me in his arms.

"I hate to go," he whispered. "I hate the thought of leaving you this way. But our relationship is ... There'll be more to come for us." His face drooped into sadness because he didn't believe it, either. "I love it here. I loved being with you in this place."

I dug down deep and came up with a miniscule amount of The Right Thing To Say. "Well, I never want you to have to choose between me and your son. I know how important that bond is."

Lies! Lies! Stay here! Stay with me and comfort me! Hold me and tell me you love me and never let me go! I'm afraid! I wanted to scream at him and hold on to him for dear life. I wanted to plead with him or cajole him or threaten him to stay.

"Is Jeremy ... sick, or something?" I asked.

"Nothing a doctor can cure." Chris kissed me on the cheek. "I feel awful about this, Marly, but I gotta go. Please don't be angry."

Anger would come later.

"What time is your flight?"

"Couple hours. I'm flying back through Miami. Listen, you don't have to come to the airport with me. Stay here with Janet and everyone. I'll call you tomorrow."

He shut his suitcase, scanned the room briefly to check for something he might've left behind—like me, pecked me on the cheek one last time, and was gone.

Chapter 13

"You mean he just left?" Janet asked.

We were all sitting together on the beach, soaking up the sun and nibbling on cheese and crackers. I was chain smoking. The little pile of Eve 120's in an empty drink cup by my side bespoke my wreck-and-a-half state.

"Something about his kid," I said and stubbed out another butt. "Yeck. These taste awful."

"Maybe you'll quit," Richard said from under his straw hat. "You know, Marly, he came to our last New Year's Eve party with that woman. What was her name, Janet?"

"Becky?"

"Yeah, yeah," Nat said. "Becky. I remember that she was sloshed before nine o'clock."

Dot looked up from her crossword puzzle. "Oh, my God, what a scene! You should have seen the look in his eyes when he tried to get her out to the car. She was a mess."

"What look, Dot?" I asked.

"I remember watching him guide her," said Janet. "She kept trying to slap his face. I think she was scared to death."

"What look was that, Dot?" I asked again.

"What? Oh. He had the look of a man trapped in hell."

I lit another Eve and thought how I'd seen that look on Chris' face the night before. Just before I drifted off to sleep, it traveled across his face.

Suddenly, I wanted to leave. Not the beach; Antigua. But the idea of being alone in my own home didn't cut it. All those echoing wood floors; all that cool, empty space. No. I needed a brisk dose of common sense. I scuttled me and my beach accoutrements to the public telephone in the lobby.

As you can imagine, placing a long distance call in Antigua takes persistence.

"No ... that's area 212, operator. No, 212. No, I'll need to bill it to my AT&T card. I already gave you that number. Why do you have to verify? The computer's down again ... hmmm, I see. Yes, I'll wait." Two minutes passed.

"Monimo? Marly. Are you guys ... No, no, everything's fine. Wait, scratch that. Lousy. Are you guys in town for a while? Could I visit for a couple of days? ... Great ... I'll call you back when I make my flight arrangements ... I love you, too."

Minutes later: "Marly? What are you doing?" Janet's body blocked the sunlight in the doorway of my room.

"I gotta get the hell out of here."

"He kinda ran out, didn't he?" she asked.

"Yeah. And I kinda laced up his track shoes for him." I swallowed tears, feeling a twinge of disgust with myself. God, I was tired of crying.

Janet shrugged. "You're doing okay, Marl."

I shook my head.

"Yes, you are."

I couldn't make myself tell her how I'd held onto his body until my arms ached or reveal how needy I'd felt. I certainly couldn't tell her about that Dante's-inferno look I'd seen on his face.

"I don't think you should go, Marl. You shouldn't be alone right now."

"I'm going to New York to see Monimo and Gramps. I'll be okay. Just help me make the plane."

Janet got me a bellman and went ahead to summon a taxi. I power-walked through the entrance hall of the hotel without even stopping to pay the bill; they had my address. I didn't detour through the pool to thank Richard or Nat or Dot or say good-bye. I didn't even check to see if there was room for me on the flight. I was just going to sit myself down on the goddamned tarmac until some airline company took pity on me and found space, even if I had to travel in the head the entire time.

As fate would have it, Felip was waiting for me in his brother's taxi. "Ah, missus, most shrewd crab purchaser. May I take you? The very, very best rates on the island and very, very fast."

I actually smiled.

"Airport, please." I turned to hug Janet and discovered tears on her face. "Don't cry for me, Argentina. A few days with Clay and Rachael, and I'll be good as new."

As Felip pulled out of the driveway in a cloud of dust, I waved at Janet's retreating figure long after I could no longer see her.

So much for Antigua.

I swear I could sense Rachael's feisty warmth while my plane was still circling Kennedy. She was so capable, so bustling.

"Marly. My goodness, your tan! Give me that bag. No, no." She playfully grabbed it from me. "I'm not decrepit yet. God, the weather! Three storms in a row. We haven't seen the sun in weeks. You must be freezing; please take my coat. Take it! Did you bring any warm clothes? Well, no matter; I'll buy you whatever you need. No arguments! Let's see ... carousel seven, I think. This way. Clay apologizes. He's beating a deadline with a stick. I've been cooking since you called. We're having quail and wild rice. Can you hear the smell?"

I felt better already.

They lived in a pretty old co-op brownstone in the west 80's. Kitchen, living room and dining room on the ground floor, Clay's office and their master bedroom and bath on the second, with guest rooms sharing a Jack-and-Jill bath on the top. I remember the first time Clay persuaded me to slide down the bannister. He ran all the way down the stairs beside me, laughing like a wild man.

What is it about grandparents? They even smell comforting. Maybe it has something to do with grandparents' and grandchildren's shared enemy?

When Rachael finally got the key to work—"Damn this lock! It needs some WD-40!"—the aroma of her fabled cooking flooded out at me, drawing me into the cozy entryway. Intricately designed parquet floors glowed yellow in the soft light of a small chandelier. Rachael and Clay had taken some of their furniture from Home Farm when they'd moved to New York from Iowa all those years ago. The rest of their furniture was a curious yet pleasant mix of eclectic bits and pieces from their travels.

In the corner of the living room, to the right of the fireplace, hung a lovely hand-knotted swinging chair they'd brought back from Pago Pago. The marble mantle came from Poland. Behind the sofa sat a lamp whose base had been carved in Ireland out of the wood from a shipwreck. I remember Grandpa Clay telling me about the Erin sweaters he and Rachael had given the family that Christmas, after their trip to Dublin. "All the clans knit these sweaters in different patterns. This one's called Donegal. They don't treat the wool, so it retains its naturally water-repellent nature. Ireland's coastline is treacherous, and the North Sea is a killer. When fishing boats crash against the rocks, the searchers can tell which clan the bodies belong to simply by identifying the pattern of the knit." His face sobered. "Often, that's the only identification possible."

Clay's travel columns were full of fascinating tidbits like that. He wasn't content to write about the surface of a place.

"Frieda? Come help with the bags." Rachael pushed her head through the swinging door of the kitchen. "Frieda?"

"I let her go an hour ago. Marly girl!" Clay swung down the stairs with that easy stride of his and swept me into his arms. "Still light as a feather. Let me look at you. Ah, you're such a pretty young woman. I like the wig. New, isn't it?"

He noticed the little things and never used them to hurt or embarrass.

"Your grandmother's been cooking up a storm. Wouldn't even let me taste till you got here."

She patted his middle softly. "You cheated!" She pretended severity. "He's supposed to be on a diet."

He kissed Rachael then and grabbed my bags. "She's too good a chef!"

The little garret room at the top of the house had always been mine. It had a three-quarter canopy bed made of sun-bleached cane. Rachael had fashioned the canopy herself out of mosquito netting tied with huge ribbons of tapa cloth from Pago Pago. Three pastel hand-braided rugs from Wales cozied up the wooden floors, and an ancient brass-studded ebony chest, whose cushion matched the tapa ribbons, sat next to the window seat. One wall of the little triangle-shaped room was covered with storyteller wreaths fashioned by artisans from the Jemez Pueblo near Santa Fe. The other wall was solid with bookcases. In fact, there were bookcases in every room of the co-op, including the kitchen. Clay's two great passions (or money drains, as Rachael would say) were books—"They're tax-deductible because I'm a writer. Isn't that something?"—and the truck he'd insisted be brought to New York from Home Farm back in 1948. "It still runs like a top," he always boasted.

"And the rent on the garage for that old relic costs as much as our house payment," my grandmother always shot back.

"God this all tastes so good. I never eat like this at home." I patted my belly happily. We were sitting at the old oak dining table in the kitchen.

"You eat too many salads," Rachael said. "I never held with salads."

As I pushed the last couple of bites around on my plate, I saw the look pass between Gramps and Rachael. "Well, I think I'll whip up an astounding meringue for dessert and leave you two to talk. Now shoo," she said.

Rachael was a pistol. I loved her dearly. But Clay had this quiet place in his heart that was perfect for secrets and sadness. While he laid a fire, I stretched out on the floor.

"You look a little tired," he said kindly. "Maybe you need a vacation after your vacation?"

"Ohhhhh, Gramps," I said contentedly.

Soon the living room was rich with dancing light. I watched the flames for some minutes, letting the mood cradle me.

"And how's Talbot?" Clay asked quietly.

"He's good."

Clay noticed something in my face. "What is it?"

With Gramps, you never had to pretend you didn't know something. "Oh, God. Let's see ... Your question made me think of Mom and Dad. You know, their marriage. How they've always been so ... close."

Clay's eyes gleamed to understand better.

"I used to have dreams, Gramps. About my life. I'd meet someone and live happily ever after. Now, I don't even know if I'll live, period."

When Clay nodded his head, I could tell he understood exactly what I meant.

"I hate my body," I went on. "I hate it. The way it looks. How it betrayed me. I'm an unholy mess."

He rested his chin in his right hand. "You're in a lonely place; a cold, hard, lonely place. I've never had a ... well, to put it bluntly, I've never been required to think about my own death. Not that I haven't. We're alike, you and I, in that way. But it was always a choice, not a necessity.

"I lost my parents early on when I was still bulletproof. And I've been lucky with friends and loved ones since then. So I've never been made to think about ... the concept of death. It tippytoed up on me, you see, and introduced itself genteelly. We got to know one another slowly, over time. Because I was curious and wanted to know." He reached forward and picked up an ancient meerschaum pipe from the coffee table. He began to work on it with a pipe cleaner and said, "Death walloped you in the stomach. Bang! You're still reeling. You may never recover. Don't judge yourself too harshly for that. You've ten times the courage I have. Believe me; I couldn't have stood what you've stood."

"I don't believe you," I snorted with self-contempt.

"That's up to you, Sweetchild." He opened his arm, and I scrambled up onto the sofa beside him. "Let me hug you," he whispered.

That's how I fell asleep, with his arm around me. I remember the sweet cherry smell of his tobacco and the popping of the firewood. I remember the pounding of the rain against the windows. And how well I remember feeling so very safe and welcome. I felt welcome for the first time in months.

In a very few days, I was back on the healing trail.

"Do you have to leave?" Rachael asked, carefully brushing the back of my wig. "We'd love you to really stay with us. We haven't been to any new restaurants. We didn't get into a poker game. And think of all the recipes we could try!"

I laughed at the sparkle in her eyes. "I'll come back soon. But whatever you do, please don't tell Miriam I was here. She'll skin us all alive!" Miriam was my literary agent, a good, old-fashioned shark.

Clay drove me to the airport in the old truck. "Be of good cheer," was all he said in way of good-bye. When he hugged me, my bones suddenly felt more substantial.

I love travel, and I hate getting home to the accumulations of modern living: mail, phone messages, dirty clothes, moldy cheese and stinky milk cartons.

After a rush-hour battle, I dragged myself into the house around seven. I could see my answering machine light blinking in the dark of the kitchen.

I'd been a good girl and left the number of the hotel in my message, in case of emergency. This was pretty thorough of me, considering I was the most likely person I knew to fall down and die at a moment's notice.

I was expecting a barrelful of messages on the machine, and I was not disappointed. My mother, asking about AstroGlide opportunities. Twice. My agent, Miriam, asking how the book was coming. She's a little peeved, because I spent the advance money without delivering a completed manuscript. Think how pissed she'd be if she ever found out I was in New York and didn't stop in to see her! Agents are a strange lot. They honestly believe that their clients are taking ninety percent of their money.

Good Ol' Don, asking how I was doing. Dr. Dent, probing whether I'd deliberately missed my mammogram follow-up. She sounded bent out of shape. Lark, wondering if I was still joining her in Mexico. And my step-sister, Jamie Sue. She's the one I glossed over a few chapters ago.

Jamie Sue was born to my father and his first wife, Kathleen. In fact, he left Kathleen for my mother either before or after my mother discovered she was pregnant with me. I always wondered what the real story was, in my soap opera life history.

"Marly? It's Jamie Sue. Call me."

It was the first time she'd spoken to me since the night I'd told her about my cancer. We're not close. To be honest, there are times we can't stand to be in the same city. She finds me too moody, too energetic, too unstructured. (Too honest? Too spontaneous? Too well-liked?) She says I'm jealous of her success.

There may be some truth to that.

I find her conniving, driven, two-faced. There's a narcissistic hardness about her, something missing in her soul. She once started foreclosure proceedings on a ninety-five-year-old man who wound up dying three days later. Legally, she was on solid ground, but it kinda makes a body wonder.

Suffice it to say that she lacks any empathy for the frailties of the human condition except her own. In that way, she's a little like Chris. She sucks up to power and dismisses anyone who can't be of some real use to her career. She's a rock radio DJ with a growing following in a big-time market, so maybe her lack of grace goes with the territory. Her will and her ego are unmatched in my experience.

I like to think we have very little in common. Except for this one trifling familial tie ... the same father. For his sake, we try to keep our mutual detestation under control, especially during family get-togethers. What a disgusting couple of geeky, air-kissing fakes we can be.

Don't think I haven't tried the "let's be friends" routine once or twice. My soul still carries the scorch marks. I also have a couple of real scars, courtesy of Jamie Sue, from the night she helped me through a glass door. While she was in high school and should have known better, I was only five. The memory of that sea of whole red blood, my blood, covering the white tiles in the master bathroom—that I will never forget. She still swears it was an accident.

After winding up two of my most soothing music boxes, I dialed Jamie Sue, who sounded sleepy. "Hello?"

"Me, J.S."

"Marly? Dad told me you were going straight from Antigua to Mexico."

"Nope. I'm taking a brief vacation from my vacation. What's shaking?"

"It's kinda late ..."

"It's only ten o'clock. What're you ... sick?"

"No, no," she said hurriedly. "Everything's absolutely fine."

"You called me, remember? I figured it had to be important. The place in Mexico doesn't have a telephone yet, so?"

"I wondered how you're ... how you are."

"Why don't we just say I'm better than I was but not as good as I will be."

"Daddy's pissed at me. Why'd you have to tell him that I haven't called?"

"Because you haven't called."

Now Jamie Sue is the kind of person who insists on being recognized as having the biggest and the most of whatever it is that's going around. If you had a nervous breakdown and cried every day for a month, she'd already had one twelve times worse and cried every day for a year. If you were diagnosed with Epstein-Barr, she'd contracted chronic active hepatitis. If you started dating a new man, he'd turn out to be only half as rich or half as charming as the man she was engaged to. You think you're busier than a one-armed paper hanger on drugs? She'll have her second assistant get you on the phone. Getting my boob lopped in half was the one area she couldn't surpass without placing herself either in a life-and-death situation or signing up for the strangest bit of elective surgery in the annals of medicine. In her mind, I'm sure my lump was a prize she could never aspire to.

Maybe it's because she's ten years older than I am. God! I love saying that. It's the thing I like about her the most.

I waited for her to go on. When she didn't, I said, "Besides the fact that dad threatened to cut you out of his will, to what do I owe the honor?"

"Did he tell you that?"

I yawped loudly.

"Was that a crack?" Jamie asked, more sullenly.

"This ain't much of a conversation. Shall we start again?"

I waited again. Finally, she burst into tears. "I think I have cancer," she said.

Quick ... what was my first reaction? If you said "Bullshit!" you hit the nail on the head. And I would have said it out loud, too, except there was always the remote possibility that she really did have cancer, and I didn't want to tempt karma.

"Tell me," I said.

"Well, I haven't had a period since January. So I went to my doctor, and he took a pap smear, and it came up with class two cells, and now I have to have some awful test tomorrow morning, and maybe they'll have to operate, and I'll lose all my female parts and never be able to have babies."

"It could just be menopause, Jamie Sue."

"Don't say that! Don't ever say that."

The woman is in her mid-forties. Also, she's not married, hasn't been for years. Hell, she can't narrow down her personal playing field to less than five. And she's worried about never having babies???

"Whoa, Jamie. Whooooaaaa; one thing at a time. A bum pap is no laughing matter. But under normal circumstances, a class two is way early in the progression of the disease. We're talking a few weird-looking cells. Take it from me; I'm an expert. The test is painless, and the odds of them finding anything serious are relatively small."

"How small?" she sniffed.

"I'm not Jimmy the Greek; I can't give you exact numbers. But small."

"Gosh! Think of it! I've had a brush with cancer!" She sounded chirpy. "So where're you going in Mexico?"

"Oh ... Manzanillo." Evasion.

"Baja peninsula?"

"Farther south." Careful.

"Manzanillo ... Manzanillo ... Wait a minute. You're not going to Las Hadas are you? What a great place! The movie Ten, right?"

Why is it that people you detest can sometimes read your mind better than people you love?

"Right. But I'm not going to the hotel."

"Oh ... well, I'm so busy this time of year, I couldn't possibly get away. I wish I had half as much free time as you!"

"Jamie Sue, I'm tired. Is there anything else?"

"I actually called to ask how you're doing, and I spend the whole time talking about my stuff. That's me, always getting side-tracked. You're really fine, though, right? I mean, you're recovering, and ... everything?"

"Yeah."

"I wish I could be strong like that. I guess I'm just too vulnerable. Well, bye!"

Byyyyeeee.

If I'd phoned my mom at that time of night, she'd have called down all the phantoms of hell on my head. My agent's also on New York time, so that'd have to wait till the next morning as well. Dr. Dent would have taken my call, no doubt, but I couldn't have taken her. Lark and Good Ol' Don were both up, I was sure. So I decided to get my Good Ol' Ex off the list first.

He always records the most asinine messages on his machine. And I swear that his accent, which thinned considerably after twelve years in California, is still thicker than crude oil. "I'm outta here, rockin' and rollin'. But after I get back and pull off my boots and set a spell, I'll holler at you. So leave the particulars, got it?"

I left my name and hung up.

I pushed my automatic dial code for Lark's number and turned on the speakerphone. When I got a busy signal, I punched the redial button and fixed myself a plate of crackers and cheese.

"Hello?"

"Hey, Larkie. It's me," I called out.

"Hello, you. You sound like you're in a cavern."

"Kitchen." I picked up the receiver. "Better?"

"You're not in Antigua?"

"Nope."

"Oh" was all she said.

"What flight are we on out of here?"

"Mexicana. Sunday at noon," she answered. "Well ... I'll call you tomorrow with the specifics."

She wanted to say more. Know more. She didn't push it.

I felt relieved ... and bone-tired. And lonely.

Chapter 14

The phone jolted me awake early the next morning. Ready to commit assault with a deadly weapon or my fist, I struggled to uncrimp my body and knocked the receiver out of its cradle.

"Hello?" I croaked.

"It's me."

"Me? Who me?" My mind was cobweb-filled.

"Jamie Sue. I didn't wake you, did I?"

I grabbed for the alarm clock and shook it, as though she could see me. "Do you know what time it is? It's six-thirty in the frigging morning!"

"I know, I know. But it's important. I wondered if you'd given any more thought to signing that agreement."

Jamie Sue's career was definitely on a roll, big-time. She'd not only taken over the number one position in Los Angeles during her afternoon drive-time slot, she'd also started taping a late-night, once-a-week local talk show that was rapidly finding the over-thirty yet still-hip viewership the sponsors craved. There were already plans to expand.

As Jamie Sue's star rose, so did her fears of exposure. She'd crawled over a lot of little people on the way up, one of the multitudes having been me. The agreement she referred to prohibited me from using any representation of her or her persona in my writing. To be fair, although it made no reference to other media, the contract also restricted her from bashing me in print.

"Why the hell didn't you mention this last night?"

"Well?" she continued, "Have you thought about it?"

Non sequitur ... non sequitur! Wait a minute ... My book was nearing completion. And I've always kept the plots of my books secret, because you get less interference from your family and friends when you pretend that all those weird characters are "fictional." Besides, since everything I write spills out from my solar plexus, I'd like to think I'd never compromise the integrity of my work for the sake of one brief volley of personal invective, however satisfying.

That's what I'd like to think.

"Gosh, Jamie Sue, I'd love to help you out. But I'll have to decline on the advice of my legal representation. Besides, I never consider contractual arrangements before seven o'clock in the morning, my time zone."

She missed the point entirely. "We'd be a lot stronger if we stood against the world together," she said.

Did I mention her persecution phobia?

"Let me explain in greater detail," I went on soothingly. "If I ever sign such an agreement, the supposition would have to be that I do, in fact, base my characters on actual living or dead human beings. Real people. It opens up a large can of worms—a Pandora's Box, if you will. The legal ramifications might be insurmountable."

I'd never consulted a lawyer on this particular subject, but it sounded like pretty good BS to me.

"All my assistants have signed it, all the people who work for me," she prodded.

This was a dig. It referred to the time in my life when I'd worked as her cleaning woman for five months. She paid me seven dollars an hour.

"I can appreciate your position," I said, dragging out more *L.A. Law* legal-speak, "but I'm unwilling to go against the recommendation of my attorneys." I jiggled the phone twice. "Oops, that's my other line. I'm expecting a call from my agent, and I've gotta take it. You let me know how your tests turn out, okay? Bye."

Byyyyeeee.

As soon as I hung up, the phone rang again. Eerily, it was my agent ... The Karmic Universe was certainly catching up with me quickly these days.

"Miriam! What a nice surprise."

"Pleeease do not be sarcastic from the get-go; it ruins my digestion," she said in her cigarette-rasp of a voice.

Miriam LeVine is a most unusual woman. She was born in Jerusalem during the chaotic aftermath of World War II, the child of Austrian-Jewish parents. Her family had somehow managed to slip through the hands of the Nazis in the mid-thirties, before the situation there turned mortally ugly. Upon reaching her eighteenth birthday, she applied for and received a scholarship to Radcliffe, where she eventually earned a graduate degree in literature.

She had lived in New York ever since, a happy expatriate barracuda who thrived on discovering and developing young writers, most of whom stayed with her once they made their mark in the literary world. They wouldn't have dared do otherwise. As she had often been heard to remark, "After all I've done for my little artists, I would shoot them deader than dead if they so much as used the word 'leave' in their manuscripts."

On the day she became an American citizen, I actually heard her say, "All those Jews trying to get into Israel and this little Jew staying out. I swim against the tide, against the tide."

"How on earth did you know I was here?" I asked, eliding over the uncomfortable factoid that I had been in New York.

"In keeping with popular stereotype, all the Jews in the world do know each other, Marly dear. It's the most ancient form of networking. I have an informant on your block out there in La La Land. A cantor, as it happens. Are you ... creating?"

She always used the word "create" instead of "work" or "write."

"Well ... not exactly."

"You thought about fibbing, didn't you?"

"Is that a rhetorical question?"

"Marly, those boys are chomping at the bit for your completed manuscript. They have already given us large sums of gelt in anticipation of through-the-roof sales. I worry about you, dear. And, my percentage, of course."

She looked and sounded as tough as steel brads. But she was a soft touch for any writer with a little talent and even half a brain. I qualified on both counts. I have a little talent and half a brain.

"Of course, Miriam."

"You're not ill again, are you?"

"No."

I heard her take a giant, hungry drag from her ever-present chain-linked cigarette. "Good. How long do you need? Don't misunderstand; I don't mind making them wait. But I want the truth. In fact, I insist on it."

"Okay ... I started the polish before I left. But there's still the living crap to get through. Mortgage payments and the new movie deal. And don't bug me about turning my accounts over to some CPA. I feel better keeping track of them myself. I don't like the producer they've hired. He's a cheapo and spends too much time at the track for my taste. Besides, he has a well-known penchant for big-breasted women, which I find particularly galling under the present circumstance.

"I'm trying to keep up with my group by tape. My sister's pressuring me. I haven't read any of the research that's been done on my next project.

My secretary's pregnant and only works part-time now. I've got the writer's conference in Santa Barbara ..."

"My, my, your defense mechanisms are in fine form today." She cleared her throat dramatically. "Let's be realistic here, Marly. This trip thing, this odyssey, I'm all for that. You can use the perspective, a change of scenery, a little slap-and-tickle ..."

"Geez, Miriam, you sound like my mother."

"A smart cookie. A survivor. You know what you need, lamb chop? You need to get yourself a wife. Men had the perfect scam going for years. So," she paused here for effect, "how much time do you really need?"

Miriam rarely tried to persuade you to take on more than you thought you could. She always made allowances for each individual's creative process. She was sometimes willing to renegotiate the time machine after the writing had begun, and she was sensitive to changes in mood, financial pressure, and that most dreaded of curses, writer's block. But once you made the ultimate no-bullshit deal with her ... the deal was the deal. Enter ... The Inquisition.

"Five weeks. I'm smiling, Miriam, over the phone. Can you hear me smiling?"

"Such a nice smile. Yes. We have an agreement. Five weeks, then. Oh, my office was contacted today by someone representing your step-sister. Shall we return the call?"

"Hey, it's your life and your grief. Do whatever won't agitate your digestion. I'll call you from Mexico."

"You always say that, but you never do it. Shalom."

I knew if I called Dr. Dent right then, I'd probably get through to her. So I detoured.

"Hey, Mom. Come to Mexico with me."

"Marly?" I heard her turn away from the phone. "Talbot, it's Marly. I'll take it in the other room. Hang this up for me, will you?" Then, "Marly? Hold on."

My mother and I haven't always been friends. Our relationship has ripened and softened more in the last three years than in all our lives together before. As I mentioned earlier, my parents always maintained a certain emotional self-possession, a coolness about the roil of life that I still find intimidating and a little confusing. Where I have always grabbed at life and suffered my victories and defeats with open passion, their joys and sorrows were undertaken with greater balance, greater equanimity. How often it has seemed that I'd been born to the wrong household.

Fierce and protective though my mother has always been, she's never been much of a one for hugging or kissing. A braggart about my achievements when I was absent, she remained aggravatingly close-mouthed to my face.

The cancer changed everything. I can remember her driving me to the hospital the day of my biopsy. How tenderly she held me, like an antique porcelain doll with a hairline crack. She clucked and fussed over my suitcase like a mother hen. "We'll insist on your wearing something pretty, something lacy. None of those rear end-exposing potato sacks. You'll see; it'll help keep your spirits up."

"What about the blood and stuff?"

"I'll buy you a monstrously expensive peignoir set as soon as the drains come out." She put her arm around me and whispered, "Scared?"

I nodded my head.

"Mother's here," she said. "Just let anyone try and mess with you."

She'd brought me a half-pound of my favorite See's candy, pecan roll, and warned me not to tempt her. Munching by the hands-ful on the way to the hospital, I told her about Mr. Fear.

"Dress him in drag. That'll teach him."

I laughed at this idea. "I could conjure him up in Little Lord Fauntleroy pants, playing the violin."

"Better the accordion. That's an indicator of taste, you know—a person who can play the accordion but chooses not to."

I remember how she held my hand while the nurse took my medical history. I remember we argued about how old I was when I got the chicken pox. (She said three; I said four.) I remember the concerned look she had on her face when a nurse, already dressed in surgical garb, gave me my local anesthetic.

My mother must have said, "I love you," fifty or sixty times over the next several days, while we waited for the lab to determine my fate. I'll never forget the flood of crocodile tears she shed when Dr. Dent told us the tumor was cancerous. And—worse yet!—that there was an indication of some unattached maverick cells in the lymph nodes under my left arm.

Those few days together, among the most terrifying and humbling of my life, had helped to heal us, helped us to put our past misunderstandings into crystal clear perspective, helped us to reevaluate our relationship and rediscover its faded glory from my childhood days.

"What the hell are you doing, calling this time of the morning?" she yelled into the receiver.

So much for rediscovered glory.

"Mother, dear! Did I wake you?" I asked in honeyed tones.

"No. But you interrupted us."

"Mother!"

I heard her rearranging herself. "So?" she said finally. "Tell me about your island romance."

It takes some getting used to, this point in your life when you realize your mother's always been a woman.

"It was nice," I said, unable to find a better word.

"Nice?"

My call waiting beeped through for real.

"Hold on, Mom. I'll be right back." I pushed the button. "Hello?"

"Hi, Marly! Lark."

"Hola, amiga."

"I can't wait to get out of this town. My children just learned they will have to spend next week with their father, and they're acting like brats! Anyhow, everything's set. We leave Sunday at twelve-thirty. Why don't you come here around noon? I'll hire a limo. Splurge."

"Lark ... I can't keep letting you ..."

"Don't be penny-pinching noble; it's tiresome. Just be here at nine A.M. Gotta run to the asylum. I'm starting in on the adult ward the week after spring break, and I've got a briefing. God, am I nervous."

"No worries. You'll be the sanest one there!"

"Very funny."

I switched back to Mom.

"I hate call waiting," she said. "If I were Harrison Ford, you wouldn't put me on hold."

"Mom, if you knew Harrison Ford was on your other line, you'd put me on hold."

"I don't have another line."

"So you'll miss out on Harrison Ford's phone call."

"So? You were up to the 'nice' part."

I told her as much as I could put together. I could feel her turning the information over in her mind. Then she said, "I think I will come to Mexico. What flight are you on?"

"There's no way you can get a reservation now, Mom."

"Please don't call me 'Mom.' You know I don't like it."

My usual morning routine has varied little over the past several years. Coffee. Newspaper. Daily crossword. That regimen was the one thing I struggled hardest to hold onto during my illness. It was a way of keeping the old rhythm. Except now the coffee is decaf, and the newspaper is full of murder and drought and savings-and-loan defaults and gang shootings and AIDS. Had I never noticed before? Most woefully, the crossword clues either seem familiar to the point of boredom or impossibly difficult. Time has marched on, oblivious of my rigorous attempts to stop it.

I used to think that someday I'd give up sugar, quit smoking, cut down on the vino, and get enough money in the bank to rest once in a while. Who teaches us these fairy tales? If I ever catch up to the s.o.b., I'll crack his head open.

When my conversation with Miriam pricked strongly enough at my conscience, I sat down at the computer and lost myself for a few hours. Thank God for my writing; it was a big-time good-luck charm and a prayer bead. It wasn't a conscious decision, but ever since the cancer, the words poured out of my guts and onto the screen like never before. Safe inside my stories, I felt like God. I created a universe and populated it. I was responsibility personified and in Complete Control.

Except when the characters refused to obey, which they sometimes did after they'd fleshed out a little and taken on a life of their own. Sometimes they'd listen but not very often.

It was the same with the men in my life. I met them and recreated them in a pre-fabbed image. Everything would roll along smoothly for a matter of weeks or months. Then, they'd flesh out a little and take on a life of their own. I'd argue my point with them, and sometimes they'd listen ... but not very often!

I'm beginning to comprehend why God gets frustrated.

Chapter 15

"Buenos dias!" said Lark, kissing me on the cheek. "Park your car in the garage and give Marty your bags. Cecilia!" she called out and ran back into the house.

Lark lives in a manicured area of Encino known as the Clark Gable Estates, right across the street from that most creative money juggler, Michael Milken. She and her ex-husband had originally bought two lots, side by side, in order to accommodate both their home and a tennis court. He got the court in the divorce settlement and still comes over to hose it down twice a week, drought or no drought. Eventually, I suppose he hopes to sell the land to home-builders. Although what anyone would want with a $750,000 plot barely large enough to hold one tennis court I can't say.

After the amount of time it takes to smoke two Eve 120's had passed, Lark ran back out of her house, shouting last-minute instructions to the housekeeper. The instructions were in English, and the housekeeper speaks only Spanish.

"And Cecilia? Please try to remember ... if we run low on something write it down on the list!" She pantomimed writing in the air. "And don't forget to empty the vacuum bag!"

"Do you have a proof of citizenship?" I asked as she plopped herself down on the seat beside me.

Lark looked at me dumbly.

"Not for Cecilia, you dolt. This isn't an INS raid. For you! Your citizenship! They're a little sticky about letting people like you back in."

"Gack!" she said and ran back into the house.

Sarah met us at the Mexicana ticket counter in the Tom Bradley International Terminal. Her travel agent, Bud, in his typical Houdini-esque manner, had somehow managed to finagle my mother a seat on our flight, at the height of the season, one day in advance.

The trip down takes about four hours. This is because all commercial airlines headed to Manzanillo are required to stop at Guadalajara in order to pass through immigration. What a pain! You deplane and are then herded onto buses that take you to a small, airless terminal. Get along little dogies, get along. Then you de-bus, get in line, pass through customs and receive an entrance visa in the form of a pretty pink slip of paper with an airplane, a ship, and a car drawn on the front. Whatever you do, don't lose that pretty pink slip. You absolutely positively gotta have it to get out of the country—that and twelve dollars. The Mexican authorities are not fools; they only charge you when you leave.

I once lost that innocent-looking slip of paper and was therefore unable to prove how I'd entered the country. ¡Qué lástima! It took the nearby American Consulate, all the influential residents I could round up from Mazatlan (not to mention a couple of infamous ones), many honest tears on my part, and some quick thinking by a flashing-eyed mustachioed immigration official with a weakness for blonds in distress to get me straightened out. I was sweating bullets for an hour or two, picturing myself languishing in a Mexican jail, my feet filthy, my hair stringy, smoking roll-your-owns.

My mother is an anywhere, anytime shopper. She finds airports particularly alluring, because they specialize in mugs, fake jewelry, tee shirts and paperback books. Her collection of shirts and the mugs fills three shelves in her den, and that doesn't count the ones she gifts. Hey, it's a matter of taste, you know? The sizes are always wrong, and the designs she picks out are, in my unhumble opinion, geekily sentimental or syrupy cute. I'll bet some of her household employees have outfitted entire families from my mother's quirky largesse, of which the tee shirts formed the single largest contribution.

She also gave away rug remnants and oil paintings that had come from flea market trades. She's been known to give away old lamps featuring fish and birds, sheet music for unknown songs, picnic hampers, sets of mismatched dishes, tea kettles with broken whistles and used tennis rackets. I haven't the faintest idea where she gets all this stuff; I only see her give it away. It is a little like the miracle of the loaves and the fishes.

It's a curious thing that most people who have worked for her down through the years have always taken whatever she offered them, including old waterbed mattresses; potholders sewn for Girl Scout fund-raisers; and the occasional glass paper weight. But nobody ever took the mugs.

My mother prides herself on the fact that she can still pick up and go at a moment's notice. Not that she and Talbot haven't collected some odd mementoes, apart from her odds-and-ends giveaways. We're talking real treasures here, selected by an eclectic eccentric. I can think of two or three shrunken heads and several rather risqué hand-painted Chinese screens, just off the top of my head. At first, these curios hold places of honor, but as they become familiar, they are inevitably replaced by newer, temporarily fascinating stuff. The age, value and utility of the object have less to do with its ultimate fate than where it sits in relation to my mother's daily path. Once it starts to nag at her, out it goes. I can't tell you how many sets of linen napkins my parents have run through over the years.

Flying makes me nervous. How else to explain that after boarding a flight, I always have to pee just after the fasten-your-seatbelt sign goes on. The lights are obviously attached to my bladder. I have tried to fix this problem by going two or three times in the terminal, which means dragging my crap all over hell and undressing in a space barely big enough to shelter my large traveling purse.

I left Lark and Mother happily browsing in the duty-free shop while I found the nearest ladies' room.

An elderly man pushing an even more elderly woman in a wheelchair was standing just outside the door. He appeared stumped, and she seemed confused. It hit me: she had to pee, and he couldn't push her inside without causing a riot. One look at her frail body told me that her making it in under her own steam was a very long shot.

"Can I help?" I asked.

He looked at me blankly.

I gestured to the door with the woman figure on it. "I see your dilemma. Can I help?"

I'll never forget the gratitude that lit up those two aged faces. It warmed me down to my toes. I know, I know. You're thinking, gee ... what a nice, even saintly, thing I did, what a truly gracious person I must be. And you'd be right, of course. Except that ever since my brush with the Big C, I've been racking up time-off-for-good-behavior points. In Eastern cultures, way back before Christ was a corporal, there are written references to a boon called a Kha Khan. It's a dispensation granted by a king or a prince that entitles the holder to be forgiven the death penalty ten times. I was putting in my Kha Khan time ... I just hoped God wasn't too busy with Her nails to make a notation on my score card.

I have spent a lot of time in Mexico over the past several years. By some weird coincidence, I keep stumbling into relationships with people who own vacation places in La Punta, a peninsular development of grand houses and an offshoot of the Las Hadas resort.

Las Hadas translates to "the fairies" in English. It's a soft, lush resort near Manzanillo on the west coast of Mexico, just below the Sea of Cortez, where the air is continuously pregnant with moisture, the houses are built open to the sea, and the people are handsome and mannered.

The resort itself resembles a Moorish castle on the coast of Spain, all stark white adobe complete with crenelated towers. The property cascades on multiple levels down landscaped cliffs to the sea, and the amenities include a small town filled with alluring shops and restaurants. You can eat pizza or pasta or just-caught fish by the boatful. You can buy haute couture bathing suits or Bustamante moons and suns or Mexican comic books. You can ride horseback on the sand, take windsurfing lessons, sharpen your tennis game, water ski, attend a fashion show or deep sea fish, all without leaving the general environs of Las Hadas.

The city of Manzanillo, a fishing port and trading center, smaller than Acapulco but larger than La Paz, is the usual third-world mix of the superrich (often foreign), middle class vendors and shop owners and struggling poverty. There are always stray dogs wandering the dirt streets, and the main roads are paved in the usual way, except for the potholes, which are almost too numerous and cleverly placed to avoid.

The entrance to the resort, between the airport and the central part of the city, is marked by a large white Kasbah-shaped sign with blue and gold lettering and a wide turn onto a cobblestone street.

At first glance, the cobblestones seem like a picturesque throwback to simpler, more aesthetic times. But after you've bumped over them once or twice and had your spine thoroughly rearranged and your jawbone dislocated, you reconsider. Some smart entrepreneur down there does one helluva business in shock absorbers.

"Isn't this quaint?" my mother said as we pounded over the cobblestones. Ah, well, she and her lower back would get it quick enough.

Mario, the butler/jack-of-all-trades at the house where we'd be staying, had met us at the airport in one of three VW Things, nee Safaris, that belong to the absentee homeowners. They are ancient, rusty, and constantly breaking down ... The cars, not the owners. Therefore, owning a small fleet of same is a necessity, as opposed to a luxury.

The road in from town is a narrow two-laner, and passing slower cars is dangerous but commonplace. This particular trek was more than usually adventuresome, because the sun was setting and many of the cars we came up behind didn't have working taillights.

Mario's English is hit-and-miss, but my Spanish does well enough to communicate the basics, so I translated for Lark and Mom. Every time Señor Mario brings someone in from the airport, he describes the exact same and rather odd points of interest along the way, like a tour guide recording stuck in one bizarre groove. We're not talking Fifth Avenue here. There aren't any museums or hanging gardens. There isn't even a McDonald's. But Mario will point out the three nanny goats of Señor Morales with the same air of awed pride each time.

When we stopped at a golf cart crossing, I explained, "This golf course is attached to the Las Hadas resort. It is pricey, and your game is often interrupted by tourists on horseback, which adds strokes to the slope rating. They are considered additional moving hazards, and if you hit one, you get a free drop and a pound of manure."

Mario nodded his head in agreement, though he couldn't have understood more than one-fifth of my spiel.

"That's the local school." I shouted the translation over the unmuffled engine once we'd started up again. "And that's the shopping center they've been building for the last two years. It hasn't gotten very far, has it?"

Mario shook his head and sighed.

We took a left and headed past the new gargoyle-ish monstrosity of a hotel that had opened the Christmas before and continued up a winding, narrow road that was bordered on the hillside by condominiums. Oh, how energetically we bounced along!

"Is this all a part of Las Hadas?" Lark shouted.

"No, although most of this land has been developed by their corporation. It's a pretty good deal, actually, because if you buy from them, you also get member privileges at the resort."

We passed the entrance to the hotel on our left and continued on up the hill. The view of the sea was spectacular in the daylight hours. At dusk, the lights across the bay begin to resemble a glistening necklace of champagne amber.

There's a guard gate at the entrance to La Punta that is touted in their literature as a security feature. In reality, the guards are no more capable of throwing a trespasser out on his rear than the Federales were of capturing Pancho Villa. Our boys did smile with mucho gusto as they lifted the railing and waved us on through, without bothering to even check our names or our destination.

Ahhhh, Mexico: the land of unbroken mañana! Where a simple ritual we take for granted, like opening a bank account, can take days or getting a telephone installed can take months. Where a tradesman from Colima will drive to Manzanillo on a work day to collect cash for his services, after the bank has mistakenly bounced your check. Quién sabe when he'll get the money otherwise.

In Manzanillo, the two best places in town for fresh fish and poultry are one-room storefront shops with no windowpanes in the windows and no air conditioning. The carcasses are packed in ice because refrigeration is still a new-fangled, high-tech concept. If you can get through the curtain of flies at the front door without turning green, you're considered a native.

It's not impossible to live well in Mexico; quite the contrary. It merely requires patience and time and a little bit of money, not to mention a willingness to learn the rules of the game and a gift for circumventing red tape. A practice called mordida is most helpful. In the US, we call it bribery.

Our destination was Casa Greca, a house built by a gargantuan Southern Californian named Harry Hughes with a booming manner and a tendency toward serial bankruptcy. It was rumored Harry'd filed for protection while the La Punta house was under construction, and that was the reason he'd had to sign on two additional investors ... to keep everything afloat. The Mexican authorities don't take kindly to gringos with shallow pockets who invest in their country.

If a hyena is an animal designed by a committee, then Casa Greca is a piece of real estate run by the Mongol Horde. The partners are few in number, but each one contributes to the confusion exponentially, like earthquake measurements on the Richter scale. I often wonder how any one of them got this far in their lives without constant supervision.

They certainly have adopted a maverick style of "conducting business." Peter has actually robbed Paul to pay the piper, and the left hand is washing the right brain and never the twain shall take the bull by the horns.

I always refer to the place as "Toon Town," a designation you could never appreciate without a) having seen "Roger Rabbit," and b) having visited this little enclave of chaos for yourself.

It's a question of management ... or should I say, mismanagement? There's never enough toilet paper. There are discomfiting wires hanging loose in the master bedroom ceiling, where light fixtures ought to go. The huge shower is totally open to the rest of the bathroom, which means the bathroom floor is always covered with water. The toilets aren't enclosed, either, making for some tense moments of enforced intimacy. The guest bedroom suite roof, built on the level of the house below the pool area, is so tall, it cuts off the view from the dining room table.

It sounds a bit like a comedian's joke about a dump. But truthfully, Casa Greca is the most compellingly romantic place I've ever visited. The structure is reminiscent of a classical temple, down to the frescoes etched into its white walls. The floors are all mauve marble and have to be mopped daily to prevent damage from salt air. The two couches in the living room area are sculptured cement topped with downy-soft lilac cushions. The dining room table, a ten-foot slab of thick glass atop two intricately carved wooden horse heads, easily seats sixteen. Best of all, in the common rooms, there are no walls or windows to keep the sea air or the tantalizing ocean vista out.

The master suite sits off by itself on the northwest corner of the property. It is bounded on two sides by a wide terrace covered with bougainvillea that sways in the ever-present, ever-freshening, salt-kissed breeze. The master suite has high ceilings dotted with skylights, and the closets are floor-to-ceiling. The spa tub looks like a throwback to the communal baths of ancient Rome.

The other bedroom suites, also large and airy, boast their very own private swimming pool and waterfall. And last but not least, a native-style canopy, made of banana palm fronds, shades the south side of the pool area. It's a glorious place to sit and watch a fiery orange ball of sun sink behind the hills across the bay while sipping one of Mario's killer, done-from-scratch Margaritas. Welcome to a decadent lifestyle, voluptuous and full of texture.

The first time I ever saw Casa Greca, I was in the throes of an emotional breakdown. I was scraped bare and beaten down by my chemo treatment schedule. The word "cancer" echoed through my head during my waking hours like a death knell. I couldn't turn off the voice of doom in my head with alcohol or sex or food. I couldn't exercise myself into a deep enough oblivion to truly rest.

At my worst point, I could only get from my bedroom to the bathroom by crawling. I went too long by twice without washing the sheets on my bed. I cried every single day for six weeks, and I couldn't bear to answer the phone, even when I could hear my mother's scared voice on the answering machine, pleading with me to let her help. That strength of soul I'd come to rely on in my teens and always regarded as my personal fail-safe had disappeared like smoke on a windy day. I didn't care to live. I didn't care to be.

Before my fight against cancer, I'd had zero empathy for the reasons people gave up. I was smugly convinced that every human being could find the strength they needed if they only looked for it.

Wrong. Not this time, brother; not now that it was me. I gave up like any weak-in-the-knees coward ... lost, gray of face and failed of character. Mr. Fear was working his seductive betrayal in spades.

I might as well have been dead.

I remember one harrowing night in particular, I was standing in front of my bathroom mirror, well into my first chemo cycle and feeling lousy. I'd just washed my hair, my golden mane, which'd been a source of vanity from the time I was a child when absolute strangers remarked to my mother on its luster.

Telescoping my face nearer and farther from the glass, I noticed how dull it looked. And when I started to brush out the tangles, the stuff came out in clumps. It fell from my tortoise-shell comb and lay on the floor like scorched wheat. Oddly, I recall wondering if carrots really did scream when they were ripped out of the ground ... if oak trees cried out when young boys hammered nails into their sovereign trunks to make tree houses. Because, you see, I heard a throbbing, moaning noise and thought it was my hair wailing for its lost youth. Until I realized it was me wailing for my lost youth.

I threw my comb at the mirror, which shattered. Wild with grief, I stumbled to the kitchen and proceeded to drink myself stupid, not too long a trek. Then I dialed the very private, personal home number of Dr. Dent and prayed to God she'd answer.

She did.

"It's Marly. Are you busy?"

I heard her take in my state. She said, "Of course not."

I knew she was lying, but I didn't care. "I'm ..." My voice shriveled away.

"Yes?" She sounded alert, aware.

"I don't think ..." Mr. Fear and his Wall of Death moved closer and pressed on my chest. "I just need to talk, I guess." I wondered if she could smell my insanity over the phone.

"Talking is good, Marly." She was casual yet cagey, not forcing, not giving in. I could feel her leaning into the phone. She waited.

I said, "It's a bad night." Hold on, hold on.

"How bad?" she asked.

"Can you tell me, why me? My hair is ..." The waterworks broke down, and my tears poured out. "It's lying on the ground."

As if that explained everything.

"Your hair?" I could sense her weighing, examining.

"Yes, goddammit," I screamed into the phone. "Are you deaf?"

No," she said carefully.

"I'm sorry for interrupting your free time." The sarcasm was an effort to regain my balance.

"Don't be an ass, Marly. Look, I've dealt with this scene for years. I can't do it. I'm hopeless. I'm not any better at it now than I was when I started my practice."

God, I'd put her on the spot! I hated myself for my own weakness—almost as much as I enjoyed hearing her struggle.

"I have a number," she continued, "for the leader of that group I told you about. She's kind of on call, you know? She's trained to ..."

I yowled into the receiver, "You're my doctor! You're supposed to help me!"

Silence. Maybe a minute of tense silence.

Finally Dr. Dent said, "I'm a surgeon, Marly. I cut. That's what I do best, and I'm good at it. That's how I heal. But frankly, you've got some wounds I know nothing about."

I hated that her speech sounded rehearsed. And rational.

"Give me the goddamned number," I said.

"Ask for Kyla."

I slammed down the phone, fumed for a couple of minutes and dialed the goddamned number.

"Is Kyla there?"

It was an act of courage. It was an act of desperation.

"Hello?" Her voice was low and rich. I liked it immediately; it was the kind of voice you know would never lie to you.

When I met Kyla the next afternoon, I wasn't surprised to find her statuesque and raven-haired. But no physical description could ever do her justice. She's full of self-mockery, a trait I have always found most appealing in successful people. She's theatrical, her hands and face like a living painting replicating her innermost thoughts.

We sat sipping hours-old coffee in the lobby of the Women's Center. Without much preamble and less emotion, she said, "Three weeks after my breast cancer diagnosis was confirmed, I got in my MG Sprite and crashed into a wall at 70 miles per hour. The car was totaled. I ended up with two broken arms. Sitting in that cold, stark emergency room, I decided that suicide attempts might not be the answer."

I gave her the lowdown on me.

She said, "I've been expecting your call. Phyl Dent warned me you were stubborn. Come to Mexico with me next week. Stay at the house. Get away from Los Angeles. It'll just be the two of us. We'll lie in the sun and bitch at each other. You can spew some bile my way and rage at the universe."

"Well ..."

"Listen to me, Marly. Are you listening? You're drowning; do you understand? You're being swept over the falls. I'm throwing you a rope. Don't be an ass. Grab on hard while you can still make a fist."

"Are you trying to scare the living piss out of me?"

"Yes."

"You do good work. I guess I can make it."

Harry Hughes' wife, Martha, had been through Kyla's therapy group during a bout with late-stage cervical cancer. Martha Hughes had been one of the few lucky ones. After surgery and chemo, she'd remained symptom-free for three years, so she was beating some very long odds. In gratitude for the indescribable emotional benefits she'd gotten from The Cancer Club (I named it, actually, in a fit of sarcastic frustration.), Martha loaned out Casa Greca to Kyla several times a year for the purpose of rescuing the stubborn ones like me. She also rented it out on the cheap to our group alumna.

Everybody in the world had a line into Martha: every suffering out-of-luck, every deadbeat, every last-chance Larry. There was speculation that her open-handed generosity was at least partly responsible for her husband's several bankruptcies.

May their children's children bless their names forever and a day.

Because during that week at Casa Greca, I broke the back of Mr. Fear and wondered if life might actually be worth living after all.

Chapter 16

Mario expertly guided The Thing down the steep, flower-bordered driveway of Casa Greca and stopped with a screech of tire. Mario's wife, Patty, had turned on all the lights, and the great open living room was awash in a soft glow.

"Wow" was all Lark could manage.

My mother was more poetic. "Wow, indeed."

The magic of that place never ceases to move me. As I walked through the living area, a full moon lit a path across the deep blue of the pool. Fresh-cut flowers poured out of free-form glass vases on every tabletop. I could smell fresh-made sopites warming in the oven.

Without asking, or needing to, Mario carried my bags to the master suite. He'd unpack me and plug in my computer as a matter of course.

Materializing out of the shadowy kitchen, Patty gathered the remaining luggage onto a little red wagon.

"Abajo?" she asked with a slight jig of her head.

"Si. Todos. Gracias, Patty."

Neither my mother nor Lark had ever seen Casa Greca, except in photographs.

"Unbelievable. This place is unbelievable!" Lark said, finding her voice at last. "Look at this view! Is the water warm? Shall we go for a swim?" She clapped her hands together. "I'm so glad you brought me here!" She sounded like a little kid on her first visit to Disneyland.

I was glad I'd brought her, too. "We'll do everything, I promise. But first, why don't we toast our arrival with some Margaritas, which should be ..." I opened the fridge by the bar, "... here. Ahhhh, good man, Mario."

I poured generous servings into chilled glasses and topped off with shaved ice.

"Then, maybe we all unpack. We've got a whole week; I figure I can let my hair down," I said, shaking my wig like a shampoo add. "Relax. Get out to Bar Social on Friday afternoon when the fishing ships dock. Tear lobster right out of its shell at Willy's ... They're scandalized when you eat with your hands. We can watch the sun set up at La Recif. Then there's Que Barbara and Pappagallo for dancing. But tonight ... I'm just gonna loll. Maybe for a couple of nights. Dangle my feet in the water and dangle my tongue in some champagne."

My mother kissed my cheek. "You drink too much."

"You're right," I said, kissing her back. "Mario! Comidas!"

We called it a night around eleven. I sat down at my computer and actually rewrote a few pages before the Sandman got me. The sea rose and fell against the shore below, until it had my breath in its rhythm and I was seduced to sleep.

"Is anybody here?"

What the hell?

"I said, is anybody here? Now don't you go leavin' me, señor cabman. I gotta make sure I'm in the right place. Hey! Look out, will you?"

I heard a crashing noise and prayed it was a nightmare. Because if it wasn't, I had a visitor who sounded, in my fuzziness, disturbingly like Good Ol' Don.

"Hey, turkey buzzard, watch that luggage! Sonafabitch! Come back here! Marly?"

I sat up and looked at the clock. Three effing eighteen A.M. Why does bad news always come at three effing whatever A.M.? Maybe if I pulled the pillow over my head, he wouldn't find me, and the Federales'd come and get him and whisk him out of the country.

"Marly, I know you're here, and I am not budgin' until you come out. And if you're not quick about it, I'll start singin'."

A catastrophe to be avoided at any cost. I jumped out of bed and threw on a robe, grumbling loudly all the while. "What in the hell does this asshole think he is doing? How did he find me?"

"Marly, honey? I can tell by those honeyed tones that I've found you! Hey, you ain't peeved, are you, Sugarbush? I need some more Jose Cuervo. Señor Cuervo? Where you hidin'?"

Oh, great, just great, Good Ol' Don was drunker than a lord. "Stay right where you are," I said. I jerked open the screen doors and advanced on him like a great bird of prey, my robe streaming out behind me, my fingers tensed into talons.

He had a sad/funny, lopsided grin on his face, and when he saw me bearing down on him like that, he melted into a puddle of alcohol-scented remorse.

"Marly, honey," he whined, "where else could I go?"

"Who told you I was coming here? I'll boil the sucker in oil. Tear his heart out."

"Miriam. It was Miriam, I tell you."

"That bitch! I'll tear her heart out!"

He crossed his hands over his face to fend off my attack. "It was life and death; she had to tell." He looked up into my face, then squinted his eyes shut against my blinding wrath. "Who else can help me?" he moaned.

"Marly?" It was my mother, calling sleepily from the door of her bedroom.

I whirled on her. "What? What?"

She took in the situation for a moment before pointing at the sodden heap that was Good Ol' Don. "How long has it been here, and how much longer does it have to live?"

"Seconds, on both counts."

"If you promise to keep it quiet, I'll make some coffee. Is the tap water safe?"

"Mother!"

Lark's door cracked open. "What's all the fuss?"

Oh, my God, this Embarrassing Moment was turning into rush hour at O'Hare.

"Lark," my mother said firmly, "help me make coffee." She pointed to Don again. "Don't worry; it's been neutered."

"God, whyever did You make women?" Don semi-yodeled.

I turned back to face him. "Shut up. Just shut up! The entire security force will show up here in a minute."

Don slapped his hand over his mouth and shut his eyes. Tears began to stream down his face.

"Great," I said with a shake of my head. "Come on, cowboy."

I managed to get him to his knees and prod him to the wicker sofa under the palapa. Ol' Don grabbed me by the arms. "Don't go," he mumbled. "You gotta save my ass."

"Why? Who's kicking it now?"

"Her name's Tawnie, with a 'i' and a 'e' on the end. She's very particular about that," he said with a little sob.

"I'll bet she is."

With Lark and my mother aiding and abetting, we got some strong, hot coffee down Don's throat. It didn't sober him as much as it woke him up. His bleary eyes turned watery, but he was able to keep them open. When it looked like he was ready to spill his guts, my mother and Lark drifted back to bed. The look on my mother's face was Highly Disapproving.

"How did you get here?" I asked.

"Well, it all started up in Alaska sometime yesterday." He scratched his head. "Or was it the day before?"

"Alaska?"

"I'm workin' the pipeline; you know that. Don't snort at me, Marly. It makes me feel like a fool."

"Okay, okay, so you're up in Alaska. And?"

"And ... I kinda got married."

"Kinda?"

"Well, she's not very old ..."

"How old?"

Gulp. "Nineteen," he mumbled.

"I see." Boy, did I. "She's not pregnant, is she?"

"No way, Jose. Hey, you got any Jose Cuervo?"

I ignored this request. "What's the problem?"

He sat back and rubbed his forehead. "What's the problem? I got to thinkin', yesterday, or was it the day before? Damn! Let's see ... well, anyhow, after the ceremony, I was wonderin' to myself what in the hell we were going to talk about for the rest of our lives." He looked up at me. "You can only fool around for so many hours a day, you know. Hell, didn't she and me find that out?"

"So you got drunk and took off?"

"So I got drunk and took off."

I poured Don some more coffee. "Why?" I asked. "Waning hormones? Machismo? Was she a virgin?"

"Screw you, Marly."

"I'm with you so far. But why come here?"

He pulled at his hair. "Because you know me, Marly, better'n anyone else. You gotta help me figure out what the hell to do."

I clicked my tongue in my cheek twice. "I don't have to help you do anything. We're unengaged. Besides, I came here for a rest. I want to sit in the sun and swim in the ocean, eat like a pig and play tennis till I drop. I want to sleep late and be totally irresponsible. I'm willing to give up two hours a day for my writing, but they're paying me big bucks, for Christ's sake! What in the world makes you think I'd waste a second for a sorrowful excuse of a man like you?"

He hung his head then. "You're the finest and smartest human being

I ever met."

"I hate it when you do that." I felt my indignity cracking. "Look," I said, sighing, "why don't you sleep here tonight? We'll ... take this up again tomorrow when you're sober."

He smacked a dry mouth. "A tall glass of water wouldn't go down too bad."

"Get it yourself." I turned on my heel. Without looking back at him, I said, "Turn the lights off."

"I don't know where the switches are!" he bawled.

"Find them."

I didn't toss and turn. I didn't stew or grumble or twitch. As soon as my head hit the pillow, I fell back into a dreamless and seamless sleep.

It was the scent of coffee tickling my nose that awakened me. The sun was high in the sky, which meant it had to have been at least ten. Don stood over me, bending down to study my face. On a tray he carried, I saw a tall glass of pink juice, a small coffeepot, two cups, cream and sugar.

"I know you didn't put that together," I said and yawned. "You better be glad you let me sleep in, mister."

"I remember how you are when someone wakes you up in the middle of the night." He smirked. "It was that Mario fellow did this." He pronounced it "Merio." "You gonna throw any of this stuff at me? Cause if you are, I'll take it right back."

For a nanosecond, he looked worried.

"Set it there." I studied his face and was surprised to see how tired he looked; listless. There were more lines under his eyes than I remembered, and his moustache showed a definite streak of gray. It also drooped. "Whenever you're ready to talk, fire away, Don."

"Don't you think you oughtta pee first? So we won't get interrupted?"

It's hell when a man like Don remembers every little thing about you. I can imagine exactly how many women he'd practiced on to whip his memory into that kind of shape. I swear, he could identify a female he hadn't seen for years a quarter of a mile away by her walk.

I got up and peed.

While I was at it, I washed my face, brushed my teeth, removed my scarf and combed my nicest wig into place. I felt a need to scrub away any lingering cobwebs.

"You look like hell," I said, settling in.

"I feel like hell and with good reason. You're gonna think I'm nuts."

"Probably," I agreed. "But then, I think everyone's nuts. Go ahead."

Don ran his hands through his hair, which was longer than I'd ever seen it. He gulped his coffee down. "I can't be married, Marly. No way. I was figurin' to get a divorce quick-like down here."

"What about Tawnie with an 'i-e?' Mightn't she have anything to say about all this?"

He looked puzzled.

"Think about it, Don. You went all those years and managed to escape getting hitched. Then, you fall hard for some nineteen-year-old with firm breasts and dewy skin. No doubt you are blaming it on the loneliness of the pipeline gig and the fact that she won't give it to you unless you marry her. So ... so you marry her."

His jaw dropped open. "I hate it when you do that," he said.

"Get in line. And you have the gall to think I'll help you slink away? Not this time. When the excrement hits the fan, you take off. That's your only way. Now I can't stop you from doing that, but I can refuse to help you."

He was having a hard time looking me in the eye.

"Besides," I said, "what if marrying her was the right thing to do? What if you actually love her?"

"I never thought of that."

Out of the corner of my eye, I saw my mother and Lark sit down on the terrace for breakfast. My mother kept glancing over in our direction, aching to be in on this little tête-à-tête.

"God, you're sexy, Marly."

"Excuse me?" I pulled my robe closer around my body.

"I'd forgotten how perfect your tits are. Even with that itty-bitty dent there. The skin is so fine and clear, you can see the veins right through." He took a deep breath. "And I still say, you taste better'n any other woman I know."

I shivered in spite of myself.

"But see," he went on, "you were always too smart for me. Oh, not the readin' and writin' part. It was the part where you'd know what I was gonna do ten minutes before I did it. It made lyin' hard. It was ... inconvenient."

"That didn't stop you from lying."

"No. But it took all the fun out."

I poured us each another cup and put two teaspoons of sugar in his. He took a sip and said, "Perfect."

We sat and stared at one another for a long while. Finally, he shifted his weight on the bed and idly scratched at his thigh.

"Can you get hold of her somehow?" I asked.

"God, she's probably sittin' in her folks' house, cryin' her eyes out. I can't stand it when she cries; she looks so lost, like." He blinked rapidly several times. "Sometimes I'm afraid I'll flatten her with this goddamned chip I'm carryin' around," he admitted.

That struck me. "So ... you finally admit to a chip. That's a start, I guess." I paused dramatically and shook my head. "She's probably a lot more resilient ... and a lot less naïve than you think. Why don't you call her? There's a phone at the house next door. Casa Rosa. Just tell them you're a guest here."

Don reached out and stroked my cheek softly with the back of his hand. An echo of pleasures long past skittered down my leg. He leaned over and kissed me on the mouth.

"Go on," I said, pushing him firmly away. "She'll be worried."

"Lookin' at you lying there makes me remember."

"You better get your ass over to Casa Rosa while it's still attached."

"Yes, ma'am."

Chapter 17

Lark and Sarah pretended not to notice when Ol' Don bolted out of Casa Greca. They were lousy actors. When my mother couldn't stand it any longer, she said, "Where did that ... that man sleep last night?" She shoved a piece of warm tortilla into her mouth with force. She'd never liked him.

"Right here. Under the banana fronds," I answered.

"Oh, really?" she inquired as she lifted her eyebrows and chewed with precision. "He wasn't lying here when I woke up." She turned her head and glanced pointedly at my bedroom.

"Mother," I warned, "don't start."

Lark cocked her head. "You know," she said, "I woke up early, just after sunrise, and came upstairs for a glass of milk. I didn't see him out here then, either."

"Well, he was probably taking a whiz, for God's sake." I scratched my neck uncomfortably. "After all that booze."

Lark turned to my mother. "Sarah, I think Don is still attracted to Marly. What do you think?"

"I think he's still carrying his dick around in his hand."

"Mother!"

"Yelling at me won't change anything. And you think he never cheated on you?" She shook her head at me, her poor daughter, who'd obviously been absent when the brains were passed out.

I stewed for maybe ten seconds. Then I jumped from the table and stubbed my big toe on the chair leg. Howling in protest, I ran up the drive and out the wrought iron gates of Casa Greca, dressed only in a short nighty and robe.

Casa Rosa is a much more traditionally styled Mexican house than Casa Greca. Usually, I stop to admire the singing sound of the fountain in the open entryway. But that day, I power-walked into the main part of the house, past Luisa and Marco in the kitchen, past the Smith family at breakfast, mouths yawped in amazement, down the first set of stairs on the right to the den. I threw the door wide with enough force to bang it against the wall and caught Don on the phone, mid-gesticulation. His eyes popped out of his head when he saw the whirlwind that was me, and he clasped the receiver to his chest.

"If you ever even think of taking advantage of me again, I will hack off all the fingers of your right hand with a pair of dull scissors and stuff them into your mouth, which I will then sew up with barbed wire." I shivered with rage. "Believe it!"

Suddenly, I had a splitting headache. Without waiting for a reply, I stumbled back through Casa Rosa, managing a weak smile to the Smiths, who waved tentatively. I slinked back down the road, hoping no one I knew would drive past, and entered Casa Greca like a fugitive, the incredible stupidity of my behavior beginning to flush the tips of my ears. I made my way to my bathroom and pressed myself into the cool shadow of the marble walls and floor. As I passed a cold washcloth across my forehead, I wondered what in the hell had happened. Was I becoming schizophrenic? Manic/depressive? Dangerously hormonal? Was it the influence of Toon Town? Or was it the tequila-drenched ambience of La Punta?

The truth was ... that I was still attracted to that slimy, no-good son of a bitch I'd almost married all those months ago. Ick. What in the hell was the matter with me?

Mexico, that's what.

I'm addled by the seductive softness of the night and the glow of the moon. Even in my present state, my appetite for life is abundant, and I find myself doing things I'd never dream of doing in Nashville or Cincinnati or Omaha.

It was the last weekend before Christmas, the year I turned thirty. I was in Mazatlan for the first time, playing a fun-and-games charity golf tournament that benefitted the local orphanages. There were some fairly famous types in attendance. You know ... "Hill Street" alumna and some Hall of Fame athletes from football and baseball. And me.

I was writing a magazine column about women's issues in sport at the time and had been invited as a token "lady" press representative. Which was fine with me; I'm a sucker for sports legends. There's nothing in the world like sitting around a table, drinking beer with a bunch of old Yankees, listening to their stories about Jackie Robinson's first season or the legendary Chicago Shirley. For those out-of-the-know, Shirley was an infamous, moneyed socialite who "entertained" star athletes on opposing teams, never her beloved Cubs.

These kinds of events do raise money. But the athletes and movie stars don't show up out of the goodness of their hearts; they show up for the perks: a free trip to an exotic locale; great parties; plenty of booze and a gaggle of pretty, bored women in every age category, looking for a better class of trouble to get into than the loud, rich men they've accompanied.

Charity events don't run on good intentions. It takes money. We're talking stiff fees for the patrons and mega-auctions and corporate sponsorships on the stratospheric level. In return for their cold-hard, the well-heeled business types get publicity for their companies and schmooze-time with all the famous folks they can stomach over a long weekend. They might even glimpse themselves on *Lifestyles of the Rich and Famous*.

He was (and still is) the best-looking man I ever saw. A slim, six-foot-four blond with a profile like a Greek god and eyes so deeply blue, you could swan dive into them. He put Sandy the Lifeguard to shame. He was wearing a suit of raw silk, checkered with small black-and-white squares. It was a little like watching an optical illusion pass through the room, this man women drooled over in public.

I was surprised when he sat down next to me at the cocktail party. I have always considered myself an odd duck. Pretty enough, but also a weird mixture of the jock and the siren, my masculine and feminine energies ever at war with one another. Great-grandmother Francesca encouraged this eccentric side, this never-settling boundary dispute between lady-like and man-powered, because she was the mold for the model. The old girl made it look easy. I have only recently come to recognize how delicate her balancing act was.

My personality put off a lot of guys, because I was intimidating to the unsuspecting guy-next-door. Hell, I intimidated myself.

And then suddenly, just about the time the 80's wound down, my character smoothed out. The sharp edges rounded. I grew my hair out from its Peter Pan cut until it grazed the top of my breasts, while still managing to keep that line of definition down my inner thigh tendon. My two warring sides declared an uneasy truce. Coincidentally, the ideal of feminine beauty as perceived by men was changing, too.

Muscle tone was in.

I was finally off to the races.

His voice was dusky. His eyes were drills that bored into my soul. He had the routine down pat.

"Isn't one of you lucky gentlemen going to introduce me to the most attractive woman in the room?" he said to the table at large, his eyes never leaving my face. By the time I found out his first name was Skip, I wasn't in the least surprised.

Almost everyone at the party had some tidbit of information about Skip:

"He's a cheap bastard. He only got to come on this trip because he set up the travel arrangements," one woman whispered to me in the ladies' room so her husband wouldn't hear. "If you say yes, you'll have a good time. Short and sweet. He isn't the type to hang around long after the ground-breaking."

"Watch out," warned the triple ex: ex-Steeler wide receiver with two ex-wives and countless ex-fiancées. "He's a great guy, but he's ... you know ... a guy."

I don't know why they bothered. Skip was obviously the single greatest example of the Don Juan type I had ever met. He should have been listed in the Encyclopedia Britannica at the top of the heading "Famous Swordsmen," with a photograph.

I'm not sure whether he loved women or hated them. I once heard him say, "In order to catch a woman, you have to think like a woman."

He looked, and was, lazy: his manner, his ambition, his smile. He glanced at every other female in the room, and yet his attention never seemed to waver from me. It was a fascinating performance, like a snake charmer. But who was the snake here?

He was proprietary, almost courtly. I decided he had to be smarter than he looked. He began calling me "Baby" within minutes, in that soft, low baritone of his, and instead of dislocating his shoulder or cutting him with a scathing remark, I smiled and purred in response.

It was a disgusting performance. Mine, I mean. His was Oscar-worthy.

After dinner ended, a bunch of us went out dancing to the hot disco in town, Valentino's. When Skip walked me through the strobe-lit room, I could feel women of all ages leaning slightly in his direction, pressing against their clothes and their dates, but not seeing or feeling their own escorts, only seeing and feeling Skip. He made their antennae vibrate. But, hey, I was a no-nonsense modern woman, and no woman-preying bum was going to seduce me.

This is where Mexico came in.

It must have had something to do with the way the moon shimmers on the sea, undulating with the tide; with the way human skin always glows there in the humidity; with the way tequila shooters soothe but never stupefy. I even wrote a poem about it:

IT FEELS LIKE HEAVEN TO ME

Take seven dead-of-summer days,
shimmering with heat,
and seven windless, sultry nights.
Add a dash of sweet temptation,
sweeter than the scent of night-blooming jasmine.
Now this is a recipe for mischief.
For fanning that dampness seeping
around all your most private parts.
For wearing practically nothing
next to your skin.
Even in mixed company.
For sleeping bare-assed,
with tossing and turning and dreams full of sin.
For skinny-dipping, all shiny naked wetness.
It cools the fever.
Maybe.
For a moment.
It's hotter than hell they say sometimes.
But it feels like heaven to me.

You get the picture.

He took my hand and led me to the crowded dance floor. We wedged ourselves into one corner, and I let the music take me. The DJ was spinning Motown, the Stones, Gloria Estefan, the Pointer Sisters, Phil Collins, Julio, Stevie Wonder, and Tina Turner. The room was gray with artificial smoke, which billowed up out of the floor at the command of some unseen light show techie.

By the time the music slowed down, we were both drenched with sweat. I remember his lime-and-tequila man smell and the way his hair fell into his eyes. I remember how his long arms engulfed me and how he towered over me.

"Sleep with me tonight," he whispered.

My mind tensed up, and my body followed suit. Oh, shit, I thought to myself, here it is. I didn't say anything, but my thoughts ricocheted inside my head like pinballs.

My two sides got into an argument. What am I, a slut? I can't go to bed with this man. I'm only asking for trouble, and I've had my share of trouble with men for this lifetime. But then, I haven't slept with a man in months. So what? Is that supposed to have earned me a medal? He likes me. He's never met anyone like me. Yeah? He's never met anyone like Bella Abzug, either, and she's not Princess Di, but that probably wouldn't stop him from seducing her.

But at least she wouldn't be dumb enough to give in.

And I wasn't either ... exactly.

We slept together. But we just slept. That is ... we kissed and rubbed naked chests first and massaged one another. On the back; no orgasms. And then we slept.

The next morning, he kissed me softly just before the wake-up call came through, "... So you wouldn't be startled out of your sleep." The rest of that day, he was so attentive. He carried my golf bag and brought me my lunch and generally acted as though we were a couple. At the banquet that evening, I remember how the short, rounded man next to me began to puff up his dewlaps when he suddenly decided I was attractive enough to impress. And I remember Skip's unconscious response ... He took my hand and lightly held it in his, never breaking up the flow of his own conversation in the other direction.

That night in bed, with the fragrant sea breeze scenting the air, the petting got hotter, heavier. Still I held out. My defenses were getting bombarded by superior fire power, but I dug in my heels. I wondered if it was truly only a matter of time before I conceded defeat and wondered how many days—hours—a fling with Skip would last—could last. He had the attention span of a gnat.

I wanted it, make no mistake, but ...

On Saturday, I resolved to lie about having my period and breathed a sigh of relief. Now there would be no question of ... whatever. I'd plead a need for privacy, retire early, get on a plane the next morning and run back to the safety of my celibate life. It'd been five and a half months since my last relationship had ended, but I figured I could last a whole year if I put my mind to it and kept the rest of my anatomy on hold.

The moment of truth came way past midnight. The streets of Mazatlan were still roiling with activity. Teenaged tourists were hurrying to one last club before closing time. In Mexico, the legal drinking age is judged to have been reached when the young man or woman in question is tall enough to plunk his pesos down on the bar without climbing onto a stool. The partiers in our group were enjoying the last night of celebration before having to return to the real world.

Skip and I clung to one another on the dance floor. He kept stroking my hair and kissing the tip of my ear. Finally he grabbed my hand and said, "Let's get out of here."

The taxi ride back to the Pueblo Bonito was full of grasping and groping. His tongue was searching, probing. His hands wandered up and down my backbone, lazily tapping a sultry Morse code of desire.

I opened the door to my room and turned to face him. I said, "Wouldn't you know it? I got my period. What lousy timing." I began to shut the door behind me.

I don't know what I expected, but his response was A First. First he laughed warmly. Then, he swooped me easily up into his arms, carried me inside, and kicked the door closed behind us.

"You don't really have your period, do you?"

Those were the last words either of us spoke until morning.

That's how I became a Skip Statistic. Like I said, Mexico. Actually, I learned a rather interesting fact in the course of my relationship with Skip. I had naturally assumed that all gorgeous men were lousy lovers. After all, how hard does any man try when he doesn't need to? Skip was mediocre, not terribly creative, with a ragged rhythm to his pumping that never let me get set in position long enough. He wasn't in a rush, but I suspect that the time he took in bed with his partner had more to do with his own ego than her satisfaction. He loved to hear the sounds of a woman moaning with pleasure. It turned him on. I know this because he told me so himself.

I heightened the skill of faking it to an art form.

We saw one another off and on for four long months until it became apparent that Skip was unable to share his emotions with me. Probably because he was too shallow to have any.

Thank God we always used a condom! No doubt out of an already-opened six-pack on his part.

With any other man, the way Skip acted, I would have sworn he was crazy about me. With Skip, that was simply the way he treated every woman he was ever with: grandmothers, maiden aunts, soccer moms, Raiderettes.

I broke a cardinal rule with Skip: never waste time with a guy whose belt has been notched so many times, it resembles Swiss cheese. When I'd had enough, I let him drift away and decided it was time for a real boyfriend. Hey, my biological clock had begun to chime "Taps."

That's where Good Ol' Don comes in, who, I now realize, was only a rougher and more shit-kicking version of Skip. He didn't look the same. He didn't sound the same. But they were cut from the same cloth: sharkskin.

I learned lots from Skip, most of it unsettling. And I'd probably do it all again.

Mexico. Merde!

Which was why, sitting on my veranda at Casa Greca and smelling the tart salt air, it didn't shock me that I found myself picturing Good Ol' Don naked. It didn't disgust me. It didn't even surprise me. On that day, in that place, it wouldn't have surprised me to find I was still attracted to Skip.

Chapter 18

"We thought we'd go down to the hotel and check out the shops. I've got to find some quirky tee shirts," my mother said, peeking at me from the bedroom hallway. "In Spanish! Want to come?"

I was slumped across my bed. "No," I said listlessly. I couldn't even bring myself to make the usual tee shirt-related crack.

My mother sighed as Lark stretched her head around my mother. "Let's go someplace fun tonight," she said hopefully.

"Right," I answered, sitting up. "I'm up for some fun." My laughter at my own joke was weightless. "Can't you tell?"

Lark and Sarah exchanged an arch look, no doubt wondering what in the hell they should do next. I struggled to raise my head three inches. "Will you go on, for Christ's sake? I'll be fine."

I imagined I didn't look so fine from their angle.

"I'll build some Miriam karma by spending the afternoon on my book."

They stared at me dumbly.

"I said, "Go on!"

Still they were rooted to the spot.

"I'll make a reservation at Willy's," Lark said. "Seven-thirty. We'll celebrate ... something?" She sounded unsure.

I laid my suddenly heavy head back down. "Right."

As they tiptoed out, I just sprawled, legs akimbo, loose-limbed, Raggedy Ann-like and worn out until I heard the sound of Don's whistling coming from outside. It was his own special brand of music.

I stood up quickly enough to drain the sad blood from my head. Everything went gray. I braced myself against the wall and waited to regain my equilibrium, a process that looked like it was gonna take the rest of my life.

"Yoohoo! Marly! You in there?" Don drawled from somewhere near the pool.

"Be out in a flash." I grabbed some shorts and a top from the closet and somehow managed to put my feet and arms through the right holes on the second try. I ran a brush through my hair and strolled out to confront

Don, still jittery. The feeling wasn't lessened by my finding him cheerful as a leech at a Red Cross blood drive.

He grabbed my hands and began swinging me around. "Boy! You are one smart woman, you know that? Tawnie and I had a heart-to-heart, and it looks like everything's gonna work out okay."

"Really."

"Well ... at least we're gonna take us a honeymoon. And really talk, see what it's all about, what we're all about." He looked at me coolly. "Without the sex, you know? Sex can be so confusing."

I turned on my heel and walked toward the kitchen. "Yes, it can," I answered. He seemed so ... happy, suddenly. Dammit, he looked almost smug. Yet I recalled that his moods were like the weather in Denver, Colorado. Don't like it? Stick around for ten minutes, and it'll change. Then it hit me. "And where will you and your lovely college co-ed be taking this honeymoon?" I asked.

He had the good grace to look sheepish. "She's not in college, for Christ's sake." He gave me his best "aw shucks" look. "I told her to come here."

"You what?"

He threw up his hands in a gesture of appeasement. "Not right here, silly. To Casa Whatever. Geez, how stupid do I look?"

"Don't tempt me, Don."

"To the hotel. Hey! I just had a brainstorm! Do you think anybody'd be using that little ol' condo of yours? The one you bought when we were still together?"

You can reason with a brick wall till you're blue in the face if you don't mind the blood from all the head-banging that goes with it.

"Let me get this straight." I paused for dramatic effect. "Your new bride, Tawnie with an 'i-e,' nineteen years old ..."

"Twenty-three."

I glared at him. "Right ... twenty-three ... who replaced me in your affections, whom you then ran out on in favor of my comfort and wisdom and maybe even the scent of possible nookie reclaimed ..."

"Marl ... It isn't like that at all."

"Don't deny it! Remember me? I know your lies before you even think them up! Whom I then counseled you to communicate with in order to save your sorry excuse for a marriage, not to mention your miserable hide ..." I took a deep breath and loaded up for boar. "This woman/child you are now bringing to Mexico for a honeymoon, and you wish to practice your connubial bliss in my condo??!!"

Don looked hurt. "You make it sound tacky."

"Gaaaaaad!" I yelled.

He studied his hands for a moment. Then, "Aw, Marly, c'mon! If you were honest about it, you'd admit you're glad you didn't marry me."

Sometimes the truth is highly inconvenient.

"Okay," I practically spat out, "if it's not rented." I shook my head.

"She knows a whole bunch about you, Marly."

"Swell."

"She'd really like to meet you ... I mean, she's read all your stuff, and she was a literature major before she dropped out. Actually, when I told her you were down here, she was the one that insisted she come. Hell, she might even feel the tiniest bit jealous."

Oh, my God, the poor thing. What had she gotten herself into? Wait a minute! I know exactly what she'd gotten herself into.

"Don, listen to me. I've had a rough year. You have good reason to know this, as you were an asshole and therefore a large part of the cause." I held up my hand to his mouth to silence his protest. "I came here for a little peace. To soul-search. To fiddle with my latest masterpiece. So ... if you promise not to bug me for the rest of my natural days, or to come around unbidden ever again under any pretense whatsoever ... particularly to my bed ... I will meet this child bride of yours for exactly ten minutes ... when I have the time and the inclination."

He ground his boot toe into the floor. "Hell, I thought maybe we could all have dinner together. My treat!" he added hastily.

"Don't push your luck. When does she arrive?"

"Two nights from now."

"I'll have Mario check on the condo this afternoon and let you know later. In the meantime, please make yourself scarce."

He smiled like a June bride, kissed me on the cheek before I could stop him, and heel-toed his way out the front of Casa Greca.

I went immediately to my computer and banged away for three hours. The work was molasses-slow, each bloody, gut-covered word taking its own sweet time. I couldn't stop all the crazy thoughts floating around in my head.

- When Tawnie and I stood side by side, people were going to think she was my daughter.

- Lark was going to recommend my involuntary commitment to the nearest mental institution, which would refuse to take me as a patient.

- My mother would finally disclose that I was adopted, because no true kin of hers could ever find herself in such a screwy situation.

- I wanted, more than anything, to share my chaotic black comedy of a life with Chris, because ... because ... I was a pathetic lump and a glutton for punishment.

"You what?" asked my mother incredulously. It was close to sundown by the time they returned, having both shopped and eaten their way through the Las Hadas environs. We were sitting by the pool, sipping Margaritas. "You invited them here? For their honeymoon? Are you mad?"

I opened my mouth to try and explain and discovered I didn't know how it had all happened and, therefore, could not explain.

"They're not actually staying here, I mean here," Lark said, with confidence. Then, with less assurance, "Are they?"

"Well, it's her condo; that's the same thing," said my mother.

"I'm sure there must be a logical explanation," said Lark, sounding annoyingly like Mr. Spock. She put her arm around me. "It's really none of our business. But are you sure you're okay?"

I snorted. "Is this Dr. Brothers calling? Look, it's Mexico. These things just happen here."

I don't think either one of them bought it.

The night settled in softly.

"Let's hit Willy's," I said, "I'm starved."

It's one of the "in" places in Manzanillo, is Willy's. Half the seating is outdoors; the food's pretty good; the service is slooooooow but polite and the prices, some of the most expensive I've found in the area, are still cheap when compared to those in Los Angeles.

I ordered lobster. I always order lobster at Willy's. They bring it in the shell, and I tear the white flesh out with my hands, dip it deep into melted butter and swallow it whole.

My mother has seafood allergies, so she had the chicken. Lark had barbecued shrimp.

I felt animated to the point of cartoonishness. I could see my hands darting about in the air like territorial hummingbirds. Jess would have been proud. My voice was a good three notes higher than usual. And I was into my vaudeville comedian conversational style: Ba-da BA. I hate myself whenever I get like that. It's pushy. It's masculine. It's soooo unattractive.

"You're doing it again," Sarah said quietly.

"What? What? I'm doing what again? Losing it?"

"Don't be such a gigantic a twit," she said. "That Yiddish comic thing you get into when you're exhausted."

Lark laughed at my mother's summation. I glowered at her. She laughed harder.

"Actually, I don't see the humor in this," I said.

"Yes, you do," Lark said. "You're a character in a farce over which you have no control. Like the rest of us." She took my hand and squeezed it.

I snatched my hand away and sipped at my wine while I considered her observation. Control: a buzzword that has haunted me all my life. Oh, sure, at times I'd head off on some tangent without considering the consequences and get myself into a mountain of trouble. But when the shit hit the fan, I'd change my tune and obsess to know exactly what was coming next and how I was supposed to react way before the fact. In other words, when things are all smooth sailing, I'm happy to go along with the wind. But when a hurricane comes a-visiting, as hurricanes sometimes do, I tighten up and try to grab onto my life with a stranglehold.

It might have had something to do with my mother and father's rocky beginnings. He was married, after all. Or it might have had something to do with my feelings about my own accomplishments.

It'd taken me forever to find myself. For most of my life, I screwed up too often between the good parts. But when I was diagnosed with the C word and pitched my tent at the edge of the abyss day after day, I learned about boundaries and how to extend them. And how to peek over the edge and admire the dangerous view.

So many cancer patients I've met speak about maintaining some sort of control over their treatment. Planning and adhering to a schedule. Making sure, say, that Christmas festivities take precedence over chemotherapy treatments even when hospital beds are in short supply, each of which is a form of Russian roulette.

My skirmish with mortal illness has spotlighted the opposite side of the coin. I learned to let go, to leave my laundry unwashed and my bed unmade. I learned to say no. I learned that trying to please everybody all the time is the quickest way to insanity. I learned about taking real care of my true self.

It was terrifying and thrilling. Like Samson, I threw off the chains of the Philistines and dragged the temple down around their heads, whoever they were. Of course, Samson died in that confrontation, hair shorn, blinded, weak and the temple collapsed on top of him, too.

The Cancer Club

I learned that I might never get what I want but that I might get what I need. Mick Jagger knew what he was singing about.

I remember my first session with The Cancer Club. It was held in a small room in the bowels of the Pasadena YMCA. We eventually had an adjunct group in Santa Monica later on. The sessions, which ran two nights a week, were open to anyone with cancer, regardless of sex, race, income level or insanity factor quotient.

I'd just returned from my first week at Casa Greca with Kyla. In Mexico, I'd hacked my way through furious energy, been frenzied, violent and totally out of control. I'd screamed and cried and thrown fits. God, how I hated the world and everyone in it!

Steady, sensible Kyla goaded me, prodded me until I couldn't help unleashing my rage. At times, I punched at her wildly, in a vain attempt to punish someone else, anyone else. But Kyla proved stubborn and strong as an ox. She pinned my arms in an iron grip and held me fast. Her patience was inhuman. On my sixth afternoon in Mexico, at precisely 3:17, the tornado finally blew itself out. With Kyla's help, I literally crawled to the guest suite, lay down on the bed, and slept for eighteen hours straight.

I awoke with a strange lightness in my head. Something of heft was missing. I think if I'd gotten on the scales, I'd have discovered that I weighed four or five pounds less. My stomach, which had knotted and cramped by turns for weeks, was placid. My appetite returned with a vengeance. I didn't feel happy or cured or whole, but I was ready to be helped.

"My name is Marly, and I have cancer."

I don't know if admitting I was an alcoholic or a coke-head would have been more difficult, but I sincerely doubt it. 'Cancer' is still a nasty word in our society. People shrink from you when they know, because you're suddenly outside the realm of so-called normal human experience. But hey, since we're all gonna die of something sooner or later, it's tough to figure out what all the tap dancing is about.

And I was the Sammy Davis of tap dancers.

We numbered twelve regulars in The Club in those days, including Kyla, seven women and five men, and we were seated in a circle in comfortable director-type chairs, which had been donated by Valerie Harper.

"So, like, what kind of cancer do you have?" asked one young woman with a reddish buzz cut.

I squirmed in my seat. "Breast. Here," I said, tracing an x to mark the spot. "Cross my heart."

"A comedian?" asked one obscenely thin middle-aged man.

I took a deep breath and tried to ignore hot pain that welled up. "No," I admitted. "I always joke around when I'm petrified."

There was some nodding.

"I cried every day for a month," I went on, "when I wasn't screaming bloody murder at the top of my lungs. I'm tired of tears. Sick to death of tears. And I don't want to be angry anymore."

"It means you can still feel," said the gaunt man, whose name was David. "It means you still care. Count your blessings."

"I don't want to feel." I stood up and walked to a window that opened onto a stairway leading to the street above us. I lit a cigarette and blew the smoke out. Nobody in that group ever nagged at me to quit or worried about getting cancer from second-hand smoke.

"I think I lost my capacity to care weeks ago," skeletal David continued. He sounded played out.

That place was depressing at first, smelling of dampness and disinfectant. I wanted to run from there, from them, to prove to the universe that I didn't belong—that I wasn't one of those sad, displaced people with the haunted eyes and the frozen souls. But there was no place I could I go and not end up facing me.

Kyla recrossed her legs, which were lush in the way of hourglass-shaped Turks, of which she was, and is, a prime example. "I can't think of one good reason why you should care, David." She shook back some emotion with a gentle motion of her head and a quick intake of breath. "Except that I want you to. I want you to feel." She worked her hands, rubbing the right fingers hard with the left ones. "God, I'm selfish! I want to know I've helped." She hung her head now.

"You're more concerned with the time you wasted on me than with me," he said simply.

"Not wasted; never wasted."

"I'll go along with that, David," said Lisa, the red buzz cut. "I started out thinking you were gonna be a real pain in the ass. Then I found out we're all of us real pains in the asses."

"So what do you want here, Marly?" asked Scotty, a nattily dressed black gentleman who had to have been in his eighties. "We're not gonna cure you, that's for sure. This deal's not about cures. Miracles abound, but we see few in this room. It's not about love. It's an ugly place." He looked around and clicked his tongue.

"I know," I said and blew the last drag of smoke out the window. "I just ... hate myself for getting sick. I'd like to stop hating myself. Need to."

"You think being sick is the only reason you hate yourself?" asked Lisa. "You started hating yourself and feeling guilty and all that other crap a long time ago. Get with the program, Marly."

I looked for assistance to Kyla, who shrugged her shoulders.

Scotty said, "None of us can marshal quite enough strength to deal with our own death, with cancer." He made a small circle with his hand. "But together, together, we could maybe cut you a deal. I have no time for lies, and neither do you. Of course, that'd be true if you lived to be a hundred."

I felt uncomfortable. "Are you mad at me?" I asked the group.

"Mad at you?" asked a dwarf-sized woman across the circle from me. "I'm not mad at you. I want to believe in you. None of us is mad at you. But since you're probably going to live and most of the rest of us aren't, what difference does it make?" She cocked her head. "If you do live and I don't, I'll be mad as hell."

There was another pocket of silence.

I looked into each face, searching for ... what? Answers? Absolution?

"When did time get to be so damned crucial?" I asked.

Nobody answered.

"Maybe I could learn how to let go a little." I felt the sweat start up on my forehead. "Just in case."

Scotty leaned back in his chair. "I'm listening."

"Marly," Sarah whispered, bringing me back to Willy's, "look at that gorgeous man."

My eyes refocused, and I turned coolly in the direction she'd pointed with her chin.

No! This was turning out to be one hell of a week.

Chapter 19

"I think he's smiling at you, Marly," Lark whispered.

"Who is?"

"Him." She squinted to get a better look. Lark had taken her contacts out to rest her eyes, and she refused to wear her glasses on vacation. "That rather hunky-looking guy. He is hunky-looking, isn't he?" She squinted harder. "Do you know him?" Lark asked hopefully. "I never saw a better-looking man in my entire life. I think ... he's staring at you."

By now you, astute reader that you are, may have guessed that Skip was having dinner at Willy's that night in Manzanillo. Of all the gin joints in all the towns in all the world ... he walks into mine.

I fussed with my wig, licked a drizzle of drawn butter off my finger and waited. Maybe he wouldn't be brazen enough to come over. He was sitting with a group of senior citizens who obviously doted on his every word. Suddenly, he stood up and towered over the restaurant and said something to his meal mates that made them laugh. Then he strolled over to our table.

He leaned down and kissed my forehead. "Marly," he said softly, "you look wonderful. I'm so happy to see you here." He grinned at Lark and Mother.

Oh, cripe city. I introduced everyone.

Skip has this habit of taking a woman's hand when he first meets her. He holds it for a moment or two longer than necessary, which sends out a tingle of electrical current. Neither Lark nor my mother were immune to his charms, although they'd both heard plenty about him in the past and should have known better.

"We're almost through over there. And I think my friends will be heading back to Las Hadas for a nightcap. I'd be the happiest man in the world if you'd let me join you."

Lark and my mother made him the happiest man in the world.

It felt crazy, sitting there with Skip like that after almost three years. Watching his eyes light up with laughter. Gauging the speed with which Lark and Sarah were being gradually won over by his personable ways. Feeling the warmth in his smile whenever he turned toward me and the hint of his curiosity at my wig.

It was as though we'd never been apart, dammit.

That was the problem with Skip. He'd always behaved as though he was crazy about me. I knew it was all part of The Big Act, but sometimes, for an insane second or two, I daydreamed that he actually meant it.

"I can't believe we never met, Sarah," he said. "Marly spoke about you so often, in such glowing terms."

"Did she?" Mom looked at me. "Maybe that's why she's always been my favorite child."

"Only child."

"Are you staying at Las Hadas?" asked Lark. There was a new note in her voice. I glanced at her face and saw her interest in Skip flushing her skin.

Holy cripe city.

"Actually, I came up from Mazatlan today with some friends. On a boat called *The Persuasion*."

Everyone thought this was marvelously funny. Ha ha.

"She's docked at the hotel marina. Hey, why don't I take you all on a private tour? She's something special." He took my hand then, right there in front of God and everybody, and looked into my eyes. "You'll love her."

"What about the owners?" I asked.

"Oh, they won't care; their yacht is my yacht." Everyone laughed again.

The Persuasion was ocean-going length at ninety-odd feet, with a permanent crew of five, including a gourmet chef. Her four sumptuous staterooms were arrayed in varying tones of washed aqua, with each boasting its very own private head with shower. Her deck was brass and mahogany, polished and glowing. Her galley boasted all the latest culinary niceties, including a built-in microwave oven, a temperature-controlled wine vault, and hand-hammered copper sinks.

Lark was into everything. She opened cupboards and inspected drawers and exclaimed over the Berber carpeting in the salon. A hidden bar sprang into view at Skip's touch. He grabbed a bottle of Cristal from the fridge and poured us each a flute-ful.

"To old friends and new friends," he toasted us.

"God!" Lark said, "I feel like I'm in a James Bond movie."

Skip gestured grandly. "They have clay pigeon release aft, so we could get in a little skeet practice. Course, it is tougher to hit them at night ... I know!

The chef is on call twenty-four hours a day. How about a little crème brûlée?"

"We couldn't," said my mother firmly. She licked her lips. "Could we?"

We did.

As the champagne flowed, so did the conversation.

"Okay, Mom, you're dying to. You know it. Just say the damned toast."

She cleared her throat. "May you cheat, steal, and lie." She paused dramatically. Then, "May you cheat the devil, steal away from bad company and lie by the one you love best."

"Ooooh, I like that one, Sarah," said Skip. His voice was buttery soft and smoky low.

At that moment, a discreet knock on the salon door was followed by the entrance of an immaculately dressed crew member. "Thanks, Jean." Skip pronounced the name in a good French accent, with a casual grace I found irritating. "That'll be all, I think. When are the Hardys due back?"

Jean's face never changed. "They have decided to take a suite at the hotel, Monsieur. If you wish your guests to stay here, please let me know, as I will have to prepare the staff." He gave a little bow and slipped away.

"What a great idea! Hey, look, ladies, since we have this little scow to ourselves, why don't you all spend the night?" He arched his eyebrows three times.

"We couldn't," I responded at the exact moment my mother said, "Let's."

"Mom, I don't think ..."

"Oh, c'mon, Marly," Lark said, poking me in the shoulder blade. "Loosen up. This is great!" She threw her arms wide and drank in the soft scent of beeswax polish and fresh roses. "Can a person be in love with a yacht? I think I'm in looove."

"But we don't have any of our stuff," I said in growing panic.

"Are you kidding?" asked Skip. "What do you need? Nightgowns? Toothbrushes? Make-up? This boat is like a floating Nordstrom's."

How to explain without raining on their parade.

"Okay," I said finally. "You talked me into it. But I'm in the middle of Clancy's new book. I'll just cab it back to Casa Greca and get it. You guys need anything?"

Lark looked at Skip dreamily. "Not a thing."

As my mother poured herself another glass of Cristal, I made my way down the gangplank.

The hotel was full to overflowing that week. Every restaurant I passed, every bar, every outdoor cafe was crammed with noisy guests, as were the cobblestone highways and byways. Normally, I would have savored the high spirits and the ever-present mariachi music. I might even have dropped in on the Discoteca and danced the rest of the evening away. But that night, my only thought was escape. I ran blindly through the happy vacationers, barely aware of the ebb and flow of bodies.

I couldn't suddenly decide to stay overnight somewhere on a whim. I needed my wig stand! I needed my specially designed and fitted sleeping bra nearby, just in case the aching started up! I had to put vitamin E on my scar, and most importantly, I had to be absolutely alone when I undressed! I thought of the smoke-tinted mirrors on the walls of The Persuasion's staterooms and shivered as an uninvited picture of perfect, handsome Skip walking in on my nakedness unexpectedly floated across my mind's eye.

You're born alone, and you die alone; I don't care how many people are in the room with you. You have cancer alone, even with a loving family and a largish circle of close friends standing solidly by your side. There are only so many favors you can call in. There's only so much sympathy you can wring out of your loved ones. That's when you start accosting strangers in shopping malls and turn to religion or Mary Kay Cosmetics. If you're lucky, maybe you realize in the nick of time that all the love and understanding in the world doesn't—can't—make it better. The big moments, the tragedies, the natural disasters in life are solo gigs. And that cavernous, echoing solitude can be a prison cell or a cocoon, a torture chamber or a womb. Or all of the above.

I breathed a sigh of relief when the taxi pulled onto my street and the soft lights of Casa Greca beckoned me with the promise of sanctuary and quiet. As I paid the driver with the pink-and-green play money of the country, I thought about a quick skinny-dip followed by a good, long sleep on clean sheets, under the soft and cooling draft of the ceiling fan.

Mario met me at the front door, which wasn't actually a door in the traditional sense, more like a gateway. "Una mujer," he whispered with a shake of his head, "durmiendo abajo."

"¿Quién?" I asked. I couldn't imagine who'd be visiting me at that time of night, much less sleeping in Martha's guest quarters.

"¿Su hermana?"

Oh, my God...

"No es possible," I assured him. "Pero pienso que ella es una amiga de Señora Martha."

There was no way in hell that Jamie Sue could have tracked me down to this place. Nobody who knew me well enough to know where I was would have dared tell her. So who else could it have been but some lost lamb needing rescue by the goodness and hospitality of Martha Hughes' wonderful Shangri-La? Question: Did I give enough of a shit to find out? Answer: No.

"Mario, mi amiga y mi mamá no están regresando esta noche."

"¿Y la extranjera?"

I shrugged my shoulders. "Mañana. Gracias."

I hurried to my bathroom, stripped off my glad rags, hung up my wig and ran my fingers through my own half-inch-long tresses. They were downy, like baby duck feathers.

As Mario would retire to the privacy of his own apartment now and not show himself again until morning, I felt free to luxuriate in pure nakedness of body and soul. You may wonder at my rather cavalier nonchalance in the face of the uninvited female intruder. But Martha was the kind of person everyone took advantage of, including me. I expected to handle the situation properly in the morning.

I slipped into the warmth of the darkened pool and felt the water lap silkily across my skin. A tingle of pleasure circled my ankle and worked its way up the insides of my thighs. I dolphined beneath the surface and watched my breasts drifting lazily from side to side as I frog-kicked my way along the bottom. I'd started working out my upper body with two-pound weights, and it seemed the dent in my boob had filled in a little, especially in the half-light of the moonlit Mexican night. I popped up through the surface at the edge of the waterfall that cascaded into the guest house pool and felt around with my hand until I located the filter return jet. With a wicked little smile no one saw, I settled myself just so, until the stream of water created a lovely, tickling sensation. Then I closed my eyes and listened to the sound of the incoming tide below.

"I know what you're doing."

I might have been startled, except that I knew that voice as well as I knew my own name. I wasn't surprised, and I had no reason to pretend false modesty. I thought briefly to cover my head, but what was the point? Without moving I said, "C'mon in."

In a moment, I heard a rippling noise as a body waded down the steps and into the liquid darkness. Even as I arched myself closer to the narrow and steady spurt of warm water, I felt long, gentle fingers touching me in all my most secret places. He hesitated for a millisecond over the scar on my breast. "Oh ... what have they done to you?"

Skip had come after me. How? Why? I hadn't a clue. But as he turned me toward him and kissed me long and deeply, I let my bones sag underneath my skin, and I folded myself into his welcoming embrace.

His left hand slowly caressed the top of my head. "Why didn't you ever tell me?" he whispered. "I could have held you. Made love to you."

"Because you're lousy at confronting the tough stuff," I said, not unkindly.

He drew back a little. "Maybe I could have learned," he said.

After the roller coaster ride Chris had taken me on, being with Skip was comforting. I knew exactly what I was in for. He gathered me into his arms and lifted me up out of the water. "Are you sleeping in there?" he asked, shrugging his shoulder at the master bedroom.

I nodded my head yes.

"Let's go." He carried me easily inside and laid me down carefully on the bed. He kissed my scar first. "Poor little tit," he whispered. I felt his warm breath on my nipple, then his tongue. His movements were unhurried, lazy. "I love this tit."

That's Skip. He never met a tit he didn't like.

He kissed me again. And again. He ran his fingers through my hair. "It's so soft. And fine. God, you look about fifteen years old."

Then his fingertips traced a zigzag pattern down the trunk of my body until they came to rest in the small patch that was left of my pubic hair. I glanced down and was again thankful I hadn't lost it all during chemotherapy. He scratched me softly, and I felt a fluttering in my stomach. I covered his hand firmly with mine and lifted it away from me.

"What are you doing?" he asked.

"I just remembered why we drifted apart."

"What are you talking about?"

I took his hand then and held it close. "I'm not angry with you, Skip. I wasn't then, and I'm not now. I knew all about you the moment we met."

"Who told you?"

I laughed softly at his naïveté. "No one had to tell me."

I felt his body tense. "I never lied about anything ..."

"Not after I'd already found out some other way."

He sat up and began to swing his legs over the side of the bed.

I stopped him. "You still don't get it," I said. "I wonder if you'll ever get it."

He sighed. "I've missed you more than any of the others. I didn't realize ..."

"And ten minutes after you leave here, you'll have forgotten your realization, whatever it is. So do me a favor and don't tell me. Just lie back down and hold me, okay? Just hold me."

"How about a massage? A real massage, I mean; you used to like that."

There were plenty of things about Skip that had proved hard to take in the past. His real massages weren't on that list. So, for the next hour, with his hands gently kneading the knots in my muscles, I told him part of what had happened to me. Finally, just before the sun peaked its rosy head over the hilltops behind Casa Greca, I drifted off to sleep, my body totally at rest for the first time in months.

"Marly?"

My subconscious oozed away from the intrusion as I rolled over.

"Marly?"

There it was again. Someone was trying to ruin my sleep by pretending to be Jamie Sue. I buried my face deeper into the pillow.

"Marly ... are you awake?"

Not too many people in the world could have asked a question that dumb. It struck me then that the voice might actually be emanating from my half-sister. I pulled the sheet over my head and felt a void where a body had lain. I slid my hand into the depression that was all that was left of Skip. I could still smell him, the perfume of his masculine sweat. I heard a rustle of what sounded like paper. A note. He'd left me a note.

"Marly?"

There it was again, that nasty intrusion. I sat up suddenly. "What?"

Jamie Sue jumped back as though I was Lazarus resurrected.

"Well?" I said without so much as a how-de-do. "What the hell is it? I'm awake now." I blinked uncertainly. Casa Greca was beginning to remind me of the body-strewn depot scene in Gone with the Wind. I mean, was everybody I ever met going to show up here?

"Are you angry?" she asked.

I rubbed my eyes and stretched. "Angry? What could I possibly be angry about?"

"You weren't expecting me, for one thing. Mario ... that's his name, right? He looked confused. He made coffee earlier. Want some?"

"Look, Jamie Sue, if you want to continue playing this scene buddy-buddy, like it's the most natural thing in the world, it's okay by me."

She plunked herself down at the edge of the bed. She looked ... what? Wary? Watchful? I noticed, because she rarely paid me the least bit of attention, even when I was sitting next to her at Christmas dinner. She never bothered mentioning that I was her sister during interviews and behaved, generally, like she was the only little girl in her daddy's life. She resented the hell out of me, always had. And the fact that she had a dozen years on me didn't make the situation any less inflammatory.

"On the other hand," I said, lying back on my pile of pillows with a thwap! "I could use a shot of caffeine. Got an IV with you?"

The humor was lost on her.

"Cream and sugar?" she asked.

"Just cream. And bring a glass of whatever juice is in the fridge, will you?"

This conversation probably doesn't read tense, but you could have cut the atmosphere in that room with a plastic airport knife. While Jamie Sue was busy hunting up cups and serving trays, a process that could take her twenty minutes, I took a pee and read the note Skip had left me.

"Maybe we should start up again," it began. "I still care for you."

Still? That was news. In the past, he'd never admitted to any feelings for me of any kind.

"You're easier to be with now, Marly," the note went on." Or maybe I've changed, too. God, you positively glowed last night."

The afterglow of radiation therapy?

"You and I are alike. You'll never admit it, but we are. I don't want to get any closer if I'm not wanted. *The Persuasion* sets sail (or, to be more precise, motors away) today. You're welcome on the boat any time. You're welcome to come with us as my guest. Separate cabins! The Hardys would love you. But then, everybody loves you.   SKIP"

"That was a gorgeous man. Who was he?" asked Jamie Sue as she set the laden tray down on the bedside table. She began to pour.

"You saw him?" I asked.

"I was up early." She added cream to my cup and handed it to me as politely as the Queen steeps High Tea. "I'll bet you're wondering why I'm here," she said casually.

"Who? Me? Naaaah."

I watched as Jamie Sue drew herself inward, steeling herself for The Confrontation. As her quivering gathered momentum, she said, "I've had the test thing, you know? The culscop ... whatever it is. And I got to wondering ... what the hell am I gonna do if I have cancer?" She sat down at the foot of the bed, sipped at the steaming cup, and stared out at the verdigris sea. "I thought you could give me some ideas. I feel like a total jerk, like I'm cracking up over nothing. All I do is cry these days."

What did she expect me to say? It was the first real face-to-face conversation we'd had since my cancer diagnosis.

"Welcome to my world. How did you find me?" I asked.

"Miriam."

That bitch! I was going to peel her skin off half-inch by half-inch!

We sat there, sipping and mutually watchful for an eternity. Finally, Jamie Sue said, "You know something? I think I like you better since your breakdown."

That might have been intended as a compliment, one along the lines of, "So, I heard you stopped beating your wife."

"On the phone a couple days ago?" she went on. "Remember?"

I nodded.

"I felt like you were actually listening to me. You never do that."

Was she being intentionally insulting? With Jamie Sue, it was impossible to tell. From everything I'd overheard Talbot and Sarah say, she took after her mother. There was something basic missing in both their souls which rendered them ignorant of the most common decencies in human behavior. This was "being nice" for Jamie Sue. You can imagine what "being nasty" was all about.

It hit me suddenly that she needed me. She needed whatever strength I'd managed to glean from my experience with cancer. And because I possessed something of uncommon value, something Jamie Sue felt she desperately wanted and needed, my sister was willing to pretend for the moment that I was a person of some consequence. Did I consider, even for a moment, that she had truly changed for the better, that these feelings were sincere and heart-driven?

Not on your life. I'd been burned by that fire once too often.

"So what do you want from me?" I put up my hand to stop her automatic protest. "Don't lie. I know you want something. Something really big. I'm not signing any of your contracts. If you've got something else on your mind, do us both a favor and spit it out, okay?"

At that moment, I wanted to be anyplace else in the world. Going over Niagara Falls in a barrel. Diving off a hundred-foot cliff in Acapulco. Jumping off the top of El Capitan with a parachute and a prayer.

She blew out a long breath through puffed cheeks. "If I discover that I actually have cancer, I want to you to help me get through it."

Holy guacamole!

Chapter 20

What was this? A peace pipe? A white flag? A red herring? My sister seemed ... vulnerable. "Why me?" Yes, that ever-present voice inside my head had burst through my lips to wonder aloud what she was really up to.

She clicked her tongue. "You know what I'm going through; you've been there. God, Marly, I'm scared. Really scared. You've got to help me! We're family, you know, whether you want to admit it or not."

Warning. Warning.

I could feel myself recoiling from her pronouncement of need and kinship as though it were some ugly physical deformity, a kind of leprosy of emotion. Ever since I was a kid, it's been tough for me to maintain a crusty dislike of another human being once I've glimpsed the emotional pain they drag around behind them. But with Jamie Sue, I didn't want to let go of that dislike. When I felt her squirming, I took pleasure in it. I'm ashamed to admit it, but that pearly cloud of moral superiority through which I'd looked down my nose at my half-sister was a security blanket. It was a distasteful situation, and I behaved distastefully.

When *People* magazine does its story on me, I'll say I'm Lady Bountiful mixed with Albert Schweitzer. That's in my mind's eye, of course. In the real world, I'm obviously a tad more venal.

I do so hate it when I have to revise long-cherished good opinions of myself.

Let me elaborate: People had always been careful around Jamie Sue, careful about how they reacted to her, how they spoke to her. She was so volatile, so off-kilter, they so often observed, she could never handle the truth. The reason this pissed me off royally was because it meant she'd gone through a significant part of her life surrounded by so-called friends, advisors and family who tap danced on eggshells and contorted themselves into pretzels and generally bent over backwards to excuse her bad behavior.

Oh, once in a while some ex-boyfriend would get fed up to here and get photographed screaming at her in a restaurant. But I don't think she's ever understood how people perceive her. Maybe no one's ever loved her bravely enough to tell her. I'm not sure she'd believe it if they had.

"You take me for a fool?" I started out. "You expect me to fall for this ... family claptrap?"

Jamie Sue's eyes grew big as saucers, a facial gesture I'd nicknamed The Doe Look. She started to speak, but I cut her in two.

"You've come to me exactly four times in my life: once when you wanted some help writing those demo interviews on Rod Carew and Bruce Jenner for NBC Sports. The way I remember it, you took the credit for the finished project even though I did all the research ... not to mention all the writing." She gasped to speak, but I cut her off. "I'm not finished yet." I rubbed my hands together in glee. "Two: you used my name to secure an introduction to my friend and film director Buddy Lazar, without telling me. He was fairly pissed about that. Three: remember when you needed to borrow twenty-five grand to pay off your boyfriend-of-the-month's wife's divorce lawyer? I'm still waiting for the balance on that one. And last, but certainly not least, the time you were pretty sure Dad was going to disinherit you. After you'd pushed me through the glass door."

"That was an accident! You always made a big deal out of that. It was an accident!"

"Whatever. I wouldn't expect you to have the guts to admit any responsibility, even though you were fifteen at the time. And when Dad asked you about it at Christmas two years ago, I saved your miserable hide." I rolled my eyes heavenward.

The yawning gap between Jamie Sue's upper and lower lips widened considerably.

I barreled right ahead. "You keep getting yourself into sticky situations through your own stupidity and cupidity. Then you run to the family and yodel for help. Usually, there's at least two items on your hidden agenda nobody knows anything about."

She started to cry. I was just finding my rhythm.

"Hey, it isn't just me. You've taken advantage of almost everybody you know at one time or another. You never bother to say 'please' or 'thank you' or even 'screw you.' You're selfish and conceited and a goddamned liar to boot."

I went to the bathroom and got a box of Kleenex. When I tossed it at Jamie Sue, she hissed at me. "You've always been jealous of me, Marly. You're vicious and narrow-minded when it comes to me. You always have been. God, I'm tired of hearing you panting at my heels."

Our argument modulated up a couple of decibels.

"All right, I admit it. I am jealous, and I'm angry!"

"You're pissed because you only have half a boob on the left side." She dug her finger into my chest. "I worked my ass off to get where I am! I'm good and I'm successful, and you hate it!"

"Bullshit! You probably slept your way up the ladder!"

She slapped my face. Not that I blame her. I'm surprised we didn't both suffer core meltdown.

"What do you know about it?" she screamed/sobbed. "What do you know about it?" Jamie Sue was enraged, full of bile, wild with pain. "Just because you don't have the talent or the guts to do what I've done, don't take it out on me."

"This is an odd way to ask for my help. I think you'd better leave." I spoke through clenched teeth. "But before you go, think about this: the concept of your own mortality is hammering at your consciousness, Jamie Sue. And enemies or not, you're looking to me for the quick fix, and you're looking for it yesterday. You weren't there for me, and I ain't gonna be there for you!"

Exit rational and caring human being, enter demon bitch.

"Either that, or you're up to something truly underhanded and despicable! I'm not gonna fall down and die this time!"

She wailed right back at me like a banshee and threw herself at my face with teeth and claws bared. Cups and spoons and glasses and bedside lamps went flying. Locked in a kind of Wrestlemania death grip, we rolled ass over tea kettle two or three times. Then we exchanged pathetic punches.

I think that's when I first noticed Mario anxiously peeking at us from the safety of the kitchen area on the other side of the house. Seeing the shock on his face snapped me out of … whatever. Like a sleepwalker, I shook myself free of Jamie Sue's grip and crawled to a neutral corner.

My chest was heaving like I'd just finished a triathlon. I slowly lowered myself onto the cool marble floor.

"You're cruel, Marly." Her voice was a whisper now. "You're worse than me, much worse. Because you pretend to be better."

I don't know how long I lay there like that, spent, lifeless, hollow. I think I must have fallen asleep, because the next thing I remember is my mother shaking me awake. "What the hell happened in here?" she asked.

Lark finished looking around the room and said, "My God, are you okay?"

"Never better," I answered as I scraped myself off the floor and collapsed on the bed. How was your stay on *The Persuasion?* Were you persuaded?"

"Marly! This is Sarah, your mother! You have some explaining to do."

"Did Skip show up here last night?" asked Lark.

So I covered the highlight tape of the immediately preceding hours.

"You have been busy," Lark said, a bit crestfallen.

I put my arm around her. "Listen, Skip and I were unsuited bedfellows a long time ago. I don't know that I feel anything for the guy now, except maybe an echo of lust." I chucked her on the chin. "So you do whatever you want about him. It's not worth risking our friendship, that's for damn sure."

Lark sighed. "Champagne always screws my head on backwards. It sets my hormones on fire, or something." She looked at me sheepishly. "But he is good-looking and seems charming. I hate it when they're charming, too."

"Tell me about it, sister."

"Speaking of sisters," my mother said, "what happened to Jamie Sue? Will they find the body?" It appears to be a flip remark written on this page, but she looked serious, maybe even a little angry.

I shrugged my shoulders.

"Marly," Sarah said firmly, "your life is a mess. And I hate this ... thing between the two of you. It's so ugly. So unlike you." She ran distracted fingers through her hair. "I feel badly about it. It worries me. It's ..."

"Mom, you should see it from over here."

"Anybody home?" It was Good Ol' Don.

"I don't remember a revolving door on the street level," my mother said in her most exasperated tone.

"Haaalloooo!" Don yodeled again.

"Just get rid of him, will you?" I asked. "Tell him he can get the key for the unit from the front desk later this afternoon. I've ... oh, I don't know. Tell him I've got a few calls to make."

The phone situation at Casa Greca/Casa Rosa is convoluted. During the latest, not to say the last, of Harry Hughes' bankruptcy proceedings, the bill had gone unpaid for over three months. The Mexican utility companies take a dim view of that sort of behavior. They don't just cancel your service; they send some axe-wielding Mestizo thugs over who rip all the equipment and wires out of your walls. You might pay a substantial amount of mordida over a long period of time in an attempt to reestablish your good reputation. This may or may not work. In the meantime, if you happen to live on La

Punta, you can receive messages through the security office, whose minions may or may not deliver them in the same week. You can get a cellular phone that comes with a three-hundred-dollar-per-month bill built right in. And that's just for starters. Or you can hassle and inconvenience your neighbors.

The Smiths were saintly about sharing their phone, although I think they were a little pissed when it came to taking messages for Mario, which happened on a regular basis. I was always careful to leave plenty of money to handle my charges and to bring Mrs. Smith signed first editions. She had an impressive collection of modern authors, which even included two or three of my own works. I didn't flatter myself about this, though. It was indiscriminate collecting. She had every Larry McMurtry ever written.

The Smith family had all gone to town for breakfast, so I left them my latest contribution: two of my mother's autographed bestsellers. Then it was time to tackle the Mexican communication system. Holy Guacamole!

After only three tries, a personal best, I managed to reach Miriam in New York. She must have known I'd be hopping mad, and I admired her courage for taking my call immediately.

"Go ahead. I know you're going to yell. I've got my earplugs in."

"Why? That's all I want to know ... Why?" I was yelling.

"Okay, okay," Miriam sighed. "Which fuck-up do you want to know about first?"

"I'm supposed to be resting down here, writing my book. You're supposed to be my barracuda, my Great Wall, not my Achilles heel!"

"Trojan Horse is a better metaphor."

It's frustrating when someone I'm yelling at agrees with everything I say. It takes the oomph out of my momentum. "Well?" I said finally, in a calmer, saner tone, "Aren't you going to interrupt this tirade with an explanation?"

"Since you put it so nicely ... first off, I've always had a motherly thing for men who are basically no-good-niks. Good Ol' Don qualifies."

"True."

"He was plotzed. I hung up on him six or seven times. Then I told him to call you at home, but he knew you were traveling. Then I swore at him, but he still kept calling back, and it was obvious he was going to keep on calling back until he got what he wanted, which was your destination. Mind, this was during working hours, yet. It was a business decision. I gotta make a real effort to scrape together a living, since you're taking ninety percent of my money."

I pictured her tapping her pencil on her stained and crumpled blotter.

"Besides," she continued, "who could have predicted the dinkus would actually show up at Casa Greca instead of faxing you like a normal crazy person? Which reminds me, I want to come down for a visit next December."

I would have laughed out loud, but I wasn't ready to let Miriam off the hook. "One down, one to go," I said sternly. "And this one had better be good."

"Your father is a handsome man caught like a rat in a trap by his attachment to four women. Through very little fault of his own, he finds himself perpetually up a creek. Okay, okay, he was the teeniest bit responsible for the unpleasantness way back when. I know, I know, that's an old-fashioned think. But your father called me out of desperation, looking for a bit of peace because she, the ugly step-sister—or is it half-sister?—was hounding him, the poor man, for your whereabouts. Even then I might not have given in ... but he presented it as a matter of life and death. Damned convincing, too. Was it one? Life and death, I mean?"

"If Jamie Sue dies shortly, it was."

"Myyyyyyy," Miriam said, drawing out the word like Jack Benny, "how nurturing of you."

"Hey! You're supposed to be taking abuse, not dishing it out."

"I'm sorry, Marly. I lost my head."

"No. I think you wanted to make sure I'd call you."

"There is that."

Dramatic pause on both sides.

"Yes, I'm working on the book, and yes, it'll be done on time. God, you're like some old biddy hen with a brood of wandering chicks."

"I like that, Marly dumpling, I'll use it at the Writers' Conference."

"Crap, don't remind me."

"I've thought of another little gem. Keeping a writer in your house is like having a tarantula for a pet: you can milk out the poison and teach him not to bite, but he's always going to be one hairy, ugly, son-of-a-bitch."

"Say goodnight, Miriam."

"Oh! You're not nuclear anymore. Bye."

Miraculously, I somehow managed to connect to my voice-mail next. A producer-director-writer called. I tend to think of him as a hyphenate and the equivalent of a female actress-model-whatever, except for an actual track record. It was my dad, to apologize. That made me smile. And Dr. Dent. Twice. I gulped and bit the bullet.

"Phyllis?"

"You were supposed to be in my office for a check-up two weeks ago."

"I know."

"You're playing a terrible game on my time, and I don't like it, Marly. I want you in here, yesterday."

"Okay."

"I'll grab my appointment book. You tell me when, and I'll squeeze you in."

I do so hate when people I'm trying to avoid are prepared with pencil and paper. It's particularly offensive in doctors, dentists and ex-lovers.

Lark was painting her toenails a fire engine red, just the right color for a '65 Mustang. She had little cotton balls squashed between her toes. My mother was drafting an article on modern marriage for Los Angeles magazine. We were all sitting by the pool, eating sopites and drinking virgin daiquiris. I was about to go for some rum.

"How can you two just sit there and write like that?" Lark asked as she studied her left big toe. "It'd terrify me, knowing I had to fill up blank page after blank page."

"Thanks a lot, Lark. You have just asked the one question guaranteed to bring on writer's block," I teased.

"But Lark, you have to write papers for your college work," my mother pointed out.

"But those topics are assigned. The papers are about something specific, something in my course that I can learn about, research. I don't have to grab it out of the air."

"Novels should be about things we know," my mother said, spritzing herself with her handy-dandy water bottle.

"I always feel like God," I said, stretching hugely. "I make the universe. I put in each flower, each tree, a house here, a mountain there. Then I populate it. I'm responsible for everything that happens. It's a kick, most of the time. It gets a little harried when the characters start running around at their own cross-purposes. That's why God makes mistakes, I guess." I stood up, reached for my glass, and headed for the bar.

My mother lowered her sunglasses. "Since when do you believe in God?"

"I don't," I said airily, waving the newly minted, icy-cold pitcher of daiquiri mix around my head. "Not in the traditional Judeo-Christian, paternalistic, bearded father-figure-crap sense."

Lark smiled. Mother said, "I see."

She always says that when she isn't quite sure of me. I decided, rather wickedly, to elaborate.

"To me, God is everything, every single thing, good or bad, past, present, or future, that exists in the universe or in the mind of Woman. I don't believe in the devil. I do believe in ignorance and stupidity and stubbornness, on the minus side. Not evil, not the devil."

I swirled a dollop of drink over and under ice cubes before sipping with smacking lips and staring at my mother. I was daring her to disagree. I believe I mentioned that she's always defended me tooth and nail. Did I also mention that she infuriates me? That she's still trying to steer my life? That she worries about me because I have no ambition? That she even criticizes my singing, for God's sake?

"I worry about you, Marly," she said, almost on cue.

"You said that already, Mother dear. In fact, you say that once every twelve hours every time we're together. You'll just have to wait your turn. There are a lot of folks ahead of you."

Lark said, "It's hard to just let your children be."

"Anyhow, Mom," I said as I opened the bar fridge and nosed around, "you don't go to church, so what difference does it make to you?"

"I almost became a Buddhist once," she said, peering over her sunglasses again. It made her look like a hip librarian.

"Really?" Lark said. "I can't imagine that. You're so ... well ... solid. Firm. Strong. That didn't come out quite the way I ... well, I meant it as a compliment, Sarah."

"Of course you did, Lark. What are you doing, Marly?"

I had extricated three pitchers of freshly squeezed juice from the fridge: cantaloupe, watermelon, guava. I had idly begun to pour droplets of juice into my daiquiri, tasting each result. A droplet, a taste, a droplet, a taste.

"Why aren't you a Buddhist now?" Lark asked.

"I don't know that I ever got completely away from it. I have strong feelings about past lives."

Now it was my turn to be surprised. "You do?"

My mother looked at me as though I'd been declared unfit to stand trial. "Yes. I may not run around doing talk shows on the subject, but yes."

Droplet, sip, droplet, sip.

Hmmmmm.

"But, to my mind," Sarah went on, "the mainstay of Christianity is love. No matter what those dolts in churches might teach. Acceptance. Understanding. Mutual respect. Not exclusion and superiority."

"Hallelujah!" I shrieked.

Lark tipped over her bottle of polish, and Mother practically flew out of her chair.

I started to laugh. "No, no, it's all right. It's just that this," I gestured at my drink, "is an Aunt Minnie's Surprise!"

I felt like I'd won the Pullet Surprise.

I told Mother and Lark about Ginevra and the crab races, which somehow led my mother to mention the AstroGlide.

"AstroGlide?" asked Lark.

"AstroGlide?" said a voice from the front doorway.

It was the perfect entrance line for Skip, if I ever heard one.

Chapter 21

"AstroGlide?" Skip asked again. "Sounds interesting."

"Never mind," I answered.

He was carrying a bouquet of flowers in one hand and a bottle of something in the other. Skip was odd in that way. While he often brought presents for no reason, he rarely brought them on birthdays or Christmas.

"Good morning," he said with that lazy smile of his. "Oops, wait a minute here," he said, squinting up into the sun, "I guess it's afternoon."

Lark sat up and sucked her stomach in. "Hello, Skip," she purred. "We all had such fun last night."

"Some of us more than others," my mother offered, beyond sarcasm. Almost cruel. I remember thinking it didn't sound like her.

"Where can I put this stuff?" Skip asked.

"Follow me into the kitchen," I said. "Can you stay for lunch?"

He didn't answer. Once we were around the corner and out of sight, he set down his peace offerings and literally swept me off my feet. It was one of his rituals. You'd be waiting in line with him somewhere, and maybe he'd get a little bored and without warning, he'd swoop you up into his arms. I always fancied I could hear the other women complaining to their escorts, "Harry, you never pick me up like that." And Harry would sigh and stub his toe along the floor and curse the big blond man with the romantic notions and the carry-on-sized girlfriends.

"This feels right," Skip said, breathing in deeply. "I'd know the smell of your hair anywhere."

And probably the smell of every woman's hair he'd ever canoodled with. Hey! Whaddya know! A zing of reality flying in the face of my unrelenting Mexico-aggravated hormones!

"I came to tell you that *The Persuasion* is pulling out early, in about an hour. You know how rich folks are."

"Like poor folks, only more so?" I answered.

He had to think about it. "Yeah ... well, they're always changing their minds. Come back with me to Mazatlan."

I kissed him on the cheek. "No."

"That word again. You know I've never liked it; you can do better than that."

"You just haven't heard it enough to become familiar with it. It's not such a bad word."

"You'll be missing a great time."

"But you won't, whether I'm with you or not. Acres and acres of women out there ..."

He set me down and pursed his lips. "Does this mean there's no chance for us to get back together?"

"Not much."

He peered at me. "Don't you usually talk more than this? Aren't you going to ask me some of your hard questions?"

I shrugged my shoulders and shook my head.

He tipped my chin upwards. "You have changed. I'll be back in Los Angeles next week. If I call you, will you see me?"

I shrugged my shoulders again. Clint Eastwood has a good thing going: His iconic characters don't explain or equivocate or even think. They simply utter monosyllables and move a body part occasionally, to show they are still alive. His roles could sound deep and look contemplative while actually being shallow as a mudhole.

Skip and I kissed then, really kissed and didn't say good-bye. He waved once, flamboyantly, and strutted off.

"I hope you didn't refuse to go on our account," my mother said. There was that tone again.

"Mother ... You were listening? Great. No," I said, whumping myself down on a pool lounge. "I need to be away from sex for a while. From the temptation and the distraction. Ooh, I believe there's some humongous shrimp in the fridge. Let's indulge."

Even the most casual meals are "presented" at the great houses of La Punta. Live-in housekeepers and gardener/drivers are trained to arrange the food artfully; replace all the cut flowers in in the house every three days; make roses out of radishes, fruit bowls out of melon rinds and glasses out of pineapples. Dining tables are king-sized. Not only do you have to entertain your friends and neighbors so they will entertain you in return, quite often the house owners travel in gaggles like geese, necessitating room at every seating for the descending Mongol Hordes.

There were only the three of us at lunch, but Mario behaved as though he expected El Presidente. He served the meal so smoothly, you would have sworn he was on skates.

Mother brushed some quesadilla crumbs from her lap. "Your father would love it here."

"It was a women-only trip."

"Don't be defensive, Marly."

That was like saying don't breathe through your nose. "I'm not being defensive, Mom."

"Of course not," she said and began unconsciously gathering up our dishes. "I wish you'd call me something besides 'Mom.' Have you given up smoking? I don't remember cleaning up any dirty ashtrays."

That was one of my mother's "things"—she didn't mind having smokers in her home, but she was damned if she'd allow any cigarette ashes.

"I guess I forgot about it somewhere along the line." That was the truth of it: it had slipped away from me in the last week without my knowing. "Just until my next anxiety attack. Don't do that." I slapped at her hand as she stood and reached to clear her dishes away. "Leave it for Mario and Patty."

Lark stood up and began to help my mother. "I don't know," she said, "I guess we feel too guilty, letting them do everything."

"That's what they get paid for!" I snorted.

Larkie. The Wonder Mom. In the old days, she'd never let her kids make a bed or tidy a den. She was one of those clean-up-after-the-housekeeper types. It might've been because Tom could find a speck of dirt on an operating room floor. Or it might've been because, in the early days, Lark's entire life worth was about being Betty Crocker and Florence Nightingale on alternate days.

"No one can make me feel guilty in Mexico," I said. "Not even you two experts." I dove into the pool and swam a lap under water, my wig wicking out behind me like octopus arms.

Mother waited until I resurfaced. "Why did you disappear last night?"

"I just couldn't be there any longer."

Lark took one look at us and tactfully retreated to her room.

Sarah walked over to the side of the pool. "Are you sure that's all it was? You wouldn't ... keep anything from me, would you?"

What a question; of course I would! "Of course not," I lied.

"I mean, you're okay. You're feeling ... everything's okay ..."

"Mom, I'm doing fine. F-I-N-E."

Hell, I was about as far from being f-i-n-e as I cared to go. But, thank God, not as far as I had been. I was just about to make a snappy reply when she veered.

"Jamie Sue's behavior was puzzling. Almost frightening."

"Isn't it always?"

Sarah gave me A Look. "You're always so unkind when it comes to Jamie Sue."

"And you always take her side. It's infuriating."

"I've felt ... I don't know ... responsible for her, in some way."

I didn't like the way that made me feel. "She's got a mother of her own."

"Yes. Kathleen—a bitter, spiteful, angry woman. I helped make her that way. In turn, she helped Jamie Sue become what she is."

"That's a lot of BS, and you know it!"

"No, Marly, I don't know anything of the kind."

"It's kind of an all-encompassing stance to take, isn't it? I mean, who elected you God?"

Sarah smiled oddly. "If nominated, I would not run."

We sat together and shared a prickly silence. Apropos of nothing, my mother suddenly turned toward me and asked, "Are you avoiding talking about Chris?"

"I'm avoiding thinking about him."

"Why?"

"Because I want him even though I know he isn't good for me. I'm needy for him, which I despise. And I keep fooling myself into thinking maybe ... if I give it some time, he'll get there, too. When I'm not there to begin with. I haven't got the strength to keep all these fucking plates spinning."

"Is there anything I can do?"

I wished I could have told her the truth. Instead, I dove back into the cool water and swam for a time, listening to the rhythm of my own breathing in my head.

Casa Greca represents the very best of Mexico and the very best of me. It's a place for soul-searching and recreating yourself. Life there has a gauzy texture that promotes intimacy and softens reality.

Later that afternoon, as the sun was beginning to sink behind the hills across the bay, I laid my soul down in the sun to warm itself. I was dozing when I heard Mother and Lark come up from the guest suites.

"Whatever made you want to write about modern marriage?" Lark was asking Sarah. "It's such a depressing subject."

Sarah laughed and slapped playfully at the bottom of my feet. "Get up and walk with us, Marly, my darling daughter. You're positively going to seed." As I sat up and stretched, Mother warmed to Lark's question.

"To begin with, I wondered if modern marriage was really such a greatly different animal from the previous incarnations. It seemed that the changing role of women would have to change the institution."

We straggled down the steps of Casa Greca and out into the heat of the late afternoon.

All the houses on La Punta are wondrous to behold, as different from one another as Fabergé eggs, and as glorious. We did a lot of "oohing" and "aahing."

"Those nice publishers also offered to pay me," Sarah went on, intoning one of our little family jokes. Then she said, "I have found marriage to be challenging and humbling. Sometimes it wears me out." She picked up her pace. "I guess, more than anything else, I'm writing an epilog," she said.

"Really?" asked Lark with interest. "How so?"

I was dismayed. "Are you saying you and Dad aren't happy together?"

My mother picked up her pace again until she was well ahead of us, the better to think. She jutted her chin out to cut the wind and the distractions. When we finally caught up to her, in front of The Blue House, La Casa Azul, she threw her arms open to the sea below. "We're certainly not unhappy." She looked at Lark. "The way you and Tom must have been."

"Tom was a jerk," Lark said.

"Exactly. Talbot isn't anything resembling a jerk. And yet our life together is not what either one of us expected."

"I don't like this, and I don't want to hear it," I complained. "You guys are a love match! He left his wife for you, and by extension, for me."

"That's a trifle simplistic, don't you think, Marly? What do you expect me to say? Marriage is a tough road. The work is satisfying but hard. You have to be lucky for it to hang together. All the good intentions and good communication in the world might not be enough. Your father and I may be two of the blessed ones, but don't think it's been all peaches and cream."

I hate it when my cynicism gets a shot in the arm.

Lark put her arm around my shoulders. "I think you're shaking her foundation, Sarah. Maybe your daughter's not ready to hear this."

I shrugged away. "That's not true. I just didn't know."

Sarah said, "Marly, you act like you're waiting for it all to fall into place. Well, don't hold your breath." She pointed to our left. "Ooooh, look at that yellow house. It reminds me of an Italian villa: so elegant!" She turned back to me. "You're probably praying that this patch of trouble you're passing through will somehow recede into the mists of time past. That suddenly, you'll wake up from the nightmare, and the dust will have settled, and you'll look around and recognize some old familiar trail markings and your old self in the mirror. It doesn't work that way. You're not ever going to get back to that place where you were dynamited off the track."

"I don't believe you! And what the hell has any of this got to do with modern marriage?"

"Everything," said Sarah.

"You're ... not going to get divorced, or anything, are you?" I felt like a little lost girl and shivered.

"Again, it's not quite that simple."

She'd thrown my heart up into the air, twirled it around two or three times, then stuffed it back into my body. I clung to her hand in the deepening mauve of the eventide. "But you guys are the smartest people I know. God, you're in love! If you haven't got it all sorted out ..."

"It's not about sorting things out, really," Lark said. "Because they never stay sorted, do they? It's about letting go. You've done it with your life, and you don't even realize it. How much you've let go of. How sane a position you've taken."

"Sane? This awful jumble of mistakes and raw emotions is sanity?" I asked. "Don't tell me that!" I covered my ears like a ten-year-old.

My mother took me into her arms and fairly crushed me against her large, warm breasts. "You're feeling ... everything. I can feel it. And here I am, giving you grief about not making choices. But your current set of predicaments has started me thinking." She smiled wanly.

"Don't think!" I said. "Do yourself and me a goddamned favor and don't think!"

I never meant anything more in my life.

When Good Ol' Don and Tawnie with an "i-e" arrived for cocktails at seven-thirty, they found us three Casa Grecans in a subdued mind-set. I had made reservations at Le Gatsby for 8:30, which meant we couldn't indulge in more than a longish half-hour of nerve-wracking fun. Not that I could bear the thought of going out, but the idea of staying "in" with the newlyweds gave me the willies.

God, she was young. Nothing jiggled or hung except her nipple-length Titian-red hair. It flowed in soft waves across her forehead and cascaded down her back like a fountain.

"You're really Marly Mitchell? I've read every book you've ever written." She pumped my hand in greeting for a seeming eternity. "When Don told me he used to ... that he knew you ... I begged him to introduce us. And here we are!" She eyed her man possessively. I think Tawnie was wondering how much Don had told me.

I was wondering how much he'd told her.

"Come in, Don," my mother said, with rather more grace toward my ex than usual. She swept them both forward with a flourish. "I can recommend the Aunt Minnie's Surprises."

"Without alcohol," Don said, "Tawnie and I don't drink."

Lark's eyes popped, but she didn't comment.

"Well, I guess you won't mind if we toss back a couple," I said.

"Oh, no," Tawnie almost chirped. "It's a generational thing, isn't it?"

I didn't fall for the bait.

"What a romantic house," Tawnie went on. "And this view! I've never been to Mexico before. But Don insisted. For the honeymoon, and all." She glanced at me from under enviable lashes.

There it was again. The Probe. She wasn't as dumb as she looked ... but a lot less confident.

"How you must love to be a writer!" Tawnie was practically gurgling by this time.

"Guacamole, anyone?" I responded.

"To live like this, I mean ... and say exactly what's on your mind and get paid for it." Tawnie, who was the only one of us still speaking on a regular basis, turned to my mother. "I don't mean to ignore you, Mrs. Mitchell. I've read *Francesca of Lost Nation*. But then I guess just about everyone in America has." Tawnie whirled on Lark. "You must feel so lucky! Traveling to Mexico with two awesome writers! Just like Hemingway and his revolving entourage! Except, of course, it was Spain in his case."

If I hadn't seen the look on Don's face for myself, I wouldn't have believed it. He was all loving attention and positively beamed at Tawnie as she prattled on. He seemed perfectly happy to let her grab and keep Center Stage.

For her part, Tawnie's hands were in continual contact with some part of Don's body, as though they were joined by an umbilical cord. And while she rarely looked at him, he rarely looked at anyone else but his bride.

I found her exhausting performance a tad irritating.

"I'd love for you to stay longer, but we'd already made plans for dinner when Don called," I said. I thought I sounded sincere.

"Don't give another thought! This has been wonderful! The highlight of my honeymoon ... maybe my life!" Tawnie spoke with lots of invisible exclamation points hanging in the air. "Thank you ever so much!" She turned to Don. "Don't you think it'd be okay now?"

He started to shake his head, but Tawnie reached down into her purse, which was large enough to hold three nights' worth of clothes. "Oh, dear! I can never find anything in here!" She practically disappeared into the bag.

"I've got it!" she said, brandishing a dog-eared copy of my first mystery, *BloodHounds*. "You wouldn't mind signing this, would you?"

The adoree rarely becomes perturbed with the adorer. "Of course not," I said.

"See, Don?" she said gaily. "I'm so happy! Thank you! Thank you for everything!"

"I'm not sure I have the energy to eat," said Lark when we were finally on our way to the restaurant. "Marly, do you remember when you had that kind of energy?"

"I never did," I answered.

"Not true," said Sarah. "You were powerfully animated as a child. It wore me out, trying to keep up."

"So?" I went on, "isn't anybody gonna say anything?"

"They seem quite different, don't they?" said Lark, the diplomat.

"She'll run him right into the ground within the year. Serves him right," my mother said.

They both turned toward me and waited.

"I think she's the best thing that ever happened to him," I said, surprising myself with the fact that I meant it. "At the very least, he'll hear every day of their married life together what a superb and talented human being I am."

This remark of certain sharpness made everyone laugh. I looked out the window and watched the harbor lights twinkle a trail across the bay.

"And at the very most, he might learn what it's like to be truly loved."

"Amen," said Lark.

"I envy them," I said, leaning over and resting my head against Sarah. The cobblestone streets rattled the taxi and bumped my head up and down on her shoulder blade.

"I do, too, Marly," Lark said quietly.

I cleared my throat. "I'm not afraid that no man will ever love me again; I'm afraid that I'll never love a man ever again."

Chapter 22

The remainder of the trip passed uneventfully. Lackadaisical tennis was played. Lousy literature was rewritten and sometimes even ended up better. I swear, at times I wonder when I get back into my computer, what third-rate hack has been messing with my stuff.

We'd visited with my Mexican friends and introduced them to Aunt Minnies. I bought a couple of tropical print shirts that I'd never wear again. (God! I was becoming my mother!) And I broke down and paid too much for a cunning little Bustamante angel, all pale pastel, looking a little like it was carved from a bowl of sherbets.

Lark, Mother and I invaded the traditional Friday celebration of payday at Bar Social. As long as you keep drinking some form of alcohol, they keep bringing food. I ate everything but the pig knuckles.

We played golf and soared over Las Hadas in an ultralight aircraft fitted with pontoons for water landings. We sat in the sun and trashed each other's men and laughed like hyenas and held hands as the sun went down.

Sometimes I went off by myself and brooded ... embracing the melancholy like a trusted friend. At this point, I even decided I'd better drop in on my group at least once before I took off for Tucson.

On our homeward trek, the three of us took turns lambasting the immigration process as practiced at Los Angeles International, much to the delight of our fellow sufferers. I always marveled at how wonderfully cynical Lark became after a few days in the bosom of my family.

"Think of all the extra money they make in parking fees, making us wait like this," she cracked as we pushed and pulled our baggage along on a small cart with a petrified front right wheel, through the woefully understaffed customs brigade.

Lark's chauffeur deposited us all neatly at her front door, and she asked us to stay for dinner.

"Mom can stay, if she wants."

"I thought I was sleeping at your place tonight," Sarah said, "and I'd prefer you didn't call me 'Mom.'"

"You are; sleeping at my place. But we're not Siamese twins joined at the hip. Stay here for dinner! I've got a ton of phone calls and laundry to do; I'm off to Tucson Monday."

Sarah elected to elongate her vacation by a coupla extra hours, and the two of them swooshed me off with hugs-on-the-run and vigorous waving.

On the drive back to my place, I cursed myself yet again for not owning a car phone. For my money, people who brandished car phones were the height of pretentiousness, and the cost was enough to initiate the gag reflex. But the telephone was a lifeline in Los Angeles, my one steady hook-up with the outside world when a cross-town trip at rush hour was a two-hour-minimum slog. I'd certainly had enough of the comedy phone routine in Mexico, and back in California, Ma Bell was once again my patron saint: She interrupted my writing often (which was good). She disturbed my bathing ritual (which was bad), but I'd recently taken to screening my calls by listening to the incoming voices on my answering machine, a habit I detested in others. It was painfully clear ... I was gonna have to break down and get me a cellular, 'cause about the time I passed the Laurel Canyon off-ramp, I was fuming over the aggravation I could already have saved myself.

Answering machine first; the usual: Dr. Dent. Checking up on me, eh, Doc? Afraid I'll miss my appointment? Skip, all crackly-voiced and sincere. He must have tried me from an airplane phone. Miriam. Paramount was making okay-okay-we-give-in noises on my BloodHounds deal. Huzzah! (Sic 'em, Miriam.) Jamie Sue (gad!). Daddy again. (Double gad!) Chris Lockehead. Hmmm. My little angel pal Sugar from Tucson. When was I'all arrivin'? And aren't all us gals jus' gonna have fun? The producer-writers attached like rubber cement to BloodHounds. I hate hyphenates, especially the ones who wear suits. They always want to redo my stuff without the inconvenience of having to consult me.

"I'm sorry. Dr. Dent is with a patient."

"Oh. Well, just tell her that Marly Mitchell ..."

"Mitchell?" the crisp voice broke in. "Please hold."

I guess the Doc had sent the posse on ahead to cut me off at the pass.

"Marly? You're coming in tomorrow, right?"

"Goddammit, Phyl, you're not my parole officer."

"I like it when you swear during our conversations; it usually means you're cornered. If you're not here on the dot, I'll hire a private detective to find you and put it on your bill."

She's so pushy.

"Miriam? Marly."

I heard her smack her lips twice. "We have a deal, my darling child. They're willing to give you cast and writer approval. If you'd have been less greedy artistically, I could have got you lots more lovely money."

"I know. But it was a matter of self-defense. I don't want to see my stuff hacked to pieces by twenty-four-year-old wise asses who never heard of Ingrid Bergman or John Huston. Or even Jimi Hendrix."

"Jimi Hendrix?" Tap, tap, tap went the pencil. "You could write the script yourself."

"I'm a novelist, Miriam."

"You can't eat art, Marly." Tap, tap, tap went the pencil again. "I hear your gorgeous friend Skip paid you a visit at Casa Greca."

"You with the CIA?" How did she do it? "Yeah. My vacation turned into a regular class reunion. Everyone from the old neighborhood showed up."

"Now there was a man you could simply gaze at. Who cared if he couldn't talk? And such exquisite manners. Is he ... pining away for you?"

"I wouldn't say he's lacking for diversion."

"You realize I haven't even mentioned the current manuscript. You see how I trust you?"

"Miriam, you're despicable."

"Thank you, dear."

Forget Jamie Sue for the moment. And Daddy. I wasn't up to facing them yet. How I detested their little conspiracies. How I hated sharing him with her.

"How can you love her, Da? She's so self-centered and cold inside. I tell you, there's something missing there."

It's a conversation we'd had, in various disguises, countless times down through the years. As I grew older, I'd grown bolder.

"It breaks my heart, the way the two of you carry on," he always says peevishly. "Why can't you at least be civil toward each other? Would it kill you?"

"It might, Da. You don't know what she's really like."

"I don't want to hear that, Marly."

"Mr. Lockehead's office."

"Debby? It's Marly Mitchell. Is Chris in?"

"How was your trip to Mexico?" Her voice was child-like and high-pitched. We'd developed something of a phone friendship over the preceding months. "He's so closemouthed, hardly tells me a thing."

"The trip was lovely, Debby."

"I've never been to Mexico. My husband's not much of a one for countries where the people are short and dark-skinned and poor and the water is suspect."

"All the restaurants and all the hotels purify, Debby. As for the poverty, check out downtown Cleveland sometime. Or don't they tolerate the homeless in your fair state?"

"Oh, we've got 'em, all right. That's what I keep telling my husband. I know Mr. Lockehead will want to speak to you. Just let me buzz."

While she was off the line, that feeling of discomfort returned. I started to fidget.

"Marly? He's tied up. Wants to call you back tonight. Will you be in?"

"Yeah."

I remembered not so long ago when taking my call was the number one priority in Chris' life. He used to love to swagger out of some high-powered meeting to talk to me. My gut turned over, and I felt, suddenly, very tired.

"Kyla? Marly. I need a session."

"You're sounding a little draggy."

"The weight of the world."

"Come tomorrow night, after your appointment with Phyl."

"This is a conspiracy! You guys have Star Trek two-way communication, or what?"

"Daddy?" I said into my parents' answering machine, "it's Marly. I'll be home tonight. Mom'll be there too, so you guys can gang up on me. Hey, I know why you're calling, but I don't think I could take it if you yell at me. I love you."

It was a little after nine when the phone rang. I was already in bed, waiting for my mother to come home.

It was Daddy.

"I know what you're going to say, and I wish you wouldn't," I began.

I heard him sigh. "It's part of my job, Marly."

My father always had a thing about duty. It meant more to him than happiness. He'd never argued about paying child support for Jamie Sue, and he probably always suffered from a dire case of the guilts over leaving his first wife. You could sense a constant war in his soul between loyalty and happiness, coupled with a standard of ethics no mortal could live up to. He was fully committed to his responsibilities as a man in his culture, however distasteful those responsibilities might sometimes be to maintain. I think we all let him down terribly but not a tenth as much as he judged he'd let himself down.

"This is serious, Marly. I wouldn't be making this call unless I was convinced of that."

"You know how I feel about Jamie Sue, and I haven't changed my mind." I sat up and pounded the pillows behind my back, because I could already tell I was in for a siege. He had his heart-to-heart voice on.

I continued to defend myself. "If anything, that little episode in Mexico only strengthened my resolve."

"I don't understand it," he said. "It's such a little thing I'm asking."

"Are you crazy?" I said, feeling hotter. "You're asking me to take a rattlesnake into my bed."

"Marly, she's reaching out for your help. It doesn't have to be more complicated than that."

"Yeah? And you still refuse to believe that she intentionally pushed me through a glass door when I was five."

"It was an accident, a childhood prank. So many years ago ..." His voice trailed off.

"She was in high school at the time, certainly beyond the age of reason."

"I will not listen to this," he said finally. "I love you, but I don't understand you, Marly. You have such a capacity for kindness and yet ..."

I pictured him shaking his bowed head, eyes closed, hands spread and pressed down into the tabletop in front of him.

"Will you at least call her when the tests results come back?" He was pleading now. I hated to have made him do it.

I sighed. For him and for me and maybe even for Jamie Sue. "I'll think about it, Da."

"Marly?"

"Chris." I was just beginning to doze.

"You weren't asleep, were you?"

He sounded far away. All afternoon long, my spirits had banged back

The Cancer Club

and forth between certainty and doubt until all I felt was a knot of conflicting feelings. He often called just before he went to sleep. But this was different. Memories of our lovemaking came unbidden to my mind.

"No."

A long pause. Our pauses had been companionable once; this one was empty.

"I had a great time in Antigua," he said, slowly as a dream-walker.

My concentration faded in and out. I opened my mouth to speak but thought better of it.

"I've been thinking about you a lot since then," he added.

My heartbeat flipped into high gear. "Oh" was all I could manage. God, I felt vulnerable.

"You're an incredible woman, Marly. A gem of a woman. I always enjoy our time together."

He listened to me wait for him to continue.

"You know," he went on finally, "every time we've been together, our relationship has deepened, moved up to a new level."

Another long pause.

"Not this time, though. I ... I've been thinking about that, too." He sounded drained, as if the few words he'd spoken had sapped all his energy.

Did he expect me to commiserate here? To comfort him? That was the moment I stopped feeling uptight.

"What's this all about, Chris? Look, if you've got something important to tell me, just say it."

"You've been through a lot, Marly. I'd hate to think I was adding to your trouble."

"Don't flatter yourself."

That got him pumped up enough to let it fly. "It's just not going to work out between us. I wanted to fall in love with you. I tried. I didn't."

"Why?" I asked.

He was expecting a rain of tears and recriminations. If I'd railed through flinty dignity, he wouldn't have been surprised. But for some reason, my question took him completely off guard.

"What do you mean, 'why?'" He sounded confused.

"Think about it. You watched me like a hawk; you must have drawn some conclusions. I think I have a right to know what they are."

"I didn't watch you, and it's not anything specific," he said too quickly. "We don't control who we fall in love with."

177

"That's not true! We don't control who falls in love with us!" I gnawed on my right thumb's writer's callous. "You don't think I'm sane enough for you, is that it? I'm too needy? Too repulsive? Too scary?"

"Jeez, you must have been pissed to say that stuff," said Lisa, "and I thought I was emotional."

Eight of us founding members of The Cancer Club were sitting in a free-form circle in the basement of the Los Angeles Women's Center, though not all of us were women. Lisa's hair was still in a buzz cut, although she'd grown out one thin wisp in the back, which fell in a curl to just above her bra line, if she'd been wearing a bra, which she obviously wasn't.

After having become skinny almost to the point of incandescence, David had died two months previously. Big and tall Bill, from Jess's Tresses, had joined us shortly after I purchased my wigs. Ancient Scotty was still hangin' in there, along with five or six others who revolved in and out of the core group depending on their treatment schedules and the precarious states of their health. Martha Hughes popped in once in a while.

And Kyla; let us not forget Kyla. She of the expressive hands and the dramatic Persona with a capital "P." A woman who had the strange grace to reduce our most swollen and grotesque absurdities down to stumbling blocks so we could take a look at them.

"Pissed. Yeah." I grabbed another tissue and dabbed at my blotchy, tear-stained face. "I am so tired of being miserable. He thinks I'm insane. Can I blame him?"

"Why are you looking at yourself from his point of view?" asked Kyla.

I turned to face her. "What do you mean?"

"Well, you keep saying he was watching you, that you could feel him judging you from outside the feelings you had ... er ... have ... I don't know ... for one another. Did you start to watch yourself in the same way?"

That was a new thought. "Well, maybe," I said. "Maybe. I don't know. So what?"

"So maybe you bought a line of twaddle," Scotty said. "Sounds to me like this guy didn't have anything much to give, so he made damn sure he wasn't going to have to give it. That way, he couldn't be found out. Anyone can see you're on the mend." He shook his head. "Except you, fool."

"Emotional bankruptcy?" Kyla mused out loud. "Wasn't there a draining relationship somewhere in his recent past?"

I remembered the alcoholic. "There was. He met her just after he finished his own five years of group."

"Well, did he ever go back and get his anger out of his system?" Lisa asked.

"Not to mention the guilt," said Martha.

I thought about it some more. Suddenly the room was wonderfully quiet. That was the best thing about The Cancer Club: past the sarcasm and the dark humor and the cynicism and the fear, there was respect, a rocking-in-the-palm-of-God's-hand respect for the other guys' search. We might all bitch and moan about all the bitching and moaning that goes on in a group like ours as a matter of course. But when it comes time for The Truth, that rather spare and chilly room takes on the aspect of a country church during midnight service on Christmas Eve.

I spoke haltingly. "Chris thought he was finished with therapy. Of course, he'd assumed that many times over the years, but his therapist insisted he had more to do."

"Don't we all hope it's over every time we come?" asked Lisa.

I rolled my eyes at Kyla. Nobody laughed. "Apparently, his therapist finally agreed, because he quit and hasn't been back."

"Maybe his therapist got worn down. The nerve of that guy," Bill said.

"Chris or his therapist?" asked Martha. She sat off to the side and listened over her shoulder as per usual, knitting too fast for the naked eye to follow.

"Take your pick," Bill shot back. "You got two control freaks pushing each other along. From what Marly's told us, it sounds like everybody's so busy watching, they've forgotten about letting the feelings be."

I'd come to have a lot of empathy for the AIDS patients who belonged to Kyla's group. As a class of people, they weren't any better or worse than the rest of us. But the deadly virus was going to rob them all of every last shred of human dignity before it was done with them. They'd become emaciated, too weak to perform even the most simple or intimate tasks. Their friends and family would shun them. Their insurance companies would cut them off. Their obituaries would deliver the final coup by revealing to the world the grim outline of their struggle.

They came to the group, under a probable sentence of death, looking for a way to die that left them a sliver of humanity. I'm not sure we were of any help to them. In fact, and shamefully, the mere fact of their physical condition brought some comfort to us. We knew there were some things worse than death that we would be spared. I can't imagine how they faced a future so uncompromisingly bleak.

"It's a lot tidier, being with people who'll never need your help," Bill went on. "It's also selfish, cruel, egotistical, insensitive, and downright nasty." Bill smiled. He had a well-developed gift for character assassination.

"It doesn't sound much like he paid a lick of attention to the various women he supposedly ruined," Scotty said. "I mean, what were they really asking for? Not for him to control their lives, surely. He gave himself a lot of power, didn't he?"

Bill said, "It sounds like they were the ones giving him power."

A timid-looking woman named Cooky, with washed-out skin and self-cut hair, shifted in her chair. "I do that. Why do I do that?" She looked and sounded defeated. "I mean, I get a little self-confidence going, and this macho guy I run into sometimes at my son's little league games asks me why am I acting so tough all of a sudden, and I practically slink away."

"It just hit me," interrupted Martha, turning to face me, "that you slept with this Chris person and this Skip whatever within the space of a few days. That would confuse me. How did you manage it? Didn't you feel guilty? I would've felt guilty. Of course, I'm married ... a different generation ..."

"Hey, you guys, this is supposed to be my story," I said, peeved.

"So? Nobody's stopping you from telling it," Lisa commented, raising her eyebrows. To Martha, she explained slowly, "She didn't sleep with both of them. She slept with both of them, but she only slept with one of them. There's a big difference. And so what if she had?" Having asked the question, Lisa appeared to ponder it for a moment. "Sex isn't a federal crime. Well, not yet, anyway. This Reagan/Bush Supreme Court'll probably change all that."

Scotty smiled. "I don't know; half of them are too old to remember sex, and the rest are too conservative to enjoy it."

"No politics, please," Kyla said.

"I don't feel comfortable talking about sex." This was Cooky.

Lisa said, "You'll grow out of it."

It was all downhill from there, as the focus of the assembly shifted to wise-cracking.

"Wait a minute here!" called Kyla. "I said, wait a minute! Hellloooo!" She stood on her chair and flapped her arms gustily. "Okay! Listen up!" The

The Cancer Club

room quieted down. "That's better. I think it's time for a break. The natives are restless."

"Yeah," said Lisa, blowing smoke from the tip of an imaginary Colt .45, "let's reload."

Sometimes the free spirits act a little too spirited. I hated The Cancer Club the first four times I went. Now I love those people as though they were my children.

After the break, I was encouraged to continue. "What can I say? Physically, I can feel improvement almost every day. I see it in the mirror, thank God. But when do I start to get better? Why aren't I kicking up my heels? Why can't I be like I used to be?"

Cheryl, a new addition to The Club, cleared her throat. She hadn't contributed much yet; still scoping out the lay of the land. "Isn't there some kind of depression that sets in when you finish a long course of chemo?" she asked.

"I don't know," I said. I turned to Kyla. "Is there?"

Kyla looked around the room. "Does anyone have any experience with this kind of depression?"

Scotty said, "It's like losing your bulletproof vest in the middle of a riot. It's paranoia time. Hey, all you can do is wait to see what's gonna happen next."

Martha's knitting needles flashed and clicked. "You grabbed onto this life rope. It bloodied your hands and burned your muscles, but pulling at it, at least you were doing something. Really fighting the cancer. No more rope ... no more fight."

I shook my head. "Sometimes I think I might shatter. Sleeping with Chris might not have been such a good idea."

Cooky asked, "Because it didn't work out?"

"Because I liked it. Because I was hungry for it but not ready for it. And I hate the thought that Chris might, in some weird way, have understood this."

"Why?" asked Kyla. "Because he's a man?"

"Because he's ... dense and thick and cruel, but that didn't stop him from being right about me."

Martha, Kyla and I went for coffee after the meeting broke up. There was a jerky little dive just down the street on Cahuenga called "Pookie's." God knows how long it had been there; fifty years? Sixty? I can only say for sure that the matching cracked linoleum on the floor and tabletops had to have been part of the original decor.

We'd come into that joint twenty times at least. Pookie, bleary-eyed and about a hundred and ten years old, of indeterminate sex but seeming male-ish, sat in his usual place beside the cash register, working the New York Times Sunday crossword.

"Evening, Pookie."

He grunted, exactly the way he always did. From somewhere in the cafe's nether regions, a pale, dark-haired girl materialized. She took our order, as she always did, without speaking. Pookie's was the place to go when you needed to feel invisible.

We sat at a table in the back, next to the jukebox. I was an early-70's music junkie and popped in quarters by the carload.

"What did Phyl say?" asked Martha. She was stirring three teaspoonfuls of sugar into her half-decaf/half-regular.

"What can she say until the test results come back?" I chomped down on a heaping pile of greasy, crispy, skinny fries richly drizzled with mayo. "But it looks good."

They waited.

I said, "You know, I've never yearned to have children. But if this recent round of tests prove me to be sterile from the chemo, well ..."

I could see Kyla debating whether she should dig further. Instead she asked, "How can you eat that and not have it show up as saddlebags?" She wasn't a celery-munching diet freak, or anything, but she dug in and fought the battle of the bulge every day. She believed in walking briskly for thirty minutes four times a week and never touched fried foods.

See's chocolate was an entirely different matter.

I poked at my thighs. "When I squeeze my skin together here, I have lemon rind just like everybody else."

Kyla snorted. "Don't make me laugh. You have the best legs in L.A. County."

I snorted back, then sipped at my guava juice. Don't ask me why a place like Pookie's would have guava juice. "Olé. It doesn't taste like the fresh stuff at Casa Greca."

Kyla took my hand, which was cool and damp from the glass. "I'm rooting for you. I'll never be able to tell you how you've opened up my life."

I was confused. She was the one who'd opened up my life! "What are you talking about?"

Martha said, "She's talking about courage."

I looked at them and said, "I am so sniveling a coward."

Kyla patted me. "You'll probably never realize the good you've done."

Martha clicked her tongue. It made the same noise her knitting needles made when her fingers were really flying. I stopped chewing and took another sip of juice.

Martha studied the Formica and said, "That's what Kyla's talking about, you dufus. You touch our souls." She never looked up at me, but I could feel her emotion.

Kyla said, "Just for once, cast yourself in the hero's role, and let's get on with it."

Martha said, "There's always a place for the truth, especially the way you tell it."

Kyla nodded. She turned to Martha and said, "Marly wrote a poem about me once; did I ever tell you?"

Martha shook her head.

"I'll let you read it someday." She cupped her coffee with her palms and let the steam rise up into her face. "I've always been ashamed of how intensely I yearned to know how I appeared to others. I've made a fool of myself on scads of occasions, trying to find out. I guess I thought that if I knew how someone else saw me, I'd know what I really was." Kyla turned back to me. "You wrote my secret dream of myself." She looked beyond Pookie's for a moment. "I never told you that, did I? How did you know? How could you know? How did you ever dare give myself to me like that?"

My soul was filled with grace. At that moment, I knew that I was supposed to be a writer. For better or worse, richer or poorer, I was on the right path.

An idea for a book niggled at the back of my head. It was a tickling sensation. I scratched and thought and hoped for lightning to strike. It didn't.

But I could smell a storm coming.

Chapter 23

Since getting to Tucson from Los Angeles without stopping in Phoenix takes the cunning of Rommel, I'd left the particulars to my whiz-bang travel agent. It was much more expensive—I might as well have set fire to a couple of hundies. But I consoled myself that I'd make it up by flying out of Ontario and parking in their three-buck-a-day, rock-bottom, long-term lot.

I swing back and forth like that. I'll buy three designer blazers at Nordstrom's because they're on sale and then turn right around and wash my own car for two months. If I'm on a swing through New York to work with my editor on my latest manuscript and staying at a first-class hotel at their expense, I'll splurge and send all my laundry out with the hotel valet, a whoppingly expensive proposition. Then, I'll make a financial U-turn and not allow myself to open my honor bar or order room service. As you can see, I cause myself untold aggravation and self-inflicted financial neuroses.

Maybe it's because my income is generated, and therefore appears, sporadically. I often receive royalties on the number of books sold, or residuals from the theatrical or television play of films that have been adapted from my works. I call it "money from home," because it's always a windfall. I can't count on it or work it into my budget until after it's appeared in my mailbox, and therefore, already spent.

Maybe it's because, subconsciously, I'm afraid that one day I'll run out of book ideas. Or out of words, period. A blank computer screen or a blank page can send me into a rage ... or a coma. It can give me amnesia or fill me with self-loathing. That empty space awaiting my word-generation represents an unadulterated point from which to restart a portion of life, a second chance. It's an opportunity to rewrite ancient history or touch up yesterday. That kind of responsibility can sometimes seem wearing and daunting over the long haul. And I wonder sometimes if I'll crack like a fresh egg under the strain.

Maybe I'm simply a fruitcake looking for a place to psychose. Maybe eccentric is more on the mark. All I can say is that, at times, I can feel the rumble of my uncertainty rolling like thunder through the Hall of the Mountain King.

It wasn't all that great a morning. I had to fight some hellish traffic, which was going the wrong way to boot. You see, in Los Angeles, at certain proscribed times of the day, any heavy traffic should only be encountered in this direction, never in that direction. So when I ran up against wall-to-wall parked cars in the middle of the freeway going in that direction, I of course wished out loud that there'd been an accident.

I didn't mean that the way it sounds.

I still had plenty of leeway to make the plane by the time I'd found the lot and a parking place. I laid my three bags on the ground and prepared to lock up my Miata, when suddenly, like a bolt of lightning, I was forcefully struck on the head with this Brilliant Idea.

I can tell you, beyond the shadow of any doubt, that when you're in a hurry and you suddenly get a Brilliant Idea, immediate and total retrograde amnesia is the only state that will save you. Here's how it all came about:

I keep my cars clean; I always have. It makes me feel upright and conscientious, and I'm convinced the car runs better longer. But I seldom wash my car before leaving it at an airport, because it will only be encrusted with L.A. grunge by the time I return. Of course, I could leave it with a long-term valet. They deliver it to you curbside at baggage claim and wash it the day you come back. But whenever I travel, I'm usually in some ridiculous economizing mode, and I just park the damn thing and pray it doesn't get stolen.

As you know by now, I'd been flying around more than usual the preceding several weeks, and my car was beginning to look like something an Okie had driven cross-country during the 1930's Dust Bowl. So I'd had it hand-washed and waxed by Ernie, a stoop-shouldered Bandy rooster of a man who stuttered when he spoke and coaxed the paint on any vehicle to mirror-glossy.

Picture this: my luggage resting in a medium-sized heap on the ground. As I reached down to gather everything into my arms, I happened to catch sight of my face in my car's finish and decided I couldn't stand leaving this shining baby car to face total grime-out. I opened the trunk and retrieved my car cover.

It was breezy that day, a regular occurrence at Ontario airport. I placed the cover lovingly over my Miata, picked up my bags, and started for the nearest tram stop. For some reason, I happened to turn back, only to discover my car cover billowing toward Mecca. It was the wrong size, you see, having been a leftover from my previous model, a Honda Accord. Another cost-saving measure. That's when the Brilliant Idea struck.

Of course, my departure time was creeping up on me, but I still figured to make it easily. I quickly considered the dynamics of my dilemma logically. I somehow had to anchor the sides of the cover. Maybe, I thought, I could slam the trunk and the doors in such a way as to catch and secure the material.

No problem. Except ... except that one side still seemed a trifle loose. I unlocked the door, adjusted the cloth, and shut the door with some force. But for some reason, I couldn't get the door shut! I unlocked and relocked. I fiddled with the latch. I kicked the door and then I kicked the tires. Precious minutes ticked past. I started to sweat. I unlocked and relocked and pushed and prodded and watched the time sweep by on my second hand. What to do? Leave the car? Sure to be stolen. Cancel my flight? Ah ... but my ticket was non-refundable, and my Scrooge personality had firmly taken root within my soul.

To go or not to go? Tick, tick, tick, the seconds raced by. Why was God testing me? Or was She? My head started to ache while inside my blouse, sweat trickled down my chest. My scar itched. I was dying to scratch, but at that moment, a tram went by.

The hell with it! I started to run.

I was Secretariat, sweeping the Triple Crown. I was Satchel Paige, moving on out and never looking back. I was the Winged Victory. I was Joanie Benoit with a Flo Joseph kick.

I made the plane with two whole minutes to spare.

So why is it that when you really don't want to chat to the person sitting next to you, they come on like Phil Donahue?

He was some kind of a freelance oil rigger from Oklahoma named Bif (I swear) who worked with high explosives. He'd spent the night before trying to spring two of his crew members who were tossed in jail for starting a bar fight. He claimed he was a cousin to Garth Brooks and owned a small spread outside of Tucson. He'd never been married and still had nightmares about 'Nam.

I learned all this before we took off.

He ordered a bourbon and water and opened up a little. Holy cripe. My make-up was dribbling down my face in rivulets. The damp cloth of my blouse nicely outlined my breasts. Finally, I broke into his monologue by wriggling past him on my way to the head. His right knee was a little too friendly, his eyes bright with Johnny Walker and delusions of conquest. He may have been harmless, bottom line, but we were talking my bottom. When I inched back to my seat, I feigned sleep with such concentration that I actually fell asleep.

I had the lump nightmare and woke with a start. Bif had disappeared. Covered in sweat yet again, I went back into the lavatory and rinsed my face with cool water. The aft flight attendant knocked on the door tentatively.

"Are you ... OK?" she asked.

I felt dreadful, positively overflowing with anxiety. It was hard to get my breath. Something was pushing at me. I don't claim to be a seer, but I can recognize something pushing on me, something coming down the pike.

"I'm okay," I said through the locked door. "But if you'll fix me a Bloody Mary, I'll be even better."

I studied my face in the eensy-weensy mirror. In a matter of weeks, I'd have enough hair on my head to qualify as having hair on my head. I thought about burning my wigs. My Bridges. There was a knocking.

"Yes?" I asked.

It was Bif's voice. "Your drink's ready."

I sighed. "Be out in a minute."

An attendant brushed past me when I opened the door. "Want me to move him?" she asked quietly. "I'll put him on to Pat in first."

"What good would that do?"

"Pat's good at handling guys like him."

"Poor Pat."

"Don't worry," she said with a grin. "She's gay."

We both laughed. "That's okay. I'll take my punishment."

Sugar met me at the gate.

"It's nice of you to take time off the job," I said and hugged her.

"Are you kidding? I'm the best agent they've got, and they know it."

At that moment, Bif sloshed by. "Here's my card. You're welcome at the ranch any time."

Sugar watched him amble away. When she turned back toward me, I shrugged. "I'll tell you later."

"You lead such an interesting life."

"Riiight."

Sugar was lovely and blond, a short dumpling of a woman with pale blue eyes and lots of teeth in her smile.

"Hey, you're skinnier," I said and gave her another bear hug. She'd lost at least thirty pounds and looked ten years younger since the old coot had died. He'd been a mean drunk most of their married life, and it always amazed me how much of her innate decency she'd been able to hold onto. "How's that young man of yours?"

"Don't ask," she said and took my computer. "God, is this heavy. Baggage claim is this way."

"Sugar, I thought you two were in love."

"We are. But his old girlfriend just won't leave him alone. He swears it's over! But ..." Sugar sighed. "I don't know anymore. I am so glad you're here."

"Love is tough," I said.

"Don't do it!" she groaned.

"What? Don't do what?"

"You're gonna give me a lecture."

I lifted my eyebrows in indignation. "Me? I don't 'lecture.' I'm not the interfering kind."

"Hah!" she said with a snort. "You always stick your nose in. Now don't get huffy, Marly. With you, I think it's a calling."

She looked at me then, as we were folding ourselves into our seats, really looked at me for the first time. "You look tired. Here I was, carrying on and on." She reached over and touched my face. "Is everything okay with you?"

I hardly knew where to begin.

You might wonder, as I recount this saga, that all my friends were so miraculously understanding of and interested in my problems. This wasn't the case, of course. I had been very determined, when planning this pilgrimage, to spend time only with those folks who had enough grace left over from their own trials to lavish some on mine.

There were plenty who couldn't stomach the details of my recovery and many fewer who could summon up any compassion. It pissed me off at first. How could they care so little, these people who supposedly loved me? Didn't they know I might die? That I was desperate? That I couldn't bear to walk down this painful road alone?

I hated them, safe and smug in their well-cut lives. I hated their guilty faces and the way their eyes never rested comfortably on my grayed and stringy self. I hated their energy and their callousness. I hated their wholeness and haleness.

After some months with The Cancer Club, I see things differently. My struggle with cancer somehow evoked scary thoughts of their own mortality that made death seem like a nasty secret, like incest. It conjured up images in their minds of their funerals and the cold ground being shoveled over their coffin tops or their ashes being tossed to the four winds. They shivered and were glad it was me and not they.

How could I blame them when it was simply a matter of fear? Mr. Fear, whispering his silken betrayal. Knowing Mr. Fear intimately, having experienced his polished brand of seduction, I forgave them. Hadn't I felt the same way about the troubles of my own friends in the past? Yes, I forgave. But I hated coming to grips with how little my presence meant in the great scheme of things, how the shifting sands of the living universe might erase the footprints of my entire lifetime.

I started to cry.

Sugar glanced over at me often as she drove. We were near the airplane graveyard outside of the city. It's a huge, eerie-looking site, a final resting place for all United States military aircraft. Outmoded helicopters and crashed fighter jets, cargo planes damaged by enemy fire. Re-fitting and modernizing them, with an eye to selling to foreign governments or multi-national companies would have crushed the American aircraft market and damaged US steel output. And so, literally millions of tons of grounded flying machines sat on the desert floor, suffering the gathering sand and rust on their once-shiny frames.

It seemed like such a waste.

"Why don't you take off that damned wig? It's ninety degrees outside. I mean, you look so hot ... and I don't mean hot." She reached down under her seat and handed me a bottle of sparkling water.

I scratched at my head. "It's uncomfortable, I admit." I took a long swig.

"I can see the sweat dripping down the back of your neck, for Pete's sake!" she said with a laugh.

"Okay, okay, I'll think about it. Geez ..."

I looked out at the winged forms we were passing. I noticed their lonely dignity. They reminded me of the Native American women in R.C. Gorman paintings. I burped.

"Carbonation," I mumbled and burped again.

Sugar laughed hard.

The car sped on through the bleak, baking landscape, now well past the ocean of useless aircraft. As many times as I've been to Tucson, I couldn't begin to tell you how to get from the airport to the Westin Hotel. Looking back, I remember that we'd turned a corner and were driving through a rougher part of town. All used car lots, ramshackle houses, brownish lawns and unkempt children, sluggish in the billowing heat.

"Stop the car!" I yelled suddenly. "Stop!" I reached into my purse and got out my thin, square billfold.

Sugar gasped and stomped on the brakes. The car swerved and fishtailed. "God! Oh, my God!" she screamed.

I was out the door before the Jag shimmied to a stop just short of a cinderblock wall topped with barbed wire. "Call 911!" I yelled back over my shoulder.

I impatiently watched the line of passing traffic for a break. When one came along, I darted across the street to a junkyard surrounded by an eight-foot-high electrified fence. The gate had a "CLOSED" sign on it.

Just inside the fence, a group of young, tough-looking Mexican males were engaged in evil sport with three brindle-colored pit bulls.

The young men had set the dogs to fighting with one another. To ensure that the dogs behaved with appropriate ferocity, they kicked at the animals' legs and ribs with the toes of their pointed boots and hurled them occasionally by turns into the electrified fence. I could hear the thud of heavy leather striking bone and smell the stink of burning dog hair and flesh. They all laughed at the hilarity of the situation.

"I'm a US Deputy Marshal," I yelled as coldly and loudly as I could, waving my billfold like a badge cover. "You're all under arrest. I'm off-duty, and my gun is in the front seat of that automobile, and my jurisdiction is intact. We have radioed for back-up. If any of you so much as looks sideways at an animal, I will immediately retrieve my gun. I will not hesitate to use it."

My heart pounded. I could see them weighing me; I must have presented quite a sight. I was so enraged ... at that moment, I could have happily murdered them all.

I believe they sensed this.

The moment dragged out in slow motion. I memorized the details of their faces, etched with amazing and indelible precision like tattoos of observation. I hated them. I wanted to beat them to death with my bare hands. Through it all, the dogs yelped and whined.

One of the youths, seemingly the youngest, perhaps in his middle teens, opened his mouth. A snide look crossed his face. But before he could speak, the oldest and coldest-looking of them all, a beefed-up bully in his middle twenties with a scar bisecting his right cheek, made a decision and hissed something to the rest. Without another word, the gang slowly edged back away from the fence.

Quietly now, I said, "You leave those fucking dogs right there. Don't touch them again." Without turning toward the car I yelled, "Bring my gun!"

Just then, the wail of a siren scraped across the shimmering heat of the day. The young men turned and ran all in a row, like retreating British cavalry, leaving their poor dogs behind, yelping in the dirt of the foul-smelling, garbage-strewn yard. I began to cry violently as I watched the bruised and bleeding animals writhe in their suffering.

Chapter 24

I made a statement to Captain Bud Griscoe of the Tucson police later that day.

"You could have been killed," he said casually, not taking his eyes from the standard complaint form in front of him. He was making some final amendments in pencil. "They often carry guns, you know. And knives. We're not talking monks. These guys're not into good works; they're into violence."

"What'll happen to the dogs?" I said. A shiver tiptoed up my spine as I leafed through the fourth heavy, plastic-covered book full of mug shots.

"They'll have to be destroyed. We call it 'meaning a dog up.'" A pit bull like that'd never attack its master, the one who tortured it. But someday, some little child will step on the dog's tail ... and get her throat ripped out. There's no way to reliably rehabilitate an animal like that." He shook his head.

Sugar sat slumped on a faded leatherette sofa behind me. Her spirit seemed to have oozed out.

I'd stopped crying by the time I arrived at the station, but I couldn't seem to stop shivering. "Could we get some cold caffeine and sugar in here, Captain?" I asked.

"I can arrange that." He ordered three Pepsis over the intercom line of his telephone. "You look like you could use a little hair of the dog." Realizing what he'd said, he had the grace to grimace and lift his hands in apology.

When his assistant brought the drink cans in on a tray, accompanied by a bowl of ice, Griscoe produced a small bottle of light Bacardi from his bottom drawer. "Medicinal purposes," he advised. "Just a touch to revive the spirit."

"Isn't this slightly illegal?" I asked.

Captain Griscoe turned his wrist over to show me his watch face. "Actually, I was off-duty twenty minutes ago." He poured, stirred, and sipped. "That was a brave thing you did. Incredibly stupid, but brave."

"Stupidity: the stuff heroes are made of, I guess." I shrugged like I confronted armed gangs every day.

Sugar swirled her drink around in her glass. "Can you believe it? I never saw anything like that in my life. Marly, you could've starred in *Alien 3*."

She stared at the liquid in her glass for a moment. "Why is this tasting so good? I don't even like rum."

I studied Griscoe. He was a tall, square man with ginger-colored hair. Solid. His smile was deceiving: so open and hearty on the face of things, there was a tough edge underneath it. A good man to have with you in a dark alley. He inspired confidence. His presence was comforting.

"You look exactly like a policeman." I paused over a photograph and looked into his open face. "I meant that as a compliment."

He nodded. "It's all I ever wanted to be. You find something?"

"This man was the leader." I slanted the book in his direction.

"Let's see ... page 146, number 7a. Okay. No question?"

"No question." I closed my eyes. "I'll never forget that face. Aside from the scar across his nose, I think it was the nothingness in his eyes ... a numb cruelty."

"Find anyone else?"

"No," I said and closed the heavy volume. When I moved to lay it back on his desk, it came off the dried sweat of my bare legs with a hiss.

"Would you be willing to come back and make an ID? Help us out at the trial? Presuming we get a go-ahead from the D.A.'s office, of course."

"You mean there's a chance that son-of-a-bitch won't be prosecuted?" Sugar asked indignantly. The drink was shoring her up.

Griscoe's chair creaked with his bulk as he leaned back. "The courts are full. Public endangerment isn't a felony. Still, he broke his parole." Griscoe smiled. "Oh, we'll get him. He's a three-peat."

I closed my eyes and thought about those poor dogs. "Will those other men ... go to jail?"

Griscoe's smile widened to grin status. "Even if we have to make it up as we go along." He stood up and reached out his hand across his desk. "Thanks. We'll be in touch." He turned and shook hands with Sugar. "You see to your friend here. She obviously needs tending."

Sugar hung her head to the right. "Bif? His name was Bif? Honestly! You make these people up."

"I resent that! I tell you, I could not get rid of the man. You saw him. Any moment now, I expect to find him peeking through that window, jabbering away, finishing up with the one three-month timespan he hasn't already told me about his life."

"Why do they all have southern accents?"

"Hell, I don't know."

I was lazing in a hot, bubble-filled bath whilst sipping champagne in a spiffy suite at the Westin La Paloma. Sugar'd stocked my room with a couple of iced bottles of Perrier-Jouët. Yum. She'd dragged two plump couch cushions onto the bathroom floor and was lounging and sipping while we kept company. We avoided speaking about the incident at the junkyard.

Conveniently, I suddenly remembered my little Miata disaster.

"You mean to say that you left your car agape—open in an airport parking lot?" Her eyes popped out of her head. "You just walked away and left it there?"

"What was I supposed to do?"

"Isn't there someone you can call?" she scolded. "Some security people or the airport police, or something? Marly …"

"Hand me the phone."

After trying for twenty minutes to locate someone willing to admit jurisdiction in the matter, I gave up.

"See? Now I'll have to pay for all those 'hotel-assisted' telephone calls, and it didn't do a damn bit of good. No doubt one of those jerks we spoke to will steal the damn thing. Are there any nuts in the honor bar? I'm starving."

"Only nut I can see is the big one in the bathtub."

We snacked on smoky almonds and a package of chocolate chip cookies.

Sugar waved the penultimate pack of Famous Amos vaguely at the steamy tub. "Feeling better?" she asked with a full mouth.

I nodded. "Except for the crumbs in the water; they itch. You?"

"Well enough to talk a little." She swallowed the last bite of cookie and brushed the crumbs off of her lap. "God, the stress. I hate love."

"So what's with this asshole?" I asked with my usual diplomacy.

Sugar is a well-off woman in her early fifties. After a twenty-seven-year nightmare marriage to an abusive alcoholic, she found herself an early widow with a sizeable inheritance. For the past ten months, she'd been seeing a younger man, a railroad brakeman who was, at that time, being paid good money not to work.

Sugar sighed. "He's not an asshole. At least, I don't think he is. I mean, I don't want to get married, or anything, so why should I care that she's wormed her way back into his life? He swears he hates the whole business."

I snorted. "In the first place, not wanting to get married and having a man all to yourself are not mutually exclusive. Don't you think you deserve to have your very own man? In the second place, him having her stay at his house, her being invited to his mother's birthday and you not ... her being invited to his sister's wedding and you not ... that's not her worming her way back in. That's him dragging her back in. Besides," I said, piercing her with my most Serious Look and popping a handful of nuts into my mouth, "I never heard of a man who got tired of two women fighting over him."

"I sent his mother the most beautiful birthday bouquet." She frowned. "I swore over and over I'd never fall in love again. I tell you, Marly, we have an absolute ball together. I never had as much fun with anybody else."

"On trips that you pay for, which he could never afford on his own," I pointed out.

"He's so precious. Everyone says we're darling together."

"In public. They also pull you aside and ask you what the hell you're doing with a man who's obviously using you."

Sugar sighed again. "I never had a climax until I met Bert."

"Hell, Sugar, that's the first remotely telling argument in his favor you've brought up. Hand me that towel, will you?" I took the fluffy sheet and rubbed my body vigorously. "Look, Sugar, I love you, but I want you to really look at this ... relationship. Don't pull a pretty pastel coverlet over anything. Don't hide any toxic creatures under a rock. When you have all the facts, you can do what's best for you. Hey, what if you didn't take him on any expensive trips for a few months? Would he still be hanging around?"

Instead of answering, she said, "I love him to death. I wish I didn't." She sipped some more. "I like your hair that length. Why don't you slap some gel on it and forget the damned wig tonight?"

I studied myself in the full-length mirror. "I don't know ..." I flapped my arms. "Ooooh, how I hate this dangling underarm part."

She grinned. "You think your underarms dangle ..."

We had a contest to see who could jiggle what gravity-laden body part the most.

"I just love being middle-aged," I said with as much overblown sarcasm as I could muster.

"You're always so ready to give me advice about changing my life." She saw me open my mouth to protest and cut me off. "Give it up, girl. I mean it. You're pounding away at something. Just give it a rest once in a while. Hell, you gotta be able to take it as well as dish it out."

I sniffed and started to say something ... sarcastic ... and changed my mind. Instead, I stepped closer to the mirror and turned my head in every direction.

"I suppose you could get along without any man at all for years and years." Sugar sounded reflective.

"You've always had an optimistic opinion of my self-discipline. Are you sure my hair looks all right?" I patted my neck. "I feel buck naked."

"For the hundredth time, you look f-i-n-e. Will you please stop fiddling?"

"Sugar, it hasn't been anywhere near a hundred times." I reached into my purse and got out my compact. As I studied my face critically in the dim light, I said, "Nobody's requiring you to become a nun. I only said it might be better to be alone than to be with some lousy man." I stuck my chin out. "Hell, they might as well call me Lantern Jaw."

"You look like a singer in a heavy metal band, with a better wardrobe. Bert is not a lousy man. Oh, shit, I don't know what kind of a man he is."

Then we were in her limo, toodling down the road on our way to dinner. Greg the chauffeur had quietly put the window up between the back seat and front when our conversation'd taken a more personal turn.

"Where're we going?" I asked.

"Daniel's. Pasta, pasta, pasta. It's one of the best restaurants in town."

"What about Tina and Serena?" I asked as I poured myself a glass of wine and noticed I was drinking a lot.

"They'll catch up with us at Burkie's."

Tina from nearby Douglas, Sugar's oldest and dearest friend, and Serena, a local TV newswoman. While I only knew Tina through Sugar, I'd appeared on Serena's *Women Today* show a couple of times in the past to promote my books. Her name means "serene," which is a laugh. She's pureed dynamite, all four-foot-ten of her.

Daniel's is an oasis of elegance in the Southwestern desert, a restaurant you wouldn't be surprised to find in San Francisco, or even New York. It's on the intimate side. The linens are weighty, and the ambience is muted action; you can smell the old money in the room. It narrowly escapes being too status quo for two reasons—first: the food, which is zestfully seasoned and a touch on the unusual side and second: Daniel, Himself, the proprietor.

"Sugar! Always a pleasure," Daniel greeted my friend, sweeping a low bow. He's of indeterminate European extract, short, bullish and graceful in the extreme. His neck is short enough to appear invisible to the naked eye. He could have been a bouncer, probably had been, or a weight-lifter. A bouncer who'd taken an extended ballet course. A weight-lifter who looked like he was born in an Italian three piece raw silk suit.

When Sugar introduced us, he turned more formal. I wouldn't have been surprised to see him click his heels. He sat us in an alcove and immediately brought a large plate overflowing with exotic antipasto.

"All your favorites, my sweet darling."

"How do you always remember?" she asked.

I suddenly found I was starving. "Wow! Wow! This is beautiful!" I speared a Greek olive and asked, "Where are you from? I don't place the accent."

He gestured to include The Universe. "Here and There. I think of myself as a Citizen of the World." I could almost hear the Capital Letters in his speech.

"Can I get you two something to drink?"

We ordered and Daniel strutted off to place the order himself. I glanced around the room and took in the soft gray walls and the charcoal Berber carpets. Occasionally, my hands wandered up to fiddle with my hair, what there was of it.

"Would you put your hands down, please?" Sugar said. "My God, you're acting like you've got Tourette's syndrome." She ate three pickled cherry tomatoes. "Now, how long do I have to give up sex for?"

"Who said anything about sex?"

"You will, sooner or later. Them that can't, teach."

"That's not funny."

I know, I know ... My life was a confusion of men, all of them driving me crazy. And none of them in my bed. What the hell did I know?

I began to complain out loud. "My feelings for Chris were never chemical. They grew out of our correspondence, which was the thing about that relationship that pisses me off the most." I bit down on a small pepper. "I did the mature, adult thing—actually taking some time to get to know the man. And where did it get me? To Heartbreak Hotel."

"Maybe we should confine ourselves to window shopping from now on," she said and glanced around. "Hmmm."

"What?"

"See that guy at the bar?"

"No."

"Marly ... Don't be difficult. Right there. Auburn hair. Trim. Sweet-looking. Now that's exactly the kind of man you need."

Okay, I admit it, I had noticed the man. He was nice-looking, in a corn-fed sort of way. "Too naïve, Sugar."

"How can you tell by just looking?"

"I can tell. Of course, he could be a psycho."

"Marly, if he was a psycho, you'd be attracted to him for sure."

"Crap and double crap!" I hissed.

"What in the hell is the matter now?" Sugar asked as though I'd been getting on her nerves for the past hour.

"I have a hole in the back of my head. Don't look! Just glance in the mirror casually. Casually. See?" I put some quiet heat into my voice. "It looks like I have a hole in the back of my head. There isn't any hair!"

"Oh, for God's sake, have a conniption. Lean over this way. Turn your head. It's a tiny little separation. There. All fixed. You look perfect. Okay?"

My eyes darted back across the room to The Man. He had a clean profile. I couldn't see his eyes, but his skin was peaches-and-cream and scrubbed-looking. Dressed in western duds, his stone-washed, snug-fitting Wranglers hung cunningly on a lanky frame. He was sipping something dark in a tall glass and keeping to himself. There was a lovely stillness about him.

"Miss Mitchell?"

I was startled out of my daydream and spurtzed some wine onto the tablecloth.

"You are that Valkyrie from this afternoon?" the familiar-looking man said, taking the napkin from the top of the bread basket and mopping up my little mess. Huh? I couldn't place him. Not for the life of me.

Sugar dismissed me with a wave usually reserved for a dim-witted relative. "Captain Griscoe," she said, "what a nice surprise. What're you doing here?"

He glanced quickly at my head and answered Sugar with a grin, "Police captains make enough in salary to come here, oh ... once a year. Besides, Daniel gives law enforcement a deal on the bread."

Sugar laughed at herself. "I didn't mean that the way it sounded. Could you join us for a drink?"

Oh, great. I grabbed my skirt to keep my hands from flying to the top of my head.

His gaze swept the room. "Actually, I'm meeting someone. J.D.!" he called out.

Was God about to play one of Her little jokes?

Another ginger-haired, scrubbed-faced stranger waved back.

Oh, great.

J.D. Griscoe turned out to be the Captain's younger brother. He was a builder by trade, who I discovered had recently handed over most of his accumulated net worth to his ex-wife in a bitter child-support settlement. I could see the pain in his eyes, hiding behind his smile.

He was also suffering the effects of the recession. At least he made one or two quiet jokes about concrete prices and flaky buyers. Then, "I thought about moving away ... trying Florida. There's a building boom in Florida, believe it or not. But my girls are here." He shrugged. "That's good enough for the present." He shook his head at himself. "Sometimes, I want to get in my truck, kick up some dust, and ride into the sunset."

The conversation was interesting, occasionally lively. J.D. was watchful. Open-faced like his brother, but more content to sit back sometimes. Delicious.

Sugar asked J.D. how long he'd been married.

"Twelve years. One day, she just said she'd fallen out of love and felt the need to move on. Gave her the cars and the house. I just took enough to give myself a leg up. Here I am, at forty years old, starting all over again."

"Think of all that garbage you won't have to get rid of in a garage sale," I said.

"There is that."

A strange peace settled over me. I even felt comfortable enough to lightly mention my recent emotional struggles.

"Hey, I'll show you mine if you show me yours." He took my chin in his finely-made hand and said, "A car accident. On top of the divorce. A little lucky to be alive." His smile spread slowly over his face. "Very lucky." He tapped at his head. "Doesn't quite work the same as it used to."

"That's okay," I answered. "Neither does mine. At least you have hair."

Suddenly, the last year of my life seemed like nothing more than that—life. I felt my world shift to the left.

Bud asked, "So how long are you here?"

"She's visiting till next week, unless I can persuade her to stay longer," Sugar answered.

J.D. said, "But that's perfect." He turned to Bud. "Did you get your weekend off? We could all ... tourist it up, or something." He trailed off and got a shy look on his face. "Ooops, wait a second. You guys might have made plans. Girl things. Wait! That wasn't supposed to sound like a put-down." He ran his fingers through his hair distractedly. "Or a come-on. I'm a little out of practice."

Bud rolled his eyes. "Rusty as a two-hundred-year-old nail."

J.D. turned to Sugar and said, "I don't want to horn in ..."

"Like hell you don't," Bud said with a laugh.

J.D. gave his brother A Look. He continued, "... But I'm not responsible for my behavior. I mean, I am ... but I don't ... I can't ... " He glanced at me.

I couldn't say which of us blushed the brighter red.

"Let me try this again." He cleared his throat. "I usually keep a serious work schedule and see my kids whenever I can. But since my kids are away on vacation, and since there isn't any serious work to speak of, I'm thinking maybe I ought to reward myself. For what, I don't know." J.D. turned to me. "Anyhow, I'm a fan of country music, and I've been promising myself I was gonna learn to dance the Texas Two-Step. You like to dance country?"

"Not really," I answered. "But I think I might like to learn."

Too suddenly, it was time for us to head off to Burkie's and the music of the Blue Lizards, where Tina and Serena would already be waiting.

Bud picked up the tab. He probably always picked up the tab. After all, he was The Big Brother. He walked Sugar to her limo, and J.D. took me by the arm.

"You know, I'm not usually attracted to women who wear their hair shorter than mine ... But I never met a writer before." He gave me that shy smile again. "You're a pretty gal." He took my hand and kissed my palm. "You never barrel raced, did you? Along with the tennis and golf? Cause if I ever found a woman who'd spun a quarter horse on its ear, I swear I'd be in love forever."

I shook my head no.

"That's okay. Can I take you to breakfast? I live right near the Westin. Pick you up any time you say."

I felt like I was being carried along by a steady current over which I had little control.

"Hmmm."

"That's a yes. Great."

I took his hand. "It must have been awful, having her leave you like that. Then, with the accident, on top of everything else ... You seem to have recovered so well. I wish I could say the same."

He cocked his head. "Don't you believe it. There are still times I want to crawl into a hole and die. But I kept thinking I might run into someone ... How does the song go? Who wants what's left of me? Besides, life's too short to be with someone who doesn't want to be with you."

I peered into his face. "Should I trust you?" I asked.

"Don't know yet."

We arranged that he'd meet me in the lobby at nine A.M. sharp.

As Bud shook my hand good-bye, he whispered, "He'd make a great catch."

I whispered back, "I'm not looking to catch anything."

Chapter 25

Burkie's was a mass of teeming humanity. The pool tables were full up, and the rowdies at the bar were hipbone-to-hipbone. We wisely left our fur coats in the limo and pushed our way through the crowd at the door. Squeezing along, we finally spotted our pals at a microscopic table.

"Yoo-hoo!" Serena yelled above the din. Boy, did she look out of place, dressed anchorwoman-style in a dark suit and four-inch heels. This made her nearly the same height as Tina, who was seated.

"You made it!" she said with a laugh and threw her arms around me.

Tina stood and drew herself up slowly to her full Amazonian stature. The combination of her hair, which she wore short but spiky on the top, and the stiletto heels on her pointy shoes raised her to six-foot and something. She was literally head and shoulders above the crowd.

Tina thrust out her long, skinny arm and shook my hand across the tops of the empty beer bottles she and Serena'd accumulated while waiting for us. "Marly," she said, her usual curt self.

She wasn't unfriendly, exactly; maybe brisk is more accurate. I wondered if she was a bit jealous of my relationship with Sugar, though she would've died before admitting to anything so ... small-minded.

The Blue Lizards, who specialize in classic rock 'n roll, were driving the beat on "I Heard It through the Grapevine." The harmonies were tight, and the familiar melody made my feet sneak to heel-toe tapping.

At one point, a couple of inebriated baby-faced Navy pilots, their scalps shining through their buzz cuts, tried whispering tequila nothings into my ear. Serena thought this was hilarious.

"Go for it, Marly!" she whispered. "They have even less hair than you!"

"Very funny," I shot back. I'd pushed them to the next table. "I'm not into threesomes this year. Besides, I'm almost old enough to be their mother."

"At least they were tall," Tina said.

We all danced until we were soaked and then we danced some more.

The Cancer Club

It was well after midnight when we stumbled out to the parking lot.

The cold air hit us hard, whiplashing us out of our sweaty intoxication. Serena and Tina followed us to Sugar's house, which sat on the high ground of the Ventana Canyon Resort. It wasn't palatial exactly, but it did boast floor-to-ceiling glass on the south side. The view of Tucson spread out at our feet snatched the breath right out of my lungs.

"I always feel like they decked out the city just for me," Sugar said. "You know, if I turn out these lights, I can see the Milky Way. Wait a minute ... Doesn't J.D. live somewhere near here?"

"No. Absolutely not." I thought I sounded plenty firm.

"Now I am sure that's what he said," Sugar pushed and then added, "When did you ever get so shy?"

"I don't feel shy. He's ... Okay, okay, I feel shy." I realized that I meant it and wondered at myself.

"I hear his legs are as long as mine," Tina said.

"He's a precious man," Sugar paid her highest compliment. "And he even has backbone!"

Tina said, "I hate you. Why do you always get all the good, tall men?"

"You've obviously forgotten my relationship history for the past umpteen years."

"Well, I think we should try to find this Mr. J.D. Whatever," Tina persisted. "It might be fun. Maybe he'll sweep you off to a castle in the sky."

I sighed. "I vote for the light show outside," I said, trying to steer the conversation to shallower waters. "I remember my first clear look at the Milky Way. I was in Hawaii, walking across the golf course at the Hilton in Lahaina, on my way to Whaler's Village. The sound of the wind rustling through the palm trees made me want to lie down on the grass and listen, which is exactly what I did. And that's when I saw it."

I walked into Sugar's kitchen and grabbed some chocolate chip cookie dough from the freezer. I sliced off some pieces and handed them around. "The skeleton of our galaxy is huge and delicate, like a fairy-lit spider's web arced across the night sky. I stared up for twenty minutes at least and would've stayed longer, except that the sprinklers came on and ruined my dress. It was worth it!" I frowned. "You can't see the Milky Way in Los Angeles these days."

"It makes a person stop and think about the so-called benefits of progress," Sugar said, licking her fingers. She reached for another blob of dough. "Why is this stuff better raw?"

Stretched out in our winter coats on comfy outdoor furniture, with a glorious light show above and below, we settled ourselves in for a woman-thing chat.

Serena was the only currently married member of our group. We all agreed that her husband, Tom, was truly a saint, as her business life kept her away from the home fires at least six days a week. Yet he never complained.

"Doesn't he get antsy?" Tina asked. "Won't he be angry that you've stayed so long tonight?"

"Maybe he needs the rest," I said.

Serena ignored me. "We've ... talked about it. But he knew exactly the person I was when we married. It helps that he's independent, too—has his own friends."

"I couldn't be so hang-it-all-out," Tina said. "Men get into trouble when they run in packs."

Serena explained, "I'm not his warden, and anyway, marriage isn't a prison sentence."

"Then how come it usually feels like one?" asked Sugar, which made us all laugh.

"Serena, if something happened to Tom, would you get married again?" I asked.

She never hesitated. "No way. I'd never find anyone patient enough ... or young enough to train." Her grin ebbed. "Truthfully? I don't know if I'd have the energy or the unbridled optimism to make the investment again." She leaned in my direction. "Why do you have such a thing against marriage, Marly? What is it that terrifies you so?"

"That's easy: Men go through a terribly difficult stage ... somewhere between nine and death. Hey, I'm not saying it isn't a great institution. I'm just not sure I want to live in an institution."

"That's a nice, flip answer," Tina said.

"Hey," I said again, "you stand up there in front of God and a bunch of relieved relatives and cynical friends and swear you'll love the guy no matter what. You stick it out through drug addiction, promiscuity, physical abuse, distance, and sometimes simply plain old loutishness. I couldn't make that promise with a clear conscience, and know I could keep it for all the coals in Newcastle. I'd do better running my finger, blindfolded, down the 'M' listings in the white pages, bonking the guy over the head, and dragging him back to my cave."

"What if you were sure he was a nice guy before you fell head over

The Cancer Club

heels?" Tina asked.

"Don't be stupid, Tina," I said, a little heat in my voice. "When was the last time you found a man who was willing to make a real effort After the Fall?" I thought about what I'd just said and sighed. "I've become so prickly over the years, I draw my own blood."

"What is that thing about two porcupines making love?" Sugar asked. It should have been funny, but no one laughed.

The conversation lulled. I glanced at myself in the window behind me. "How do you like this hair?" I asked blithely.

One of these days, I'll learn to be more careful with my questions.

"I think it's awful," Tina said. "It makes you look ... awful."

"Tina ...," Sugar said, "I told her to wear it that way."

But the tall woman shrugged her friend off. "God, she always has to tell us about it. Or show us. Whatever it is. Hair. Unrequited love. Cancer. That hole in her boob, for God's sake. She has to make fun of it." She stared at me. "Your life doesn't look so bad to someone like me." She stuck her jaw out.

I felt my face flush. "Hey, no problem. I'm sick of myself, too; sick to death." I laughed convincingly. "Be back in a sec."

Sugar stood up, but I motioned her off with a smile. "Look, I'm tired and therefore about to rain on this nice parade."

Tina said, "Marly ..."

"It's okay. You're probably right ... I just can't deal with it right now."

As the limo worked its way down the snaking road, I opened the moon roof and gazed upward. Tina'd struck a nerve. Why did I have to make sure that everyone knew why I was so unpleasant, why I was such a mess?

I stood up through the opening and drank in the crystal air. As the cold felt fresh tickled my skin, I wondered if this might be the least fouled-up my life would ever be again.

Now there was a scary thought.

I looked up into the Great Beyond and said a little prayer under my breath. "Dear God, I don't know what else to do. I have tried so very hard to get better. But all I feel is lonely and beat-up. Could you help me? I wouldn't ask unless it was really, really important."

I didn't hear an answer.

The phone was ringing when I got back to my room. I waited until it stopped, then dialed the front desk. "Please hold all calls until eight A.M. tomorrow morning, at which time I'll need a wake-up call. Thanks."

J.D. was prompt. He pulled up in front of the lobby just as I got there. "I'm glad you decided to come," he said with a mile-wide grin. "We can eat here if you like, overlooking the golf course. That way, when Sugar comes in, she can join us." He peered into my face. "Are you hung over? Or is it something else? You look tired."

"Thanks."

His face clouded over. "I only meant ..."

I patted his hand. "I know what you meant."

He said, "I didn't sleep too well, either. Scotch goes down smooth, but it sweats out painful. Let's be lazy-ass and drive."

As I climbed into the front seat of his red pick-up, the concierge ran out. "Ms. Mitchell! So glad I caught you. Serena Estevez is on the phone. It sounds important. You can take it at my desk."

Without preamble, Serena asked, "How are you?"

"Gun-shy."

"I feel terrible, Marly."

"Why? You didn't do anything."

"I hopped onto the bandwagon."

"It's a big bandwagon."

"Sugar was teed. She and Tina got into it afterwards."

"Ooooh," I said. "Sorry I missed the fun."

"Ooooh, the sarcasm. You're getting too good at sarcasm."

"You can never be too good at sarcasm," I said cheerfully. "Is there something else on your mind?"

Serena's next guest for Women Today had cancelled last-minute. "Uncontrollable at both ends, with this flu thing going around, and absolutely positively unable to get here tomorrow for the taping," Serena explained. "Can you please pull my frijoles out of the fire and do the show? Please?"

"But what'll we talk about?"

"The new book?"

"Not close to being finished."

"Superstitious?"

"Youbetcherass."

"Fair enough." There were thirty awkward seconds of silence before she continued, "I'm late for an appointment down at City Hall. I'll find you later, and you can help me think of a replacement."

I slapped my hand on the concierge's desk, startling the poor man. "Okay, okay, you've out-guilted me."

"Good! You're a doll! An absolute doll! I promise I won't put you on the spot."

Riiiight.

"What's it like doing a talk show?" J.D. asked as we settled onto our lawn chairs at the edge of the clubhouse patio. The narrow, hilly green of "Lumpy Loma's" eighteenth fairway rolled away below us like hand-scissored carpeting. "I think my tongue'd wind up in knots."

"It's easier than it looks, especially with someone seasoned like Serena. She does her homework."

"Listen, little Miss Smartypants, you have to be brave to talk about yourself in front of millions ..."

"Thousands ..." I interrupted. "And that's stretching it."

"Well ... tens of thousands of viewers. I couldn't talk on television to some stranger about grades of gravel, much less personal stuff. How do you know what to say?"

"I don't," I answered truthfully.

He whistled a salute. "It doesn't seem ... I don't know, seemly."

The waitress came and took our order.

When she'd gone, J.D. went on. "It's funny, but for some reason, you don't feel like a stranger. I have this crazy feeling that I could tell you the truth."

I waited while J.D. rolled this over in his mind. Finally he said, "I never played around on my wife. Not once."

I nodded.

"Women have this idea that marriage ought to be romantic over the long haul. I'd like to think that was possible, but what actually happens has a lot more to do with how often life ... gets in the way. Colicky babies. Back injuries. A big monthly nut during lean times. I know about these things."

He leaned back a little, warming up to his own story. "Eventually, we settled into a routine. I liked it. My baby girls came. My business was booming. Eventually, I went out on my own and made even more money. Then life got more difficult, but I figured that's the way it's supposed to be." He lifted his left eyebrow and said, "This is the shortened, good-parts version, you understand."

I nodded again.

"Then Judy—that's her name, Judy—she started to get bored, I guess. She went back to school and got a part-time job, and the kids went to day care in the afternoons. I hated that."

"Studies show that the children of working moms are more outgoing and independent ..."

"And happy mommies make happy babies. I know, I know."

"Then what?" I asked.

"I hate to think it was all man ego." He turned toward me. "I could feel her getting restless."

The waitress brought our food, and J.D. picked at it while he talked.

"I didn't know how to ... tell her. I tried to stop her from getting so far away, but I couldn't admit that I needed her. I could only criticize. Then one day, she announced it was time to leave, and she thought it was me who should do the leaving."

"Just like that?"

"Just like that."

"Was there somebody else?"

"She hadn't slept with him yet, but she wanted to be free to try it." I could see the pain in his face. "So I went to my daughters and told them Judy'd found someone she liked. That their mother wanted to date the guy to find out exactly how much. And we had to let her."

"You didn't ... I don't know, fight for her?"

"Life is too short to be with someone who doesn't want to be with you." He gave a grunt. "They can put it down on my tombstone when the time comes."

"It would have devastated me," I said.

J.D. grinned. "Someday soon, I'll tell you all about the hospital I checked into where they take away your razor blades and shoelaces."

"Wow" was all I could manage.

I started to eat then and found I was ravenous. J.D. nodded approval and said, "That's good. I don't trust a woman who thinks food is her enemy. Have another biscuit."

Sugar caught up with us during dessert. She was smart enough not to go into any gory details of the night before, but she did give me one of her "Are you sure you're okay?" looks. I leaned across the table and squeezed her hand, which seemed to satisfy her.

"Well," she said, "my work's done till later, my dears, and I am ready to play." She stared at the littered table. "The two of you couldn't possibly have eaten all of this food."

J.D. patted his stomach. "Every last morsel."

Sugar turned to me. "You'd better give him a tennis lesson before all that butter lands on your thighs."

"I haven't played tennis in a dog's age," J.D. said. "I won't remember which end of the racket to use."

Which wasn't too far off the money.

J.D. was wild. You could tell he had good coordination and reasonable reflexes. But he set a record for the most balls struck on the racket frame for a non-blind player.

"Oh, shit," he mumbled every five or six shots. "Now I remember why I quit." Zing! Over the fence. Bam! Middle of the net.

It's impossible to play tennis when you're laughing your head off.

"Okay, okay! I've had enough!" he cried. "I want a cigarette for the first time in three years. Really punish myself. Can you imagine?"

"Marly just gave them up herself." I started to protest, and Sugar pointed her finger at me. "Yes, you did, Marly, even if you didn't mean to. She's hardly been bitchy at all."

"Thanks a lot, Sugar."

That night, Sugar treated Tina and me to dinner at the Westin. A peace pipe ceremony.

Tina glared at me, and I pretended to ignore her. Sugar rolled her eyes and looked eager to throttle us. Finally I leaned over and grabbed one of Tina's big hands. She squirmed, but I held on.

"Of course, we could put on the boxing gloves," I said. She hung her head in truce. "I admit I get waaaay off course sometimes. But let's not let my self-pity and your rudeness ruin a good party."

She clicked her tongue. "You're not nearly so bad off as you think, Marly. I get mad at you sometimes, because you don't know how lucky you are."

I felt the prick of truth upon my conscience.

"Come on. Let's do the toast," I said, taking up my glass.

"I don't feel like it," Tina said.

"Oh, for God's sake! Will you two cut it out?" Sugar said and picked up her glass.

So ... we recited together: "Friends may come and friends may go and friends may peter out, you know. But we'll be friends thru thick and thin ... peter out or peter in."

Tina, who couldn't hold on to her anger a minute more, guffawed and slapped me on the back, knocking the wind out of my lungs. Calm descended. At least for the moment.

After dinner, George picked us up in front of the hotel and drove us to Rick's Oasis. They play rap and heavy metal there, which I find tiring. But it's the kind of place to experience twice in your life. The dance floor is Sardine City. The clientele is all about tattoos and torn jeans and pierced noses. And brother, is it loud! When I called Serena and told her where we'd be, she said, Jack Benny-style, "Oh, my."

You might wonder why we decided to go there. Actually, it was Bud's suggestion. He said he'd set up the whole deal, and he and J.D. would meet us there about ten. When Sugar mentioned the joint's reputation, Bud grinned and said, "How much trouble can you possibly get into, sitting with a police captain?"

Which was a good point, as far as it went.

We arrived to find J.D. and Bud waiting at a reserved table surrounded by several pitchers of slushy Margaritas. It didn't take long for things to get interesting.

It started as a simple shoving match down on the dance floor. I remember seeing a kind of wave-like current of humanity snake from one end of the place to the other. I thought I heard shouting, but that might have only been the rest of the folks in my own party, trying to be heard over the music.

Things settled down for five or ten minutes before somebody bumped our waitress and sent her sprawling with a tray of drinks. I don't remember how long it took before I saw the flash of the knife blade. I do remember that Bud, Sugar, Tina, and Serena had disappeared.

"Let's get the hell out of here!" J.D. yelled.

"I can't leave my friends!" I yelled back. "I have to find them!"

"Not without me!"

He grabbed my hand, and we began to elbow and knee our way through the crowd. The second moment of violence had ebbed away, but I could still feel the tension in the room. The music started to pound inside my head. I remember feeling a trickle of sweat start down my chest.

"Do you see them anywhere?" J.D. yelled in my ear.

"No. Is Bud still here?" I yelled back.

J.D. shook his head, and the movement was punctuated by the crack of a gunshot.

As the scene clicked into slo-mo, J.D. wrestled me to the ground. I vividly recall screaming, a spurt of blood, more shoving, and the shout: "Look out! He's got a gun!"

There was a confused stampede for the door, at which point Bud stalked back in, drew a bead on the troublemaker, took his police-issued gun from under his coat, disarmed the guy, spotted us, and jerked his head in the direction of the rear exit.

We didn't need a second invitation to leave.

Once we were outside, we heard the wail of an approaching siren. I ran through the parking lot, but George and the limo seemed to have disappeared.

"Those bitches!" I screamed in frustration. "They left me here! After I practically risked my life!"

J.D. grabbed me from behind and steered me roughly in the direction of his pick-up. As he fast-walked me, he said, "Hey, hey ... Bud probably insisted they go. Now get in the damn truck."

We'd only got two blocks away when we started to laugh. He said, "Hey, my cousin's doing a great job of keeping the city safe, don't you think?"

"I hope he's not an elected official."

We laughed and laughed until finally he had to pull over. He rubbed his mid-section. "God, does that hurt."

"Laughter works better than sit-ups."

J.D. studied the night for a moment, then turned to me and said, "Don't say I'm not a classy date. On top of everything else, I've got us lost!"

Fortunately, it was a simple matter of J.D. using his cellular phone to call Captain Bud, who was by then at the station, making a report.

J.D. described our whereabouts in general terms. "We're in the middle of the goddamned desert, that's where we are."

Apparently, they'd locked up the young man with the gun and "some other Bozo with a knife." Bud hoped my crime-laden visit to his city hadn't turned me sour.

J.D. jabbed at his brother with glee. "Jesus, Bud, she might as well be in Iraq."

"Put Marly on and let me apologize."

I took the phone.

"I'm really sorry," he said. "Tucson must seem like the crime capital of the world."

"Now that you mention it ..."

"I think I already made it up to you. I called a pal over in Pomona P.D. Your car has been located in the extended parking lot and fixed. It'll be waiting for you, good as new, except filthy dirty of course, when you get back. Okay?"

What could I say? "Come to the taping of the show tomorrow. It'll be fun."

J.D. grabbed the receiver. "Hey, don't go trying to butter up my woman. We'll see you at the station about four o'clock. No. The TV station."

Back at my room, J.D. hesitated at my door. "Maybe we should call it a night; it's late, and you'll need to ... grow some hair, or something, before your big performance."

I felt bashful. I didn't know what to say ... or what to feel.

"I ... had a great time," I said.

"I did, too ... It'd be unnatural of me not to think about getting lucky. A woman like you ... I already got lucky." He kissed me softly but lingeringly on the mouth. He had good lips. "See you for lunch?"

"Absolutely," I said.

"Why don't you call Sugar? She's probably worried to death."

"Nope. I want to make her feel guilty."

"That's my girl," he said and disappeared into the night.

Chapter 26

The taping was scheduled to take place at four P.M. in Studio number 2. Through the day, Serena and I tossed possible ideas for discussion back and forth over the phone. At about 12:30, I was called away from my lunch with J.D. and Sugar.

"Are you sitting down?" Serena asked without preamble.

"Yes."

"Good." Silence.

I waited and felt a knot tie up in the pit of my stomach.

"Marly, why don't you talk about your cancer? Wait ... wait; before you yell at me, think about it: there are millions of people out there who could benefit from your experience. They've had it with discrimination. They've been dehumanized by the medical community. You could address those things with some knowledge. And some heat."

"I haven't beaten any of that. I'm still in the middle of the deep, dark woods."

"Well, you are and you aren't. But you could also talk like a pro about the deep, dark woods. About the fear of not knowing how it's gonna come out, how you're gonna come out. And you can lay out all those baby steps you've taken since the beginning."

"This sounds rehearsed."

I think I embarrassed her. There was a taut quality to her silence. Then she said, "We could set it up and take live callers."

I rubbed my hand across the top of my head. "No wig, I guess."

"I know this is a terrible question, but do you have any photographs anywhere?"

"No. It was hard enough looking at myself in the mirror without letting myself be captured on film. A photographer in New York chased me all over Manhattan a couple of months ago. I wanted to hang the s.o.b. up by his fingernails."

"I think you should tell that story." I could hear her lean into the phone. "So ... will you do it?"

The little cocoon I had so painstakingly knitted for myself was about to be torn to shreds. From this day forward, I wouldn't be able to control who knew and who didn't. Not that I'd kept my experiences a CIA eyes-only secret, or anything. But I'd had some privacy. I sighed from my toes and told Serena yes.

"Let's get at it," she said. "I'll prepare an outline. Remember, you don't have to answer a question if you don't want to."

"I'll remember." Mentally, I kicked Mr. Fear in the groin and went back to the table.

Sugar saw my feelings in my face. "What is it?"

"We're gonna do a show about the ... uh, my cancer," I answered.

J.D. leaned back in his chair like someone'd knocked the wind out of him.

"Are you positive you want to do this?" Sugar asked.

"I'm pissed at Serena for talking me into it." I shivered.

"Cancer?" J.D. finally asked. "Is it serious?" He smacked himself in the forehead. "Jesus H. Christ! What a dumb question."

I patted his hand. "I'm used to it. Although it's irritating, I do understand about the ... well ... morbid curiosity."

"Jesus H. Christ," J.D. said again.

"J.D., darling, under the circumstances, I'll forgive you if you don't want to come to the taping," I said. "Truth? I'm not sure I want to be there. No hard feelings. Promise. And you'll probably want to call Bud. Warn him."

I stood up and stretched my back and shoulders.

"Listen, you guys," I said with a coolness I didn't feel, "I'm not hungry anymore. Why don't I see you later?"

Sugar stood up, too. "Are you absolutely, positively sure you want to do this?" she asked.

"I'm absolutely, positively sure I don't want to, but I'm gonna."

She hugged me. "I'll be here at three to pick you up." She hugged me again. "If you need me in the meantime, you know where I'll be."

The Westin La Paloma sits smack in the middle of the forbidding Sonoran desert. The kelly green of the golf course is bounded on all sides by cactus-strewn sand and rattlesnake hidey-holes. There are little signs on every fairway, warning the players not to look for errant golf balls. It's rumored that hotel staff is trained to administer a venom antidote. Even if it wasn't true, it gave the place just the right amount of rugged mystique.

The grounds of the La Paloma are rambling yet discreetly manicured. Most of the vegetation is indigenous to the area, which makes for a spare, natural look. Since the scraping, vast blue of the sky was somehow comforting, I decided to walk the grounds. I drank in the scrubbed smell of the air and the rustling noises of an occasional cottontail. I recall the heat of that particular day as unseasonal for April and how it billowed up off the pathway like a living thing.

There was a big old ball of dread at the pit of my stomach. After all, if I ended up losing this battle for my life, I wasn't sure I wanted the world to know my failure or my weakness ... but especially not my rage ... unless I could involve the whole enchilada that had been my journey. That's when and where the idea for this book hit me, struck me like a bolt of lightning from the Creator's Hand: on that mesa top, overlooking the desert. The great vista embraced me, putting the trials of man, and therefore my own, into a manageable perspective.

No heavy weight was lifted from my shoulders; the bile in my belly didn't ebb away. But the challenge of dramatizing my struggle, of setting it down on the page, of trying to make it readable ... of trying to make someone get it ... I'd found a place of strength from which to beard the beast.

TV stations in Tucson don't enjoy lavish budgets. As I awaited my trial by fire, there were no make-up artists, no hairdressers, no wardrobe mistresses. There wasn't even anyone waiting to greet us, so when Sugar and I got to KMTQ, we asked directions to Studio 2. Since it was close to show time, we were shuffled in the general direction by a balding man biting down hard on a felt-tip pen.

Inside Studio 2, there were a couple of techies, with longish ponytails, who handled lighting and sound. When I stepped through the heavy, soundproof doors, quivering and faintly nauseous, the crew was scurrying around, adjusting lights, testing sound and hooking up the telephone line to their broadcast audio system.

Serena looked confident, the queen of all she surveyed, and took my hand firmly. "This is a good thing," was all she said in greeting.

"Yeah, fine," I whined. "You'll win an Emmy, and I'll look like a fool."

Serena tsked me and then showed Sugar and me around the stage setting, familiarizing me with the audio monitoring system. "There's a delay, of course. My producer will try to weed out the nuts and the obscenities." She gestured vaguely. "Wave to Linda over there." I obeyed, my arm feeling heavy as a bowling ball. "She'll be running the booth and screening the calls."

I remember the look on Sugar's face. It reminded me of Janet Leigh in *Psycho*, after she'd discovered that the dear old lady who lived in the creaky house on the haunted hill was actually going to kill her.

I mused, she thinks she's scared ...

Five minutes to the hour, I sat in the hot seat. Techie #1, Dave, pinned the mike onto my coat. "Can you give us a voice level?"

I wondered if I'd be able to talk. "Hamlin town's in Brunswick, by famous Hanover City." I looked to Dave, who motioned me to continue. "The River Weser, deep and wide washes its walls on the southern side. A pleasanter spot ..."

Dave gave me the A-OK, and there was nothing to do but wait.

"Don't worry, chica," Serena instructed. "It'll all come out in the wash."

"Do me a favor? Get right to it? I don't want any long introductions."

Then I heard the theme music and felt, rather than saw, J.D. and Bud move out of the dark perimeter of the studio. How long had they been there?

The cameraman started the countdown. "Ten, nine eight, seven six, five." The last four numbers were done silently, with hand signals. Then he pointed to Serena, and it was Miller Time.

There was a standard pre-recorded announcement introducing Serena and the show. Then the little signal light on Serena's close-up camera went red. "Good afternoon and welcome to *Women Today*," she said. "My very special guest for this live broadcast, which will be aired again during its usual Sunday time slot, is award-winning and best-selling novelist, Marly Mitchell."

She turned to me then and smiled encouragingly. "I'm so very glad we're able to do this show together, Marly. I guess the most obvious question is ... are you any relation to Margaret Mitchell?"

It was unexpected. "No." I think I smiled.

"But writing is in your DNA, isn't it?"

"Yes. My mother, Sarah Mitchell, is quite well-known. As is my grandfather, Clay Morgan. He writes for travel magazines and has his own column with *The New York Times* syndication."

Serena glanced at her notes. "I'll say in advance that I'm envious of your courage. That I appreciate your coming here today to talk about a very tough subject. Let's dive right in, shall we? Is there life after cancer?"

My heart skipped a beat, and I hurled myself off the edge.

"I don't know." I mentally shook myself to bang the fast-rising editorial voices out of my head. "I mean," I went on, "that I'm obviously still alive. But maybe your question is, am I living, really living? And my question

The Cancer Club

back at you is—is anybody really living?"

Serena knitted her delicate eyebrows together. "The 'C' word must have changed your life. Can you talk specifics?"

The ten previous months stood out in my mind like a stage setting. "I learned to live without hair. Without sleep or sex. Without courage, whatever you may think. Without the breast on my left side. I didn't laugh at all in the beginning ... not for countless weeks. I didn't lose all sense of joy, I guess, but it doesn't seem to come now without a tinge of melancholy mixed in for good measure."

Serena waited.

"Well," I continued, "of course, it wasn't bleak every second ... It just seemed like it."

Serena tapped a gold Paper Mate against her jaw. I heard the soft splat of metal hitting skin. "Why come out with this story now? I mean, haven't you attempted to keep your illness a secret?"

I grinned and leaned toward her. Softly, I said, "You made me! You dragged me here, kicking and screaming. For an Emmy nomination!" I turned and faced the camera for a moment. "She really did make me."

Serena had the grace to look embarrassed. "Caught like a rat in a trap," she said and shifted slightly until all her attention was focused on her close-up camera. "As you can see, we're in for quite a little ride here. Stay with us for more surprises right after these messages."

The red light on my camera blinked off.

Serena said, "You're doing great," at exactly the same moment as a tensely worried look flickered across her face. "Will you please let go of that chair? You're white-knuckling. You'll get a cramp."

"I need a Kleenex."

Serena bit her lip and said, "I don't have ..."

"I need a Kleenex!"

Serena stood abruptly, yanking at the mike chord that was attached to her seat. "Someone get her a goddamned Kleenex!"

Dave the cameraman said, "But we haven't got time before we ..."

"A Kleenex!" she screamed.

I'll bet they heard her in Cleveland.

Linda ran out of the control room and threw a handful of the stuff at me. I was just mopping my forehead when we went back on the air.

Serena shifted once again in her chair, tucking her right leg underneath her. "Why is it so difficult to talk about having cancer, do you think?"

she asked. "Why, in these so-called enlightened times, is it still treated like such a dirty little secret?"

"Odd, isn't it?" I said. "I think it's because a cancer patient's diagnosis somehow ends up being about everyone else's mortality. I bet you get a ton of negative reaction to this show, a reaction designed to teach us to put the subject back in the closet. To really talk out the experience, I had to go to a group of fellow sufferers. And if it sounds like I'm grousing, I'm not. I've learned the hard way that some experiences are simply outside a normal life."

"What's been the worst part of this experience?"

I dabbed at my face with the now-soaking, shredding Kleenex. "Not knowing and being afraid to hope. I think I could come to terms with a death sentence, yet I have to believe I'm cured. I went through hell, hell, and that belief is my reward for having been a good girl. Still, you can't help wondering ..."

Serena ticked a check mark next to a line of the printed sheet on the clipboard in her lap. "How do you think your attitude helped or hindered?" she asked.

"It helped, when I could keep ahold of it. The fear is still the most paralyzing thing I come up against. I think of fear as a person, with physical features and a seductive character. Gotta kick him in the kneecap sometimes."

"Interesting. It's a way of focusing?"

"It's a way of fighting back at something you can't see except on an x-ray or a scan."

"But you're getting through it."

"I made it through what there has been of it so far but not without suffering one helluva breakdown in the process."

She considered this for a moment. "Breakdown. You're talking a good, old-fashioned nervous breakdown?"

"You bet. The only way I could get from my bed to the bathroom was on my hands and knees. I cried every day for a month and every other day for the next month. I thought seriously about suicide."

"What stopped you?"

I shrugged my shoulders.

She was silent for a long moment and then observed, "That sounds like a good, old-fashioned breakdown, alright."

I ripped the last little piece of Kleenex into littler pieces and continued. "I've come this far due strictly to: the help of my friends and family way past the point where they couldn't give any more; the support and wisdom of my group; the kindness and acceptance and yes, the constant and irritating insistence of my counselor, Kyla. And to God, who helped out whenever She wasn't too busy someplace else."

Serena turned from me and faced the camera squarely. "When we come back, we'll be taking your calls on the number you now see flashing on your screen. See ya then."

I sipped water from a Styrofoam cup and listened to my heart thud. I actually wouldn't have minded some light chitchat, but the air for conversation seemed to be stuck halfway down my esophagus. I closed my eyes and visualized Mexico.

Serena said, "Can I get you anything?"

I shook my head.

"You hang in there, chica."

I nodded.

"We're back and taking your calls. Hello, you're on the air. Caller?"

"Hello? Hello?"

"Go ahead, you're on the air."

"Marly, I've read all your books. I love them. But it's been ... what? A couple of years since the last one? Did your ability to write get affected?"

"Writing is a good way to get shelves built in your office." We all laughed. "Most writers welcome any excuse to interrupt their writing. Getting cancer was a most extreme example of this ..." I sighed and went on. "... Actually, it was a terrible interruption. I still don't feel well physically. My energy level is still lower than whale blubber ... The entire process seems harder. My ability to concentrate has been damaged—though the result is probably better, in some ways."

Serena said, "Thanks for calling" and pushed another button on the phone. "You're on the air."

"Marly?" The voice was low and cigarette-raspy.

"Yes?"

"It pisses me off, all this bellyachin' in public. Why don't you just go on about your business?"

"Since I'm a writer of fiction, I believe that mankind is my business."

"It dudn't set good with my way of thinkin'."

"What's your way of thinking?"

"Everybody dies alone. That's the way it's always been."

I wanted to yell at him. Instead, I said, "But maybe it shouldn't be. Have you ever been really ill?"

"What's that gotta do with it?"

"Have you? I don't think you should give an expert opinion unless you've been there."

"Yeah, I been ill."

"You probably didn't ask for help. Maybe you hated that look of pity in the eyes of your friends and family. I sure as hell did. But maybe, if they'd have made it easier for you to ask, you would have found some relief from that pain in your soul. I don't want to sound too tough about this, because I respect and understand the choice you made for yourself."

Serena said, "I mean, that's why we're doing this show: throw a little light on the subject. Maybe find out why people are so reluctant to get involved."

I heard the man catch his breath. "Yeah, well, you best pull yourself up with your own bootstraps. People don't like to be burdened with the troubles of others."

I said, "True. But I don't think it should feel like a burden, listening to someone in pain, being there for someone else. We should all have to do it at least once a week. I mean, some people don't have arms to pull themselves up by their bootstraps, so they need a boost. Now believe me, I'm not saying people shouldn't learn how to help themselves or that ultimately, you're not alone. I agree with you. My solution was group therapy. We all helped each other while we were helping ourselves."

There was an awkward silence, and Serena reached for the phone button. I stopped her. "I'm just sorry that no one was there for you," I said. "That you couldn't ask for help. Sometimes I took advantage of the people who said they loved me, because I was stubborn and refused to suffer by myself. I realized I couldn't do it all by myself. But that's just me."

The man hung up without saying another word.

Before we broke, I told the story about the photographer in New York who'd chased me around the city one day, hoping to snap a picture of me without hair. And I told a little about my time in Mexico and The Cancer Club.

I started to feel comfortable. I got on a roll. Some calls were supportive; some weren't. Some were intrusive; some were downright rude. They began to pour over me like water.

- "What you need is a man in your life."
- "What you need is a woman in your life."
- "What you need is to receive Jesus Christ as your Personal Savior.

And God is not a she!"

- "You've given me hope to go on."

- "Why do you sound so negative? You're sending the wrong message here. You're wallowing in self-pity. Get on with your life!"

- "Can you recommend a counseling center here in Tucson?"

- "Do you think you'll ever be in a relationship again? I mean, how can you be ... physical with a man now?"

- "Why haven't you had reconstructive surgery?"

My honesty and the vulnerability I admitted to felt liberating. It felt right.

Then ...

"Peter Haskell here. *Tucson Post*. How do you feel about your half-sister's suicide attempt?"

Serena and I looked at one another.

"I beg your pardon?" I asked.

"Jamie Sue Mitchell. It came over the wire a couple hours ago. You didn't know?"

Serena said, "Mr. Haskell, I'm not sure this is the time or place to discuss ..."

He interrupted. "Is it true there's a feud? And is that what brought on the attempt?"

"For God's sake, is she alive?" I yelled.

"I believe so."

There were still four minutes to go in the broadcast. I said, "You mean you don't know? What hospital?"

"Ms. Mitchell ...," he started.

"What hospital?"

"The Huntington in Pasadena."

"Thanks. I have no further comment, Mr. Haskell. And I do so appreciate your tact in this matter." I disconnected his call, stood up, and undid the mike from my jacket lapel. "Serena, I'm sure your viewers will excuse my hasty exit."

Serena turned toward the booth. "Linda, go to commercial." When we were off the air, she said, "We'll make a reservation. Back to Ontario?"

"Might take too long, with the stopover. Get me anything direct to LAX." I just stood there for a moment, frozen to the ground.

Bud said, "I'll drive you. We'll handle your stuff later. Serena, call me on the car phone and let us know what flight."

As I hurried out of the station, J.D. caught up my arm. "Make it two reservations," he called back over his shoulder. Then to me, he said, "I'm going with you."

Chapter 27

We got to the airport in record time, thanks to Bud's maniacal driving and blaring siren. I didn't bother to thank anyone as I jumped from the car with J.D. right behind.

"Look," I yelled back to him over my shoulder as I ran into the terminal, "they're going. See them leaving the airport? Go with them."

"Don't be so damned stubborn."

"I am not being stubborn!"

We were still arguing when we got to the ticket counter. "I don't need your help!" I hissed at J.D. for what seemed like the tenth time. "I don't want it."

"Tough. Read my lips: I am going with you."

Our tickets'd been prepaid by the station and were ready and waiting.

"Baggage?" asked the bored-looking agent.

"Hey!" I explained, trying to remain calm, "we only have ten minutes to make the plane. Can you hurry? It's an emergency, a matter of life and death."

The agent gave me A Look. "Baggage?" she asked again, with more tone.

"I tell you, this is an emergency!" I insisted.

"Isn't it always?" she asked.

"We don't have any goddamned baggage, okay?" J.D. yelled.

Just beyond the security checkpoint, J.D. grabbed for me as I sprang forward. "What is it?" he asked.

"What is what?"

"The reason you don't want me to come. Tell me the truth. If it's good enough, I'll stay here." I gave him a look, and he assured me, "You'll make the damn plane."

The words poured out. "It's going to be awful. My sister and I have never liked each other. You see ... it's a long story. The press'll be swarming all over us. And my father, my poor father ..." I threw my hands in the air.

"Oh, OK. I'm going."

We made the last direct flight of the day with three minutes to spare.

It was night by the time our cab pulled up in front of the Huntington Memorial Hospital. J.D. and I hadn't spoken much on the ride across town. What was there to say? Until I knew whether my sister was alive or dead ... I'd tried to phone my parents once I got off the plane, but no one was home. The hospital refused to give me any information, because I couldn't prove I was a relative.

It was all giving me a head-banger.

"Jamie Sue Mitchell? She's a patient."

Mrs. Forsch, the blue-haired volunteer, looked up from a long printed list and pursed her lips together. "Are you a relative? Access to that room is restricted."

"Then she's alive! Thank God. Yes, yes, I'm her sister. Where is she being held?"

"We don't hold our patients. We treat them. May I see some identification, please?" She examined my license, which looks like a candid photo of a refugee from a chain gang. "All right. Sorry about the third degree. Room H673. Follow this map."

"Excuse me, Mrs. Forsch," Ron asked, "but why is the room restricted? Intensive care?"

"We've been holding back an assault by the press," she answered and went back to her list.

The elevator opened on the sixth floor of the H wing. The lights in the corridor were too dim to read by. I followed a sign to the H6 station.

"I'm here to see Jamie Sue Mitchell," I said.

"Just down that way. But you'll have to wait until the nurses are finished." The woman looked down at me over her glasses. I don't mean she was tall; I mean she looked down at me.

"How is she?" I asked, feeling antsy. It was that damned hospital smell ... and my general state of mind. "Is she going to be okay?"

"I'm afraid I can't give you any information. You'll have to speak to Dr. Marxer. Why don't you try the waiting room?" I swear she pointed, with her pointy, looking-down nose.

I ran my hands through my hair. I felt grimy. "Is there a cigarette machine somewhere?"

"Cal-Oaks drugstore at the corner. The hospital is a non-smoking zone."

Well, excuse me! I slapped the station counter loudly. "Thanks!"

I'm not at my best in hospitals ... Can you tell?

J.D. shook his head, but he didn't say anything.

The Cancer Club

"I told you how it was going to be," I hissed.

He took my hand. That was all, just held it.

We made our way down the corridor. The floor was inky and shiny and smelled of disguised astringent.

I wasn't prepared. I should have been, I know, but I'd shut myself down during the previous four hours. Because when we turned into the waiting lounge, there were my mother and father, sitting side by side on two leatherette chairs. They were facing away from the door, leaning in toward one another with their heads almost touching, like two life-mated elephants sharing ancient secrets. I thought of how often I'd seen them this way during my lifetime ... so self-contained in their love.

I wanted to run—to disappear, just like that night at the Marine Room in La Jolla so many years before. A vision of that fiasco, when Luis walked in and caught me with Sandy, flashed before my eyes in Technicolor. How many times I'd screwed up in between!

But this was A Beaut.

They sensed my presence and turned. My father's face was drawn, and he sagged with exhaustion. "She'll live," was all he said.

My mother hardly looked at me. "You selfish bitch," she said with real venom.

Dad jumped in his seat and grabbed mother's hand. "Sarah!"

"Don't be an ass, Talbot. Sometimes, you're such an ass."

Behind me, I sensed J.D. step to the side. He backed down the corridor and fell heavily into a chair by the window. I stood stock-still, barely breathing. Thank God it wasn't too long a wait.

The two most remarkable traits about Dr. Marxer were his bushy unibrow and his grasp of medicine. He'd been our family doctor for years. When I was a kid, I remember that just seeing him helped me feel better. And I appreciated that he'd always given me my shots himself, because although his manner was gruff, his touch with the needle was quick and smooth.

When he promised it wouldn't hurt, it didn't.

Dad stood up, still holding onto Mom's hand, to hear the medical verdict, almost as though he were accused in court.

That was the moment Kathleen showed up.

You could tell Dr. Marxer didn't know what the hell to do next. His mouth gaped. Kathleen didn't waste any time making like a six-hundred-pound gorilla. After sizing up the situation for five seconds, she bellowed, "How is my baby? Will she be all right?"

I noticed that no one ragged her ass for not being there sooner.

Dr. Marxer said, "We believe she will make a full recovery." As he subtly loosened his collar, Dad's shoulders relaxed with relief. He took a small step away from Sarah, who gave him back a spiteful look in return.

"There's no apparent brain damage," the doctor went on, perspiration showing on his face now. "We got it out of her in time. Under the circumstances, I feel very strongly about her need for professional help. In fact, I insist on it as a condition of Jamie Sue's release. I've made a few suggestions. And we'll need to go after the cancer yesterday."

Kathleen whirled on me. "Why didn't you help her? She needed you! This is all your fault!"

Dad reddened with exasperation. "Now, Kathleen ..."

"Oh, shut up, Talbot. See what your weakness has brought us all?" Kathleen spit out the words. "Do you see?" She sank onto the window seat.

I looked to Talbot for support, but he was in his own personal hell and didn't have any depth of spirit left over to give away. Nobody said a word for what seemed like years, and then Dr. Marxer cleared his throat twice. He turned toward me. "Actually, it's Marly she wants to see first. Alone."

Kathleen jumped up. "Impossible. Does she know I'm here?" she shouted, at the same moment my mother yelled, "I don't believe that for a second!"

They were pissed.

"Where is her room?" I asked warily.

"Just go down the hall to the right, turn left, first door on your left. Don't worry. I'll hold off the vigilantes."

"Thanks, Dr. Marxer."

The only solid contact I remember having with the physical universe was the moment J.D. took hold of my hand again and squeezed it hard. I floated into Jamie Sue's room, quietly shutting J.D. out in the corridor.

She was as pale as a ghost, and the skin on her face was drawn taut, as though she'd visited some ghastly plastic surgeon. I stood there, waiting—for what, I couldn't have said.

At last, she opened her eyes. "You came." Her voice was soft and raspy from fatigue.

"Yeah." I could taste the acrid mixture of uncertainty and guilt in my mouth.

She closed her eyes again. "When I saw you in Mexico, I already knew

The Cancer Club

about the cancer," she said.

"Why didn't you tell me?"

"You wouldn't have believed me."

I walked over to her bed. "You're probably right."

She looked up at me then. Her eyes had sunken into her skull. "We've never ...," she started but trailed off.

"No, we haven't."

"Am I gonna die?" she asked, quite seriously.

"I don't think so." After a moment, I said, "Sometimes I'm a stubborn old pig."

The light came back into her eyes for a moment. "It runs in the family." She chuckled dryly and asked, "Are Mom and Dad here?" I nodded. She asked, "Can you ask them to come in?"

"Of course. Can I do anything else?"

"You're here; that's enough for now," she said with a long, low sigh and let her head go slack on the pillow.

"I'll be back tomorrow."

"I know. You're my sister, and there's nothing you can do about it."

I hesitated for a second, then leaned down, straightened up, leaned back down and brushed Jamie Sue's forehead with my lips. The corners of her mouth turned up.

Shaken, I returned to the waiting room. As I peeked around the door jamb, I could see and hear that it was war. Dad had his hands over his ears; Kathleen and Sarah were yelling at each other; and the nurse was clapping her hands, trying to get them to be quiet! I would have turned and run if they hadn't noticed me first.

"Well?" Kathleen asked with venom, as the nurse sped away.

"She wants to see you and Dad."

I didn't wait for a reply. I swung myself around, took J.D.'s hand, and got the hell out of there.

"You're shivering," he said as we walked back through the entrance.

"Excuse me, Ms. Mitchell?"

It was the blue-haired volunteer. "We have a message for you. Your Miata is in the lot here." She sounded puzzled. "The attendant outside has your ticket."

J.D. laughed. "Bud's a great guy, isn't he? A cop down to his toes. He always takes it personally when a friend of his gets shot at."

I laughed. "You're behaving incredibly well."

"I got hit by a lightening bolt."

"Really."

"Yep. So don't think this is good behavior. Just can't seem to help myself. I am also a hungry guy." His stomach gurgled. "See?"

"I could eat a horse myself. There's a primo Mexican food place just down the block. Mijares'. You like Mexican?"

"I've always been partial to those little white-hot peppers." J.D. said, "Even when they bring tears to my eyes." First, he took the key ring from my hand and opened my front door. Then he looked around for a minute and nodded his head. "This place looks like you." Finally, he leaned down and gathered up my mail from the floor. "Where should I put this? Kitchen table? God, you're tidy. My place is strictly Early Bachelor."

Then we stood there, looking at each other.

Finally, J.D. said, "You look a little tired. Beautiful, but tired. See? I mastered my 'tact' lesson from the other day. Why don't you show me where the guest room is? I'll lay my head down and be asleep in five minutes."

On the one hand, I was bushed. On the other, I was slightly miffed that he was going to let me sleep alone without putting up even a token resistance. But after a nanosecond's reflection, I realized I was too worn-out to care. "There's toothbrushes and shaving stuff in the guest bathroom," I mumbled. "The towels and sheets are clean."

He took me in his arms and held me. "I'll be fine. Really. Now get in there and go to bed." He kissed me softly on the lips, turned me around and pushed me through my bedroom door. "And don't you dare get up early on my account."

I can't ever remember feeling that exhausted before, but sleep wouldn't come. Scenarios of trouble kept marching across my mind. I wondered if Jamie Sue would recover, if my mother would ever forgive ... whatever unforgivable sin I'd committed. What this mess would do to Mom and Dad's relationship. I thought about J.D. I worried and worried until I'd worried myself to Slumberland.

Chapter 28

I found myself back in my own shower with the yellow tile. Garth Brooks was singing, "And I'm glad; I'm glad I didn't know the way it all would end, the way it all would go. It's my life; it's better left to chance. I could have missed the pain, but I'd have had to miss the dance."

The lump in my left breast grew. I pushed down on it as hard as I could, but I couldn't stop it from sucking the life out of me. That's when the noise startled me awake.

I didn't know where I was at first. I lay in the bed, trying to get my bearings and finally realized my own phone was ringing in my own bedroom. Drenched in sweat, I grabbed for it and knocked the receiver onto the floor.

"Shit."

Glancing at the clock, I leaned down and scooped it up. "This better be good," I said. "It's seven-thirty!"

"It's Miriam, darling." She hesitated. "I'm sorry, but I ... Are you okay?"

"Oh. Miriam. What is it?"

"I'm under attack. The press is swarming all over the story. What should I tell them?"

"Tell them to do something anatomically impossible."

"OK."

"No, no ... wait a second. What do they want to know?"

"About your cancer. About Jamie Sue's cancer, her suicide attempt, the feud. I spoke to your mother."

"And?" I asked.

"You tell me. What in the hell is going on?"

"My mother's ... in a rage."

"This I already know. But why?"

"Oh, shit. Look, just no-comment me around till I figure something out. Maybe I can come up with a statement ... I am a writer, after all. Hey! I'll make something up! I promise I'll call you later."

"If there's anything I can do, Marly ..."

"Yeah, yeah."

I dragged myself to the closet and grabbed my Old Faithful terry robe. Then I remembered I had Company.

"Oh, merde!" I toyed with the idea of putting on something more presentable. "The hell with it."

I often talk to myself when I'm exhausted.

I washed my face and cleaned my teeth. Fluffed up my wispy hair with my fingers. Feeling slightly less deceased, I peeked out into the rest of the condo, but there were no signs of life. That's when I smelled fresh coffee. Following my nose, I walked into the kitchen.

"Good morning."

I pivoted in my socks and discovered J.D., sitting on the living room sofa, glancing through the want ads in the *L.A. Time*s.

"Coffee's on. Toast warming in the oven," he said.

"Looking for a housekeeping job?"

His smile sobered. "May have to, one of these days. But actually, I'm checking out the antique motorcycles. Indians, mostly. It's a thing with me."

He went back to his paper.

The coffee was hot and strong, just the way I like it. I turned back to J.D. "Listen," I said, motioning to the blinking light on the answering machine, "I have some fires to put out."

"Go ahead."

The next two hours found me at the eye of a hurricane. I called my parents first. My mother refused to come to the phone, and my dad sounded distant. I collected my messages, which were mostly from "friends" in the news biz sniffing out a scoop. I contacted Kyla, who agreed to meet me at the hospital for lunch. I prepared a written statement about the situation and faxed it to Miriam. It was quite a work of fiction.

Around noon, I was almost caught up. "Listen, J.D., I have to get to the hospital. It might be better if you left now. I'll order a shuttle, or something. I mean, I appreciate everything you've done ... but I ..."

He pierced me with his eyes, and they shred a longing way, deep down in the hidden center of his self. For ... me? For a connection?

"What is it?" I asked.

He didn't say anything.

"Have I ... Are you angry?"

"No," he answered at last. "I know I should go. Because you need to attend to your life here. But I might never see you again. That would be hard." He took me in his arms. "You know me so little. So let me say what I gotta say." He took a deep breath. "And listen good, 'cause I'm only gonna say it once. If you ever think about getting married again, I want you to think about marrying me."

It was a sweet kiss, seasoned with melancholy. He didn't give me time to respond before he was out the door. I wondered if he knew where the hell he was going.

"Momma, he's crazy ..."

Kyla was already at the hospital when I arrived. "Oh, my dear," she said with her usual warmth.

"The excrement, as they say, has definitely hit the fan, Kyla. Let's eat some delightful cafeteria food, and you can tell me what in the hell I'm supposed to do now."

I bought an onion bagel hard as a diamond. The stale cream cheese didn't help the stale taste. Kyla poked around the pre-made salads and found one slightly less wilted than the rest. "Is it safe?" she asked the cashier as she speared the offending greenery with her fingernail.

"Three ninety-five, including tax" was the only response forthcoming.

"There are sick people here," Kyla observed as we sat down. "Now I know why."

"It is kind of disgusting, when you think of the cost of staying in a hospital these days. Why is the food always so bad?"

"Tradition?"

Kyla's voice is throaty. You couldn't recreate her tone with ten packs a week and a fifth a day. I sometimes picture her in kindergarten, explaining life to her teacher in smoky basso tones more suited to Orson Welles.

"I don't know where to start," I admitted.

"I do. Let's see ... Catastrophes bring out the best in you. I figure the dust with Jamie Sue will settle eventually; there was nowhere to go but North. It's this blow-up with your mother that concerns me."

When I attacked my bagel with a plastic knife, it shattered. The knife, not the bagel. "She wouldn't speak to me this morning," I said as I bashed the roll on the tabletop. "Which is odd, because, you know, Jamie Sue is my father's child by his first wife. It doesn't make sense. God, this bread is hard," I said and banged the offending rock-like roll on the table again.

"That's why they call it irrational behavior ... I could have a little chat with Sarah, on the order of a fact-finding mission. Does that appeal?"

I finally managed to bite off a hunk of bread. I gnawed and thought for a moment. "I feel guilty."

"About what?"

"I should have helped her. Jamie Sue, I mean. I just should have bit the bullet and helped her."

"She's as much responsible for your relationship as you are—for the distrust and the dislike. But just for the sake of argument, why didn't you help her?"

I was still chewing. "Because she's burned me once too often. Because I don't trust her. Because I don't like her."

"All good reasons. Like I said, the distrust and the dislike."

"Oh ... is that where I heard it?"

"Are you glad she's ill?"

"That's not funny."

"Wasn't meant to be," she said and pushed her half-eaten salad away. "Are you?"

"Well ... no. Not in the way you mean. At least I don't think so." I looked into my heart for a moment to see what was there. "I guess I hope it'll humanize her a little, that she'll recognize that she needs help."

"She did need help. And recognized it. And came to you, remember?"

"Oh, yeah."

"I'm not here to punish you, Marly."

"I don't need any help."

"I know you quite well, and I honestly believe you're trying your damnedest. No one can ask more."

"It's hard, Kyla. She's never been there for me. Not with my cancer and not with my life. We're enemies."

Kyla toyed with a wrinkled tomato wedge. "What do you want me to do?"

"I'm not ready to let my defenses down. If you want to take her into the group, okay; that's your decision. But I have no desire to share that experience with her."

"Because she'll find out too much about you?"

"No. Because I'll find out too much about Jamie Sue."

"That's a bad thing?"

"Couldn't be badder. Because once I taste the pain that makes her do the awful things she does, once I know what she's dragging along behind her through life, I won't be able to dislike her anymore."

The Cancer Club

"Mmmhmmm." Kyla speared the tomato and examined it more closely. "Actually, it might be better for Jamie Sue to start with us privately, anyhow. I'll think about it. Now, about your mother ... "

About my mother.

Of all the things that had happened to me since the cancer, my mother's current disgust with me over this was the most devastating. What shocked me was that instead of breaking down, I was actually royally pissed about the whole thing, a reaction Kyla found encouraging. "You're getting your sea legs back under you, and you're reacquiring that high-maintenance assurance you thought was gone forever. Frankly, I think your mother's behavior is puzzling. It's understandable for you to feel upset with her."

"It feels like a betrayal, Kyla. She's blaming me. But why? What for? She doesn't even like Jamie Sue."

"Is it a betrayal?"

I had to think about that. "I don't know. She appears to be taking Jamie Sue's side against me. What would you call it?" I began tapping the table for emphasis. "Look, forget my mom. I'm bitterly disappointed in me."

"Maybe your mother is disappointed in you, too. And maybe you're not the only one she's disappointed in." Kyla let this idea sit with me a while before going on. "Does Jamie Sue have any close friends?" she asked finally.

"That's hard for me to answer without prejudice."

Kyla nodded.

"Aside from whatever current male escort might be hanging around, I couldn't tell you," I said. "We've kept our lives separate. I think there's a girl named Susan in New York. Or maybe she's in L.A. now. Ask Dad; he'll know."

"There're other things I'll need to know. Will he tell me?"

"Kyla, you could charm the music out of a flute."

I let her go up to Jamie Sue's room ahead of me so I could gather my wits, which seemed to be so much flotsam and jetsam strewn around the universe.

I wandered aimlessly for a time, looking for ... I couldn't have said. Guidance? Direction? Answers? I felt ... wonky, upended. On the one hand, my life was in the most serious, crisis-ridden period I'd ever experienced. But weirdly, I wasn't afraid. I remember thinking—quite calmly, mind you—that it was time for God to step in and do Her stuff. Obviously, I was quite incapable of running my own life. Fine. No problem. I'd just plop myself down by the side of The Road and see what came around.

I suddenly found myself in front of a large wooden door. A discreet sign on the wall said "Chapel." Hmmmm, I thought to myself, what have we here? I opened the door and stepped into the dark.

It was a pretty room, candle-lit and quiet. It wasn't a church, in the strict sense of the word, but a place to meditate. There were no crosses or altars or Stars of David. There were no Torahs or Korans or Bibles.

There were two small, free-form stained glass windows tinting the soft light that filtered in. I was alone. Alone with my God and my confusion and my anger and my exhaustion and my self. It was pretty crowded.

I sat down in a pew toward the back and waited.

"I don't know whether You can help me or not," I finally whispered. "Or whether You even want to. I honestly don't know what else to do." The quiet of the place filled my cranial cavity. "I can feel my weakness, and I hate it."

I closed my eyes in concentration. I felt the air going in and out of my lungs. "I'm not saying I didn't contribute to Jamie Sue's misery. I do feel responsible, but I'm not sure why, exactly. What in the hell am I supposed to learn from ...," I hesitated, "... all this?"

That's when I saw The Circle that was my life—that was everyone's life, for that matter. A giant wheel that encompasses all of existence, which is in turn divided into smaller wheels ranging in time frames from seconds to millennia. From generation to generation, the problems of our world remain the same: greed, jealousy, racism, hatred, condescension, fear, ignorance. The actors look different with each new span of time, but the results are always the same. Rodney King's arresting officers go free, and the rain forests dwindle, and the president is selling arms to our enemies and bails out the S&L's but turns a blind eye and a cold heart on the inner cities and the victims of incest. A woman is most likely to be the victim of violence from someone she knows. Forty percent of the children in America grow up in poverty.

It seems like we haven't learned a thing.

For me, the beginning of this particular bit of wheel was the first time I suffered through the Lump Nightmare. Now I was coming around to a beginning again.

But the beginning of what?

A new relationship with my step-sister? Was I ready for that? To start the new book? When I hadn't finished the one I was rewriting?

Oh, those things would come in time and sooner than I expected, no doubt. But this solemn and quiet moment was A Time for Something Else.

Suddenly, I thought about my parents. Something tugged at my heart, and a flash of need shuddered through my body, raw and coarse. I could feel it scrape across my nerve endings, but instead of shaking it off, I just sat with it for a time, there in that quiet place, and felt something sharp piercing my soul.

I knew they loved me. I'd never had any doubts about that. They'd supported me in their way and yet, and yet ... there was something intermingled with our feelings for one another that needed to be separated out and looked at. It wouldn't solve America's drug problem, but three little souls might find a road to healing.

I realized that whatever it was represented a big chunk of my resentment toward Jamie Sue. I couldn't stand the idea of relinquishing one iota of my parents' affection for me, because I'd never felt I'd had enough to spare.

I closed my eyes and let the sweet, cool dark of the chapel wash over me. As I relaxed my body, one part at a time, I asked for help, guidance, a sign that I was loved.

A feeling of peace began to envelop me. It came on slowly, gently, like the gentle lapping of a tideless sea. Time became eternity—one moment, all moments; the wheel turned finely, inexorably. Lost in a kind of reverie, I was only subliminally aware of the chapel door opening. A woman stepped hesitantly inside. I saw her outline in my mind's eye and smelled the delicate fragrance of Fracas. Then a familiar arm wrapped itself around my shoulders and crushed me against an ample bosom. I heard my mother say, "Marly."

How had she found me? Why had she sought me out now, at the one moment in my life when I needed her love above everything else?

I opened my eyes to thank her and found I was alone.

Chapter 29

I felt rested, refreshed. Tremors, present in various muscles for days, subsided along with the scratchy feeling behind my eyelids. I looked around in awe one last time, to make sure I was truly alone, and silently thanked God for my little miracle.

It was the first real peace I'd felt in months, and I hated the idea of disturbing the mood. But I was convinced I'd received A Sign From Above, and since I don't screw around with Signs From Above, I made my way to Jamie Sue's room and peeked in. My mother and father were visiting, talking quietly. There was no sign of Kathleen, thank heaven. Boy, did I mean that literally!

"Am I interrupting?" I asked. I waited and gauged the sentiment. Something had definitely changed. Or was it me who had changed?

"Hey," I said hesitantly, "why don't I come back later?"

I pulled a U-ey, but before I got two feet past the door, Kyla grabbed me from behind. "Not so fast, my little rabbit," she whispered. "You can't run forever."

"I'm not running," I whispered indignantly ... "Am I?"

Kyla shook her head at the naughty little girl that was me and said, "No matter where you go, there you are."

"Wow, let me write that down."

I turned back toward Jamie Sue's room and discovered that everyone was staring at me. I laughed weakly.

"I'll be right behind you," Kyla whispered and poked me in the back with a bony finger.

"So you can use my body as a shield when they start shooting?" I asked over my shoulder. My folks were looking at me oddly now.

"To block your escape." She grabbed me again and pulled me closer. "Listen, you idiot, I had a chat with your mom. Did you ever stop to consider that she might be in worse emotional shape over this brouhaha than you?"

Only Kyla could get away with a word like "brouhaha." I held my tongue in answer.

"No," she went on, "I didn't think so. Sarah looks strong; is that it? She sounds so sure of herself. Bushwa! You should know her better than that

The Cancer Club

by now, because she's been your mother for the entirety of your miserable life. Have you considered that maybe her anger doesn't have anything to do with you? Ah! I see I have touched upon a novel concept! Good! Just be in that room with her for a few minutes, okay? You don't even have to smile or say nice things. Then you can lace up your track shoes and get the hell out."

"But ... she doesn't want me there."

"Don't be a dodo."

I made a quick deal with myself. "Maybe I could get through a few minutes ... as long as it wasn't more than, say ... seven. Seven minutes, then. And I mean seven minutes."

I took a deep breath and was surprised to feel again that lovely peace from the chapel when I stepped back into the room. "Hi, everybody, me again." I decided not to embrace Sarah and cleared my throat instead. "Mother." When I air kissed her cheek, she stiffened but didn't turn away.

My dad smiled and stood up to hug me. "I'm glad to see you." I noticed that he was wearing the sweater I'd given him last Christmas. It was a signal to me, and I was grateful to see it.

Jamie Sue was ethereally pale, almost angelic, an optical illusion undermined by the bruised, charcoal tinge around her eye sockets. Her skin still had the taut look of medical trauma, and I noticed how still she lay. Her eyes were startling in their depth of blue. Talbot's eyes. Our father's eyes.

A male nurse, sensing the crackling electricity that accompanied my arrival, laughed nervously and hastily exited with his thermometer and blood-pressure machine.

That's when I noticed that Kyla had suddenly disappeared, leaving me to face The Enemy all by myself. That bitch! The selfish, heartless bitch...

There were no chairs left, so I sat on the bed, careful not to touch Jamie Sue. "What does Dr. Marxer say?"

My mother answered, "If you'd been here with the rest of us, you'd know what he had to say."

"You're right, Mother."

At least she was speaking to me.

Close up, Jamie Sue looked even more exhausted. "They think they've found it in time," she said without emotion.

That was the first moment Jamie Sue's distress seemed real to me. She turned toward me then and said, "Surgery day after tomorrow. I guess I'm over my ... my accident. They're hopeful—about the operation, I mean." Then her face closed over, and her energy ebbed inward.

I recognized her shame and her fear as unfamiliar empathy welled up inside me. "I'm sorry. For ... whatever distress I caused you. I didn't know you were ... We haven't ... We aren't ... I still can't. Oh, shit." I took a deep breath and started again. "I understand you'll be seeing Kyla. Good. She's the best. She's helped me a lot." I held Jamie Sue's hand for a moment.

My sister still looked flat, two-dimensional. She said, "If it hadn't been for you, Marly, I wouldn't have had the tests, whatever Sarah says." My mother sniffed. "I might never have found out in time." Her voice was a monotone.

"I'm glad you did. And it is in time; you gotta keep hold of that. I'll keep hold of it, too. Listen, I have to get to my book for a while. But I'll be back."

Just in front of the elevator, I checked my watch. "Hmmm," I said under my breath. "Eight minutes, twenty-two seconds. Not bad ... Not bad at all."

A young candy striper pushing a book cart had heard my little exchange with myself from somewhere behind me. After we got in the elevator together, she stared down at her feet in embarrassment.

"Don't pay any attention to me," I said. "Middle age, you know. It softens the brain."

And maybe the heart.

I went back home and fixed a gigantic snack of refried beans, salsa and chips with melted cheese slathered over the top. It tasted awful, so I poured it down the garbage disposal.

On the floor by the mail slot, I found a note from J.D. "Marly, I was glad to be of some help. I miss you already. I'll call you."

He'd put his telephone number below and had started writing a postscript, which he'd crossed out. I held it up to the light, but I couldn't make out any of the words.

A most unusual man.

I spent the next several hours with my manuscript. For some reason, the words and images poured out of me like gushing spouts at Niagara Falls. I located two big-as-houses story holes in the early chapters and plugged them solid. And when I came up with a sweet story from my own childhood to illustrate a point about the protagonist's character, I was rollin' on down the road.

I took a break around four and called Miriam in New York. I knew she'd still be in the office, slaving away.

"Damage control is under way," she said. "I've calmed the storm for the moment. And we should have the contracts on the film project by the end of this week. Oh, did I tell you? Glenn Close is very interested in the part. I like her. She's a reader, you know. Of books, my dear. I sent the manuscript to her agent last week. Without telling you."

I wondered why everyone called me "my dear."

"You're the best, Miriam," I said. "A marvel."

"I agree. How's Jamie Sue?"

"Hangin' in there."

"And you? Are you hangin' in there?"

"Better than that. The book will be done by the end of next week." I hung up the phone on her gasp of delight.

Sugar called, too. "Where in the hell have you been, Marly? Didn't you get my messages? I hate it when you don't call back. What is going on out there?"

"I've been ... up to my ass in alligators."

"I've been worried sick about you! Is Jamie Sue going to be okay?"

"They handled the suicide thing—the physical part, anyway; an overload of pills, I guess. Kyla's going to start helping with the rest."

"God, she must be going through hell."

"Yeah."

"And ..."

"They're hopeful about the cancer. They caught it early."

"Thank God."

"Listen, call Serena for me, will you? And thank her for the plane tickets ... and everything."

"You got it."

I had a brief conversation with Lark.

"So when does the Great Neo-Therapist make her next appearance?" I asked.

"I start back next week, taking classes in adult therapy. The kids were tough enough. I am excited, but I'm really nervous."

"You'll be great; I know it. You're so patient with people. Now you'll have patients who'll pay you for being patient."

"Why do I get the feeling you have more confidence in me than I have in myself?" she asked.

The doorbell rang. "Ask your analyst," I said. "Gotta run."

"I love you, too."

I went to the door and found my father on the other side.

"Dad." I could hear the wonder in my own voice.

He looked tired. He was holding a small box of See's candy. "For you."

"Come in, come in. Light chocolate molasses chips! Oh, boy!"

He took me in his arms and hugged me for a long time. "Am I interrupting ...?" he asked.

"You know me; I welcome any reason to take a break. Writing a book is the best way to get shelves built in the garage."

"Your mother's the same way."

"Is she? Where is she?" I asked.

"Still at the hospital."

So he'd come by himself. It was so unlike him, coming to me like that. Oh, he has plenty of backbone, but he didn't make a habit of playing The Peacemaker.

"How about some wine with our chocolate?" he asked.

I opened a nice bottle of Pouilly-Fuissé, and we settled ourselves onto the couch in my living room. Knowing how unused he was to rescue work, I was curious as to where he'd begin.

Finally he said, "You remember that fishing trip we went on together? When you were ten?"

"And I got my period," I said, laughing. "Boy were you shocked and not too thrilled about going to the market for me, either."

He nodded in agreement. "I've never been good with that female stuff. Besides, you were still my little girl. What business did you have being a woman?" He closed his eyes for a moment. "You always will be my little girl, even if you live to be a hundred."

I waited, my curiosity growing.

He opened his eyes again. "Your mother is the most compelling person I've ever met." He took a chip, broke it in half, and popped it into his mouth. "I recall vividly the first time I ever saw her," he said as he chewed. "It was the summer of '58. In La Jolla, at the Beach and Tennis Club. She was twenty-one."

I poured myself another glass of wine, careful not to upset the delicate mood that had fallen over the room with the twilight.

My father went on. "She'd come down to the beach with your grandparents, who were staying at the hotel. I still picture them, Rachael and Clay, laying out fluffy, blue beach towels. You can't imagine the glory of your mother in those days: so full of life, bursting with life."

He stood up and walked to the window. The failing day covered his face with pastel light. "I was already married then, with an eight-year-old daughter, and I wasn't unhappy. But something about your mother touched a place in my heart I didn't know existed. A wellspring was tapped inside me."

He reached to the wall and turned on the bank of track lights on the ceiling above him. The pale shadows of dusk were rounded out with the warm pink of the bulbs. I saw the daydream of that other time pass across his eyes, infusing them with a glow and his face with color.

"I had always thought of myself as an ethical person; I was raised that way. Duty, responsibility, morality. My life was carefully planned, and I knew who I was and where I was going." He shook his head at his own youthful naïveté. "But in that moment, everything I had known, had been, was turned on its ear. Without doing a thing, your mother reached inside me and captured my soul. I had to have her forever, no matter the consequences. And there were heavy consequences, as you know."

I nodded.

"That is to say," he continued, "you know a small portion of the story. I agonized three long days before telling Kathleen, who was dumbfounded. She kept asking me what she'd done and refused to believe that I had done little more than meet this girl. She couldn't understand how a man like me could throw away a good marriage, a family, and every tenet I'd held dear for a woman who might not even want me when the dust settled. I couldn't explain it to Kathleen then. I couldn't explain it to her now ... after more than thirty years." He shook his head in wonder.

To get the blood going again in my head, I drank down the rest of my wine. It was hard to picture my father overcome with violent emotion of any kind.

"Kathleen left me that very day and took Jamie Sue with her. I wrote Sarah a letter, explaining everything, and left it for her at the reception desk. She called my room and agreed to meet me.

"We went for a walk on the beach. I remember the tide was coming in. We spoke of inconsequential things: the weather, the Beach Club, peanut butter and banana sandwiches. That we both adored peanut butter and banana sandwiches seemed absolutely miraculous."

Dad walked over and sat down beside me. He took my hand and held it lightly before going on. "When I asked if I could see her again, she said yes without any hesitation. And the day my divorce was final, Sarah and I were married. Two weeks later, Sarah discovered she was almost three months pregnant. With you."

He kissed me. Then, "I've never spoken of these things to anyone. Jamie Sue only knows what Kathleen told her. But I decided it was time for you to know the truth. Because you see ... your mother ..." He thought for a moment. "Your mother needs our help now."

He stood up again and began to pace. I could see him picking his words carefully out of the air.

"Your grandparents were against our marriage in the beginning. They were horrified. Not so much by the scandal, I guess. They were worried about Sarah ... and no more than I was. In fact, I was the one who left, the one time we were formally separated. I had it in my mind that I'd ruined her life and that leaving was the only decent thing I could do."

He stopped and gathered his thoughts. I remember wondering how long he'd planned this speech. I could see how hard it was for him to share it with me. "And my life fell apart. I couldn't eat or sleep. I couldn't work. Because in all the years Sarah and I have spent together and apart, I never could have been with anyone else, once I'd seen her. And your mother knew that. My love for her is shameless, complete. Total. It's that fact, maybe more than any other single thing, that's the reason we're together now. She rescued me from my loneliness. She saved my life—literally, by giving me hers."

"What are you saying?"

"That she's carried the burden of my monumental and overwhelming feelings all this time. You can't imagine the weight or the responsibility. It would have crushed a lesser person."

My dad looked interested in his own monologue, like he'd just figured all this out for the first time ten minutes ago, like his life and my mother's had never made sense before.

"I will always belong to her. She owns me. One of us leaving won't change that. And though she probably wishes her life had been different, especially her relationship with you, she kept her part of our bargain even though she's never felt about me the way I feel about her."

He stroked his chin and waited for his words to sink in. After a minute or two, he said, "You must have a million questions, but honestly, I don't have any answers. I can tell you that I welcomed your coming, that I'm proud of you, that I loved you in my own way. But for me, there's never been anyone like Sarah. And I've hurt her and hated her and blamed her for the mistakes I made. She's hurt me, too. And hated herself. But the love ... so much love … It's been a damn good relationship." He was done and grinned shyly.

I didn't know quite what to make of all this, and I'm not sure my father did, either.

He kissed me lightly on the cheek and walked to the front door. He said, "I love Jamie Sue, you know. She's a part of me; I can't help it. But no man ever loved a daughter more than I've loved you. How little we know each other these days. I'd like us to do something about that."

And then he drifted out into the night.

Chapter 30

Chris telephoned me that evening. Through the miracle of modern technology, word of the giant snafu (situation normal ... all fucked-up) that was my life had grapevined all the way to the wilds of Cleveland, Ohio. I spoke to him briefly, feeling curiously detached, and said that everything was Fine, Just Fine.

It was by way of a brush-off. I got the impression he was expecting emotional fireworks and that he was let down when he didn't get them. Did he expect me to pine away for his company? Men...

By the time I dropped in on Jamie Sue, visiting hours were almost over. The hospital was uncommonly quiet and emptying out. Jamie Sue was alone and sleeping so peacefully, I decided not to wake her. Instead, I wrote this joke on a paper towel roll:

A little Jewish man named Sam, whose general contracting business was in deep weeds because of the recession, took to visiting the synagogue each night to pray for a miracle.

"Help me, Lord," he begged. "Let me win the lottery. Please! Pleeeease! I'll donate money to charity. I'll send my mother on that trip to Miami Beach she's always nagging me about. Just please, pleeeease let me win the lottery. Pleeeease!!"

Four long days and nights Sam spent in the synagogue, praying and weeping and gnashing his teeth. Finally, dejected and worn out, Sam gave up. He decided to go back to his house and sleep. What more could he do? On the way home, the clouds in the night sky parted, and a voice boomed out, "Sam ... do me a favor, will you? Meet me halfway! Buy a ticket!"

And then I wrote: "Jamie Sue, You bought a ticket; you'll win the lottery. Love, Marly."

I've always been fascinated by the machinery of life. I burn to know why people do what they do and what makes the world the way it is. Unfortunately, there are rarely finite answers to these questions, only glimpses of truths and half-truths too powerful and subtle to define with hard edges.

It's been frustrating. I frustrate myself! But once I have my little fists around something, I can't seem to make myself let go, no matter how bollixed-up things get.

I know that's another reason why I'm a writer. I like to tinker with mechanisms, but I'm no good with screwdrivers or nuts and bolts or electrical wiring or pipes. I'm good with people, the workings of the human heart ... when I'm not pissing someone off, that is. I can disentangle emotions and passions and behavioral patterns quite nicely. I can determine where the fear began to fester into rage. And I get so damned fascinated; I have a tough time just being with someone. Enjoying them. Instead of eating Raisinets or playing Liar's Poker together, I prefer to delve down into their inner workings and watch the gears mesh or grind. 'Why,' 'why,' and 'why' are my three favorite words in the English language.

You can see why this pisses people off or exhausts them. And even though I'm careful about not judging, my friends get edgy when I poke and probe too much. Kyla once said that my whole life was a group therapy session with all the other folks in the group banging on the doors to get out.

So I had no idea in the world what in the hell I was going to do about my mother.

Should I call her? Would she talk to me? What if she got fed up? She was already fed up, of course, so I didn't have much to worry about on that score. Maybe I ought to wait. That idea made me nuts.

Hmmmm.

So I waited. And made myself nuts. And waited some more.

In the meantime, I signed the contracts on BloodHounds and sent Miriam two round-trip tickets to Antigua as a bonus. Sugar had a knock-down, drag-out blow-up with her much younger man. She called me hysterically, claiming that he'd stolen her car. I extracted a promise from her to visit me pronto, with a view toward mutual man-bashing, raging, and sobbing.

Jamie Sue had the operation. I visited her twice a day, and we spoke about inconsequential things. Dr. Marxer said he was encouraged by the results and that the prognosis was good. Since he wasn't an accomplished liar by trade, we were encouraged.

When she started on her chemotherapy, I brought her a gorgeous and frivolous wig. I let Kyla do all the necessary prying and tinkering into my sister's psyche. And made myself nuts because I itched to hear.

But not quite as nuts.

My father and I took a fishing trip together. The good news was that I unexpectedly got my first period since coming off radiation therapy. Which was coupled by an announcement from Dr. Dent on my answering machine that I wasn't sterile after all. The bad news was my dad had to go to the market for me and buy "plugs and pads" (his words). He still wasn't any good at female stuff, but he was a damned good sport.

"O.B.? Is that a brand name? Unscented ... What the hell does the other kind smell like? No! Don't tell me! No applicator? What's an applicator? Never mind! I don't even want to think about that. Why do they put the pads in wrappers? And how do I tell if they're wrapped? Why do they need to be wrapped?" He hung his head like a little boy.

"Ask the manager," I answered.

"Damn," he said and slammed the door to my motel room.

Later, at dinner, we discovered we both adored mayonnaise on our French fries. And felt badly for Wynonna Judd. And missed Johnny Carson, Cary Grant and Amelia Earhart's mystery.

I didn't ask him about Mother.

J.D. didn't call for two weeks. And I waited while resigning myself to waiting. Until I couldn't wait any longer. I tried the number he'd given me.

"Hello?" his machine answered. "This is the old cowpokes' home. J.D.'s out roundin' up eggs for the Easter Bunny. He may be gone for a while, but if you leave a message, his attendant will be sure and pass it along."

I started to speak. And decided I wasn't ready to stop waiting. I wasn't getting good at it, exactly. But I'd convinced myself that waiting was a form of doing something.

I wrote feverishly and sent the completed manuscript to Miriam three days early, along with an outline of my cancer story, which I had taken to calling The Cancer Club. She took everything with her on her trip to Half-Moon Bay Hotel.

Boom! My desk was suddenly clean. I didn't have a rewrite or research or a contract deadline staring me in the face. I decided I deserved a rest from banging my head on my computer keyboard.

So I played. Tennis and golf first and then I started back on my workouts. I went to the Western Connection, a cowboy hangout, and took their dance lessons. I learned the Ten-Step and the Tush Push and the Cowboy Cha-Cha. I practiced the Electric Glide and the Achy-Breaky. I waltzed and swung (East Coast and country) and generally had a ball.

Just about the time I resolved to give up on the son of a bitch, J.D. finally called. "So how's the book coming?"

He acted as though he'd seen me the day before.

"Done," I answered, biting off the rest of my reply.

"You're kidding. But that's great! Why didn't you call and tell me?"

Huh?

"I know," he continued enthusiastically, "why don't I come to town and help you celebrate?"

I had to laugh. "Why don't you?"

"Is ... everything else going well?"

I laughed again. "Yes."

We both waited for a moment.

"I've been thinking about you," he said more softly. "How about I come see you this very weekend?"

"Yes."

"I'll call you later with my flights. You still the prettiest woman I've ever seen?"

"You make that decision when you get here."

I picked J.D. up Friday afternoon. We didn't fall into one another's arms like we'd never been apart. We didn't pick up where we'd left off. No, we circled one another like wary animals perched to bolt.

"God, I'm glad I remembered you the way you actually are," was the closest he came to a compliment.

It wasn't until after dinner that I felt the thaw come. I was drinking a shot of Patrón for purely medicinal reasons. He was sipping a tall scotch and water.

I watched him watch me. He drew in his breath and said, "I didn't call."

"No."

"You didn't, either."

"No," I said again.

He took my hand. "My life's a mess right now. But I figure, by the time we really get to know each other, I'll have all that crap straightened out. You would like to get to know me better, wouldn't you?"

"Yes."

He looked relieved. "Well, that's all right, then."

I nodded. "You didn't know if I felt what you felt."

His eyes glowed. "Yes." He took my hand and held it in his tightly. "Yes," he said again.

The sex between us was like nothing I'd ever experienced before. He was tender, gentle. And yet he was on fire with his need for me. He kissed me and stroked me and touched me and stared at my body.

When I finally gasped and tried to pull away, he laid his head on my belly and exhaled soft, warm air into my groin.

When he was finally ready, I saw the liquid look in his eyes as he pushed his way slowly inside me. I had never been so wet, a mixture of my juices and his kisses. We rocked back and forth in the cradle of love for lush minutes. I remember the tremor in his thighs whenever he'd stop moving to hold onto his control. "It's too good," he whispered. "I don't want to stop yet."

But there was something beyond sex: a climax beyond orgasm and a feeling beyond any physical pleasure. The greatest part of the experience was his obvious regard for me, a respect that I felt from him in a way I had never felt it from another man. He couldn't hide it, and he didn't want to hide it, and he didn't try to hide it.

Somewhere in the middle of all this ... the telephone rang. Don't worry; I didn't answer it.

But I should have.

Chapter 31

About ten minutes in to our horizontal dance, I heard a key turn in my front door. The universe down-shifted into slow motion, and thirteen conclusions flitted across my mind in the space of a heartbeat. My parents had a key. My hugely pregnant secretary had a key, but what would she be doing here? So it was either Dad or Mom, and I hoped to hell it was Dad.

Now remember, all these things flickered across my consciousness as J.D. and I were uncoiling. I also remember thinking we would've been fine, just fine, if we'd only waited to get to the bedroom. As things stood, however, (You should pardon the pun.) my mother entered my apartment and caught us bare-assed and red-faced.

She and I had carefully avoided being alone in the same room together for weeks. Of course, we weren't exactly alone in my living room. I'll never forget the look on her face. She paused in the doorway for a good twenty seconds before finally stepping inside and closing the door firmly behind her. "I guess I should've tried calling again." Her voice was muffled but decipherable.

I crab-walked into my room just behind J.D., dragging garments as I went. In the safety of my bedroom, I sat on the floor for a moment, trying to catch my mind up as it galloped away and seeing myself as my mother had just seen me. Oh, my God!

"Think she'll ... go? Just turn around and go?" he asked in a hopeful whisper. "I sure as hell don't ever want to see that woman again." His face was strawberry pink. "Actually, I don't want her to see me."

"It was awkward, wasn't it?" I whispered back. I touched my own cheeks and felt the heat. "There's no way she'll leave. She obviously came here to wait for me, not knowing I was already home."

"How's the book coming, Marly?" my mother yelled through the shut door, thus signaling her intention to wait us out.

"Finished it last week," I answered loud enough for her to hear. "See?" I whispered to J.D. "She's too much like me to walk out on such a juicy situation."

"I don't get it," he said. "If she's not speaking to you, what the hell is she doing here?"

I had stumbled to my bathroom and was running a soapy washcloth haphazardly over all the pertinent parts of my body. "I don't know!"

As I whipped on a warm-up suit, J.D. jumped into the shower. "Coward!" I yelled in at him.

"You bet your ass!" he yelled back.

I let her in.

She made herself at home on my Santa Fe sofa and extended her hand to invite me to go first. No way.

"Miriam says *The End of the Trail is* the best thing you've done." She sounded sincere and non-controversial. "I'm so happy for you." Meaningful pause. "I mean that."

"Thanks." I cleared my throat and straightened up. Head back, chin up, put on a good show, you know. Like my parents always have ... I leaned against the fireplace mantle. "How about some ... tea?" I asked and headed to the kitchen.

I heard her following behind, her footsteps hesitant. Her voice was surer. "Tea? Yes ... well, actually, I think I'd rather have a Mexican Mary."

"I think I might join you."

She was skillfully avoiding my eyes as I poured generous drinks into a couple of long glasses. She gulped hers half-down, and I took a sip of mine. I pointed over my shoulder. "I better check on my ... friend."

She nodded.

J.D. was sitting on the edge of the bed. Actually, he was perched and ready to bolt. "I don't feel like coming out," he said.

"So don't."

"How long will she be here?" he asked.

I shrugged my shoulders.

"Is there a back way outta here, Marly?"

"Through that window there and down the drainpipe."

"Oh." His shoulders sagged. "Got any recent suicide manuals?"

"I collected them for a time. I also have cable TV: fifty-something channels. You could die of boredom." I felt ridiculous. "I feel ridiculous," I added for good measure.

He grinned then. "Life's a bitch."

I mussed his wet hair. "I'm amazed I can still face you."

"There're lots of worse things than being caught naked by your mother."

"Name one."

"Can't."

"What am I gonna say, J.D.? I haven't got a clue."

"You could always try letting her talk first."

I flashed a look into the living room, where I discovered that Mother had poured herself another Mexican Mary and was now reclining across my sofa. "I always liked this piece," she said, rubbing her fingers across the nap of the cloth and then dandled her foot over the side. I noticed she'd taken off her shoes. "Why is tequila so soothing?" she asked herself. "Must be the cactus juice," she answered herself.

I finally dredged up the nerve to reenter my own living room and asked her, "How about your article?"

She tossed her head back. "My article. I'm ... still working on it. Like the French chef whose very first baked potato exploded in the oven, eet's a leetle more coamplicated than I thought."

I waited.

She closed her eyes and said, "I ... I've had some new thoughts on the subject of modern marriage."

I still waited.

She said, "I ran into Kathleen today."

"Oh? At the hospital?"

"Yes. She spoke to me without yelling. Can you imagine?"

"After all these years? That's pretty amazing."

Sarah frowned. "She was touched by my concern."

"Of course she was. Mother, it happened such a long time ago."

She arched her eyebrows. "Mother? Not 'Mom' any longer?"

"You never liked 'Mom.'"

"Oh, I didn't mind nearly as much as I pretended."

She gestured theatrically in the direction of the kitchen. I inferred I was to bring her the bottle of Patrón, and I complied.

We hadn't said anything deep. Yet each time we spoke, I felt the dynamic of our relationship changing by millimeters. How to describe it? I began to really look at her. Not as a child looks at a mother, with total adoring acceptance and absolute belief in her power to protect, but as a complex human being with problems and weaknesses. I really listened to her nuance of tone, and I watched the way she turned things over in her mind. I noticed how she struggled and hesitated before verbalizing her thoughts. I studied the way she moved and thought about the way she looked at Dad when he smiled. How often she intimately took his hand and stroked his fingertips with hers.

"Your father is an uncommon man," she said and shivered. "A possum just walked over my grave."

It bowled me over then how little I knew her, apart from our common umbilical cord—as a separate entity, sovereignty, an autonomous soul who didn't have all the answers and who was sometimes usually smart enough to know she didn't have all the answers.

"He awakens things in me ... I am still ill-prepared to deal with," she said.

I was unsettled to catch her sexuality. There was crackling electricity about her as she considered the man who was my father and her husband. It was weird to think of them coupled and sweating, gasping out their moans of satisfaction.

I looked for the glory Dad had seen in her all those years ago and found it immediately in her smile and in her laugh. In the wistful melancholy that sometimes tiptoed across her face when she thought no one was looking.

I was curious, suddenly, about a woman I'd taken for granted all of my life.

"Tell me about the article ...," I ventured. "Maybe a fresh viewpoint would help."

She looked at me closely. Was I prying? I saw the transaction take place on her face. I was, she decided.

"I was quite young when I met your father," she began. "But I was quite independent. The places I'd been with Rachael and Clay! Europe. Africa. New York City, which may have been the most exotic and dangerous destination of all. I was a virgin, but I was sophisticated, a neat trick. In fact, I wondered throughout my teen years if I'd ever meet someone fascinating enough to marry." She wriggled her toes. "Rachael worried about me, a mother's primary function ... worrying. Not to show it, but to do it.

"My father was the neatest man. He always believed I'd land on my feet even through the ... the trouble."

She brushed some imaginary cobwebs away from her mind and continued. "The article, yes. Well, actually, I've come to a rip-roaring halt. I'm stuck in a bog, which is a metaphor for my own shifting sands." She tapped at her head. "It's a real pisser; I mean, when do you ever finally get there?"

"I haven't the faintest idea."

"I wish I'd never met your father." She was matter-of-fact calm. "I would have been a much fuller person if he hadn't taken so damned much of me."

She set down her glass on the table and had to sit up to do it. "Modern marriage is full of heartache." She hung her head. "My heart aches for you. And for me."

"I don't understand."

"I don't, either. Let's go for a walk."

"Huh?"

"A walk. I feel like walking. Tell your friend you'll be back later."

I found the bedroom through a fog. J.D. was flipping through a back issue of *World Tennis*.

"Marly? Are you okay?"

"What a stupid question. Do I look okay to you?" I glared at him for a moment. Then, "I'm sorry. My parents're ... they're ..."

"Acting weird?" he asked gently.

"Yes. Exactly. Weird! It's scaring me."

"Why?"

"What do you mean 'why?'"

"Can't they act human?"

"No. They're not supposed to." I clicked my tongue at myself.

"Don't beat yourself up too bad, Marly. You're doing okay." He waggled his finger at me. "You hear me? I mean it." He gave me a yummy kiss.

"How come you're so smart about all this?" I asked.

"Two reasons," he answered. "When my sister went through Betty Ford for coke addiction a couple years back, she asked me to go with her. As an out-patient, to kinda help her. I did. Learned a lot about ... trouble. And that my sister wasn't the only one who got screwed up in the last thirty years. That's the first reason."

"I'm listening."

"Second reason is ... since this is your mess, it's easy for me to talk a good game, 'cause I'm not in the middle." He kissed me again. It was yummier. "I'll be here when you get back. And remember ... You gotta suffer headaches in this life, but you don't have to bash yourself over the head."

My mother had always liked to walk. Along the beach or in the city, on dirt roads or blacktop. She spent her first ten years on a farm near Lost Nation, Iowa where everyone did a lot of walking and figures she just never got out of the habit. "You might come across something interesting you wouldn't see from a car or a plane or even a bicycle. I once found a gold

Bulova watch on the sidewalk at Fifth and Lexington in the middle of Manhattan!"

Sarah made straight for the small park three streets over. It'd been there a long time; you could tell by the size of the trees.

"I've always liked the rose beds here. Most city parks can't be bothered with roses these days." She took in the rich scent. "God, that's good."

"Do you miss Iowa?" I asked, out of the blue.

My mother looked at me keenly. "I've been thinking about Home Farm a lot lately; how did you know?"

I shrugged. "Do you still miss Francesca?"

"Oh my, yes. She was the dearest person I ever knew. I don't miss her every hour of every day ... but when I think of her, when the feeling of her suddenly sweeps over me, I still cry. It's not even sadness, really. She was the best friend I ever had."

I hugged her and felt her heart racing. "What is it you want to tell me?" I asked.

"Odd. You suddenly seem like the parent, while I feel like the child. Let's go sit on the swings."

She pumped herself gently into the air while I drizzled my feet across the dirt.

Back and forth went the swing. "I came here to tell you ... that your father and I are separating." Back and forth. "I don't think it's forever, but I'm not sure." Back and forth. "I need to ... be apart from him." I heard the catch in her voice. "Live by myself for a time and spend time with you, just the two of us. Visit Rachael and Clay. Maybe spend some time on Home Farm. Maybe we could spend the summer there together; it's such a wonderfully healing place."

"I remember," I said.

She turned her face toward me. "You're a ... a remarkable child. Woman. I wonder at the little I had to do with that." She turned away. "You always seemed so self-sufficient. I wished you'd come to me the way you used to go to Grandfather Clay. The way I used to go to Francesca." Back and forth. "God knows we've argued enough these past years to have settled seven tons of dust. But there might be more ... What do you think?" Back and forth. "Aren't you going to say something?"

"This soul-searching shit seems to be catching."

"Your young man has a gorgeous behind."

The minute Sarah left, I called Dad. "Is it true?"

"Yes," he answered.

"I don't understand."

"Didn't she explain?"

"Yes."

"Well, then, you know as much as I do."

"That's it? That's it? That's all you're going to say?"

"I love you, Marly; we both do. We always have, and we always will. What more do you need to know?"

I heard the dial tone but couldn't seem to put the receiver back on its cradle. What in the hell was happening to everybody?

"Marly?"

"What? What?"

"Testy. That's because you're starving. All that emotional stuff stirs up the juices. I could do with a meal myself. Why don't we go out somewhere nice? Any place you like. Put on some fancy clothes and do it up right. What do you say?"

"You don't expect me to eat? Now? I couldn't possibly eat now; my life is falling apart."

"Why suuure," he said with extra drawl. "All the more reason."

"They can't do this. You don't understand, J.D.! They can't do this!"

He put his arm around me. "I guess they don't know that." He kissed me. "Hmmmm. Let's do that again."

I don't know why I let myself go. Maybe it was the way he said, "Hmmmm."

When we finally came up for air, it hit me like a ton of bricks: I was hungry ... for everything. For the adventure that waited ahead, for the sex between J.D. and me, for family arguments and holiday meals and all the books I still had to write. I was hungry for life.

But all I said was, "You like Greek food?"

Epilog

Shortly after I started writing this book, I decided not to sit in with the Cancer Club for a while. I figured it might be better artistically and soulfully to try it on my own, sort out what's what, see if I could practice in my life and set down on paper what everybody and their brother'd been preaching at me for the last year or more ... and at least some of what I'd been feeling. The very next day, her antennae quivering, Kyla called and asked if I'd be interested in working at the center on a consulting basis.

"What the hell does that mean?" I asked.

"Who knows? Interested?"

"I'm amazed you think I can help. Of course I'm interested. I'm not sure I have enough ..."

She interrupted, "Patience? Empathy? Knowledge? Think you're too angry? Get in line, girl."

"But ..."

"But nothing. Let's take the facts, ma'am: You ask a lot of questions; you're inconvenient that way. In fact, you're often infuriating. But that can be a good thing. You're a novelist with real credits; some messed-up person might eventually be persuaded that you know something about human nature. You're passionate when you believe, and you have a good heart. Twisted but good. And boy, have you been there. We can definitely use you."

"Okay, okay. You bullied me into it."

How do you thank someone for your life? You get up off your butt. And you know me ... I could have such a lot of fun running around asking why, why, why, driving everyone nuts ... and still make a real contribution.

I was hoping to come up with a big, bold end to this story, something dramatic and earth-shattering: a cliff-hanger, a lottery win, a fairy-tale wedding.

Unfortunately, my life isn't cooperating.

Hell, I can't even tidy it up. Picture all these little tapestry threads of various thicknesses and colors wafting in the breeze, unresolved and autonomous. Let's see...

The Cancer Club

After three long weeks, Sugar finally arrived in a quivering mass of wine-assisted self-pity. She ranted and moaned and wailed and flayed his ass verbally by turns. I bit my lip practically in two, but for three loooong days I never probed or poked for any deeper meanings or realizations.

She kissed me when I put her on the plane back to Tucson, feeling rested and centered and ready to flay his ass for real. "I never realized what a good listener you are," I remember her saying.

Janet and Richard, back from extended travels, have added another weekly therapy session ... which means they're up to three: one for him, one for her, one for them.

My end with Chris marked the beginning of the end of my breakdown. At this time in his journey, he doesn't have enough heart to empathize with human frailty. If five years of therapy didn't do it, I'm not sure there's a power on earth that can do it.

I deserve better.

Lark began her internship for real. She's busier than a one-armed juggler on roller skates and is, therefore, too busy to even think about how she's doing, so I don't ask. I don't get to see her much, either, and I miss her. I can see how our paths have separated, and I wonder about the future of our friendship.

Good Ol' Don called to tell me Tawnie with an "i-e" was pregnant. So past being surprised when he asked if I'd mind their naming the baby after me. It was Tawnie's idea, apparently. Obviously God has been working overtime on Her comedy routine.

Skip called to say he was thinking of getting engaged to a girl he'd met in Colorado six months ago. Which meant she and he had already known one another, in the biblical sense, when he'd asked me to go along with him on The Persuasion. I patted myself on the back for my superb judgment and moved him from my DayRunner to my Rolodex.

J.D. is still behaving like the kindest man I ever met. He also has a slight pathology in the money department—a character flaw he readily, almost cheerfully, admits. And his business has turned an encouraging corner.

He wants me to move to Tucson and marry him, not necessarily in that order, and I'm thinking about it. I'm not a cynic; I'm willing to admit that happiness exists. But not in a vacuum. You can't have happiness without all the human slings and arrows of outrageous fortune. I feel unaccountably peaceful with J.D. Peace is good. It remains to be seen whether peace is enough.

The sex ain't bad, either.

Jamie Sue and I have tacitly agreed to a truce. These days, she hasn't got the energy to hold up her part of the feud, and I have acknowledged the stupidity of trying to hold it up by myself. She lost her uterus and tubes in the surgery, which puts her squarely into menopause. On the plus side, she attracted the emotional interest of the surgeon, a good guy with a great sense of humor. He's married. Oh, well.

My mother's having one helluva time. I ache for her. She is being incredibly rough on herself about the screw-ups in other peoples' lives, as if she were personally responsible. She'll get worse before she gets over it.

My father is doing a lot better than I expected. Of course, he already had his mid-life crisis, and he's absolutely, positively sure he and Sarah will end up together. I have come to consider them separately, which feels odd, and try not to think about their splitting up after all these years. I am keeping my mouth shut unless asked a direct question ... which feels even odder.

As for me? All my life, I thought I had this gift for living that made me special. I was sure that someday I'd make some startling contributions to the human condition. Believing this was important on many levels.

It's come to me this last year through my group that I might not end up changing the world with the sweep of my hand. I might not even effect one iota of significant or meaningful change in this world before I die. Unless maybe it's by reaching one person at a time. I now understand that's the most basic and pure reason for my writing; that's why I can't help it. The stories and the people running around in my head won't let me rest until their hard-learned truths are free to infiltrate the consciousness of others.

I feel more vulnerable, now that I've fought for my life and won. You'd think it'd be the opposite, but I'm humbled because I now grasp, at a gut level, how fragile life is, how unpredictable. And there's a melancholy accompanying this realization, but it's not the end of the world. In fact, I actually appreciate, in a way I couldn't before, how I've somehow managed to restructure my life. It was part accident, part grace. And you know something? I'm very proud of my priorities. Humanity in all its forms comes first. Although I wouldn't mind suddenly finding myself filthy rich.

Sometimes the learning process is painful and unavoidable.

Like Garth sang so eloquently: you can miss the pain, but then you'll miss the dance. I'm here to dance. Always was, always will be.

I think I'm saner than I was. The hole in my boob doesn't define me any more than the fact that I had a Major Breakdown. Whatever I've recovered, whatever I've learned, there's no guarantee I still won't go berserk someday and end up spending the holidays confined in a small space with people who behave no better than myself. I'm human—the saint and the sinner. Since God knows this, I guess I'll let Her figure out the tough stuff, and I'll just do the best I can each day. The one thing that stands out is that each step is more significant than where I end up.

"Life is not a problem to be solved; it's a mystery to be lived." Amen. Gotta go. The music's starting up again ...

Eren Ozker, 1948-1993

*Eren Ozkar died on February 25, 1993, after celebrating
one final Christmas. Her spirit inspired
and lightened everyone who knew her.
- Lucinda Sue Crosby*

**Following are Bulletins Eren Ozker wrote her friends
and family during her battle with cancer.**

Letter to My Friends   Bulletin #2

Here we are again: Notes from the Cancer Club!

I wrote the last bulletin just before starting chemo treatment. "Chemo" is short for chemical i.e. drugs. The drugs used in chemotherapy target and kill rapidly multiplying cells – like cancer cells. (And the cells that line the inside of your stomach and mouth and the cells that become the hair on your head.) Everybody reacts differently to chemotherapy. All the doctors can do is to list the "side effects" that might occur, with emphasis upon those effects he is pretty sure you will get to experience. This, I here testify, is a doozy of a list. It would give Rambo the heebie-jeebies.

Doctors talk of chemotherapy in terms of "courses." In my case, a course is supposed to last 21 days. Two to four days in the hospital (receiving drugs via IV), then for the rest of the cycle – unless some horrible infection complicates things – I just get a simple blood test once a week. After two courses, I will get a CAT scan, which hopefully will tell us if the treatment is working.

This is what it has been like:

Chemo Course #1: First I had a surgical procedure to get rid of the fluid in my chest, then they gave me chemo. Getting the drugs was a cinch. Most of the time I was happily seated. After two days, they took the IV out of my arm and shooed me out of the hospital. The really hard part was the first four days at home. No nausea. No vomiting. None of the disgusting side effects the doctor had so carefully prepared me for. But there was an awful, ferociously aggressive depression to battle and an intolerable "empty pit" feeling in my stomach plus a maddening zooming in my ears. Gradually these symptoms lessened until I began to feel more or less like a normal person ... who is very tired and who has recently eaten a dead puppy. Raw.

Eight days into my first chemo course, I pulled my wobbly self together and ventured into Mid-town for a therapy session. Felt very weird walking down the street – as if I was piloting myself by remote control, a space lien belonging to a different dimension from all the other people on the street. I felt invisible. It was freaky. After my session, I wandered over to Saks Fifth venue – where I have ALWAYS felt invisible – and that calmed me down. (I also bought a winter coat there. Shopping can be good medicine.)

Later that day, Fran "Meals On Feet" Brill appeared at our door carrying a casserole.)Fran is a very good cook and casseroles are terrific medicine. Not cooking is very good for us invalids.) In the course of our conversation, I mentioned my Mid-town adventure. Fran says it's not the chemotherapy. She says everybody feels that way in Mid-town Manhattan.

Ten days into my first chemo course: not bad! I take long naps. I have a persistent, runny nose and unless I take Tylenol, my joints ache in a very flu-like manner but aside from these symptoms, each day I feel a little peppier. The blood test shows that my white blood count (as expected) is disastrously low. Can't be around crowd of children because of the risk of infection. No problem. Neither crowds nor children are flinging themselves in my path.

Days 13 and 14 are great – I actually work as a puppeteer on an industrial film. God, it felt good! And my hair didn't start to fall out until it was over …

Days 15 to 20. My blood count is coming back up to normal right on schedule. Dr. Blum is very happy. (The count coming up means, you see, that his estimate of how big a dose of the drugs I could tolerate was right on the money and that he is a very brilliant fellow. I could have told him that.)

I live in a continual shower of falling hair. Bill hauls out the Dustbuster every hour or so and vacuums me off. I have my remaining hair cut to about an inch long. Very Gertrude Stein, Gertrude Stein. And still it rains hair. I take to wearing very large earrings and lots of bracelets in the vain hope that no one will notice my bald patches. (Oh! For a T-shirt that reads: I Usually Look Much Better Than This. Honest …)

As always, however, there s a silver lining: I haven't had to shave my legs in ages and there is no longer any need to pluck those pesky middle-aged hairs out of my chin!

Day #21: Back to the hospital for Course #2. Here we go again!

Chemo Course #2

Hey! Wait a minute! I thought this would be a repeat – with ugly variations – of the first course! What a letdown! No martyrdom here! The dead puppy tummy is back but I feel terrific after only five days! I'm positively bouncy! I wonder if this is normal … I'd better cal Dr. Blum and se if it's OK that I don't feel rotten … Anybody want to go out to dinner? I feel perky. God, this is weird! Perky is not my normal state.

I still find it a shock to look in the mirror. With a tambourine and a sheet I could go out to the airport and sell posies. (Where are all the Hara Krishnas these days? I haven't seen one in ages.) At first, after all the hair fell out, I wasn't exactly bald. There were lots of little hairs about a half-inch long sticking out perpendicularly from my scalp. But none of them were really close to each other. Bill kept insisting I was CUTE this way. He says, with my lasses on, I looked just like Adlai Stevenson. Every woman's fantasy role model. Forget it.

So I asked my friend, Bonnie Erickson, to shave my scalp for me. I no longer look pathetic. Instead, I look unnerving. Like a convict. Or someone who might be a terrorist. Have you seen the movie, "The Witches?" Nuff said. I am careful to wear pretty shoes.

I do have The Wig but it's taken me a little while to get used to it. It seems like such a lot of hair somehow, like an ersatz country/western singer …

I keep in mind what my Aunt June asserts: other people are really far too busy thinking about themselves to notice whatever it is you think is so glaringly wrong with you. She must be right. Nobody stares at e like I have a wig on when I have a wig on. And I have discovered the secret to successful no-hair-underneath-scarf-wearing: carpet tape. Great stuff. (I discovered carpet tape the day after my scarf blew off in a taxi cab. It was a silk scarf and it merrily danced around the back seat enjoying the breeze while the driver, who was too polite to mention my suddenly bald head and too fascinated to remove his gaze from the rearview mirror, narrowly avoided four different collisions in as many minutes. I speak for both myself and a very shaken cabbie when I say it seemed to take forever for me to capture the errant scarf, unknot it and recover my head.)

I go to Cancer Care (a wonderful organization) for individual therapy and for my weekly support group. And I have a "visualization" (guided imagery) coach. I have joined a second support group at the Manhattan Center for Living. The support groups are the best medicine imaginable.

Such gutsy, loving people, all helping themselves by helping each other. They fill me with awe; the human spirit at its best is a wonderful, a holy thing.

And I am getting used to the wig. It helps that the weather is getting cold and that I, unlike most cancer patients, have had experience wearing and grooming wigs. This is one of the many Advantages of Having Once Been An Actress When Fighting A Serious Illness. (I bet you thought I'd never get around to this.) Here are a few of the other Advantages I have found:

1) All doctors and nurses give directions. "When I do this," they say as they prepare to poke or puncture you, "just relax." Well, a trained theatrical can take directions! All those muscle isolation exercises we had to do (why?) twenty-some years ago on the floor of a dusty rehearsal stage come flooding back just when we really need them and we can actually relax the necessary body part. This is immensely useful. (This also helps when dealing with bedpans. I am quite good at bedpans.)

2) The evidence is that cancer patients who are active in a support group do better and live longer. But some patients are shy and afraid to express themselves "in public." Guess what ... I have no problem with it t all! To an ex-actress, Group is not a scary experience – it's a captive audience! Once a week, you get to say the most outrageously private things to an audience that knows exactly what you are talking about. Imagine! Getting praise for talking about yourself! You get to cry! You make people laugh! Isn't this what I went onstage for all those years ago?

3) You get better nursing when the staff of the hospital has recognized your husband or your visitors as actors they have seen on TV. You get really good service if one of your visitors has recently appeared on a soap opera.

4) When you are lying in the hospital bed unable to fall asleep a 2 a.m. and you are tired of meditating and bored with listening to your Self Affirmation for Cancer Patients cassette tapes, if you were once an actor, you have endless resources for creative thinking. This is the time when old audition monologues spring forth from whatever depths they have been lurking in all these years, eager for revision and resurrection. It is amazing

the insights that come to you ten or twenty years too late, enhanced by wisdom born of age and suffering and the delicious detachment known only to the happily retired. At last, the meaning of "I am a seagull!" is clear to me – and for $25 I will share the secret of Nina's cry! (Hey, this is valuable stuff, you don't expect me to give it away, do you?)

    We finally got word on the CAT scan. The tumors have stabilized (they haven't shrunk any – but they haven't spread either!) which is good news. My doctor says this is encouraging and he is pleased. So now I get to have more chemo, at lease two more courses, then we'll check again.

    Bill claims he knew we'd get good news. Not me. I was terrified. But I bought that winter coat and two more wigs – so I think I've decided that I'm going to live! I feel very good and I can do almost everything I want to (except during the first few days of chemo). So don't be afraid to call or visit us – life is pretty normal for Bill and me. But if you're coming over, please specify which wig you'd like to see: I have the Suburban Dressy Look, the Columbia Graduate Student Look and the Carol Burnett look. I feel like that character in "Ozma of Oz," who chooses a different head (and the personality that goes with it) the way most people choose an outfit. I no longer aim for consistency of character, so be prepared!

    Bill continues to be the most wonderful man in the world. And he sends his greetings.

    Love, Eren

Letter to My Friends　　　　　　　　　**Bulletin #3**

I have stopped blaming my illness for the recession in retail marketing in Manhattan and started to put the blame where it belongs, on unseasonable weather and the Reagan Administration. I have done my best. If Macy's goes bankrupt, it isn't because I didn't try to buy Xmas presents there. In fact, I can offer this in evidence of my ultimate survivability: in spite of the cancer, in spite of all the chemotherapy and in spite of the upset and distress, I have never been too sick to shop or eat. Conclusive proof that I'm doing pretty well.

The CT scans are not so conclusive but they are "encouraging" – which means that the tumors might have shrunk just a bit … or maybe … maybe we should hold these X-rays under a stronger light … well, let's take another CT scan in six weeks … say, is that …? … no, that's just a smudge … let's schedule a scan again after the next course of chemo … (SIGH) ARRGH! Very frustrating. Meanwhile, we get to celebrate the fact that things are at the very least stable and that hope is still galloping onward!

Bill and I had a perfectly wonderful Christmas but it took a little dong …

Two weeks before Christmas, I was in despair. My chemotherapy routine had been thrown drastically off schedule at Thanksgiving time. The hospital simply didn't have a room available. After a delay of nine days, I was getting rather worried, so when a bed became free on Thanksgiving Day, I hopped right into it and was properly Thankful even as I was throwing up my hospital-provided turkey lunch and watching the anticipated pleasures of a family dinner with old friends dwindle down to a short (and – on my part – heavily sedated) phone call. But what, after all, is Thanksgiving? A meal invented by Pilgrims; an excuse for Native Americans and recent immigrants to overeat together. If it must be sacrificed for the sake of chemotherapy, so be it.

Christmas was to me, however, a different matter.

Christmas is important. Christmas is what the rest of the year is there for. A year without a big Christmas celebration is like eating all your lima beans and cauliflower and then being told we've run out of desert. But if December brought a similar delay to the availability of hospital beds at chemo time, I might see all my cherished Christmas plans ripped out from under me. I know my cancer is a bad thing but somehow the thought that cancer might be a big enough thing to wreck Christmas suddenly made it very real. And inescapable. And far, far too grim.

I kept remembering the time my older sister gave my nephew, Zachary, a powerful, battery-operated, obstacle-climbing toy vehicle for Christmas. Zachary was only two or three years old. He had spent hours with his new building blocks erecting an edifice of truly impressive height. Confident that his proud monument would stand forever, the little Masterbuilder then turned to the next toy, the battery-operated vehicle, and for the first time switched it on. To his horror, it roared immediately into action. Undeterred by rugs, furniture or other toys, it climbed and shoveled a remorseless path straight toward the beloved tower. Poor Zac-o was helpless. He couldn't read instructions. There was no time to call his mother. He had no way to stop the monster. All he could do was throw back his head and howl, "NO TRUCK! DON'T!!!"

That's just how I felt watching the inevitable clash of Christmas plans and chemotherapy. The hospital was even more crowded than it had been before Thanksgiving. Every day I called the Admissions Director at the hospital and ever day I heard, "Sorry, no bed today. (Pause.) Maybe tomorrow!" Time started to run out as Christmas got closer and closer and the day of our annual

Christmas party seemed likely to be the same day I'd get into the hospital. But if we cancelled the party and I DIDN'T get into the hospital after all, I'd feel utterly cheated. The cry rose to me throat, "NO TRUCK! DON'T!!!"

So Bill and I talked about what to do. The only way not to risk not having plans ruined is to make no plans in the first place. Which is not only no fun, it is also an admission of defeat before the battle can begin. We wanted to fight for our Christmas. Delaying chemotherapy is a terrible gamble. But I finally decided that giving our usual Christmas party – although we would have to warn our guests that there might be a last-minute cancellation – was too important to me. I just couldn't give it up. Nor could I bear to spend Christmas Eve and Christmas Day in the hospital. I could, however, stand to suffer the aftereffects of the treatment – the depression and the dead puppy tummy – on those special days. Even if I had to lie on the sofa feeling rotten, not even having the energy to open presents, at least I could look at MY tree and MY husband and that – if we could have the party first – would be Christmas enough for me.

So, I made a deal with Dr. Blum. The logistics were a bit complicated but he ultimately allowed me to delay the chemo until after our party. That would enable me to get out of the hospital at noon on Christmas Eve Day. You know, I thought at the time that I was just fighting for my Christmas pleasure. But I think Dr. Blum recognized that I was gong through what must be a classic phase for cancer patients – the sudden, stubborn need to take control of my life back. Just for a little while, I wanted things MY way and damn the doctors and phooey on the hospital! Just for a little while ... and then I'd go back to being cooperative.

Our other big problem was that my energy level is not dependable, so we knew we'd have to ask people to help us. Kitty Parks and Connie Day were our Christmas Angels. They offered to help put up the tree and to do most of the setting-up and the pre-party running around, to clean up afterwards. They also offered themselves as designated Hugger-and-Kissers in case I was in a phase of low immunity when the day of the party dawned. They made the party possible.

Everything turned out beautifully! We had the biggest and the prettiest tree we've ever had. (Kitty ran out to the shops four times during the trimming to buy more lights.) With Connie and Kitty doing most of the hostess work, we gave the party and 56 people came, which is a record turnout. If anything, the celebratory mood was enhanced by the threat of cancellation. Bill and I were giddy with relief and had a marvelous time.

And hallelujah! The much desired bed was available right on cue the next morning! I was dosed and out by noon on Christmas Eve.

I didn't even have to go through the depression and the puppy tummy! This time I was sent home with a small supply of steroid pills and voila! No side effects! Well, except for the "steroid crazies." (Remember that second chemo course when I felt so perky? Steroids! Turns out they're in the chemo mixture. Move over, Flo-Jo!) This time I turned into the Mad Housekeeper. I couldn't sleep. I couldn't sit still. I couldn't stop doing housework. It's a control thing. An out-of-control thing. Bill became a little alarmed when I started to vacuum the Christmas tree a second time but I was perfectly happy ... as long as no one took my appliances away from me. Bill and my sister, Denise, (who stayed with us and made Xmas dinner) were terribly tolerant and slightly terrified of me for a few days there. I had a wonderful time. And I got lots of presents. I've never had so many wonderful presents.

I am now willing to be a good, cooperative patient again. For awhile, anyway.

I wanted to give you definite news of my condition and of our plans, so I have waited to send out this bulletin, hoping one of the CT scans would turn up solid evidence that the chemo is working.
Every six weeks since September I've had a CT scan. They have been inconclusive. I just got the results of this month's scan: inconclusive again. The good news is that the cancer is stable – it hasn't spread any further. Also considered good news is the fact that I'm tolerating the chemo treatments very well; I feel well and pretty energetic. The bad news is that Bill and I will have to continue living from chemo to chemo, scan to scan, unable to plan beyond three weeks at a time. It is sometimes unbearably frustrating.
Know anyone who would like to sublet our LA apartment?

I am going back into the hospital today for Chemo #7 and to have a lot of tests done. It looks like, whatever happens, I will be on some form of chemo until the late Spring. Bill sends his love and greetings. He wishes NY had more work to offer a fifty-five-year-old actor with a lot of very handsome gray in his beard but he's getting a few jobs here and there and is holding up under the strain heroically. I'm nuts about him. I'd rather have him than hair on my head.

I wanted to sum up all that I have learned from my experiences of the past year, to pass on to you as a sort of New Year's present. I wanted to say something terribly profound and helpful. But after many hours of thought, all my new-found wisdom boils down to this suggestion: Life is never long enough so don't hold back. Use the Waterford crystal every day. And let yourself be loved.
Happy New Year.

Love, Eren

Letter to My Friends   Bulletin #4

It's been a long time since I sent out one of these letters – I hope you weren't too worried when you didn't hear from me. I'm actually doing very well. Everything is still "stable." In fact, I feel remarkably healthy.

I have now been taking chemotherapy for almost a year. In February, I prepared to join a clinical trial at the Dana Farber Institute in Boston. But the CT scans continued to be inconclusive so after many tests and much soul searching, we decided that it would be better for me to continue with the treatment I was getting at NYU. It was a great relief to come to a firm decision.

By April, the intermittent dreadfulness of chemo had become merely routine and my situation began to suffer from a serious lack of high drama. Science came p with a wonderful new drug (Zophran) that counteracts the worst of the side effects of the chemo. No more sedation! Fewer steroids! Quicker recovery! The down side is that, without sedation, I become aware enough to realize how intensely BORING it is to lie around a hospital room for three days.

The high point (amusement-wise) of the last six months came about three months ago, two weeks after getting one of my chemo doses, my blood counts fell alarmingly low and I had to and I had to get a blood transfusion. It was a wonderfully weird experience. (Didn't hurt.) NYU has an outpatient blood transfusion unit. They have a room lined with chaises longes from each of which sprouts an IV pole. I reclined on one of these chairs facing three other patients, all of whom (I think) suffered from AIDS. We were all terribly anemic, extremely pale.

We each got hooked up to plastic bags containing some anonymous person's generously donated blood. The chairs were placed just far enough apart so that conversing with one's neighbors was physically uncomfortable. I found that once I finished my bag lunch and read a little, there was nothing really for any of us to do over the next three-and-a-half hours but watch each other grow gradually pinker as the blood dripped in. It was very peculiar. We actually changed color, all of us!

I also learned to have some respect for the research that went into those old Dracula movies. Do you remember how the Count's lips always turned dark red after sucking up somebody's blood? Yup! That actually happens! When Bill came to pick me up after the transfusion, he couldn't stop staring at my lips ... and he wouldn't let me kiss his neck.

Back in February – miracle of miracles! – I shot a commercial. The timing really sowed signs of Heavenly Intervention. The auditions fell on the few days in the month when I happened to feel like a relatively normal human being. My dear friend, Bonnie Erickson, was the puppeteer consultant on the job. This helped a lot. (I do not know what she said to the producers and director about me. I can only tell you that when I entered the room for the audition, they all turned and bowed slightly. And they were not Japanese.) On shoot day, I was rather anemic. But it didn't matter because I did the entire job reclining in a comfortable upholstered chair! And this was "bare-hands puppetry" – no actual puppet's heaviness to hold aloft. The only weight I had to support was the double coat of polish on my nails and a small lump of latex on my right index finger. It was the most enjoyable day I have ever spent on a commercial set. God bless Dr. Scholl's Clear Away Wart Remover! May its sales increase! And may its residuals continue …

I am about to go into the hospital again for my thirteenth and final chemo dose. Then my doctor will want me to have a lot of CAT scans and X-rays. These will serve as a basis of comparison over the next phase of my medical life. I will be closely monitored but as long as my condition remains stable, I an stay off chemo! Hooray! I cannot wait to be free of those drugs. Free to grow hair. Free from the nausea and fatigue and the odd physical tension I carry when my body is struggling with all those chemicals. Free from the crabbiness that overtakes me while I am waiting days for a hospital bed. (Like now.)

My doctor warns me that this new phase can be quite stressful, that paranoia can take over very easily as one waits, feeling unprotected by the lack of treatment, to see what will happen next. I know from listening to patients in my support groups who are (or were) in remission, the sweetness and the terror of that particular kind of hope and the brutality of hope betrayed. I am just "stable" (the tumors aren't growing or spreading but they're still there); not "in remission" (the doctor tells you that you're cancer free) but even so … hope is an incorrigible rascal.

So I try to focus on every day that I have without chemo as a wonderful kind of "freebie." I am not bothering to look very far down the road. I am just concentrating on feeling good and having a good time.

Bill and I are planning to return to Los Angeles for a few months after I finish with the last chemo course. We'll leave New York mid-September and return here just before Christmas. We both need to get a lot more work and a little more sunshine. So we're off to the land of la! Bill is gong to lay a lot of tennis. I intend to sit around wit a hand mirror and admire the nice effect that having eyebrows again has on one's face.

We hope you are having a glorious summer.

Love, Eren

P.S. Shortly after I sent off the last Bulletin, an article about the dangers of drinking from lead crystal glasses appeared in the New York Times. Apparently, wine and spirits can leach the lead right out of the crystal. So maybe don't use the Waterford every day! It was only a metaphor, anyway. (This sort of thing takes all the fun out of being Wise About Life …)

Letter to My Friends   Bulletin #5

It's been a while since I wrote to you like this. A lot has happened.

The last Bulletin I sent out was in August of 1991. At that time, I had just finished 12 months of very toxic chemotherapy and was looking forward to once again possessing a hair-do that didn't have to spend the night perched on a stand on my dresser. I was expecting a period of "stability" (in which the tumors in my chest, though they hadn't gone away, would simply maintain the status quo). Within weeks, however, Bill and I fond ourselves sitting in Dr. Blum's office looking at my latest chest X-rays and trying to absorb the news that the tumors were growing. We asked a lot of questions. Dr. Blum gave us, gently, as many answers as he could. My tumors were growing fast. I couldn't take any more of the chemo I'd had before and there was no other treatment available, standard or experimental, that showed any evidence of working on my kind of cancer. Bill cried. I was numb. I tend not to let these things sink in until I am safely back at home. Bill often does the feeling for both of us these days.

Are you depressed yet? Hang on, hang on!

The one hope my doctor could offer us was that he was anxiously awaiting permission to begin a clinical trial of a biological compound (not a form of chemo, this is an entirely different, revolutionary approach to dealing with cancer cells) that had shown some laboratory success in fighting sarcoma. All we could do was wait for the start of that trial.

So we went on with our lives, doing the things we had planned, all throughout September, October and November. The clinical trial kept getting postponed. The October X-rays showed more tumor growth. We visited friends and family. We went to several weddings. I made two trips to Los Angeles to finish up my Puppeteer Caucus business. I thought I was doing a pretty swell job of coping with the knowledge that I was rapidly getting worse. Ha! The truth is, I was a complete nutcase. I look back on some of the things I did during those months and I'm appalled. I got very weird. Very weird and very wired. I cried a lot. I felt extremely dramatic inside. Remember Bette Davis in Dark Victory?" Uh huh, you got it.

Dr. Blum told me I might begin to experience "symptoms" by November and indeed, I did. More pains; increased shortness of breath. (The thought of not being able to breathe terrifies me.) I became tremendously paranoid: every lump, bump, twitch or tickle meant that the caner was gaining on me! Apparently, it is possible to have cancer and be a hypochondriac at the same time.

So it was a huge relief – and to be honest, a bit disconcerting – to learn at my end-of-November check-up that this time the X-rays showed no new growth! Dr. Blum then told us that the trials for the biological compound had been pushed back until the Spring ... but that within hours of receiving that disappointing news, he got word not one but TWO other clinical trials I could join – brand new chemotherapies, each of which offer a real chance of helping me.

Isn't it amazing? At the beginning of November, there was nothing medical science could do for me. By the end of the month, there were two treatments, immediate options, plus a back-up possibility (the biological compound) ready to pop up with the crocuses. It just goes to show: no matter how bad things look, it's always too soon to give up.

We decided that my best option was Topotecan. This is a drug that was tried 20 years ago. Apparently, it was vey effective against a variety of tumors. (Unfortunately, it also killed all the patients, but hey! You can't have everything!) For the last 20 years, the researchers at NYU Hospital have been working on Topotecan to detoxify it. Eureka! A breakthrough just in time to an me back from the brink! (Well, I wasn't exactly at the brink but I could definitely see the edges of the chasm in the near distance ...) The logic of this particular drug is unusual. Most chemotherapies target rapidly reproducing cells and poison them. That is how they kill cancer cells. Topotecan damages the DNA in all the cells but in such a way that the normal cells can repair the damage. The cancer cells can't repair themselves, so they die. Now, isn't that elegant?

Anyway, a clinical trial was set up immediately. I started on it the first week in December. I've had two courses now. This Topotecan is great stuff. It's not toxic so there's no side-effects to cope with (other than low blood counts, so I have to be careful about infections). I get to keep my precious new hair. And the best thing is that it is administered entirely at home. No more hospital stays! Once a month, a "home-care" nurse arrives at my door with a portable pump (about the size of a Walkman) and a few days' supply of the drug. Once I am plugged in, I am completely mobile. The pump infuses me with tiny amounts of Topotecan 24 hours a day for seven days. During that time, I am utterly free to move about, go to the movies, out to dinner ... it's wonderful! I don't even have to go to the hospital for blood tests: one a week, the home care nurses come to my apartment to draw blood, gossip a little and go away again. I feel like some wealthy dowager having everybody come to me and tend to my needs … it's heaven!

I have been stable since November, isn't that great? And I feel quite healthy, better than I have in a long time. I don't really know how much the suffering I endured this Fall was due to the cancer and how much was caused by Fear. I do know that I am extremely lucky to have found a doctor who has access to all the latest scientific breakthroughs. I've gotten so used to the idea of being sick and getting sicker that it is dawning on me little by little that I may not have to settle for that, I may not have to settle at all. I am beginning to toy wit the thought that I could actually get, well … well! It's a possibility, isn't it? Anything can happen!

Love, Eren

P.S. Bill and I have covered a lot of territory in the past two years (that's how long we've been dealing with all this cancer stuff). There are so many twists and turns to this journey that it is increasingly hard to keep track of where we've been and where we might be going. Preparing my thoughts for these bulletins is like clambering to the top of an outcropping of rock: I get a chance to look up from the path, to see the shape of the land and regain a sense of the journey as a whole. And when I search for a way to resent our experiences to you in a positive light, I often find that a new path opens before me, a higher and happier path. It helps me a lot. (Guess this metaphor makes you the rock.) Thanks. Thanks for reading all this.

ADDENDUM:

How very lucky I am to have so many good people giving me love and support over the past two years! Assistance, the practical and the quixotic, has come from all sides: doctor references; support system information; cassettes (audio and video) on alternative healing and relaxation techniques; books, newspaper articles and pamphlets on cancer cures have flooded in. I have been lent willing hands and feet and been given the gift of precious time from busy people. Delicious meals have been cooked and delivered for me, flavored with love (but no salt, no preservatives). I have been sent teas, Native American herbal remedies, crystals, healing stones and an amulet that looks like it has tiny dead bodies in it. I have been shiatsu'd, had hands laid on me and been sincerely and touchingly prayed at via both AT&T and Sprint lines. (Couldn't hurt and made me feel very cared for.) I was offered a source for "energized" buffalo meat which was guaranteed to cure anything and a vial of powered shark's cartilage. (I'm not sure what I was supposed to do with that.) An ex-brother-in-law that I haven't spoken to in years wrote that he was sure I would be healed if only I'd accept Jesus as my Savior. (Too bad he doesn't believe in paying child support – it gives a man such a nice air of credibility.)

I have been, above all, frantically urged, begged and cajoled to BELIEVE. In the power of Mind Over Matter. In the ability of Messrs. Groucho, Harpo and Chico to build p my immune system. In nutrition. In the Holy Trinity. In the natural healing strength of crystal and stone. Sometimes, all this concern about my spiritual life has been quite maddening. Sometimes it has given me a good laugh just when I needed it most. I certainly know some uninhibited spiritual adventurers.

A few dear friends have battered away at the door to my soul with a zealous disregard for the principles of reverse psychology. But most have simply, even shyly, offered prayers or had masses said o my behalf. My friend, Sister Francesca, (yes, even a heathen like me can have a nun for a friend. Of course, Sister F is an unusual nun. Actually, Sister F is an unusual human being …) has an entire convent in Indiana praying for me. You don't need to be very religious to be greatly comforted by the thought that an entire convent in Indiana is raying for you.

One of the nicest people I know is a public school teacher in Los Angeles. She is sweet and funny and kind. I don't know what church she belongs to but she teaches Sunday School there and this year she gave her

Sunday School students each a copy of the Little Golden Book of the Twenty-third Psalm for Christmas. On a whim, she wrapped up an extra copy and sent it to me. I think she thought I might be unfamiliar wit that greatest of all prayers. Not so. The 23rd Psalm and I are old fiends. I thought some of you might be interested in my reaction to my friend's gift, even those of you who are too discreet to, even hesitantly, inquire into the state of my immortal soul. I sat down to compose a thank you note to my friend and this is what came out instead:

Dear Lou,

Good heavens! I haven't looked at a Golden Book in years! Shades of long, long ago when my older sister and I went to Sunday School back in Dearborn, Michigan! There was an Episcopal church not far from our house and, although I never knew my parents to set foot in a church unless it was for a wedding or a funeral, we girls attended Sunday School sometimes. I remember a photograph my father took of Suzan and me, aged six and five, in our Easter outfits, standing all dressed up I little gray coats, little white gloves clutching basket-like purses, in front of our one-story brick tract house on Syracuse Street. I had a lovely, pale yellow straw hat with white straw daisies on t and long ribbons that streamed halfway down my back. We were all ready for the Sunday School Easter Egg Hunt.

In Dearborn in those days, everyone was white. Al respectable families went to (Protestant) church on Sunday, and everybody's father worked for one of the Detroit car companies. Foreigners were looked on with a degree of suspicion. People in Dearborn took pride in being as ordinary, as much like one another, as possible. My parents were not ordinary. My father, who did not work for a car company, spoke elegant, accentless English. But he was undeniably Turkish, which was considered a pretty outlandish thing to be. My mother had a Masters degree in Archeology burning a hole in her conscience. She was the smartest woman I have ever known and she was definitely unenamoured (sic) of motherhood as a career. She was not the bake-sale type. My handsome father was remarkably adept at blending in, although his continental elegance – combined with a too gleeful embrace of American colloquialisms occasionally betrayed him. And Mother, chafing, did a pretty good job of acting like a regular housewife most of the time. It was the fifties, the McCarthy years, and even my parents had to conform a lot. I suppose that is why we were sent to Sunday School. It was certainly not to learn about God or Jesus. My parents held themselves aloof from organized religion and encouraged skepticism in their children. All I remember about those church-gong days are Easter and the Golden Books and their pictures of light-haired, blue-eyed Bible characters.

In 1959 when I was ten, we fled to the suburbs, seeking to live among other college-educated professionals and their presumably enlightened families. My parents' intellectual sophistication was clearly suited to life in an upscale, contemporary "sub-division" where houses were constructed largely of redwood and glass and more people had the Encyclopedia Britannica on their bookshelves than back issues of the Reader's Digest. Mother politely offered to find us a Sunday School in the new neighborhood should we choose to continue attending, but, as she pointed out with an admirable air of personal disinterest, we were now old enough to decide for ourselves how we wanted to spend our Sundays. That was the end of my formal education in any religion. Spiritual belief was, apparently, something that I could choose dispassionately and unencumbered by convention, when I grew up. I knew what my parents believed. Mother, raised in Church of England Episcopalian, believed in Science. My Moslem-born father believed in Mathematics. We did not say "grace" at home except on Thanksgiving Day when my mother's parents were with us. Praying out loud at any other time would have seemed vulgar, like burping in public.

My parents made many sacrifices to bring their growing brood of daughters out of what they thought of as the narrow-minded strictures of Dearborn into the intellectual and moral liberation promised by the shining new developments of Farmington Hills.

Think, then, how horrified they would have been had they suspected what was going on in my new suburban fifth-grade classroom! Mrs. _____? Was my Teacher. I cannot remember her name now but her image rises unfaded in my mind's eye as I write this. Her nose was thin and sharply pointed. Her hair was black streaked with gray and gold, wire-rimmed glasses hung on a chain around her neck. She was very, very thin. And she was a good deal older than the teachers I was used to. But she had the loveliest clothes, all soft colors and delicate, silky fabrics. On the morning I entered my new classroom for the first time, she was wearing a blue dress sprigged with tiny, white flowers and the sweetest, little narrow belt circled her waist. I thought the Teacher's dress was so pretty!

It was mid-semester in the second half of the school year, a bad time to be the "new girl" in any school. I didn't know where to sit so I stood by the Teacher's desk, waiting until the bell rang. She smiled at me and went to close the classroom door. I smiled back, relieved that she seemed so nice. Then in a pleasant, refined voice she introduces me to my classmates. And I heard her explaining as I gazed out at the room full of strange children, that WE WERE ALL SWORN TO SECRECY. No one was to tell our parents. In This Class, she said, placing slender fingers on my shoulder and looking me sweetly in the eye, we begin the day in a special way. We always say the Twenty-third Psalm, the Lord's Prayer and then we pledge allegiance to our flag.

Did I understand that this was just for us to know?

Rather dazedly, I nodded.

Then I could go to my seat (the Teacher pointed to an empty desk towards the mid-back of the room) and we would begin ...

The children all stood up. As soon as I reached the designated desk and placed my pile of books on its surface, the prayers began. I had head the "Our Father" one before but I certainly didn't know it. The other one, the Shepherd thing, was utterly new to me. And the words weren't written on the board or anything, so I couldn't read along like I knew you could do in church. I was apparently expected to know them already. That first day, and for many days afterward, I faked my way through mouthing the unfamiliar words of the two prayers, sneaking side-long glances at my classmates to see if anyone suspected that I didn't know my lines, lines that tumbled with the ease of long practice from the lips of every other child. I tried to make up for it by Pledging the Flag good and loud.

It was the start of a very odd time.

I wanted, as all children do, to like my Teacher. She seemed so ladylike. And I loved to look at her clothes. But she had a lot of Rules.

There was one retarded kid in the class, a big, clumsy girl named Judy. She had wiry red hair and a smeary-looking mouth. The Teacher often seemed to go out of her way to pick on this girl. It shocked me. I never knew what to do or where to look when Judy was in trouble and the Teacher's voice got nasty. None of the other kids seemed to be uncomfortable when it happened. I saw some of them smirk. My discomfort made me even more aware that I was an outsider, an observer rather than a participant in this place, with little chance of becoming One Who Belongs before the school year would end and a lonely summer would begin.

I vaguely knew that the Teacher was doing something wrong by having us recite prayers in school. And I remembered the Golden Book pictures of Christ surrounded by children. Even though in those pictures the children were all blonde and pretty, I was sure Jesus would have been nice to a retarded girl and would have been mad at anyone who wasn't. The Teacher was a Christian; I new that because she talked about it. I had heard my parents say that Christians were often hypocrites and I was rather relieved to know that I was not one myself. A Christian, I mean. I couldn't be since my parents weren't. It was like with politics. In grade school, if your parents voted for Ike, you were a Republican, too, although you didn't know what that meant. However, in this strict new society where children knew the words to grown-up prayers, I thought I had better keep my family's religious eccentricity confidential.

"My parents are Non-Practicing," I explained loftily in answer to the queries of Susan Cox, whose new house was five lots down from my new house. Susan was in the other fifth grade classroom in my new school. She was the only person I ever told about the Teacher's behavior to the retarded girl. I told her that I didn't think my Teacher was really a Good Christian. I never told her – or anyone – about the prayers. None of the children did. A promise is a promise ...

And I wanted my Teacher to approve of me. Just as I wanted to think that Jesus would have approved of me if I was one of the children in the Golden Book pictures, even though I didn't go to church and didn't now anything really about him except the Christmas stuff and that people called him Good. Even my mother referred to him sometimes as an Important Teacher and the respectful tone she used meant she too thought he was Good – even if he was only a culturally interesting phenomenon and not God like some people thought.

I wanted my classmates to like me, too. I had always made friends easily. It was only a few days before some of the girls indicated that it would be alright for me to sit with them at lunch and to join them on the playground afterward. We weren't friends yet but it was a beginning and I felt glad, confident and glad.

Then one day at recess, Judy fell off the jungle gym.

She landed in the dirt with an audible thump and the other kids,

The Cancer Club

once it was clear she wasn't actually hurt, began to laugh. She was so huge, blinking and dirty and disheveled, her moth gaping open as she lumbered to her feet. "Darn!" she bellowed. "Darn, darn, darn, darn, darn!" It was an ugly noise she made. Too coarse. Too big. I couldn't tell if she meant the words to express anger at the children who had laughed or to cover her embarrassment at falling with a pretense of anger at the climbing equipment or whether she was simply aping the kind of thing adults say when they have blundered in some way.

One of the boys gasped and shrieked, "I'm telling Teacher!" and he ran toward the school building. I had no idea what he was talking about.

When recess was over and we were all gathered once again in our classroom, I was surprised to see that our Teacher liked grim and angry. She stalked over to the classroom door, shut it firmly and whirled around.

"Judy!" Her voice landed like the lashing of a whip. I jumped in my seat. Poor Judy's head jerked up, confusion and far swamped her wet, brown eyes. Her mouth dropped open.

"I a told," intoned my Teacher," that on the playground during recess, you swore!"

Swearing, we all knew, was Against the Rules. Swearing was Very Bad.

"I didn't," Judy said in a dull tone, swinging her head ponderously from side to side.

"You are lying." This was stated as a matter of fact. The Teacher raised her chin, pulling her mouth all tight and mean and sent a shriveling look down at that poor mess of a girl. Silky fabric made a soft swish as she leaned in for the kill.

The world went into slow motion in my head and time stretched itself out, as I have since learned it sometimes does. There are moments in one's life when turning points come and you recognize them as such while they are happening. At such moments, everything slows down, almost stops, while your life waits for you to fall in one direction or the other. The direction in which you fall will, you know in the long instant before the fall comes, shape you forever. The shape of my life, my inner life, has grown like a picture emerging from lines drawn from dot to dot in a children's game, each dot on the chart is a second of suspended time, of slow motion, of falling.

In this long stretched moment, I had time to register all that was going on in the classroom. I saw the Teacher's meanness, her glee and I knew she was glad that Judy had broken a big rule and could be punished harshly. I saw the satisfaction that coated the boy who had tattled and sensed the breath of children all around me held in excited anticipation. I knew then that if I spoke, if I defended this clumsy, damaged girl, I would be forever tied to her. I would be one with her, considered somehow like her and barred forever from any hope of acceptance, of easy camaraderie with the prettier girls in this school, in this neighborhood. I would have Chosen Sides. And it would be a long, long time before I would get to a chance to choose again.

I also knew that if I said nothing, the Teacher would not hit Judy. Her punishment would only consist of words. But the words would be vicious and they would sting, sting cruelly. And I knew that the words would stay with me always, hitting me as hard as they hit their intended target. They would make me smaller inside. I would have to spend a large chunk of my life running away from the memory of not speaking. Children, you know, yearn most of all to be heroes, to believe that when the test comes, they will be found on the side of the angels ...

So, time snapped back to its usual state and I fell toward the lesser of two dooms. And discovered, though it gave me no joy then, that I could not take what I wanted to have if I could not be who I wanted to be.

"She didn't lie," I protested, yanking myself to my feet. "She only said darn; I heard her."

Judy's big head swung in my direction and I could feel her memorizing the features of my face. I knew, of course, that I was doing the right thing, the noble thing. But there was no glory, no grand sense of heroism to swell my heart; there was only a dull ache and a leaden acceptance of what was to come.

I was right, too, in what I had foreseen in my Long Moment. From then on, Judy clung to me with the damp persistence of an affectionate dog. None of the other kids ever made friends with me. Today I can't recall even one of their names, although some of us ended up going to Junior High and High School together. Judy literally dogged my footsteps all through sixth, seventh and eighth grades, too, until to my great relief, her parents sent her off to a special private school. I was always ashamed of how much I resented poor Judy's attentions, but even though I tried not to be unkind, I avoided her whenever possible. Fear of "identity by association" is the curse of the junior high years.

The Cancer Club

But getting through what was left of my awful fifth grade year was, ironically, made possible by that Teacher's illegal prayer sessions. Each morning in class, after that terrible confrontation, I found myself listening to the words of the Twenty-third Psalm as they came by rote out of my own mouth:

The Lord is My Shepherd. I shall not want. He maketh me to lie down in green pastures. He leadeth me beside the still waters. He restoreth my soul. He leads me in the paths of righteousness for His Name's sake ...

I savored each line, wondering at the beauty of the language and at the strange power that words have to hurt or to heal. Why was it that the sound of the words, the sound alone, like the ringing of bells, was soothing? It was a poem but finer and truer than any other poem I knew. The Lord is My Shepherd ... what did that mean? My shepherd ... my shepherd, even mine. The assurance of God's understanding – even in the face of hostile fifth-graders – and the surety that it was mine as long as I tried to do right, gradually wrapped around me then and it has sustained me ever since. The Words sing out that Truth even though a hypocrite taught them to me.

In all the times of my life, the words of that Prayer have remained true. Line after line is colored by the specific circumstances that have led me to them again and again, for comfort:

Yea, though I walk through the Valley of the Shadow of Death, I shall fear no evil, for Thou art with me. Thy rod and thy staff, they comfort me.

That is the part, of course, that has rung home to me most often lately. And when I see all the good things that have happened in the midst of my illness:

Thou preparest a table before me in the presence of mine enemies. Thou anointest my head with oils. My cup runneth over.

Isn't it funny that I can't remember the name of that teacher but I've never forgotten Judy's name. Her last name was Golden, like the Golden Rule. Like the Golden Books. I hope she eventually found someone who was truly her friend, someone who, unlike me, brightened with gladness when they saw her coming towards them.

Sometimes I struggle with:

Surely goodness and mercy shall follow me all the days of my life.

But then the last, daring line offers me once again, despite my failings, the ultimate solace:

And I shall dwell in the house of The Lord forever.

Amen.

I'm still not "a Christian." Or any specific thing else.
But I don't believe God minds.
Do you?

Love, Eren

Letter to My Friends   Bulletin #6

Well, as the lady boasts in the Sondheim song:

I'M STILL HERE!

But it's been a bumpy ride …

This was the worst part:
Experimental drug #2 (Topotecan) worked beautifully for a month or two and then, inexplicably, in the middle of March, the tumors began growing again. They spread so quickly that Bill and I were caught unprepared. For the first time, I knew what it was to be really, really invalided by this disease. I wasn't ready to be so sick. Fluid began building in my chest cavity again, this time on my left side. Breathing became a luxury item …

So I had to go back into the hospital again for another pleuradesis. (This is the same operation I had two years ago just before my first chemotherapy began.) In 1990, I accepted this surgery with no apprehensions; it seemed no big deal to suffer or to recover from. But back then, I had a basically healthy body – which happened to have some cancer in it. Now I have a body that has a lot in common with Flanders Field before the flowers began to grow back … it's pretty well ravaged. This time I entered the hospital feeling very ill indeed; feeling that I had run out of breath, out of strength and maybe out f luck, too.

I lay I that hospital bed for seven days. I thought about trying to get myself ready to die. I was – need I mention? – depressed. But I was also pitifully weak. The mental and spiritual preparedness needed for going out with dignity seemed to me, at the time, to require an outrageous amount of energy. I just couldn't summon the necessary oomph! Besides, even in my wooziest state of consciousness, I could recollect this uncomfortable truth about myself: All the most dramatic moments of my life have been sideswiped at the last second by burlesque comedy of the lowest order.

Chances were that this moment would be no different.

Too much self-awareness can be a prickly bed fellow.

I lay there, feeling really, really lousy and I yearned to be like the Noble Old Indian who, sensing that the final hour of his life had come, distributes to his fellow tribesmen all his worldly goods, bids his loved ones a tender farewell and strides out into the desert until he reaches at last the sacred ground, where his simple prayers are spoken and he lays himself down giving his spirit its final freedom …

That's how dying ought to be. One ought to be prepared. In control. No surprises. Dignity intact.

But damn, I just know that if I was a Noble Old Indian, I would give away all my beads and my pots and my arrows; I'd tearfully kiss my dear ones good-bye; I'd march ever so tragically off in the direction of the setting sun … and then, about three weeks later, I'd have to sneak back into the village and beg somebody for warm clothing to get me through the winter, since my timing was turning out to be the weeniest bit off …

My whole life long, every time I have taken myself too seriously, I have put my foot down on a banana peel …

So I thought I would risk less ridicule if I didn't try to die.

Good thing, too, since it turned out I got better after all.

It took a long time, though.

When Bill brought me home from the hospital, I thought I was gong to be a real invalid, bed-bound, house-bound forever. It didn't seem possible that I could recapture the semblance of a "normal" life. Bill counseled patience. Patience! But he was right. About four weeks after the operation, I was sitting in my kitchen with the morning sun shining through the window and the pleasure of being alive just poured over me. I eventually discovered two or three positions which I could use – cautiously – to cuddle up with my husband as we sat on the sofa watching television after dinner … And life got good again. I can do the grocery shopping. I can go out to dinner with my friends. I've started purchasing Christmas presents – not because I might not be here in December but because the recession has made this a good time to buy …

I am astonished and grateful to have made it back so far.

I am grateful, too, to the Topotecan trial. It didn't save my life but it gave us a joyous, hope-filled Christmas. And maybe bought me an extra month or two.

Here is the good part:

The steroid bloat has finally disappeared. I am thinner but not unhealthy looking. In fact, I look terrific. Well, at least my hair does. The "chemo-curl" everybody tells you about has finally happened to my hair. (When your hair grows back in after the chemotherapy treatments have ended, it is supposed to be darker, curlier and thicker than it was before.) Si I had been very disappointed to see my new hair grow in looking just like my old hair: brown, medium in density and straight. My friends, I swear to you that when I went into the hospital for the pleuradesis, I had straight hair. When I was discharged seven days later, I looked like those photos of Bill Clinton during the 60s, only darker. I've always wanted hair like this.

Sometimes I suspect that when God hasn't been able to answer one of your big prayers, He answers one of your little ones – just so you know He's there and is paying attention. OK! So maybe some of you think it's superficial of me to put so much emphasis on looks ... but after those 13 months of chemo-induced baldness, I cannot help but find good hair spiritually significant.

July

During the darkest days of March and April, I wrestled for the first time with intense pain. Fortunately, I have access to very effective pain killers. (Let's hear it for narcotic drugs!) My tumors seem to grow in bursts. The worst pain (which I haven't, thank goodness, suffered very often until recently) happens during these sudden growth periods but it is readily defeated by good old-fashioned morphine. Initially, it took a week or so to establish the correct dosage. I had to develop a tolerance for the stuff, to create a balance between erasing the pain and zonking myself out. But now, everything is under control and I don't dead the pain. I do, however, carry a dose of morphine about with me, just in case. (Bill bought me one of those hollowed out canes. It not only holds my liquid morphine, it earns me – when I'm tired or in pain – a seat in the handicapped section at the front of the bus with no questions asked. Didn't I marry a clever fellow?)

Just in case you are curious, I get, alas, no "high" from the morphine. Apparently, when it is used to relieve pain, morphine has no entertainment value at all! My experience with the stuff, however, leads me to a potentially unique and intensely personal interpretation of Mary Tyrone's behavior in "Long Days Journey Into Night." I think the poor woman was going nuts with constipation!

See, here we are back at the yin/yang, tragic/ludicrous theme again. Constipation is the banana peel of narcotic drug use. All narcotic painkillers act like glue upon one's intestinal plumbing. So I have begun to explore the twisty lanes of Laxative Land. Suddenly, television commercials using words like "gentle" or "regular" or "dependable" command my complete attention. Friends race to share their favorite Recipes for Regularity with me. Many friends! Many remedies! This astonishes me. How come everybody I know has expertise in this area? Don't you all eat enough roughage?

I am now in the middle of another clinical trial. This is the long-awaited "MCSF," a biological compound made by the Genetics Institute of Cambridge, Mass. The initials stand for Macrophage Colony Stimulating Factor. Macrophages are the blood cells in the immune system that eat up tumor cells. (They really eat them. Just like Pac Man.)

There is as yet no sign that the treatment is working for me. Sometimes I get very discouraged. But most of the time, I just ignore the Big Picture. Somebody Bigger Than Me will have to take care of that. I just concentrate on taking good care of myself and getting as much pleasure as possible out of every day. It's not a bad way to live.

August

The MCSF didn't work for me. Now I'm on something called DTIC. It is a standard chemotherapy and I am – so far – nauseous almost all the time. I will soon be starting radiation therapy to try to reduce the size of one particularly pesky tumor that is causing me a lot of pain.

It is harder to find the concentration needed to write or read these days. Sometimes I try to work on what I call "The Last Bulletin" – all the stuff I would like to say to my friends that I need to write out now while I can still sit at my beloved computer.

(All those of you who at this point are covering your face with your hands and shrieking "Oh, no! She's not thinking POSITIVE!!! should just please go sit in a corner until you grow up.)

Here are some of the things I'd like to put into that Bulletin:
1) When you want to feel close to me, buy yourself some white

tulips, eat a piece of really good chocolate and read (or re-read) "Little Women."

2) My death is not very important. My life is important. So one day, when you get the news, don't think about endings, put the focus where it belongs. Please think to yourself: "What a terrific person just lived!"

I hope you won't be too depressed by this letter. I'm pretty sure I've got another Christmas in me. And nothing, nothing is going to take me out of the running before "Murphy's Revenge" hits the air! That's for sure!

Love, Eren

If you enjoyed this book please provide us with an Amazon review. To learn more about the author, visit: www.luckycinda.com.

You might also enjoy reading her fun romantic adventure novel, winner of five literary prizes, *Francesca of Lost Nation*.

Available: On Kindle and Paperback

http://amzn.to/1diT33c
http://amzn.to/1aviI6m

About the Author

LuckyCinda
www.luckycinda.com

**Selected in 2011:
"50 Authors You Should be Reading"**

Lucinda Sue Crosby is an award-winning journalist and environmentalist as well as a published and recording Nashville songwriter. She's also a former professional athlete who worked as a sports commentator for the women's Tennis Association via InDemand Pay-Per-View.

Other books by the author:

Francesca of Lost Nation

The Adventures of Baylard Bear - a story about being DIFFERENT

Why is Pookie Stinky? - Book 1 in the "Silly Puppy" series

Water in the West - the Scary Truth about Our Precious Resource - An Enviornmental Essay

Sell more Ebooks - How to increase sales and Amazon rankings using Kindle Direct Publishing

These titles are available at Amazon

Printed in Great Britain
by Amazon.co.uk, Ltd.,
Marston Gate.